Tiny Precious Secrets

SAMANTHA CHRISTY

Athena
Books Publishing Group

Saint Johns, FL 32259

Cover designed by Maria @ Steamy Designs.

Tiny Precious Secrets

Samantha Christy

Chapter One

Allie

Christopher's ice-cream cone drips down the sides of his hands. He doesn't mind. He's mesmerized by the Disney characters, the brightly clad dancers pirouetting their way down Main Street, and the huge Dumbo float that slowly drifts by.

His eyes are as big as saucers. "Mommy, it's Dumbo. He fwies wif his ears!"

I tousle his longish blond locks and smile. "He sure does, baby."

Pluto—or someone wearing the amazingly detailed costume—spots Christopher and comes over, reaching out a hand, or paw as it may be, tickling him under his sticky chin.

Laughter dances out of my son. It's infectious. Virulent. Highly contagious. And I can't help but laugh along with him.

Christopher's smile fades, as does his whole body—the parade too—as arms come around me.

"Mmmm," a deep male voice mumbles against my neck. "I've never heard you laugh in your sleep. You were smiling too. Better have been thinking about me."

Needing a minute, I pull away. "I uh, need to pee. Like now."

I pad to the bathroom, shut the door, and turn on the faucet, praying the tears don't come. I love dreaming about Christopher almost as much as I hate it. Breathing in and out several times to calm myself, I do what I said I was coming in to do and then join Asher back in bed.

"Actually," I say with a wink now that I'm composed, "I was thinking about meeting that famous old baseball player last night. What was his name? Sawyer Mills?"

"Hey now." He looks offended. "Watch who you're calling old. Mills isn't all that much older than I am."

I snuggle close and slap my hand on his bare ass. "Sometimes I forget how ancient you are with all your parts working as well as they do. Four times last night? That has to be a record."

He flips me on my back and hovers over me. "Care to go for another? I'll show you exactly how this old guy can keep up with the rest of them."

"Don't you have an early flight?"

"It got pushed back until later this afternoon."

I scrunch my brows, concerned about his daughter. He's away so much on business. "What about Bug?"

"She'll be fine. I'm sure she's more than happy to stay at Mel's all day." His phone rings and he scoots off me to check it. "Speak of the devil."

He swipes to answer the video call as I race to the bathroom to hide as usual.

Bug—or Darla as she insists I call her—is his feisty thirteen-year-old. And as far as I can tell, I'm the only one who she insists uses her given name.

I lean against the door, eavesdropping on their conversation. I love the way he is with her. And she adores him. They take care of each other as much as any father and daughter I've ever known. It kills him to be away from her when he travels. But he's in high demand, so he goes where he's needed. Luckily, his job is also flexible, allowing him to work from home when he's back in Orlando. And when he's there, he's full-on dad.

Or so I hear. I haven't actually seen it myself. I've never been invited.

I'm not bitter about it. I get it. Bug has been hurt by women. She's not exactly begging for a stepmom, or even a significant female presence in Asher's life. Which is fine by me. What we have—occasional nights together in Manhattan, where a lot of companies contract for his business—is perfect. And it has been for the last fifteen months.

I take the opportunity to brush my teeth and put on my running clothes. Whenever I come to the city, I make it a point to run in Central Park. Sure, Calloway Creek has some great running trails, but even those get boring and mundane. This is Central Park. There's nothing boring about a place with 132 acres of woods and meadows with 58 miles of pedestrian pathways.

By the time Asher is done talking with Bug, our breakfast has arrived.

The smell of coffee assaults my senses and my eyes close as I inhale it in. I remove the domes over the plates, hand Asher his bacon and eggs, and bite into my oversized blueberry muffin, rolling my eyes as the fruit explodes along my taste buds.

"Mmm mmm mmm," he says around his food. "This never gets old. Thanks."

He doesn't need to thank me. I ordered and paid for breakfast. Always have. It's the least I can do since he covers the hotel room. Or his company does. At first, I offered to upgrade us. Maybe I was trying to impress him back then. The younger woman who didn't need a man to pay for anything. But Asher Anderson is not easily impressed. Not by money anyway.

I've learned over the past year what does impress him. Kindness. Integrity. Generosity. And maybe the ability to have multiple orgasms.

He wolfs down the rest of his breakfast as I tie my running shoes.

I look up. "Why the rush if your flight got pushed back?"

"I want to go running with you."

I laugh. Because in all the times we've done this—which adds up to what, a dozen? Two?—he's never gone running with me. He's always on an early morning flight back to Florida.

"You?" I chuckle again.

He throws a small decorative pillow at me. "I run, Al. I run all the time. I run in ninety-degree heat."

Eyeing his two suits hanging in the corner and his more casual khakis draped over the chair, I ask, "In what, exactly? Chinos and a Ralph Lauren button down?"

He shrugs. "There's a shop downstairs. I'm sure they have something."

"Ok, fine," I huff, noting his still full cup of coffee. He's a slow drinker. "Finish your coffee. I'll run down and get something."

"You don't know my size."

"Asher, I've had my arms around you a dozen times. I think I've figured it out by now."

"Fourteen."

I look at him oddly. "I didn't know guy sizes were in the teens. I was thinking thirty-four waist and large shirt."

"Impressive." He nods. "You got it exactly right. But you said you had your arms around me a dozen times. It's fourteen. We've met here fourteen times, not including the two times we hooked up at your place."

"Oh. Well, I'll be right back."

I quickly leave, not knowing what to think about this new piece of information. He's been counting the times we've been together? Or maybe he just knows how many trips he's made to New York City.

Down in the hotel shop, there isn't much to choose from. I smile when I come across a display of cheesy touristy T-shirts. I pull one out and check the size. Then I grab a pair of athletic shorts, choosing the ones with the shortest inseam. The man has nothing if not amazing thighs.

Back in the room, Asher is coming out of the bathroom with freshly washed hair.

"Most people prefer to shower *after* they run," I say, shoving the bag at him.

"Most people didn't have their head between the legs of a beautiful naked woman half the night."

I put my hands on my hips, pouting. "Are you saying I smell bad?"

"I'm saying I don't need to get a whiff of you when we're running and end up with a hard-on in the middle of Central Park."

I giggle at the thought. Especially considering the thin running shorts he's about to be wearing.

He rummages through the bag and pulls out the shirt. "Seriously?"

I shrug. "Pickings were slim."

He shakes his head in mock disgust but slips on the shirt anyway. It's now when I realize this man could make anything look good. Even a T-shirt emblazoned with a huge red apple with a bite taken out of one side.

Shedding the towel around his waist, he pulls on a pair of light-gray boxer briefs and then the running shorts. He looks down at himself. "I thought you said you knew my size. Allie, my legs are way too long for these."

"I know your size, Asher." I walk around him in admiration, then I pinch one of his butt cheeks.

Deep rumbles of masculine laughter bellow out of him. "Okay, Montana. But just know, payback can be hell."

"Do your worst, Mr. President."

He rolls his eyes.

When Asher's sister Marti—soon to be my sister-in-law—first introduced me to him, I told him his name sounded presidential. It's been an ongoing joke between us ever since.

"Come on." He takes my hand and pulls me toward the door. "Let's get in a run. And if we're lucky, we'll just have time for another kind of workout before I have to catch my flight."

I smile knowing today's run might just be a little faster than normal.

Chapter Two

Asher

"Dad!"

Bug doesn't even wait until Mel's mom pulls out of my driveway before hugging me.

I love that about her. She may be thirteen, a young adult, but she still likes to hug her old man.

I squeeze her tightly as I wave my thanks to Barb, Mel's mom. "I missed you, Bug. Sorry my flight got delayed."

"That's okay. It's not like you had a choice."

I swing her bulging backpack over my shoulder, amazed she fit four days of clothes in it. My daughter is pretty low maintenance compared to what I've seen of other girls her age. She doesn't wear much makeup. Isn't interested in the latest trends. Doesn't beg me to upgrade her phone every time a new one comes out. Hell, she rarely even asks for money over the reasonable allowance I give her.

Her only irrational demand is her hair. It has to be blue. At *all* times. She hates it when more than a half inch of brown shows along her part, so she insists on getting it dyed every single month. As the father of a hormonal daughter, I know things could be much worse. Just ask Barb. And who am I to deny my only child the one thing she ever insists on. Besides, even I have to admit she looks pretty damn good. Probably because the salon she goes to costs me an arm and a leg.

I unlock the front door, drop our bags inside, and pick up the mail scattered across the floor beneath the mail slot. Before I can even open the first piece, my phone rings. It's my boss.

"Hey, Rich. What's up?"

"Feel like a trip to Milwaukee next week?"

I walk into the living room, out of Bug's earshot, and sigh into the phone. "Rich, we've talked about this. I won't do back-to-back weeks away. I don't even like more than one trip a month. Is it something I can manage from here? Over Zoom calls?"

"They don't work like that. In person only with these guys."

Bug walks through the room, gets my suitcase, and rolls it into the laundry room where I hear the washer start moments later. I smile thinking of how she always takes care of me. How we take care of each other.

"I'm sorry to have to let you down, but I literally just walked through the door."

"I knew it was a long shot, but you're my best guy. And this company is desperate to fix their vulnerabilities. Cyber-hacker got in and messed with all their client data. Huge clusterfuck."

"I'm sure it is. Can Arjun handle it?"

"Probably. Can you back him up if needed?"

"As long as it's from sunny Florida."

"Fair enough. How is your daughter?"

"Good." I lower my voice. "I think she's discovered boys, so I may be having my mid-life crisis a bit early."

Laughter echoes through the phone. "I hate to tell you this, but as the father of two teenage girls myself, she most likely discovered them years ago. You're probably just finding out about it now."

"I'm *so* not ready for this." I rub my temples. "Short of being Arjun's backup, do you have anything else for me next week?"

"Check your email. As long as Arjun doesn't run into any roadblocks, it may be a light week for you."

"I could use one of those."

"Later, Asher."

"Bye."

When I turn, Bug is standing in the doorway, sneering. "I have *not* discovered boys."

"Good to know," I say, not calling her out for listening in on a private conversation. After all, Allie does the same thing. "Guess I have my little girl for a bit longer."

"I'm not a little girl, Dad. I'm just saying, boys aren't in the picture."

I take a step back and study her, wondering if this is going to be one of those moments that defines our relationship from here forward. I try not to show any conflicting emotions when I say, "Okay, girls then."

She snickers. "I'm not gay, Dad. But I'm not opposed to it. Mel is gay."

This has my eyebrows touching my hairline. "Mel. Your best friend?"

She shrugs. "It's no big deal. It's not like she tries to stick her tongue down my throat or anything."

"I… uh…"

Easy, Asher. Do not handle this the wrong way. But the thought of anyone, male *or* female, putting their hands or tongue on my baby makes me want to go all ballistic protective dad.

"Okay, well, I guess good for her. But, you know, if you ever want to talk about things…"

"Ewww. No."

I step over to the couch and sit, thinking what a terrible father I am. I've never had 'the talk' with her. "Bug, I'm sorry you don't have a mom to ask all those important questions. I wish there was someone you could trust with all that… stuff."

"I'm not sorry." She gets a coke from the refrigerator and sits on a barstool overlooking the couch. "I like it just being us. Besides, Aunt Marti talks about *that stuff* with me."

"She does?"

I'm served with a huge dose of teen eye rolling. "I'm thirteen, Dad. Aunt Marti has been talking to me about stuff since I was eight."

The more she says the word *stuff*, the more I transpose it with the word *sex*, which has my fucking head in a complete tailspin. This is my baby we're talking about. I still see her as the toddler I'd push on the swing. The little girl who would run to me when she fell and scraped her knee. The pre-teen who cried when she came in last place at the rock-wall climb at a friend's birthday party.

She's thirteen. Thirteen-year-olds can have sex. Hell, they can have babies. Where has the time gone? How has she grown up so quickly right under my nose?

And with Marti living in New York now, there's no one here to act as a mother figure for her.

Immediately, my mind goes to Allie. Why, I'm not sure. Allie has never, not for one second, ever mentioned, suggested, or eluded to wanting the job. What we have is fun. Easy. Convenient. It's something I can keep separate from my life with Bug and her complete and total aversion to females in my life. Though with Allie's brother marrying my sister, those lines are converging.

In fact it's become harder and harder to separate my… *relationship?* with Allie from my life with Bug. Especially when Bug and I go to Calloway Creek so we can visit Marti and Charlie—my five-year-old nephew and Bug's only cousin.

The last time we visited, it was all I could do to keep my hands off Allie. I got the idea it was the same for her, which is why we tried to avoid each other. We avoided each other for the sake of my temperamental kid.

But the funny thing is, Bug *isn't* temperamental—until it comes to women I take up with. In fact, she's growing up to be just like my sister. Generous with her love and her time. Understanding of the shortcomings of others. Respectful of those who don't necessarily share our cultural, religious, or political beliefs. She's a daughter I can be proud of. One I'm close to. She's the most important person in my life.

She is a pitbull, however, when it comes to any woman on my radar. Sabotage is not hyperbole when I think of the crazy shit she's done to keep me from having long-term relationships.

Maybe that's why I go to great lengths to try and keep what Allie and I have from bleeding over into my day-to-day life. If Bug's tactics were to ruin what I have with Allie like they have with so many others, I know it would leave a huge hole in my life.

I lean back into the couch and sigh, knowing how even though we just parted ways this afternoon, I already miss Allie. I miss her long, honey-brown hair. I miss her million-dollar smile. I miss the way her lips dance around my cock. I miss her long, slender legs, and her toned calves. I miss the way she gets hiccups after almost every meal. I miss… everything about her.

"Dad?"

I look up. "Yeah, sweetie?"

"Are you okay? You look sad. You're not going to stop me from hanging out with Mel are you?"

"No. Of course not."

"What is it? Work stuff?"

I lie to her with my nod. Because how could I possibly tell my overprotective teenager that I think I just realized I'm in love.

And not only that, but that I'm in love with the much younger woman who has shown zero interest in making this—whatever it is—more than the incredible, hot, occasional, fuckbuddy, friends-with-benefits thing she believes it to be.

I am so completely screwed.

Chapter Three

Allie

I'm early. My Wednesday was light and my last wine tasting tour of the day got cancelled. Which I'm fine with considering I'd been anticipating hopping on the train and meeting Asher in the city since breakfast.

I love my job as the events manager at my parents' winery. I don't mind working late nights or weekends even. One day, I'll own the winery along with my brothers Lucas, Dallas, and Blake. It's the best job in the world if you ask me.

But that doesn't mean my panties haven't been soaked today as I had thoughts of what Asher was going to do to me tonight.

He got to town yesterday. I had a late event, so I couldn't see him until today. As it turns out, I don't have to be at work until late morning tomorrow, so I can stay the night.

I love it when I can stay the night and wake up in his arms. More often than not, I have winery obligations, or he has work dinners, or he has to fly home to Bug, or I'd promised to babysit one of my brothers' kids.

Not today, however. I'll have sixteen whole hours with him.

I cock my head, wondering when I started counting such things. It reminds me of what he said last time about knowing exactly the number of occasions we'd been together.

Part of me wonders if this is quickly treading into relationship territory.

Hmmm. Would I be okay with that? I've had a few *things* over the years, but nothing I'd call a relationship. Not since Jason.

Then again, Asher has never given me any indication he intends for this to be long term. Why would he? He probably laughs with his work buddies about how he has it made. Booty calls in the city whenever he wants. Zero strings. I wonder if he brags about being with a woman twelve years his junior. Not that I care about our age difference. Other than the faint lines on his forehead and around his eyes, and the ever-so-slight-and-sexy beginnings of gray around his temples, he doesn't seem forty.

"Good afternoon, Miss Montana," William the doorman greets as he waves me through.

"Please, William, call me Allie."

It's funny how all the workers here know me by name despite the fact that I only visit about once a month.

Or fourteen times to be exact. I roll my eyes thinking of his words.

"Sure thing, Miss Montana."

I giggle as I make my way to the elevator. Asher texted me his room number earlier. Texted, not called. That's another indicator of our relationship status. We never speak on the phone. We always text. And I'm fine with that. I guess. Yes, yes, of course I am. Long-term relationships lead to things I'm not ready for. Things I'll never be ready for. Like kids. I'm perfectly fine being the fun aunt.

William comes after me. "Mr. Anderson is at the bar, Miss Montana."

"Thank you, William."

"Pleasure."

It's only five thirty, and Asher isn't expecting me until seven. I stop at the entrance of the bar when I see him talking with a woman. She throws her head back and laughs. He's smirking. I can imagine she asked him what kind of work he does. He gets his kicks telling people he's a 'penetration tester.'

The funny thing is, that's the actual technical name for what he does. He's a dark web hacker. He gets hired to test tech infrastructures for vulnerabilities. And he's very good at what he does. He's high in demand. Companies from all over the world want to hire the man who single-handedly stopped a virus from draining the bank accounts of billions of people who shopped at the largest online retailer in the world.

That was before I met him. But his reputation runs far and wide. And despite how much money he's offered, he never takes overseas jobs. Not unless he can do them remotely. He has a rule never to leave Bug for more than a week, and never to be more than a six-hour plane ride away. That pretty much limits him to the continental United States, parts of Mexico, and some of the Caribbean Islands.

I have to admire him for what he's done. Not work-wise. That's all secondary. He's raised a daughter almost entirely on his own. Before that, he raised his sister after their parents died. At one point in his twenties, he was not only raising an infant, but his teenage sister. All by himself. I can't even imagine.

The beautiful redhead puts a flirty hand on his shoulder, wiping away something I'm sure isn't even there.

I roll my eyes.

I'm not the jealous type, but seeing him talking with another woman has me wondering. When he's done with me. With this.

When Bug is older and he allows himself to be in a real relationship. Will he marry again?

I can't see Asher staying single forever. He just has so much to offer. He truly is the entire package. And some woman out there will be lucky to have him when the time comes.

Ignoring the twinge deep inside me, I cough. Asher turns and smiles like he's five and I'm Santa. He quickly shakes the woman's hand, pays for his drink, and saunters—yes, *saunters*—over.

"Well, aren't you a sight for sore eyes."

I nod to the redhead and joke, "I doubt your eyes are sore after looking at Emma Stone over there."

"Al, if she's Emma Stone, then you're Cleopatra."

It's strange the way he's looking at me right now. I know it's been a minute since we've seen each other, but it's not like it's been any longer than before. Yet the way he takes me in is just… different. His eyes travel over me slowly, making time stand still. I did cut a few inches off my hair last week. That must be it.

I push my hand against his chest. "Stop it. You're ogling me."

He takes my hand and guides me toward the elevator. "I'm going to be doing a lot more than that in about three and a half minutes."

I laugh. "What, no dinner first?"

"We're ordering room service."

We step into the elevator. And we're alone. He leans close and inhales. "You're early. I like surprises."

"You do, do you?"

I cup the front of his pants. He's already getting hard. I push him into the corner of the elevator right up against the buttons. An alarm sounds when I reach around him and press the emergency stop. I ignore it and unbuckle his belt, opening his pants just enough.

He says a few choice words as I take him into my mouth and suck him off like I've never sucked him off before. In less than a minute, he's coming down my throat. I swallow, wipe my lips, zip up his pants, and answer the lady who finally comes over the speaker to ask if everything is okay.

"We're fine," I say, trying to sound calm and collected. "Some kid was playing with the buttons."

The elevator starts moving again. Asher is speechless as he finishes buttoning his pants and buckling his belt. I've stunned him into silence. I smile at the small victory.

When we reach our floor, we stroll slowly to his hotel room. Once inside, he finally speaks.

"I can't believe you just blew me in an elevator."

I shrug. "You said you like surprises."

He laughs heartily, shaking his head as if still absorbing what just happened. "Jesus Christ, Al." He laughs again. "You know they have cameras in there. They know you're full of shit saying what you did about a kid being the culprit."

I cover my mouth in total embarrassment. "Do you think they saw the whole thing?"

"Probably not. I think the camera was in the panel behind my back. But I take no responsibility if we end up on some porn website."

"If that happens, I know a guy." I wink.

Now we're both laughing. How I love his laugh. How I love the way he makes me laugh.

Before Asher, I honestly can't remember laughing. Okay, so I've been through something traumatic. That would make anyone not want to laugh. But even the man's texts make me laugh when I'm sitting at my desk all by myself.

"I love your laugh," I say.

"I love yours."

His gaze becomes intense. Too intense. Maybe I shouldn't have said what I said. I quickly follow it up with something I know will change the subject we most definitely should not be talking about. "Know what else I love?"

He waits expectantly.

I untie the drawstring on my dress, kick off my shoes, and pull down my silk panties. "Your tongue. I love your tongue. And I want it on me. *Everywhere.*"

His eyes both darken and blaze fire all at once. "Do you trust me?"

I pull my dress up and over my head. "That's a silly question to ask someone who's standing here naked demanding an orgasm."

"Al, just answer the question."

"Yes, I trust you, Mr. President."

He chuckles. Then he walks to the dresser, sets his phone up on a stand, aims it at the bed and starts a video.

My jaw drops. "You're recording us?"

"It's a long time between visits. I'd like to be able to see you when I, you know… need to relieve some stress."

This is new information. We never talk about whether or not we see other people or scratch the itch in between the times he comes to the city.

"Plus, you should see yourself when you come, Allie. It's the most spectacular thing I've ever witnessed in my whole goddamn life."

I look from him to the camera. "Okay, fine. But if you get to video me having an orgasm, I get to video you." I put my phone on the nightstand knowing we'll have two different vantage points.

His smile is a mile wide.

We spend the next several hours burning up our phone batteries.

They are the most erotic hours of my entire twenty-eight years.

Chapter Four

Asher

Our breakfast arrives all too early. I don't think we got more than a few hours' sleep between watching videos, making more at better angles, watching those, and, well, it just went on and on.

Still naked in bed, I shovel eggs in my mouth then take a sip of coffee. A work text comes in, making me think of all the videos on my phone. Instead of watching them again, I set up a shared, password protected folder in the Cloud and move all the videos into it.

Shit. Just the knowledge they're on there gets me hard, which surprises me considering how much of a workout my cock has gotten over the past twelve hours.

Allie looks over my shoulder. "Oh my god, please don't watch those again. I think you broke my lady garden that last time."

I snort out laughter. "Lady garden? Woman, I'd call it more of an organ grinder."

She raises a brow. "I didn't see you complaining at the time."

"And I'm still not. The whole night was just…"

"Beyond."

Our gazes lock onto each other. "Yeah." When my cock swells further, I shake my head and look back at my phone. "Anyway, I was just making sure prying teenage eyes won't ever discover these videos."

"Good idea." She shoves her phone at me. "Do it on mine, too. I'm always letting Charlie and Maisy play games on this. Can you imagine the wrath I'd get from my brothers if they came across one of these?"

He pales. "Maybe we should delete them. Your brothers would have my head on a spike if they knew."

She swipes her phone back. "Delete them? Are you crazy? After all that time and energy we spent getting just the right angles? I was thinking we should change careers and get into porn production. Besides, you're the tech guru. I'm sure nobody will get past your algorithms and cookies and firewalls."

I take her phone from her once more. "Better leave the technical stuff to me. You really have no idea what you're talking about, do you?"

She continues watching over my shoulder. I upload her videos to the same place, then show her how to access them.

"You're sharing your Cloud with me? Big step, Ash. What's next, a ring?" She giggles.

I don't laugh with her. Because those words conjure an all-too-clear image in my mind of me down on a knee looking up into her gorgeous eyes while slipping a rock onto her finger.

What the fuck is wrong with me? It has to be the upcoming wedding. Every time I talk to my sister, it's all she can talk about. *I can't wait to marry Dallas. The ceremony is going to be so beautiful. Charlie is going to have a dad again.*

Not to mention Bug's excitement as well. She's going to be a bridesmaid. And she's super excited about going to Antigua.

Even Allie talks about it. She's a bridesmaid, too. Everyone in my life is all *wedding this and wedding that*. It's no wonder I've got love on the brain. That's all this is.

I'm silent for so long, Allie's entire demeanor changes. "I didn't mean…" She hops out of bed and puts on a T-shirt. "It was just a stupid joke."

She's totally misreading the situation.

"Sorry. I was just wondering if there were any ways someone could break into that private folder."

"Oh." She sits back down. "Bug doesn't have your password, does she?"

"I don't share my internet passwords with anyone."

"Except me."

I cock a brow. "Not really. I created a special password just for this."

She taps her temple. "Smart. Because I'd probably go in and watch *all* your sex videos."

"You'd be hard pressed to find any. These were the first."

"Reeeeealy?" she says, as if not quite believing a man so much older than she is hasn't done such a thing.

I nod. "Don't let my age fool you, Al. Last night I experienced a lot of firsts. First sex tape, first blow job in an elevator, first… what did you call that position?"

"Reverse cowgirl."

My cock twitches. "We are definitely doing that again."

Her nose turns up. "It wasn't very flattering on video."

"Are you kidding? That might be the one I watch the most."

Her head tilts. "Are you really going to watch them?"

"Hell yes."

"Don't guys prefer to watch girl on girl porn?"

I tug her against me. "I'll put up our videos against anything any day of the week."

She smiles proudly, but her words have my mind cycling.

"Hey, that reminds me. Apparently Bug's best friend is gay. Should I be worried?"

"Worried that she'll influence Bug's sexuality?"

"No, I don't think that's a thing. But she is growing up, and now I'm worried about someone… *anyone*… trying to make a sex tape with my kid."

Her eyes roll. "You worry about her too much."

"She's thirteen. That's a very worrisome age. You have no idea because you're not a mom."

Allie swallows, her playfulness gone in an instant like a curtain is drawn over her face. Maybe my words offended her because she's a tried-and-true aunt who spends a lot of time around kids. *A lot.* It makes me wonder if she's ever thought about having them herself.

"Hey." I run a hand down her arm. "Just out of curiosity, do you see kids in your future?"

She blows out a long, drawn-out breath, as if I'd asked her the meaning of life. "Children aren't in the cards for me."

"Ever?"

She shakes her head.

"But you're so young."

"Ever," she reiterates in a tone that tells me this is not a topic for discussion.

I'm not sure if the question freaked her out because of *us*, or if it's something deeper. Can she not have kids? Does she have a medical condition that would prevent her from getting pregnant? With as much as Stella and I tried and failed to give Bug a half-sibling, I know personally how hard it can be for some people.

Sensing the need for a change of subject, I say, "Bug can't stop talking about the wedding. She's never been out of the country."

Allie's shoulders visibly relax, apparently glad I'm not pressing the situation. I guess I need to learn to keep my mouth shut when it comes to talking about the future. Because maybe she just doesn't see me in hers.

Now I'm the one who's depressed.

"So how's it going to work when we're there?" she asks. "Is it going to be like when the two of you come to Cal Creek?"

"You mean are we going to avoid each other so you aren't on the receiving end of my kid's wrath?"

"She's not stupid, Asher. You know she suspects something. It's why she won't let me call her Bug."

"I guess we'll have to figure something out. Ways to keep her occupied." I pull her close. "Because I'm not about to be stuck in a tropical paradise without making love to you under the stars."

Finally, she cracks a smile again. "Under the stars, huh?"

"And maybe in the ocean."

Her nose crinkles. "Water sex is overrated."

I stiffen, trying not to think about *any* sex she's had in the past. I brush it off. "Is that so?"

"Most of the body's natural lubricants are water-soluble, so it can get pretty abrasive down there."

Okay, so no water sex. But not because of any so-called abrasiveness.

My thoughts are overstepping the boundaries of our relationship. Who am I to be possessive about a woman I haven't even had one single conversation with about the future?

"You know"—she smiles deviously, oblivious to my internal musings—"I think I have a way to keep Bug busy. My whole family will be there. Lucas and Regan are making a honeymoon out of it.

Dallas and Marti will be busy with preparations. Blake and Ellie will probably treat it like a second honeymoon."

"Yeah, so?"

"So they all have kids. And they'll need babysitters. Say… some teenager who would be happy to earn twenty bucks an hour for playing with children."

I lean in and kiss her below the ear. "It's brilliant."

"I'm just protecting myself, Asher. I do not want to end up on your kid's shit list. The things you've told me she's done to the other women in your life." She gives me an exaggerated shiver. "What was it you said about her replacing your cologne with fish guts?"

I laugh. Bug is nothing if not creative. "It was fish-gut water. And holy shit, I couldn't get the smell off me for days, even after showering."

"I take it you never went on that date."

"Oh, I did. But after explaining to my date what happened, she ghosted me. I guess she didn't want to deal with a rambunctious ten-year-old."

Her eyes widen. "She did that when she was ten? Geesh—gotta give her a little credit. She's determined." She giggles and shakes her head slightly. "I love the one when she called the restaurant and had the staff put the wrong name on a birthday cake and then had them tell your date you arranged the entire thing."

I shake my head at that too. "At least that one waited to dump me until we left the restaurant. Did I ever tell you about the one where Bug had a drink sent to me at dinner along with a note thanking me for 'last night'?"

"And your date read the note?"

"The waitress who brought it over made sure to drop it in the center of the table. Guess she thought I was a lying, cheating pig. I tried to explain to my date that it was my daughter. She threw the drink in my face and yelled at me for blaming my daughter to try and cover up my manwhoring."

Allie giggles. "I'm sorry. I shouldn't be laughing."

"Oh, it gets worse. She used my phone more than once to reschedule dates via text. The women thought they'd been stood up. And then there was the time she had flowers sent to a woman and put the wrong name and details of an encounter on the card."

She covers her mouth, trying not to laugh again. "Is it wrong that I like Bug just a little more now?"

"She's the sweetest kid, Al. I wish you could see that side of her. She just doesn't want a woman in my life."

"It's understandable. Her birth mom signed away her parental rights, and then her stepmom divorced you after she'd bonded with her for years. I think it's more about not wanting a woman in *her* life than in yours."

I stare at her, wondering if she's onto something. "I don't know. I think a lot of it is her not wanting to share me. She's gotten used to it being just the two of us. And maybe a part of her is protecting me from another Stella."

"But she's really protecting herself. *Her* heart. She doesn't want to be let down by a third mother figure."

I sigh and run my hands through my hair. "Do you think I'll have to wait until she's eighteen to bring someone into her life?"

"Eighteen?" She guffaws. "Try thirty-five. I'm twenty-eight and still think my dad walks on water. If he and my mom weren't together, I'd… well, I'd probably still be pulling adolescent pranks to keep him single."

I deflate like a balloon. "I love my daughter more than anything. But capitulating to her insecurities for another decade or more just feels like I'm letting her walk all over me."

"You are." She leans in and kisses my cheek. "But it's kind of sexy how protective of her you are. The sexy single dad. The 'penetration tester.' The secret meetings in the city. I'd say I'm one lucky girl."

And there it is. She likes it this way. Secret meetings. Me keeping my life with Bug separate from… this.

Me? I hate it this way. I want to be here with Allie *and* be home with Bug. I want both of them. I want both of them all the time. *Together.*

But even knowing Allie doesn't share my feelings, my desires for a future, my hopes and dreams, I still find it hard to get myself out of bed and walk away from her. And I know as soon as I walk out that door, I'll miss her even more than the last time I left. Because the last time I left, I missed her more than the time before.

These feelings I'm having are too much too soon. Yes, it's been almost sixteen months. But we've only really been on fifteen dates, if you can even call them dates. Hookups maybe. Encounters. But damn, I remember every single detail about each one of them. And this one, this one tops all the rest.

I push my emotions aside and climb on top of her, wriggling against her. "The next time I see you, you'll be wearing a bikini on the beach."

She shimmies her hips up into me, licks her lips, and raises a sultry brow. "Or maybe I won't."

Chapter Five

Allie

Antigua is a beautiful island. It's not the first time my family or I have been here. Ever since we were little, our parents would take us on fun, exotic, educational vacations.

Although it's been more than a dozen years since we came here, the white sandy beaches, breezy trade winds, and million-dollar views are what drew Dallas back to the place where he'll make Asher's sister his wife.

I'm currently looking at one of those views right now. My beach bungalow sits up on the side of a hill. There are exactly seventy-three steps winding down to an exclusive beach tucked back in a bay, protecting us from the harsher ocean waves. That barrier makes it easier to see the outlines and shadows of sea life beneath the blue-green water, and at the moment I'm tracking a stingray as he flies just underneath the surface.

It truly is paradise.

A slow smile creeps up my face as I remember what Asher said he wanted to do to me here. He arrives later tonight. Along with

Bug. I'm not as worried as I was about getting alone time with him. She'll want to spend every moment she can with her cousin, Charlie. Plus, what teenager wouldn't want to spend her days on one of the best-rated beaches in the world?

It's the nights that concern me the most. Will we be able to sneak away and accomplish Asher's 'under the stars' wish?

I find myself fantasizing about all the things we'll do if we get the chance. He's texted me a few times since our last meet-up. Mostly to tell me how much he's been enjoying the videos. I have to admit, I've watched them a time or ten myself.

Mia Cruz, my best friend, once forced me to watch a porn movie when we were teens. I found it mostly funny. And at times, a bit scary. The cocks on the guys in those movies are massive, and they put them in places I thought they definitely shouldn't be putting them.

I silently chuckle. Because Asher and I have most definitely been testing the limits of sexuality. And even though he's older and a lot more experienced, it's felt like somehow, we'd both been waiting for that person who was so sexually compatible, it made all those things way more fun and not the least bit embarrassing.

Mitchell makes a noise, shifting in my arms. I avert my gaze from the stingray to my eleven-week-old nephew and sigh. Every time I look at him, touch him, hold him, memories from my past bombard me. But no matter how painful those memories are, they can't keep me from this amazing, tiny, perfect human. I gladly babysit whenever needed. And this week, it's been needed a lot.

While my mom has been tasked with keeping Maisy and Charlie occupied, mostly by following them around at the beach as they add to their growing collections of shells and sharks' teeth, my job has been Mitchell. And I do it willingly. Even as it sends shards of white-hot pain right into the center of my heart.

"Are you hungry, little guy?"

He confirms my suspicion when he arches his back and lets out a ravenous wail.

I laugh. "Okay, okay. Lunch is coming."

After fetching Mitchell's bottle of breast milk, I settle back outside, once again enjoying the view as I feed him. When he's finished, I watch his little eyes flutter open and closed. He's milk-drunk and sleepy. I hold him in one hand and pull the bassinet out onto the lanai with my other. There's surely no better place to get a nap than here.

Gently settling him down, I lie on the outdoor couch next to him, watching him through the white mesh side of the cradle as his little mouth puckers and his hands twitch as he falls into a deep sleep. I find the sight of him mesmerizing as my own eyelids grow heavy.

He's cute. He's amazing. He's perfect in every way.

"Miss Montana. Mr. Platt," the doctor says, looking anything but joyful. She gestures to the two chairs opposite her desk. "Please sit. I have some concerning results to go over with you."

Jason and I share a look. I shrug. What could be concerning? My heart thunders. Maybe we're having twins. Oh my gosh, how fun would that be? Mom would probably kill me, though. She's going to kill me as it is. Just as soon as we tell her I'm having a baby at nineteen.

Knowing how people are in Calloway Creek, Jason and I decided to keep this a secret until we get married—which will happen exactly three weeks from today. We could have done it sooner, which would have made it so much easier. Because at twelve weeks, I'm going to start showing soon, and I still have to hide it for three more.

But Jason insisted we get married on June twenty-eighth. It was his parents' wedding anniversary. They died when he was fifteen. Killed by a drunk driver. It's his way of honoring them.

My high school sweetheart, Jason and I started dating at sixteen. He lives with his aunt, who basically has no rules, so it's been easy for him to sneak around. And I live at my parents' house—Montana Manor—over one of the banks of garages with a separate outdoor entrance. It's every hormonal teenager's dream setup. My parents have never suspected that Jason sleeps over pretty much every weekend since we started having sex two and half years ago.

My best friend, Mia, is the only person who knows about our present situation, and she's been sworn to secrecy. Being a twin herself, she would totally flip out if I had twins. I know she'll be a huge help. She's even insisting on being called Aunt Mia.

Dr. Miller shuffles a few papers around. I like the way she never judged us from the start. We picked her from a google search. We needed a doctor outside of Calloway Creek. No way were we going to someone local. Despite those laws that are supposed to keep medical information private, everyone knows everyone else's business in our small town. So we've been coming to the city that's just a short train ride away.

When it seems like the doctor has been hesitating far too long, I ask, "Are we having twins?"

She shakes her head. "No, not twins."

Jason sits up straighter. "Triplets?" he squeaks out.

"No," she says. "What I have to tell you is going to be difficult to hear. The blood work we did last week revealed your baby likely has a genetic disorder that occurs when a person has three copies of chromosome eighteen instead of two."

"Wait, no," Jason says, clearly upset. "Are you saying our kid has Down's Syndrome?"

"Babies with Down's have three copies of chromosome twenty-one," she explains. "Your baby is showing markers for what is called Trisomy 18, or Edwards syndrome."

I swallow hard, feeling like the ceiling is about to come crashing down. "What exactly does that mean?"

"First off, I'd like to schedule you for an amniocentesis in three weeks, that will give us confirmation."

A relieved sigh bellows out of me. "Oh, good. So you aren't sure."

"Allie." She looks at me with sympathetic eyes. "The blood tests are very accurate. They measure free fragments of fetal DNA in the bloodstream. The detection rate of the NIPT blood test showing Trisomy 18 is around ninety-seven percent. That means, in all likelihood, your baby does have it. We just do the amnio to be one hundred percent sure."

Jason reaches over and squeezes my hand. "Okay, so assume the baby has it. What does that mean? Will he or she have issues like a Down's Syndrome baby?"

"He or she"—she looks down at her file—"do you want to know the sex?"

"Yes," Jason and I say in tandem.

"Okay, he then—it's a boy."

"Oh my god," Jason murmurs. "I'm having a son."

"Allie. Jason. You need to understand this genetic disorder is not the same as Down's Syndrome. Life expectancy with Down's Syndrome is sixty years."

I swallow again. Harder this time, as if there's a walnut in my throat. "And with this? What can we expect with our baby?"

She sighs big, as if not wanting to answer. "Anatomically, babies with Trisomy 18 can be low birth weight, have smaller-than-normal heads, clenched fists, short breastbones and extra skin folds at the back of the neck. Physiologically, they can suffer from heart defects, seizures, high blood pressure, and kidney problems."

My hand flies to my mouth as I absorb this information.

"There's more," she says sadly, and my eyes seal shut, not knowing what could be worse than what she's already said. "Only about fifty percent of babies with Trisomy 18 are born alive."

I'm gasping for breath, barely registering the rest of her words when she says, "Ninety to ninety-five percent will not survive the first year. Most of them will pass within the first two weeks of life."

I almost slide out of my chair. I want to fall to the ground and be swallowed up. I want to wake up from this nightmare.

Jason drops my hand. He's stunned into silence. Shell-shocked like me.

The doctor is quiet for a beat as we process what we've been told.

Jason is the first to speak. "Is there anything we can do? What do most people in our situation do?"

Dr. Miller sighs. "Statistically, a great number of women choose termination considering the life-limiting consequences of the diagnosis."

My eyes snap open. "You mean abortion?"

She nods.

"That," Jason says. "Let's do that."

I sneer at him and his quickness to agree to such lunacy. "I'm not aborting our baby."

"You heard the doctor. Odds are, he'll die before birth anyway. And if by some miracle he doesn't, he will shortly after. Why would you put us through that, Allie?"

"Because he's our son." I put a protective hand over my belly. "And the test could be wrong. Right, Dr. Miller? You said ninety-seven percent. That means there's a chance it's wrong. Three percent is not nothing. The test could be wrong."

The doctor nods but adds, "Allie, I don't want you having false hopes here. Over my career, I've never seen that happen. Of course you should wait for the amniocentesis to make any decision. There is another test you could do today even. It's called chorionic villus sampling. It involves inserting a thin tube through the cervix into the uterus to collect a sample of tissue. Both tests would confirm the diagnosis, but each comes with a statistically significant chance of miscarriage."

I stand and put distance between myself and the two others in the room. "I'm not killing my baby. I don't care what any test says. In fact, I'm not going to have any tests. Especially not ones that can cause a miscarriage. I don't care what he has. If he dies inside me, so be it, but I'm not killing him."

"If that's your choice, I'll support you and help you any way I can," Dr. Miller says. "But to be clear, and just so you fully recognize the severity... Allie, Trisomy 18 is a chromosomal abnormality that's incompatible with life. Do you understand what I'm saying?"

I nod.

"Your baby will not survive. If he makes it to delivery, it will still only be a matter of time. A day. A week. Probably not even a month. If you choose to continue the pregnancy, you will have to live with that certainty."

"I'm not getting an abortion."

Jason stands, walks over, and puts his hands on my shoulders, looking me straight in the eyes. "Allie, there isn't a choice here. You have to get one. The alternative is horrific. I won't just sit around and wait for him to die. It's crazy. It's inhumane. And it's not fair to any of us."

"There is a human being growing inside me." I'm sure I sound a bit hysterical, but I'm unapologetic as I'm apparently the only one here set to fight for this baby. "He's our son, Jason. I can't just kill him."

"And I can't just sit around and watch."

"No one's making you."

His hands drop from my shoulders. "Is this your final decision?"

"Yes. No matter what happens, yes."

"Then you're on your own." He goes for the door, not bothering to look back. He walks through and shuts it, abandoning me—his fiancée—and his unborn child.

I hate him right now. I hate him as much as I love the little boy growing inside me. I crumple to the floor, sobbing for what was. What could have been. What's going to be.

Arms come around me. It's Dr. Miller. "Is there someone I can call, Allie?"

Through my sobs, I nod. "I want my mom."

Cries from a baby wake me from my nightmare. For just a split second, I think it's Christopher. But once the beautiful tropical vista fills my vision, I remember where I am.

And that the baby crying is not mine.

Picking up my nephew and snuggling him close, we cry together. Me more so than him. I cry until I can't cry another single tear.

Chapter Six

Allie

I wipe my eyes and answer the door to find Mom standing there, looking all tan and much younger than her years. She's wearing a two-piece bathing suit, the bottoms covered by a pair of sheer lounge pants. Her hair is escaping a tangled bun, an indicator of just how windy it is outside. She looks really pretty.

Everyone says I look like my mom. I hope that means I'll also look a decade younger when I'm in my fifties.

"Those kids are going to run me ragged," she says, stepping over the threshold while searching through her bag, for a hairbrush most likely. "I just dropped them off with Blake for a few hours so I could come check on you and—"

She finally looks up at me, and her head tilts as she studies my face. Her eyes soften as she runs a finger down my cheek. "You've been crying." She looks over at Mitchell, who's lying in his bouncy seat. "Bad day?" Taking my hand, she pulls me toward the couch. "Come sit."

She doesn't have to ask why I'm having a bad day, and I don't tell her. She knows. She's one of a select few people who know what being around Mitchell does to my heart. That it both expands and breaks at the very same time. That it makes me want to laugh yet scream. That being around any baby solidifies my stance to never become anything but a doting aunt.

"Why don't I take him and let you get some rest?"

"I'm fine, Mom. And I don't need rest. I just had a nap." I glance outside. "Which is why I was crying."

"Oh, honey, were you dreaming of him?"

I nod.

She squeezes my hand. "I know it's not the same, not even close, but to this day I still sometimes dream about the baby I lost before I got pregnant with you."

I nuzzle into her shoulder. "You never told me that. I mean, I knew about the miscarriage, but not that you had dreams."

"After what you went through, I didn't think it was fair to bring it up. There's just no comparing our experiences."

"What are your dreams?"

"Mostly about you having an older sister. Maybe that's what I mourn the most. The boys all had each other, but you never got to have that special bond."

"I had *you*," I say, looking up at her. "And I'm lucky to have three brothers I get along with so well."

She smiles. "So, what are your plans for the rest of the day?" She must see a certain look in my eyes, because her smile becomes brighter. "Oh, right. Today is the day Asher and Bug arrive." She hops off the couch and starts gathering Mitchell's things. "You'll want to shower and shave and primp and all that."

I roll my eyes. "Whatever."

Mom stops folding the portable bassinet. "You *are* happy he's coming, aren't you?"

"Sure."

"Allie, we don't talk about it much, mostly because you seem to change the subject every time I ask, but what exactly is Asher to you? Is he a… phase? Or are you thinking long term?"

I can't tell which answer would please her more. She's been aware of Asher and me hooking up since the beginning. I mean, I do live in her house, and she did catch him doing the walk of shame that first time. And even though we never talk details, she knows about my monthly-ish visits to Manhattan. Sometimes I wonder if it bothers her that he's so much older. Strangely, it doesn't seem to bother my brothers. Then again, maybe none of them believe anything will ever come of it. And they'd be right.

"He has a kid. They live in Florida. We don't talk about things like that."

Her head cocks. "You've been together over a year and you've never talked about your relationship?"

"We're not in a relationship, Mom."

Her gaze scolds me. "Honey, you drop everything and run to the city every time he's there. Sure, we don't speak of him much, but whenever you say his name, there's a certain twinkle in your eyes. And, Allie, when he visits Calloway Creek with Bug and I see him look at you from across the room… Anyone can see what you have is a relationship."

"So we're hot for each other."

"I think it's more than that." She shakes her head as she stuffs burp rags into Mitchell's diaper bag. "You young people. You never want to define your relationships. Things were different when your dad and I met. You had a boyfriend or you didn't. There was none of this in-between stuff."

I laugh. "You led a sheltered life, Mom. I hate to break it to you, but people have been doing the friends-with-benefits thing for hundreds of years."

"Friends." She gives me a sharp stare. "*That's* what you are? Come on."

I shrug, not wanting to get into this with her again. As close as we are, I do not want to have another conversation with her about me and guys. She obviously wants me to be happy, and she thinks I need to be married to accomplish that. But she should know better. She should know there's a part of me that can never be happy.

She picks Mitchell up, resting him against her shoulder, and grabs the diaper bag. "Can you help me bring his things over to our bungalow?"

I get the bassinet and bouncy chair, then remember the other bottle in the fridge, and follow her out the door and across a courtyard to their palatial rental that's five times as big as mine. It makes me wonder where Asher and Bug will be staying. I know some wedding guests will be down at the main building of the hotel. It's where my friends Ren and Addy are staying, along with their husbands and kids. Most of the Calloways are making the trip here. They're our cousins, and our families have always been close.

We pass the large stairway that leads down to the restaurants, bars, and pools in the center of the massive hotel complex. I can almost see Asher climbing the stairs, maybe even taking two at a time in his excitement to get to me. After the videos, I know we're both chomping at the bit to see what's next.

"Allie?"

I hadn't realized I'd stopped walking and am staring at the steps.

"What? Yeah, coming."

After leaving Mom and Mitchell at her place and returning to my own, I get a call from Mia.

"Has the sex god arrived?"

I laugh. She's the only one I talk about Asher with. My other friends ask about him often, but it's hard for them to understand why I like things the way they are. Mia knows. She knows about all of it. Jason. Christopher. My aversion to anything permanent. "Not yet."

"I'm going to need details. I'm seriously suffering from FOMO here, Allie."

"You could have come, you know."

"Ha! A Cruz at a Montana wedding?"

"Dallas has nothing against you."

"Still, it would have been weird. But I want pictures. Do you have your dress yet? I'll bet the sex god is going to flip out when he sees you in it."

A smile creeps up my face. We have picked up the bridesmaid dresses. And I do believe Mia is correct and Asher might just want to tear it right off me when he sees me up there. If the plunging neckline doesn't do the trick, the amount of thigh that'll be showing through the long slit up the side ought to do it.

Bug's dress is like mine—a blue-green shade that matches the sea—minus the sexy neckline and thigh-revealing slit.

It's going to be strange, Bug and me standing up next to Marti as her two attendants. Marti didn't have many friends before coming to Cal Creek. Since her move, we've gotten close. And Bug is her niece. It only made sense that we'd be standing up with her at what will be a small, intimate ceremony. Still, it will be a bit awkward being right next to Asher's daughter—the kid who hates me because she thinks I'm stealing her dad's attention.

Sometimes I wonder if it would make things better or worse if I told her this is nothing more than a long-term fling. Would she be relieved that I'm not going to be a permanent fixture in their lives? Or would she be pissed that I'm using her dad to satisfy an itch?

"Allie?"

"Sorry. Still here. Yes, I'll send pictures."

"And you'll call me tomorrow? You know, after whatever happens with the sex god. I'm dying to know how he's going to top the video thing."

I laugh. "Yes, Mia, I'll call you tomorrow. Sorry, no pictures of that."

She huffs a pout. "I still say as your best friend I should get to watch the videos. It's not like I haven't seen you naked, girl." She pauses. "Or maybe you're being a bit territorial about the sex god?"

"Will you quit calling him that?"

"You're the one who started it, way back when. If I recall, you texted me those exact words the morning after you first hooked up."

"Yeah, but you've said it like a hundred times in the past few minutes. It's weird."

I hear someone shouting at her in the background, something about towing a car. She must be at work. She and her brothers own an auto repair shop. I kind of love that about her. She's not afraid to get her hands dirty and that makes her one badass chick.

"Hey, I gotta go. Tomorrow!"

"Okay, okay. I promise I'll call you in the morning."

She ends the call, and I'm left staring down at the bay, searching for more stingrays, wondering if Asher is making plans to 'top' the videos. Or maybe I'm not wondering at all. Maybe I'm *hoping*.

I toss my phone onto the couch and pull out the outfit I may have shopped way too long and carefully to find yesterday. The outfit I plan to wear when Asher arrives. The one that will show my tanned legs when I'm sitting nonchalantly at the hotel bar hoping to be noticed. The one I hope he tears off me when he does god-knows-what to me after sneaking into my bungalow.

I stop myself right there. Because I'm getting too excited. There's nothing different about this time. It's the same as all the others.

I glance out the window knowing it's not. This one is happening in paradise. In a place people come to get married. A place where people fall in love.

Closing my eyes, I sigh, once again trying to push away the feeling that niggles my insides. The one that presses against my heart as if knocking on a door to try and get inside. Because I know I'll never, *ever*, open it.

Chapter Seven

Asher

It's been a long day. Bug and I got up at six this morning to catch a nine o'clock flight from Orlando to Atlanta, which seems totally counterproductive since our final destination was Antigua, but that's how the airlines roll. Then our flight from Atlanta was delayed by two hours, extending our already long layover. After the four-hour flight to get to the island and then the taxi ride to the resort, Bug is definitely getting on my last nerve and I'm in serious need of an adult beverage.

We check in and make our way to our room. Along the way, I look around, wondering where Allie is staying. The resort is huge, so she could be anywhere. I doubt very much that she—or any of the Montanas—got a room like mine. I'm sure they're in the executive or penthouse suites or whatever the swanky rooms are.

We find our room and Bug swipes her key card, drops her shoulder bag near the couch, and beelines to the window. Her shoulders slump a bit and disappointment settles in. "I can't see the ocean."

"I think it's just beyond those trees," I say, sidling up next to her. "I had to compromise. It was either a regular room with a view of the ocean, or a suite with a garden view. I thought you'd want your own space." I nod to the couch. "It's a pull out, and my bed is just through there." I tip my head in the opposite direction then give her a gentle nudge with my elbow. "Hope you don't mind sharing a bathroom."

She unzips her suitcase and throws her stuff into the dresser under the television. "Want me to unpack *your* stuff?"

"What am I, five?" I wink playfully. "Seriously, Bug, we're here to have fun. You don't always have to look out for me, you know. That's *my* job."

She shrugs. "It's no big deal. I like it."

It *is* a big deal. I'm not sure if I'm just now realizing it or what. But she does a lot for me. Like this morning, she got up extra early to make sure we had a good breakfast before our day of travel. And yesterday, she made a checklist for me so I wouldn't forget my dress socks and the tie that matches her bridesmaid's dress. At thirteen, she should be more worried about forgetting her phone charger than her father's packing needs.

She plops down on the couch, as if we haven't been sitting on our asses for ten hours already, and gets out her phone. "Seems like a pretty cool place. Hope the Wi-Fi is good."

"I'm glad you approve."

Based on her reaction, I know she might be a little disappointed that we came all this way and don't even have a view of the water, but she'd never outright say it. It's not that I couldn't afford it—most of this was paid for by travel points anyway—but I've never been one to splurge. Not on a big house, or fancy car, or lavish vacations. I put away every single penny I can. For the piece of my heart sitting on the couch. For her wedding. For her future.

That's not to say we don't live nicely. We do. While our three-bedroom house doesn't hold a candle to Montana Manor, it's not exactly a broken-down shack. I drive a nice four-year-old convertible. And Bug has been to the Rocky Mountains, the Grand Canyon, Yellowstone, and just about every beach in Florida. This is, however, her first time out of the country.

It's my second. Well, my second actual vacation out of the continental U.S. I've traveled to Mexico, Puerto Rico, and a few other islands for work. The only other pleasure trip I've taken abroad was when Stella and I honeymooned in Australia—a wedding present from her parents and the only time I've been away from Bug for more than a week. Thankfully, my sister and most trusted babysitter was able to stay home with her.

"I thought I'd go check out the resort. Maybe grab a bite to eat. Want to come, or should I bring something back for you?"

She shrugs, tucking her phone into her pocket. "I could eat."

"Great." I clap my hands together. "I'm hoping to eat some good conch while I'm here."

Bug giggles.

"What?"

"It sounded like you said cock."

I sigh and roll my eyes. "My thirteen-year-old, people." I put a hand on her shoulder. "Would you please *please* never say that word again? I know you could never understand this, but as a father, it's one of the worst things I could hear my daughter say."

"Fine. I won't say cock anymore." She laughs. "I mean after that one."

I shake my head on our way out the door.

Winding paths lead in every direction. Thankfully, there are also signs posted at every pedestrian intersection. We stop at one to get our bearings. The beach is to the right. The pool is to the left. The convention center, spa, and fitness center are straight ahead. There are names of a few restaurants along with directional arrows toward them as well.

"What do you think?" I ask.

She points. "This place by the pool maybe? Surfside Eats sounds like a good place for *conch*."

The way she sounds out the word so it's most definitely distinguishable from *cock*, is hilarious.

"Sounds good. Let's go."

Surfside Eats is right up our alley. Casual outdoor dining with a great view of the massive pool and bar area. We order, and I have to keep myself from texting Allie while I'm awaiting that drink. Because here's the disappointing part: she knew when my flight was due to arrive. I'm two hours late, yet she hasn't inquired as to my whereabouts.

"Your drinks," the waitress says, placing my double whiskey and Bug's soda on the table.

"Thank you."

Bug watches her leave. "She's pretty."

I narrow my eyes. Bug never comments on women. Especially not to compliment them. "I suppose."

"Do you think Charlie is still awake?"

"Probably. I texted Aunt Marti when we landed. She and Charlie and Dallas were out to dinner somewhere off resort property, but she said she'd find us after."

"I can't believe Aunt Marti is getting married in two days. Do you think she's going to have another kid?"

"I don't know, Bug. After what she went through with Alex, and after what Dallas went through with losing his family, I'm just not sure."

She sips her soda. "I think one kid is perfect. Don't you?"

"Yup," I say without hesitation. I smile. "Especially when that one kid *is* perfect."

She smiles back at me.

Our food arrives, and Bug dives right in, biting into a conch fritter as if she hasn't eaten in days. "Uhmygod," she mumbles around her food. "These are sooooo good."

I pop one into my mouth and bite down. Then I stop chewing when I see Allie at the bar. And she's not alone.

Thank goodness Bug is playing on her phone, because I can't tear my eyes away from Allie. She's so fucking sexy. Her short sundress shows off toned and tanned legs. Her hair is long and loose, and every so often, it gets caught in a breeze and she has to swipe it off her face. When she tilts her head to brush it away, I have visions of running my tongue along her slender neck.

She's eating at the bar. And so is the guy she's with. He takes a piece of food off the plate they're sharing, and every instinct has me wanting to stride over and push him away. They both break out in laughter. I can't hear it because I'm too far away, but I can see their bodies shaking jubilantly. And then... then he touches her shoulder and my blood boils.

It's a jealousy I've never felt in my entire life. Not even when men used to talk to Stella when we were married. I've never felt a need to punch a man in the face more than I do at this very moment.

Every laugh they share is a knife to my heart. Every smile, a bullet to my soul.

For sixteen months I haven't had to deal with this. Every encounter we've had was at the hotel in New York City or at Montana Manor in Calloway Creek. I've never had an occasion to see her out and about flirting with other men.

She knew I was coming, yet she's out with this guy. Perhaps even on a date. With a much younger man than me. Maybe the sex videos were too much. A bridge too far. Or maybe this is just what she does when we're not together.

No matter how much it hurts to watch, I can't bring myself to turn away.

Bug finally notices where I'm staring. "Oh, great, it's Hannah Montana."

"Would you stop calling her that?"

Ever since the two of them met in Calloway Creek the Christmas before last, Bug hasn't been silent about her aversion to Allie. She calls her Hannah Montana as a dig at our age difference.

"Allie then." Her eyes roll defiantly. "And wow, that guy she's with is hot."

It's now when I break my gaze and look back at my daughter. "Hot? I thought you weren't into guys yet."

"I'm not. That doesn't mean I don't know a hot guy from a dud." She studies Allie. "They look good together, don't you think? He even looks younger than she is." She smiles and says a little louder. "You go, girl."

"What's gotten into you? I thought you hated her."

She shrugs. "Maybe it's the salty air. I just think she looks happy with him. Don't you think she looks happy?"

I don't answer. Instead, I eat another fritter, watching Allie flirt with my new enemy.

Since the day we met, I've felt connected to her on some surreal level. As if we were destined to be together. But for months now, I've waited and wondered. When will the day come when she doesn't meet me in the city because she's met someone new? In the back of my mind, I've wondered if maybe I'm a placeholder. The older guy she's having fun with until she meets Mr. Right. The good-time guy she passes time with while she's waiting for the one she really wants.

Fuck. I eat my entire dinner wondering if the three days I'll be here will be pure hell instead of the heaven I was anticipating.

Then Allie sees me. She smiles and bites her lower lip. But then she looks at Bug and her demeanor changes. It's only obvious to me because I know every nuance of her face. Her body. Her smile. And that smile fades ever-so-slightly.

She picks her phone up off the counter. Seconds later, I get a text.

Allie: Welcome to Antigua!

How can she be so blasé? She's eating, giggling, and flirting with another man.

I do something totally juvenile and don't text back. I just lift my chin and order another drink. But then I get another text.

**Allie: Bungalow 4. West end of the property.
You know, if you can sneak away.**

I don't know whether to be elated or pissed that she's expecting sex with me after being on a date with the baby-faced moron. But I'm not about to be a doormat. And I damn well don't want to share her with anyone. Which means I have no choice but to back away.

I shake my head, knowing tonight will consist of a few more drinks and me licking my wounds like a lame puppy.

It's the last straw when the guy leans in and kisses her cheek. He gets up to, I don't know, take a piss or something, and Allie looks back over. I can't hide my disgust. She narrows her eyes. Then she widens them as she looks from me to the guy walking away. Her head shakes from side to side, almost violently. She picks her phone back up.

My phone vibrates a few seconds later.

Allie: Asher, that was my cousin, Storm Calloway.

I've been on this earth for forty years, yet I've never been more fucking relieved than I am in this moment. All the tension in my body fades as I laugh at myself and how horribly I misread the situation. Allie was eating and laughing with her cousin. Not a random man at a tropical resort.

When I look up and we lock eyes, she smiles and laughs at my visible one-eighty. I pinch the bridge of my nose over my adolescent reaction.

Me: Thank the Lord. Because I may have been about to commit murder.

She giggles when she reads it. My attention gets drawn away when little arms wrap around me from behind. "Uncle Asher!"

Charlie is here. Along with my sister and her fiancé. "Hey guys."

"Heard your flight got delayed," Dallas says. "You must be exhausted."

My eyes flash back to Allie for a second. "Yeah, not so much."

Marti doesn't miss the brief interaction. "Hey, Bug," she says, winking at me. "How about you come for a sleepover? Charlie has really missed you."

"Please, please?" Charlie begs. "Wait until you see. There are bunches of steps down to the beach and there's even a kitchen. Will you come, Bug?"

Bug looks over at me. "Go ahead," I say.

Of course I let her go. Because that means I won't have to do any *sneaking* at all. I can walk right over to Bungalow 4 and live out my fantasy with the girl who is apparently the woman of my dreams.

Me: Give me thirty minutes.

Chapter Eight

Allie

A half-hour later, almost to the minute, there's a knock on the door, and I swing it open.

Asher is standing there with a bottle of champagne, two glasses, and a small gift bag. And one huge, shit-eating grin.

I wave him inside, laughing. "Did you really think I'd be out with someone the night you were going to arrive?"

He comes through the doorway, takes in the entire bungalow from wall to wall, then sets the bottle and glasses down, whistling at our surroundings. "Nice pad. And I was thinking maybe you thought I stood you up."

"I knew you'd be late. You texted me your flight information a few weeks ago. I was tracking it."

"Ahhh. Right." He looks pleased as he eyes me up and down. "So this incredible dress. It was for me?"

I feel my cheeks heat. Of course it was for him. But I'm not sure I want it going to his head. "Just something I had lying around."

His chest dances with laughter, like he knows I'm full of shit.

My gaze falls to his left hand. "What's in the bag?"

His devilish grin is full of delight. "Just something I'd like to see *you* lying around in."

I swipe it from him and look inside where I see a few small scraps of pink fabric. Upon further inspection, I realize it's a bathing suit. If you can even call it that. More like a micro-bikini. I hold it up by the tip of a finger. "What is this?"

"We'll call it payback. You know, for the running shorts?"

I smile and nod, sure he hasn't quite thought this through. "So you want me wearing this to the resort pool?"

The edges of his mouth turn down. "I, uh… On second thought…" He rips the bikini out of my hand and tosses it in the trash. "I'm sure the resort shop has plenty of modest one-pieces you can wear."

I giggle silently then pick up and examine the bottle of champagne, curious as always about any competition to our winery. "I'm glad you could get away. I wasn't sure you'd be able to."

"Marti took Bug for the night." He takes the bottle from me, puts it back down, and steps close, pulling me tightly against him. "But let's be clear. My kid is thirteen. I would have zero issues leaving her alone for a few hours to get some of this."

"This?" I wiggle against him.

He lowers his head, and I feel his lips against my neck. My eyes close of their own volition as his mouth devours my clavicle, the delicate divot beneath my ear, my exposed cleavage. Just when I'm getting all worked up, he pulls away. "Do you have a blanket?"

I look at him with a sideways glance. "That made you… *cold?*"

His smirk is out-of-this-world sexy. "I was hoping we could take this champagne to the beach and make love under the stars."

My insides quiver. What is it about a handsome, older guy saying the words 'make love' that is so, so yummy?

"I know just the one." I go to the couch and pull a throw off of the back. When I turn, I note he's been watching my every move. So, to fan those flames, I reach under the bottom hem of my sundress, hook my thumbs around my panties, and lower them until they fall to the floor. Then I step out of them with bare feet. "For easier access."

"Christ." He shifts his stance, and I just know he's already getting hard. "I'm not sure how we'll ever get to the beach without everyone we pass seeing how turned on I am."

I pad my way to the back door. "We don't have to pass anyone. I have my own private stairway down there."

He grabs the champagne and the glasses and follows me, stopping in his tracks when he sees the moonlit bay below. I'm surprised he didn't check out the view the second he got here—it's what everyone usually does.

"Amazing, right?" I ask.

"It sure the hell is."

But when I look over at him, he's no longer looking out at the ocean. He's looking directly at me. And there's a fire in his eyes I'm not sure I've ever seen. He must be really excited to mark this one off his bucket list.

He leaves his shoes by the top of the stairs and follows me down. "Bug would die for this view. She didn't tell me as much, but I know she was bummed our room doesn't have one."

"She seems like a good kid. Not as demanding as most teenagers I know" —I toss him a playful look over my shoulder— "except maybe when it comes to *you*. I do hope she has fun this weekend."

"Maybe I shouldn't be telling you this, but she was quite happy earlier when she saw you at the bar with another guy. She made no secret of voicing how she thought he was hot and 'age appropriate' for you."

I stop my descent. "How much do you think she knows? We've been good at hiding it when you come to Cal Creek."

"She's a smart kid." He bypasses me and continues down the stairs. "And maybe she still goes through my phone."

"So change the code."

He sighs big time. "I want her to trust me."

"Do you know *her* code?"

"No. I've never asked."

We step onto the soft sand, and I start scoping out a spot. "Seems backwards, Asher, her having access to your phone while you don't have access to hers."

"She needs her privacy."

"So do you." I spread out the blanket. "But hey, at least if she thinks I'm into someone else, she won't obsess over keeping us apart."

"I suppose," he ponders, admiring the way the moonlight appears to cut the bay in half. "But we shouldn't have to lie to her."

"So tell her."

He sets the bottle and glasses on the blanket and draws me near. "Tell her what exactly?"

I press my forehead against his chest. "Well, shit. I walked right into that one, didn't I?"

He chuckles. Sixteen months. Fifteen dates. At least three dozen orgasms. And we've still never defined what this thing is between us. Now here we are, in decidedly one of the most romantic spots in the universe, about to make love under the stars. By anyone's standards, this is the perfect time to define our relationship. The ideal setting to tell each other our feelings.

Which is why I feel anxiety eating through my body like cancer.

In an attempt not to spoil the night, I reach between us and cup my hand over his crotch. He quickly hardens under my greedy touch while his eyes shift around skimming our surroundings.

"Allie, are we going to be arrested for public indecency?"

"I've been down here every night this week. And believe me, if I didn't get caught the other night, I think we're good."

His whole body stiffens. His eyes no longer look at me with excitement. More like sadness. He steps back and runs a hand through his hair, reciting what I think are curse words under his breath.

I mentally replay the words I just said and realize why his whole demeanor changed. He thinks I've been out here with another man. It's the second time tonight he's shown signs of jealousy. And I try to decide if I'm okay with that. This one moment in time could be a determining factor in this whole… situationship.

If I'm okay with him being jealous, does that mean I'd be okay with this actually going somewhere?

Instead of going down that rabbit hole, I say, "Don't get your panties in a twist, big guy, I was by myself. Watching *our* videos."

His eyes brighten. "Seriously?"

I bite my lip and nod. "And I may have gotten a bit… vocal."

Now *he's* the one laughing. He sweeps me into his arms, picking me up off the ground before he puts me flat on my back on the blanket, hovering over me. "Damn, Al. Now I'm going to have fantasies about you down here on the beach. Alone. Touching yourself." He grinds into me. Then suddenly, he's gone. He scoots off me and opens the champagne.

I watch him intently. "Has anyone ever accused you of having ADHD? You're kind of all over the place right now. One second your tongue is down my throat. Then you're pouting because you thought I was here with another guy. Then you throw me down like you want to devour me. Then you want to have a drink."

His deep, throaty laugh seems to echo and bounce off the trees and hill behind us. He hands me a glass. "Quite the opposite. I'm usually very focused. Shit like that only happens when I'm around you. Guess you make me kind of crazy." He takes a sip. "And I don't pout."

"Oh, but you do. I've seen it a few times tonight."

"So sue me if the thought of another man's hands on you is not on my top ten list."

I take a long drink. "Mmm. This is pretty good."

He finishes his glass then pours himself another, topping mine off as well. "You're avoiding the conversation."

"I'm enjoying the champagne."

"Have there been?" he asks, looking at me with an intense stare. "Other men's hands on you?"

"Well let's see." I scrunch my brows together. "My dad hugged me yesterday. Blake tried to help me surf the other day, but neither of us were any good at it. Oh, and I believe Storm may have kissed my cheek earlier."

"You're a brat. You know that, right?" He takes my drink from me and puts both our glasses onto a flat rock by his shoulder. Then he flips me on my back. "Allie, answer the goddamn question."

I might like this game a little too much. Seeing Asher get all worked up is kind of a turn on. "If I say yes, is that going to change what happens here?"

His gaze goes from my eyes to my neck. He loves to kiss my neck. I think it's one of his favorite places on me. Amongst a few others. And his hand is getting dangerously close to one of those other places.

"I said we were going to make love under the stars. And we will." He moves his hand up my thigh and easily slips a finger inside me. "I just need to know how hard I need to make you come to ensure you forget about anyone else."

I groan when his thumb lands on my clit, and he moves it in slow circles with varying degrees of pressure.

He leans close to my ear. "How hard do I need to make you come, Al?"

"Hard." I arch my back into him. Then I reach up, grab the back of his neck and force his lips to mine. "But not because I've been with anyone else recently. Because I love the way you make me come."

He kisses me so fiercely, I'm sure my lips will swell. His hand comes out from under my dress, and he uses it, along with his other, to hold my head in place and devour my mouth in a way he never has before. Like he's claiming me. Like he's branding me as his. Like he's… professing his love.

When he's had his fill of my lips, he moves to my chest, shoving the neckline of my sundress down so he can draw one of my stiff nipples into his mouth while his fingers manipulate the other.

I reach out and try to find his belt buckle, but he swats my hand away. I know what that means. It means this first one is just for me. It means he's going to wait, the gentleman that he is, until I've been satisfied. It means he always puts me first.

I'm drenched between my thighs when he finally returns his attention there. "Jesus." The word comes out in a sigh when he realizes just how worked up he's gotten me. As his fingers test the waters yet again, he stares at me. "You are so beautiful."

It's hard to smile when I'm about to explode with an orgasm, but I do. Then, as he makes me come with just his fingers, in a way that only *he* knows how to do, I look up at the stars and shout into the night, knowing this is only the appetizer. The first of many. One in an endless line of mind-blowing detonations that he's going to provide me under his skilled fingers. His strong tongue. His incredible cock.

"Christ, Al. I have to be inside you."

He pushes down his shorts and rolls on a condom.

"Wait," I say, urging him onto his back. "You need the full 'under the stars' experience." I lift my dress, straddle him, then let it fall back down, the hem surely tickling his abs and thighs with every bounce of my body.

He grips my hips, guiding me up and down at his desired pace. It doesn't take long to get him there. His face contorts and he bucks up into me as he erupts with pleasure.

And it's not lost on me that here we are, on this amazing beach surrounded by beautiful palm trees, salty night air, and what I can only describe as the most exquisite night sky I've ever seen. Yet Asher's eyes never once stray from mine as he rides out the waves of his orgasm. The moon reflects in them as he looks up at me. And although it's dark outside, I swear I can read more in his gaze than I ever have before.

What I'm reading excites me. What I'm reading terrifies me. But most of all, what I'm reading fucking envelops me like a warm blanket on a snowy day.

Chapter Nine

Asher

If I wasn't sure of my feelings before tonight, I am now. I'm one hundred percent in love with Allie Montana. Locked and loaded. Head-over-fucking-heels. And I'm a goddamn dead man walking if I find out she doesn't feel the same.

Which is why I don't ask. And it's why I won't tell her.

Better to live in naïve bliss than be tortured by the knowledge of loving someone who doesn't love you in return.

She hasn't been with other men. But for how long? Months? A year? What does 'recently' mean. Since we first hooked up sixteen months ago?

The champagne is long gone. The moon is much lower on the horizon. Gentle waves crash upon the beach. We've been here for hours and not another living soul has wandered by.

I rise on an elbow and watch Allie watch the sky. This truly is paradise.

"There!" She grabs my arm. "Asher! Do you see it?"

I look up to see a faint white streak darting across the sky. A shooting star. If that isn't a sign, I don't know what is.

She releases me. "Did you know shooting stars aren't even stars at all?"

I chuckle. "Thanks for ruining the moment, Al."

"Oh. I didn't realize we were having one," she says playfully. "We did have a lot of *other* moments tonight, however."

I pinch my chin. "Let's see, if I remember correctly, you had four moments and I had three." I swipe a piece of hair off her face. "Okay, Ms. Smartypants, tell me about shooting stars."

"They are actually meteors burning up as they enter Earth's atmosphere."

"How have I gone over forty years without knowing that?"

She shakes her head. "Sometimes I forget how old you are. And it kind of makes me feel smart to know one thing you don't."

I let the 'how old you are' comment roll off me. As a rule, I try not to think about our age difference. I'm pretty sure it's the main reason I'm keeping my feelings to myself. I've had a wife. A family. I have a teenage daughter. Hell, I worry about things like how much I'm saving for retirement and Bug's wedding. Things Allie has probably never even given a second thought to. I feel like I'm on a trajectory to the end of my life while hers is just beginning. She has so much ahead of her.

"You *are* smart," I say. "You know a lot of things I don't. Especially about wine. Do you know I'm always worried whenever I order wine around you?" I motion to the empty bottle. "I hesitate to tell you how long I mulled over which bottle to buy tonight. But honestly, the hotel shop only had three kinds of champagne, so it wasn't too terribly painful. What did you think of it?"

"Fortunately for you, I'm not a wine snob like Lucas," she says. "He's the worst. Blake and Dallas aren't so bad. I couldn't care less.

I mean, yeah, I want people to buy from us, and I do like a great glass of wine, but I'll never complain about what you choose to bring. And, for the record, it was really good. Brut has always been my favorite."

"Duly noted."

"Noted for what?"

I hop up and extend my hand to pull her to her feet. "Future encounters under small pieces of space rock."

"I didn't say *all* stars were space rocks, just shooting stars."

"Flexing your space knowledge again?" I say as she grips my hand and I use her momentum to hoist her over my shoulder.

"Asher!" she shrieks as I start climbing the stairs.

"Shhh." I lift her skirt and swat her bare ass. "You'll wake the neighbors."

"But the blanket and stuff."

"I'll come back later."

Ten steps into our ascent, she says, "You can't carry me all the way up. There are seventy-three steps, you'll give yourself a heart attack."

I stop and set her down. "You think of me as old enough to have a heart attack?"

"Umm… no." She looks guilty as hell. "It was just a saying."

I tilt my head. "Does our age difference bother you?"

"*Bother* me? Asher, I think our age difference is hot. So do all my friends."

I feel ten years younger as I hoist her back up on my shoulder. She talks about me to her friends. I'll take that as a win. "I'll give *you* a heart attack as soon as we get up to your bed."

She giggles as I bounce her up the next sixty-one steps.

~ ~ ~

I'm shaking sand out of the blanket, reliving the best moments of last night, when I hear an all-too-familiar voice.

"Dad?"

I turn to find Bug, Charlie, and Maisy standing near my sister, who has a massive smile on her face. Marti must know whose bungalow is up the stairs behind me. And my uber-romantic little sister has always favored Allie and I getting together, even if she does keep to herself on the subject. Mostly because every time she brings it up, I tend to redirect the conversation.

"Uh, hey, Bug. What are you doing here?"

"What are *you* doing here?" she asks defiantly, eyeing the blanket and empty champagne bottle. "Our room is at the other end of the property."

"I, um…"

"Ash? Oh, there you are. I thought you left."

I spin around and look up the stairs. Allie is about fifteen steps up, wearing a short, white robe emblazoned with the resort logo. It shows off her tanned legs as well as a good bit of cleavage as she's not secured the tie very well. As soon as she sees the others, she pulls the tie tight, giving me an apologetic look.

I close my eyes. This may well be the worst *dad* moment of my life. My daughter has just caught me red-handed. Bug doesn't want any woman in my life, but she seems hell-bent on me not having a relationship with Allie in particular.

I realize now that it's because she must sense my feelings for her. Either that, or she *has* been reading my texts.

"This time of day is the best for finding sharks' teeth," Marti says, trying to break the tension.

Maisy leans over, picks something up off the sand, and smiles. "I found one," she signs excitedly.

"Good job," Marti says and signs to Allie's deaf niece.

Bug looks down at her hand where there must be a half-dozen black sharks' teeth. She throws them into the water and stalks off.

"I am *so* sorry," Allie says, still up on the stairs.

"It's not your fault, but—" I look in the direction Bug went.

"You should go after her."

"Yeah. I…"

"We'll talk later."

I nod and race off down the beach.

I find Bug sitting in the sand a few hundred feet away. She's picking up shells and throwing them into the water.

I plop down next to her, pick up a shell and throw it. "I know what you must be thinking."

"No, Dad. You don't. Because if you did, you'd know that I was thinking how convenient it was that Marti invited me for a sleepover so you could go have a booty call with the slut who probably just slept with that other guy a few hours before moving on to you."

I take a deep breath, knowing I need to tread carefully. "Darla, you will *not* call Allie a slut again. It's very disrespectful and absolutely untrue. Do you hear me?"

She knows I mean business—I rarely use her given name—and nods. "Did you arrange the sleepover?"

"No, sweetie, I didn't."

"But what about that other guy she was with?"

"It was Storm Calloway. Her cousin."

She visibly deflates. "Great. Just freaking great." She throws a large conch shell, and it makes a big splash.

"Bug." I take her hand and hold it in mine. "I really like Allie."

Her head shakes over and over. "It's gross. She's practically my age."

"She's more than twice your age. She's a grown woman. And I'm a single man. There's nothing wrong with what we're doing."

"You see her when you go to New York City on business."

It's not a question.

"Yes. I do."

"And when we visit Marti and Charlie, you sneak away and spend time with her."

"I guess I shouldn't be surprised that you've picked up on all that."

"Is she using you?" She pulls her hand away and throws another shell. "Are you using her?"

"Nobody is using anyone. It's just… complicated."

"Complicated how?"

If I can't answer that question for myself, I sure can't explain it to Bug.

"Hey, you two." Allie's mom, Sarah, comes up behind us. "Welcome to Antigua."

I stand and kiss Sarah's cheek. "Thanks. It's really beautiful."

Bug scoffs and mumbles something unintelligible.

"Bug, I have your dress in our bungalow. When would be a good time to try it on? We have someone on hand to make alterations if it doesn't fit properly."

Bug looks at me like she's as relieved as I am that our conversation came to an abrupt halt. Is she worried about Allie becoming a permanent fixture in my life? Am I worried that she *won't?*

I swear to God both questions loom in the air between us before she spins to Mrs. Montana. "I'd like to do it now if that's okay."

"Now would be perfect." Sarah raises a hand. "I'll see you at the rehearsal dinner tonight, Asher?"

"Sounds like it's going to be a lot of fun."

She turns back to Bug. "Are you excited?"

"Oh, yes. But mostly I'm excited about after. Dad promised me a movie and said we'd get a tent and sleep on the beach and then go hunting for sharks' teeth at dawn. He's a great dad."

I raise my brows.

"It sounds like the perfect father-daughter date," Sarah says. "Well, let's get going, Bug. I'll bet you're going to look beautiful in your bridesmaid dress."

As they leave, Bug turns to see my reaction. All I can do is shake my head knowing I've been railroaded by my own daughter.

Well fucking played, Darla.

I turn and walk back up the beach wondering where in the hell I'm going to find a tent.

Chapter Ten

Asher

Bug and I spend the afternoon with Marti and Charlie while Dallas and the other Montanas head to an island winery. I cherish every minute I get to spend with my sister and nephew. I've missed them a lot since they moved to Calloway Creek.

It's been hard living so far away. Marti and I were rarely apart growing up. Mostly because I was the one who raised her after losing first our mom when Marti was little and then our dad when she wasn't even as old as Bug is now. My sister has always been there for my daughter and me. She was my rock through the infertility treatments and miscarriages with Stella. She was the pillar of strength Bug and I needed through the divorce that followed.

Sometimes I think of moving closer. But Bug likes our house. Our neighborhood. Her best friend.

On the way back to our room to get ready for the evening's festivities, we run into Allie's brother Blake and his wife and daughter.

"Nice to see you," I sign to Ellie, who, like Blake's daughter Maisy, is deaf.

"Nice to see you," she signs back. Then she looks at Bug. Blake interprets, "I like your hair. The blue suits you. Very pretty."

"Thanks," Bug says, always eager to get compliments on the unusual color.

I wave at six-year-old Maisy. "Hi, Maisy. Did you find"—I turn to Blake and ask him how to sign 'sharks' teeth.' He shows me, and I complete the sentence.

Maisy smiles and signs back as Blake interprets.

Our conversation is short. Mostly because my ASL sucks, and Maisy hasn't yet learned to read lips like Ellie. They trot off, all of them holding hands, Maisy sandwiched between her parents.

I look after them, thinking about the unique circumstances that brought them together. Blake didn't even know he had a child until she was dumped on his doorstep a few years ago. It sure makes my problems pale in comparison. My life is a piece of cake if you put it up against what they've gone through. Not to mention what Dallas and Marti have overcome to get to this point.

Have I seriously been feeling sorry for myself when my biggest problem is that my hormonal daughter wants me all to herself?

Okay, maybe that's not my *biggest* problem. The winner of that award might be that I have no idea how the woman I'm in love with really feels about me.

"Dad?"

"Mmm?" I tear my eyes away from the retreating happy family.

"Since when do you know ASL?"

"I don't know a lot, but I learn what I can."

I leave out the part where Allie has been teaching me a little bit here and there. And I definitely leave out the part where some of what she's been teaching me has to do with dirty words. My thoughts instantly flash back to one specific time when I asked her to show me the sign for 'sex.' One sign led to another, and before we knew it, we'd had our own little version of ASL foreplay.

"How come?" Bug asks, suspiciously.

"Well, let's see." I start walking, contemplating the best answer. "Maybe because tomorrow, Aunt Marti will become Maisy's aunt and Ellie's sister-in-law."

"I get why *she* needs to learn it. But why are *you?*"

I thumb back in the direction of Blake's family. "Because of situations like that. Because when we go to Calloway Creek it's nice to be able to say hello to them. Because Maisy needs people in her life who speak *her* language. You spent time with her this morning. Didn't you say anything to each other?"

She shrugs. "Not really. Aunt Marti did most of the talking. ASL seems pretty cool though. I was thinking about taking it as my language elective in high school next year."

I stop and look down, not wanting to think about the fact that my daughter will be entering high school in the fall. A huge high school. In Orlando. With thousands of other students.

Pushing aside my fatherly fears, I try to focus on the here and now. "Really? That's fantastic. If you like it so much, why the third degree?"

"We should go. It's going to take me forever to wash and curl my hair."

Her non-answer says it all. She thinks I'm learning it because Maisy is Allie's niece.

"Bug." I put a hand on her shoulder.

She shrugs it off. "Fine. Whatever. You're learning sign language. Who cares?"

She stomps off toward our building, her blue hair blowing in the breeze, as I wonder once again if there is any universe in which Allie, Bug, and I could somehow become a family.

~ ~ ~

The rehearsal dinner is packed with Montanas and Calloways. With Allie and I keeping our distance from each other, I've gotten more of a chance to get to know her Montana cousins—the ones who aren't in the wine business. They own the Calloway Creek Golf and Country Club.

While Allie and I aren't directly talking to each other, that doesn't keep us from staring at one another. Is she thinking about the beach last night? Because I haven't been able to get it out of my head. How beautiful she looked straddling me against the backdrop of the moon and stars. How her soft, tanned skin prickled under my touch. How her third orgasm perfectly aligned with my second, her walls squeezing my cock in spectacular synchronization.

I have to look away before my dick gets any harder. But I still hear her talking with a few Calloways. Her voice is as soft and sensual as her skin.

"So, which is better," Serenity Calloway asks, "Australia or Antigua?"

"That's hard to say," Allie replies. "They both have so many wonderful qualities."

I close my eyes and absorb her voice as I listen to her make comparisons between the two. I wasn't even aware Allie had been to Australia. She's never mentioned it. She's spoken of other family trips to amazing places like Switzerland, Thailand, and Fiji, but never Australia.

I pick up on a few facts I didn't know about Allie, as in she spent many months Down Under doing an internship for a winery when she was nineteen. But then something strange happens. The more I listen to her talk about Australia, the more inaccuracies I pick up on. I should know. I've been there.

I open my eyes and study Allie as she speaks. It's odd. She's not even excited about it when Serenity prods her for more information. It's almost as if she doesn't even want to talk about her time in Australia. Maybe something bad happened when she was there.

But when Cooper Calloway asks if she liked Vegemite, and Allie has no idea what that is, I know something's off. There is no way in hell you can travel to Australia, especially for as long as she claims to have been there, and not tried Vegemite. It's practically a staple to the locals.

She catches me watching and finally her frown turns into a smile. Since Bug is nowhere to be found at the moment, I walk over. "Mind if I steal Allie for a minute?"

"Not at all," Serenity says, sharing a secret look of 'I know what you two are doing' with her husband.

"Care for a drink?" I ask Allie.

She glances around. I know what she's looking for. Or more specifically, *who*.

"She's off somewhere with your mom and Charlie I think."

"I could use a drink."

I wave over a waiter carrying a tray full of champagne and grab two glasses. I take a sip and nod. "Brut. Your favorite."

"So you *were* paying attention."

I lean in to whisper, "I always pay attention, Al," and her arm brushes mine.

Damn, how I wish I could pull her against me. Put my arm around her. Sit and talk with her all night. Part of me says *fuck it*, Bug should have to learn to deal with whomever I choose to spend time with. But the other part, the part that knows how fragile these years can be, that's always the part that wins the battle.

We stand at the bar as if we're both ready to bolt in opposite directions should we be spotted by my tenacious daughter.

"You never told me you've been to Australia."

Her smile falls. Her posture slumps. She even sets her glass down. It's like all the air has been sucked out of the space around her. "It was a work thing."

"I spent two weeks there."

"Mmm," she mumbles, looking anywhere but at me.

Ordinarily, when two people find they've visited the same uncommon place, they'd talk about it. Compare experiences. Ask things like 'did you do this?' or 'did you see that?' But Allie looks like she'd rather have a root canal than talk about her time there.

"I heard a rumor," she says.

"I hate rumors."

"But this one is about *you*."

I raise a questioning eyebrow.

"You and Bug are camping on the beach tonight?"

I sigh and run a hand through my hair. Then I apologize. "I'm sorry. I know we were going to try and meet up. After Bug saw what she did this morning, she kind of backed me into a corner in front of your mom about the whole camping on the beach thing. And then she told Marti, and apparently... *everyone*. So now I feel it has to happen or people will think I'm a horrible father."

Her hand covers her laugh. "Oh my gosh. She forced you into it so you couldn't spend another night with me? You have to admit, your daughter's got a lot of spunk."

"Spunk. That's what you call it?"

"Determination then. But hey, it's my fault for going down to the beach half-naked this morning."

I put a hand on her hip. "You should always be half-naked." I smile and wink. "Unless you're *all* naked." Leaning away, I continue, "There's no way you'd have considered the possibility of my kid being down there."

"I'll bet she really hates me now, huh?"

I'm not about to tell her Bug called her a slut. "I don't suppose you're on her list of all-time favorites."

She laughs. "No, I guess I'm not."

Getting irritated, knowing this is not a laughing matter, I toss back a long drink. "Why are we letting my thirteen-year-old control what we can and can't do, Al? We're grown adults and she's old enough to understand things."

"We?" she asks. "There's no *we* about this. She's your kid, Asher."

"I know. It's me. I'm the one who's letting her walk all over me."

"I get it. You're a single dad. You want to protect her. And you put her happiness before your own. Things are great between you. As good as it gets between a father and daughter. You don't want to rock the boat."

"But there's more to life than keeping my kid happy. I mean, you look fucking amazing in that dress and all I want to do is kiss you. I want to kiss you right here and not care who sees."

She leans against the bar, looking all sexy and inviting. "Then do it."

Our eyes lock and her gaze pulls me in like a tractor beam. I want to look around for Bug, but it's as if Allie is issuing me a challenge. Kiss her, and the world be damned. But it's almost like she's also offering me an invitation. An invitation to officially make this—whatever this is between us—public.

Without breaking our stare, I accept the invitation—or challenge as it may be—and kiss her. Putting my hands on the small of her back, I tug her to me, closing the gap between us. I lean down, finding her pink strawberry-flavored lips with mine. And I kiss her. I kiss her out in the open as if we're together. A couple. Boyfriend and girlfriend. Lovers. And for just a moment, I get lost in the dream.

The moment is broken when I hear a high-pitched scream.

"Someone fell in the pool!" a waiter yells.

I turn to see a pale-blue dress floating atop the surface before a head of wet blue hair pops up from under the water. "Dad, help! My dress. I can't swim."

Bug can swim. She can surf. Hell, we've even been scuba diving. But I'm not about to stand here and let everyone think I'm a loser for not 'rescuing' my daughter.

I run over, tossing my phone and wallet on the ground before jumping in and ruining one of my best suits as I swim out to the deepest part of the massive pool where Bug grabs onto me for dear life. She's very convincing when she sputters out water. "I thought I was drowning. My feet got caught in my dress."

I don't reply. I tow her to the side where a dozen people help pull her out and cover us with towels. They're all asking if she's okay and if we need help.

"I'm fine," she says. "We were playing tag and I slipped."

"Who was playing tag?" I ask.

"Me and the other kids."

I glance around, seeing no other kids. I pick up my things, take her elbow, and say sternly, "Come with me."

Allie is looking at me as we pass her. Guilt is written all over her face. It's quite possible we're the only two people here who know we've just been played. "Guess I'll see you at the wedding," I tell Allie.

Sorry, she mouths.

I close my eyes and sulk, embarrassed that Bug caused a scene and ruined the rest of our night.

And I dread what's going to happen next. Because I know it's time to grow some fucking balls and stand up to my manipulative daughter.

Chapter Eleven

Allie

I haven't slept much. Guilt has wreaked havoc on me. It was my fault Asher's night ended early. It was such an adolescent thing to do, asking him to kiss me right there in front of everyone. And the worst part, the part that makes me a terrible human, is that I knew Darla was there. I caught a glimpse of blue hair right before I challenged him to kiss me.

I roll over and watch the sun rise through my bedroom window knowing I royally messed up.

I could very well have, in one fell swoop, ruined not only his relationship with Bug, but *our* relationship—whatever it may be.

The other thing that had sleep eluding me, and something that's occurred to me more than once over the past twelve hours, is what if somehow I wanted it to happen. Us being put in a precarious situation that could potentially blow up this thing we have. I mean, the stuff he's been saying recently. The way he's been acting and looking at me. It's all so intense. Am I subconsciously ruining this? Am I sabotaging it?

Even as all of that was going through my head, I was also disappointed. I wanted a replay of the night before. Us on the beach. Him making love to me. The two of us wrapped up in each other so tightly nothing was between us. Not my past. Not his daughter. Not my inability to let him in.

I crawl out of bed knowing there's somewhere I need to be. My brother's wedding. It's at eleven o'clock this morning. An unconventional time, but they wanted Charlie and all the kids to be able to enjoy the reception, which will be a champagne brunch on the beach right after the ceremony.

Everything about this wedding is the complete opposite of when Dallas married his first wife, Phoebe. That wedding took place at the winery at sunset and was a very formal occasion. Nobody wanted any similarities to the wedding where Dallas married his high school sweetheart—the woman who died tragically a few years later, along with their infant son.

Their infant son.

My eyes close and I hold back the tears that threaten every time I think about Dallas's son. Because thoughts of DJ inevitably lead to thoughts of Christopher. I push away the flashbacks that start creeping into my head. Today is not a day for mourning. It's a day of celebration.

After a long, hot, soul-cleansing shower, I grab my makeup bag and head over to Mom and Dad's bungalow where they've set up the bridal suite in one of the bedrooms.

Mom greets me at the door. "Good morning. How did you sleep?"

"Don't ask."

She wraps an arm around my shoulder, escorting me inside. There's a huge spread of pastries along with coffee and mimosas in their kitchen. She picks up a mug. "Coffee?"

I sit on a barstool, noticing I'm the first one to arrive. "Please."

"You and Asher were quite the topic of conversation last night." She hands me the mug. "You'd have known that if you hadn't rushed out so quickly. But it's not like it really came as a surprise to anyone."

I let my head fall to the countertop and bang my forehead against the unforgiving granite. "Can we not talk about this? There are more important things going on today."

Her hand brushes across my back. "Just because your brother is getting married doesn't mean we can't figure out your problems."

"Problems?" I lift my head and take a drink.

"I saw Bug jump in the pool, sweetie. Teenagers can be tough. Maybe you just need to talk with her. You know, woman to woman."

I laugh. "She hates me, Mom. She's not going to listen to a word I have to say."

"She just needs reassurance that you aren't taking her father away."

As if to add insult to injury, the door swings open and Marti and Bug come through, laughing. It dies quickly when Bug sees me, however. She completely ignores me and goes to the spread of sweets, picking out a gooey cinnamon roll.

"You're lucky you can eat that," I joke. "You'd better enjoy it before you get older when every one of those will have you running an extra five miles."

She stares daggers at me. "Are you calling me fat?"

"No. Of course not. That's not what I meant at all." I stumble over what to say that won't have me putting my foot in my mouth. "Are you okay today? I was worried about you after you fell in the pool."

"Why would *you* be worried?"

"Well, for one, because I like you and I don't want anything bad to happen to you."

She studies me like I'm a freak. "You *like* me?"

"Sure. What's not to like?"

Her eyes roll. "Whatever."

I have to do something to fix this. I have no idea what happened between her and Asher after they left the rehearsal dinner. Based on the look on his face when they were leaving, however, she might just be grounded for life. Something I'm sure she's blaming *me* for. And she should. It *is* my fault. I caused whatever rift is now between them.

"Hey, how about I do your hair? I could curl it for you and then pin the front part up." I pick up a piece of blue hair and hold it up against the back of her head. "Like this."

She shrugs me off like my touch burned her. "Uh, no. Aunt Marti is going to do it."

"Marti's the bride. She has other things to worry about. Why not let me do it? It'll be fun. I'm really good at doing hair. Ask anyone." I stand up and hold out an arm in invitation. "Come on, Bug. We'll stuff our faces with cinnamon rolls and put our hair in curlers."

She doesn't budge. "You're *not* doing my hair."

"Why not? Give me one good reason."

"Because you don't know how to do it. You're not my mom. You're not *anyone's* mom, so you can't possibly understand."

Her words hit me right in the chest, piercing my heart and taking all the fight right out of me.

"And my name is *Darla*." She stomps across the room heading for the bridal suite.

Mom and Marti stand nearby, having heard the entire exchange. Mom gives me the same empathetic look she gives me whenever I'm reminded that I'm *not anyone's mom.*

Marti looks horrified over her niece's outburst. "Allie, I am so sorry. I'll talk to her. She shouldn't be that disrespectful."

I shake my head. "It's fine. I feel like I ran right into that one. I'm not sure what I was thinking trying to be her friend or whatever after what happened last night. Don't be too hard on her, okay?"

"Give her some time. She'll come around."

"Will she?"

Marti takes a sip of her mimosa. "She's just mad that Asher said she couldn't go to the eighth-grade dance next week."

Guilt crawls up my spine. "Oh, no. She must be devastated."

"She'll get over it."

I nod even though I don't agree. I'm not sure she will get over it. The eighth-grade dance is a big deal. And she's going to blame me. For everything. The dance. The special father-daughter night they had planned that most likely got ruined.

Maybe this is all becoming way too complicated.

"Hey," I say, picking up my own mimosa, "this day is all about you. Now let's go get ready. I can't wait for you to be my newest sister-in-law."

She smiles big. "I'm soooooo ready to marry your brother. Truth be told, I've been ready since the day we met after my car skidded off the road and stranded me with him."

"I know. I could tell that about you from the moment we met."

Her smile doesn't fall as she cocks her head.

"What is it?" I ask.

"I could say the same thing about you, you know. The moment you and Asher laid eyes on each other—it's like time stood still. I could practically *feel* it. It was intense, Allie."

I think back to that very moment. When I was on the steps of the winery and Asher came driving up with Marti. She's right. Time *did* stand still. My breath catches in my chest just thinking about it.

Oh, what a simpler time that was.

"Come on." I pull her toward the suite. "Let's go make you the most beautiful bride who ever lived."

~ ~ ~

Three hours and zero additional conversations with Bug later, I'm smiling as Charlie, the ring bearer, and Maisy, the flower girl, walk down the aisle. After them, Bug and I carry our bouquets past the small crowd of friends and family.

Then I turn and my breath catches as Marti comes into view, looking even more captivating than when I left her just ten minutes ago. She's glowing as Asher walks her down the aisle toward my brother.

Well, it's not so much an aisle as it is a shell and flower-lined path in the sand, the sparkling bay as a backdrop. But it's perfect. The sun is high in the sky. There isn't a cloud to be seen, and everyone's eyes are on the gorgeous bride.

She isn't the only one who's gorgeous, however. Holy hell. I've never seen Asher look so handsome in his beige linen pants, crisp white dress shirt, and tie the exact color of my blue-green dress. But I think what makes him so incredibly beautiful in this moment is the pride on his face. The love he has for his sister is so palpable I'm almost jealous of it. For all intents and purposes, he's been Marti's father since she was twelve. And he did an incredible job raising her.

I look to my left, where Bug is standing as Marti's maid of honor. He's doing an amazing job raising her, too. And here I am throwing a wrench in all of it.

Asher kisses Marti's cheek and hands her off to Dallas, who has a smile on his face and tears in his eyes.

I never thought there would be a time I'd see my brother happy again. Marti and Charlie, though, they've brought him that happiness.

Sometimes I wonder if I could ever have that.

Happiness.

It's such a foreign concept to me now. Has been for all of my adult life. Sure, there are times when I laugh, smile, and feel joyful. But being truly happy—like all the time—is an unclimbable mountain, an unfathomable feat.

I stare at Asher as he takes his seat in the front row. Since I'm just a bridesmaid and have no real duties here, I have nothing *to* do but stare at him. I stare at him as his sister pledges her life to my brother. Then, when Dallas says his vows, speaking of love after loss, it hits me like another arrow to the heart. Marti and I have such similar stories. The main difference is, she doesn't hide her loss. She wears her loss on her sleeve like a badge of honor, whereas I keep mine locked up in a little compartment in my heart.

And despite how much I'm drawn to the gorgeous man who's now staring back at me, that compartment takes up so much room, I'm not sure there's any space left for anything else. Not even for the man who's looking at me like *he* wants to be the one standing at the altar reciting vows of love and destiny. Like *he* wants to be gazing into my eyes speaking of forever.

A glimpse of blue hair in my periphery breaks the spell I was caught in. The dream I was lost in.

Asher's eyes are telling me what he wants. But I'm not capable of what Marti and Dallas have. I can't do happy. And I certainly can't do forever.

Things like that can't exist for me. They simply can't. I'm a shattered woman. And not even the love of an amazing man can put me back together when pieces of me will be gone forever. Because if I'm not mistaken, he *does* love me. He's never said it, but his eyes don't lie.

Which is why I have to look away and put my focus where it should be, on Marti and Dallas, the two people who actually have a future together. There are no secrets between them. No hurt that hasn't been overcome. No angsty teenage drama to get in the way. No hoops and hurdles.

Using Bug as a convenient excuse, I push aside any hopes and dreams of a future I know isn't possible.

But even as I try to blame Bug, I know full well she's not the reason I should end things with Asher. It has absolutely nothing to do with her, no matter how much I try to tell myself it does.

And if I can't blame anyone else, there's only one person I *can* blame.

Chapter Twelve

Asher

Allie barely said two words to me at the reception. Is she mad at me? For leaving the rehearsal dinner after our interrupted kiss? For not calling her after?

The two texts I sent this afternoon haven't even been read as far as I can tell. Tonight is my last night here. Whatever is going on with her, I'm determined to figure it out.

After leaving a pouting Bug with Sarah, who's babysitting Charlie and Maisy for the evening, I stop at the shop, buy a bottle of wine, and head over to Allie's bungalow. We didn't officially make plans, but it was implied that we were going to spend whatever time we could together.

But that was before she almost completely shut me out today.

Approaching her door, I hear a baby screaming. She's not alone. When my knock goes unanswered, I check the knob. It's unlocked, so I go in. I expect to see Regan and Lucas since I'm sure it's their baby, Mitchell, who is exercising his lungs right now. But the two of them aren't here. It's just Allie and the baby. And what I see causes a flood of emotions, even more than what I felt at the wedding.

Allie is trying to comfort Mitchell. He's cradled in her arms and she's swaying him back and forth, singing to him so softly it's hard for me to hear over the child's cries.

Finally, after another minute or so, he calms. And that's when it happens. Her voice pierces my goddamn heart, solidifying her place there as if she hadn't already taken up residence. Quietly, she soothes him with a lullaby as she looks out over the impressive view.

Her back is turned to me and I remain quiet so she doesn't know I'm here. I don't want to ruin this moment. The moment that has me envisioning a future with her unlike any I've ever imagined. Because watching her body sway as she holds him, I can almost picture her in a different room holding a different baby.

After Stella, I never thought I'd want to go down the road of trying for another child. I decided Bug was enough and put all my efforts into raising her. But watching Allie with Mitchell, a longing deep inside me percolates to the surface. I want this. I want it with her.

But then I remember what she said about kids not being in her future. *Ever.* But, Jesus, she's a natural. My heart aches thinking she may never have the joy of comforting her own child or the incredible happiness of bonding with another person in a way only a parent and child can.

She leans down and kisses him. "Sweet boy," she says softly. "My sweet, sweet boy. God how you remind me of him. Your little Montana nose. The curve of your mouth. You're… perfect."

The last word comes out squeaky like she's crying.

And I'm confused. *He reminds her of him?* Her brother? Kind of a strange thing to say.

"Hey, Al."

She spins, surprised to see me.

I hold up a hand. "Sorry. Didn't mean to scare you. I knocked."

She eyes the bottle of wine I'm carrying and looks… sad?

"I got stuck babysitting." She walks over to a bassinet and lays Mitchell down. "My mom was going to watch all the kids tonight, but Charlie was feeling sick, so I offered to watch this little guy so he wouldn't be exposed to anything."

I go over and gaze down at him. "He's a cute kid."

"He's the best," she says, leaning over to gently rub his back. Her momentary smile fades as she closes her eyes. She takes a deep breath, her shoulders slumping as her fingers run across the soft cotton fabric of his sleep sack.

Then it strikes me. What she said about children not being in the cards for her. Maybe it's not a choice at all. Maybe it's more like a curse.

And that makes me sad. For her. For potential babies who won't get to have her as a mom. Because obviously she'd be great at it.

"You've got an amazing voice."

Her cheeks pink. "Just how long were you standing there?"

"Long enough."

When she looks sad again, I try to lighten the mood. "We should definitely go to karaoke sometime."

Instead of laughing, though, she sits on the couch and pulls a throw pillow onto her lap. Something is wrong.

I set the bottle down on her kitchen table. "Hey, what's the matter?"

"I messed up last night."

"Is that what this is all about?" I go over and sit next to her.

It starts to make sense now, why she was avoiding me today. It was for Bug's benefit. She didn't want to throw fuel on the fire. Then again, it doesn't explain why she didn't text me back. Unless maybe she's been stuck with Mitchell since the reception.

Still… it seems there's more to it than that. I can read it in her eyes.

"Don't worry about Bug. She'll get over it. Besides, you did nothing wrong. What happened is on her. I'm the one who should be apologizing for my kid making a scene."

"It wasn't her fault."

"Of course it was. What she did was childish and selfish."

"But she *is* a child. And maybe she's allowed to be selfish when it comes to you. You're all she has, Asher." She sinks back into the couch. "*I'm* the adult here, yet what I did was even more childish."

"What do you mean?"

Her eyes close. "I ruined the entire night. Your father-daughter campout. And her dance. You should let her go to the dance. What happened wasn't her fault. It was mine."

"How is what happened possibly your fault? Because you wanted me to kiss you? Al, I wanted to kiss you all night. So if we're placing blame, at least we can share it."

"Yeah, but you didn't know any better." She looks at me, guilt oozing from her eyes. "I knew she was there, Asher. It's why I asked you to kiss me. I *wanted* her to see us. I'm not even sure why. It was petty and stupid and I'm so sorry."

I find it hard to hold in my laugh. "That's what all this is about?"

"I just think"—she looks out the window—"maybe this is all getting too complicated."

Instantly, my delight disappears. "Wait, what?"

"Aren't you tired of sneaking around? Of lying to your daughter? Of her acting out and now me doing ridiculous things because, what, I'm *jealous* of her?"

"Okay, listen." I grab her hand. It's stiff at first, then she relaxes it into mine. "First, you didn't ruin our night. We still pitched a tent and slept under the stars. She may not have spoken to me much, but she didn't need to, I did most of the talking. Allie, I told her about us. About seeing you when I travel—which she already suspected by the way. She knows I... like you. And she knows you're the only woman in my life."

And there it is. It's a conversation we've never had. Never—not once—has she asked whether or not I'm seeing anyone else. I've never brought it up because I'm afraid of her reaction. But right now, with her seemingly wanting to pull away, I have to tell her.

"Al, I can't promise Bug will be accepting of this. But at least she knows. And I've asked her to be more respectful of my choices. But really, after tonight, it won't matter much because the only time you'll cross paths is when we visit Marti and Charlie. And I understand why you did what you did. Sometimes I forget how this must be hard for you. I'm this older guy with a teenager. You rarely get to see that part of me. When I come to the city and we're together, you get all of me. When I'm at home in Orlando, *she* gets all of me." I wave a hand around. "It's these times when my two worlds converge where it gets messy. I'm sorry you got caught up in the mess."

"Out of curiosity..." She picks lint off the pillow, not making eye contact. "Since when have I been the only woman in your life?"

I pull her onto my lap. "Since the day Marti and I drove into Calloway Creek and I saw you on the steps of the winery."

She stares down into my eyes and I swear I can see a battle going on behind her baby blues. Is she trying to figure out if I'm worth it? Me and all my baggage? Is she asking herself if she's willing to deal with the occasional messiness of my life so that once a month she can have *all* of me? Or is she still thinking it's all too complicated?

"Allie." I cup her cheeks. "You don't need to overthink this. I want you. You're all I can think about since seeing you in that dress earlier. I want you whatever way I can have you. And right now, I want to have you here on this couch."

The battle ends as she leans down and crashes her lips to mine. Relief overtakes me. I know how fragile this thing with her is. I've felt all along that it could end at any moment. With a text. With me being stood up at our hotel in the city. With none of those, but instead just… nothing—poof, gone. Because we never defined this. She doesn't owe me anything. But why then, do I want to give her *everything?*

There is a hint of salt on her lips, confirmation that she was crying earlier when she was holding Mitchell. It makes me want to grab her and never let go. Tell her that whatever she's thinking, whatever she's feeling, I'm here. I'll be with her. I'll protect her. I'll love her.

But all I can do is convey those feelings with my lips. My touch. I pull down the spaghetti strap on her shoulder and let my mouth devour her neck. Her clavicle. The upper part of her chest. She lets her head fall back as I explore every inch with my tongue. As I taste her sweet skin, savoring it as any delicacy should be savored.

I'm growing painfully hard, a situation I'm confident she's aware of since it's her movements on my lap that have caused it.

I lift her sundress up and over her head, and, Jesus, she's braless.

It doesn't matter how many times I've seen Allie in all her naked glory, every time is like the first time. I cup her creamy white breasts in my hands. "You're fucking beautiful."

She cracks a smile. "I'll bet you say that to all the half-naked ladies who straddle you."

My laughter bounces her in my lap. I'm glad to see she's recovered her sense of humor. And I don't bother with an answer. She knows now that she's the only one.

"I'd prefer you to be *wholly* naked."

I lift her off me so she's standing right in front of me. Leaning in, I lower her panties to the floor then kiss her stomach and let my tongue blaze a trail down to the tippy top of her tiny triangle of curls. "I like this," I say, licking the smooth surface around her manicured area, wondering if she waxes all the time, or just when she knows we'll be together.

I urge her right leg up onto the couch next to me. Then I place her hands on my shoulders. I glance up with a confident smirk as my fingers find her slick folds, parting the way for my tongue.

It's damn sexy the way she watches me. Even when I can't see her stare, I can feel it. She moans my name when I suck on her clit. She almost stumbles when my fingers find the spot inside her that drives her wild.

Her fingers dig into my shoulders, incenting me to work harder. I reach up and pinch a nipple. It's that motion that pushes her over the edge, and her hands move from my shoulders to my head as she grabs my hair and holds me in place while her entire body vibrates with an orgasm.

I move my hand from her breast to her hip to keep her from collapsing. She comes hard, and I can tell she's struggling to keep herself from screaming my name. Or maybe God's.

She doesn't want to wake the baby. Which I'm grateful for, because in about twenty seconds, my clothes will be off and I'll be burying myself inside her. And I surmise in about thirty, *I'm* the one who'll have to hold in shouts of pleasure.

~ ~ ~

"I'll just be a minute," she says, gathering her panties and dress then disappearing into the bathroom.

I toss the condom into the trash and am pulling on my shorts when Mitchell starts crying. It's not a wail like earlier, more like a reminder that he's there. I pad over, not even fully dressed, and pick him up.

It's been a while since I've held an infant. Years. But it's just as wonderful as I remembered it to be.

"Hey, little guy."

He stares up at me, fortunately still too young to be frightened of strangers. My heart stands still as I gaze down into the innocent eyes of a beautiful child, longing for something that will probably never happen for me again.

The bathroom door swings open. Allie's mouth hangs agape when she sees me holding her nephew. She's frozen in place, looking entranced. Shocked. Scared.

"I, uh… he was crying. He seems fine now." When she doesn't move, I add, "You know I have experience holding babies, right?"

Her head shakes as if she was somewhere else entirely and not right here. "Yeah. Of course."

I go over and hand him to her. "It's been forever, though. Not since I held Alex." I sigh when I think of it. "It was the day before she died. She was only a week old."

Allie's entire body shudders. She knows how my sister lost her infant daughter. "I… I'm really tired, Asher. It's been a long day. And this one needs to have a bottle."

I study her as she goes into the kitchen. She's been all over the place tonight. Changing from cold to hot and back to cold at the drop of a hat. I come up behind her, kissing her bare shoulder. "Our flight leaves at nine. This is probably goodbye."

"Okay." She pulls a bottle out of the fridge.

Okay?

"So, I guess I'll see you in a few weeks? I already have a business trip planned for May eighth."

"Sounds good."

I walk around to her front so she has to look at me. "Allie, we just made love. The least you can do is kiss me goodbye."

"Sorry. It's just that he's really hungry."

I look down at a very content baby. Then, over the top of his head, I pull her close. "I'm hungry too."

When I kiss her, it's not like before. I guess she's concerned about doing this and holding Mitchell. The kiss is over all too soon.

And even before I'm out the door, I miss her.

Making my way back to my room, passing couple after couple, I'm confronted by what's come to be one of my greatest fears—not having Allie in my life. And I swear right here and now, the next time I go to the city, I'm going to tell her. I'm going to tell her how I feel. And what's more—I'm going to make her listen until she hears it.

Chapter Thirteen

Allie

I look out the window at the shrinking island, glad to be putting distance between myself and the place that now holds so many more new memories.

I can't believe I caved to his charm. I was ready to end things. I *should* have ended things. His relationship with his daughter is what he should be focused on, not booty calls in the city.

But every time I close my eyes, I see him. Not just him. Him holding Mitchell. And sometimes my mind plays tricks on me and it's him holding Christopher.

I stare out at the clouds. Asher never would have up and left like Jason did. He's not that kind of man. He would have stood by me through every fear, every diagnostic test, every last contraction. And he's the one who would have been by my side as Christopher took his last breath.

The way he was holding Mitchell, it was gentle and kind. It's the same way he is with Bug, even though she's so much older. He rarely even raises his voice at her. Even when she does stupid shit like jump into a pool in the middle of a rehearsal dinner.

The man was born to be a dad. It makes me feel kind of bad for him, knowing what little I know about his past. The two of us don't really talk about it, but Marti has become a good friend of mine and she's told me about the struggles he and his ex-wife went through. She told me how torn up he was when Stella left him. Because apparently, not only was Asher Anderson born to be a dad, he was born to be a husband.

My stomach flips over when the plane hits a tiny bit of turbulence.

I feel sick knowing that the longer Asher and I keep doing what we're doing, the longer he has to wait to become the husband he deserves to be—something he simply can't have with me.

I'm the only one he's seen since the day we met. While it's the same for me, I've never told him as much. I've never told him because what we're doing we're doing for very different reasons. His reasons I can see in his eyes every time we're together. And those reasons are becoming stronger, especially since watching Marti and Dallas get married. He sees a future. Marriage. Maybe even kids. It's a future I can't give him. But one he deserves.

My stomach in knots, I quickly unbuckle my seatbelt and race back to the bathroom, barely making it in time to lose my breakfast into the cold, hard, steel toilet.

I splash water on my face and rinse out my mouth. Then I stop at the minibar on the way back to my seat.

Mom leaves Maisy and Charlie with some paper and crayons and takes the seat next to me. "Everything okay?" She brushes hair out of my eyes. "You look a little green."

"I think I might have gotten what Charlie had a few days ago."

She glances back at Charlie, who is now officially her grandson. She's been tasked with babysitting him for the next week while Marti and Dallas remain in Antigua to honeymoon. Her eyes narrow. "What Charlie had a few days ago was a case of eating too much wedding cake."

I glance back out the window. "Must be the turbulence then."

"Mmm," she mumbles. "Or maybe you're just missing him more than you'd like to admit?"

When I don't acknowledge her question, she adds, "I've seen you out wandering the beach, Allie. You've seemed sad these past few days. Like when he left, he took a piece of you with him." She pats my arm. "I'm sure you'll see him soon enough."

I don't tell her what she said is spot on. I do miss him. And he did take a piece of me. I also don't tell her that's the reason I *won't* see him soon enough. I've let this go on too long as it is. He's caught too many feelings. I've caught them too. But we're not in the same place. We'll never be in the same place. And it's not fair to keep stringing him along. Eventually, he'll want more. He'll want all of me. He said so himself when he declared we shouldn't let Bug keep us apart. That means he's ready for the next step: being together.

In a perfect world, we *would* be together. In a perfect world, he'd move to Calloway Creek and ask me to be his girlfriend. In a perfect world, we'd go on regular dates and walk around town holding hands.

In a perfect world, his daughter would warm up to me and we'd become friends, and someday, family.

But my world is far from perfect. Perfect died for me when I held a tiny little boy in my arms as he drew his last breath.

"Excuse me." I jump out of my seat, stride back to the bathroom again, and throw up until there's nothing left inside me but the emptiness I feel.

Chapter Fourteen

Allie

I'm grateful it's a Monday and there are no events at work today. Because I'm not sure I want to leave the warm snuggly feeling of my comfy bed. Mondays are slow days at the winery for me. I usually catch up on paperwork and prepare for the week's tastings. If we have any parties or weddings scheduled for the upcoming weekend, I'll make phone calls and make sure everything is on track. All things I plan on doing from home today. And maybe even from bed.

Besides, I can rely on Natasha, my assistant, to pick up the slack. Something she's had to do a lot lately.

It's not lost on me that I've felt this way for weeks. Ever since returning from Antigua, to be exact. The desire to work, to exercise, to eat, hell, to even shower, it's just… gone.

For as long as I can remember, I've been a runner. It doesn't matter if it's snowing or raining outside, or even if it's a hundred degrees, being out on the trails of Calloway Creek has become a part of my daily routine. But lately, nothing about my life is routine. And the lack of running is definitely showing on my waistline.

It's like there's this divide in my life. It feels a lot like when Christopher died. Back then, I defined everything in terms of 'before Christopher' and 'after Christopher.' But today, and for the past month, it's felt like I'm in the 'after Asher' phase of my life.

But the funny thing is, *he* doesn't even know we're in the 'after.' I'm the only one privy to that piece of information. He just thinks I was tied up with work obligations when he came to the city last week.

I roll over and pull a pillow tightly against me, squeezing my eyes shut, knowing it's better this way. A clean break. For him. For me. And definitely for Bug.

Okay, so maybe I should be an adult about it and just tell him it's over. But every time I pick up my phone, it's like my stomach lurches up into my throat and I feel sick.

As if my phone is trying to tell me to get on with it, it vibrates. *Please don't be Asher.*

Mia: You're not bailing on me again, are you? I've been waiting for fifteen minutes.

I lean into the pillow. Right. It's Monday. Every Monday morning for the past five years, Mia and I have met at the trailhead behind the Calloway Creek playground to run five miles. Our schedules differ so much, it's the one time we could coordinate it. Mia's hours are all over the place as she and her brothers take turns manning the tow truck, but she always saves Monday mornings for us. Which makes me feel guilty for bailing. Again.

But not guilty enough to get out of bed and put on my running clothes. Maybe I'll just do some yoga later. That will make me feel better.

Me: Sorry. I'm just not feeling up to it.

Mia: You haven't run with me in weeks. Sulking over him isn't going to make you feel any better. If it's that hard to be without him, don't.

I close my eyes and let my head fall back against the pillow. Mia is the only one who knows I'm done with him. Sometimes I regret telling her. Because she brings it up all the time. And whenever she brings it up, my stomach rolls like it's telling me what I'm doing is wrong and I'm a terrible person. But I know deep down, what I'm doing is right. He deserves better. He deserves more. And I'm really tired of talking about it with her.

Me: Is this you being supportive?

Mia: I'm just saying, you're a different person now. You never want to go out. You came back from Antigua with an awesome tan, but it's like you're pale all the time. It's strange. And you don't like to do all the things you love. Allie, I think you're depressed.

Me: I'm not depressed.

I'm also full of shit from the top of my head to the bottoms of my feet. Because I'm totally depressed. I'm so depressed in fact, that the only other time in my life I've ever felt like this was after getting the horrible news about the blood test when I was pregnant with Christopher.

I drop my phone and sit straight up in bed. Oh, holy shit. *No, no, no, no, no.*

Reality hits me like bricks falling off a skyscraper. I've been tired. Cranky. Nauseous at times. And definitely putting on weight. All things I attributed to the abrupt halt of my exercise routine.

I swallow hard, trying to remember my last period. It's never come like clockwork due to the progestin-only pills I take. But since most other birth control pills cause me to have migraines, they are the only ones that work for me. And those types of pills tend to come with side effects like irregular bleeding, spotting between periods, or no periods at all.

Progestin-only pills also aren't as reliable as regular pills. It's why I've always insisted on using condoms as well. Together, the two should be a virtual fortress against pregnancy.

My stomach rolls when I remember that time Asher and I got so rough and playful, we actually lost the condom. As in I had to dig it out from deep inside me. It was embarrassing and super awkward, but we just laughed about it. That was... I think back and suddenly feel better when I realize how long ago it was. Months. Maybe even three. I'd be in the clear.

But... but...

Something inside me just knows I can't explain away how I've been feeling.

I can't push it off as sadness over a guy I may or may not secretly be in love with but who I'm trying to spare a life full of regrets.

With my eyes closed tightly, I reach up and grab my breasts, praying they won't be tender.

They are.

Of course they are.

I roll over and curl up into a ball, ignoring the texts Mia continues to send. Because my life is shit. And this situation is shit. And everything is shit. And I just… can't.

~ ~ ~

Footsteps echo in the back hallway, on the outside staircase to my apartment over my parents' garage. Then there's a banging at the door.

"Allie!"

When I don't answer, my best friend rips open the unlocked door. Within seconds, I feel the bed shift under her weight. The sound of her shoes hitting the floor prepares me for what comes next, her arms curling around me from behind.

That's all it takes for me to burst into tears and break down into sobs, my body shaking against hers. I'm crying so hard, I can't even tell her why. Like a sister, a best friend, a protector, she just holds me and lets me get it all out. She thinks I'm sad over Asher. That I've finally reached the point of having a meltdown.

I don't even know how long she holds me, but I get the idea she'd do it forever if that's what I need. Mia Cruz is my one true ride-or-die friend. She knows me better than anyone. She knows my heart. My soul. My secrets.

So it makes sense she's the only one I can tell this to.

"I…" I rub my palms over my eyelids. "I th-think I'm p-pregnant."

"Oh, Jesus." She buries her head into my shoulder, squeezing me even tighter.

Her reaction is spot on. Others might say 'think of this as a second chance' or 'everything will be okay.' Not Mia. Mia knows this will destroy me. *Oh, Jesus* is right.

"What can I do?" she asks after a few more minutes.

I close my eyes and sigh. Because what can anyone do? It's a sentence. A punishment. Some sort of twisted karma for breaking up with the most amazing guy who doesn't even know he's been broken up with.

"Have you taken a test?"

I shake my head.

"Then maybe you're not. It could just be the whole Asher thing. Or maybe you picked up some rare exotic disease in Antigua."

If I weren't so completely devastated, I might think it's funny how Mia believes an exotic foreign disease would be preferable to being pregnant. It would, however. In fact, there isn't anything in this world I can think of that would be worse. Not even a terminal disease. Because going through what I did before *would* kill me.

The only thing running through my head right now is what the doctor told me so long ago. "You can try again. Most Trisomy 18 cases are not inherited genetic mutations."

Most.

Not all.

It's strange how powerful one small word can be when it means the difference between life and death. Sanity and madness. Peace and utter turmoil.

I turn around and finally look at her. "I am. I know I am. I can feel it all the way to my soul."

She pulls me in for another hug. Then she releases me. "I have pregnancy tests in my glove box."

Any other time, I'd laugh. Because I know the tests she's referring to. And they've been there for like ten years. They're there because when I was nineteen and missed a period and was afraid to buy one myself, she did it for me. In fact, she bought five. At the time, I only needed one.

"No way are they still good."

"Do pregnancy tests expire?"

We stare at each other, neither of us knowing the answer.

She hops off the bed. "It's the best we've got."

Within ninety seconds, she's back at my side pulling one out of a plastic bag so old it practically crumbles apart. She examines a test and shrugs. "It expired seven years ago." She shoves it at me.

I push it back at her. While she was gone, I googled it. "Old tests can show false negatives or false positives."

She empties the bag of the other tests. "Then take all of them. We'll go with majority rules."

I glare up at her. "This isn't a game, Mia."

Her hands go to her hips. "Do you want to know or not?"

"Actually, not."

"Ignoring the problem won't make it go away. And if you're not pregnant, at least that weight won't be on your shoulders and you can just go back to being Ms. Lonely Broken Heart."

I glare some more.

"Oh, come on. Everyone who knows you knows you're head-over-heels for the guy."

"Can we stick to one problem at a time please?"

She picks up the four tests. "Just take them. If it's a tie, I'll go buy another one. Knowing is going to be better than not knowing."

I get what she's saying. But she's wrong. Not knowing is better.

Not knowing if there is a life inside me that I'll grow to love. Not knowing if that life is going to be ripped away so painfully that it will leave a permanent scar. *Another* permanent scar. Not knowing if I'd be able to go on living after going through that a second time when the first nearly broke me. Not knowing if I'd be able to step away from the edge of the bridge this time, but that I might just let myself fall fifty feet into the rocky ravine below.

Instead of telling Mia any of that, I take the tests from her and go into the bathroom, throwing up three times before peeing on them.

Chapter Fifteen

Allie

Mia brings me a piece of dry toast. "Try this."

"I don't want to eat."

"Allie, you've thrown up ten times in the past hour. You have to eat something." She shoves it at me and I take a small bite to appease her. "I ran into your mom in the kitchen. I told her we're taking a girls' day. She said it sounded like a good idea since you've been off lately."

"Off." I stare at the four positive tests. "That's one way to describe it." I rub my red and swollen eyes. "What am I going to do, Mia?"

She hands me my phone. "Maybe call the guy you're in love with? You know, *the father?*"

I take it but toss it on the bed. "No."

"You're not telling him?"

"I can't even wrap my mind around it. I'm not going to burden Asher with this."

"If you think it would be a burden to him, you don't know him very well. Allie, that guy would marry you today if he knew you were pregnant."

I pull my knees to my chest. "I'm not putting him through this."

"So, what? You want an abortion?"

"I don't know what I want."

"How far along do you think you are?"

I shrug. "You know how whacky my periods can be. I have no idea." I close my eyes and sigh. "I could be four weeks or four months."

"You are not four months. You'd be showing. I remember Maddie Calloway once saying she showed a lot earlier with her second because she'd already been stretched out once before."

I run a hand across my middle. "Here's the thing, though. I think I already am. My clothes are tight. I know I've gained weight. I thought it was because I wasn't running as much."

"There's only one way to find out." She pulls out her phone. "My cousin can be discreet. I know he'd see you privately."

I belt out an incredulous scoff. "Hudson McQuaid? Are you fucking crazy?"

She shrugs. "He works with high-risk pregnancies. And he's proven he can keep his trap shut. Remember when Jaxon Calloway knocked up two women at one time?"

"I'm not going anywhere in Cal Creek, Mia."

"Okay then, who was your doctor last time?" She opens a browser, ready to do a search.

"Miller. In Brooklyn."

"Hmmm." She types, reads, types, reads, then sighs. "There was a Dr. Lauren Miller. OB/GYN in Brooklyn. Retired five years ago." She taps her screen, and I hear ringing through the speaker. "We can still try her old office."

I listen as Mia tries to get me an appointment, but the lady on the phone insists the soonest is three weeks.

"Three weeks?" I cry when she hangs up. "I can't wait that long."

She tries a few more offices and the quickest appointment she can get is twelve days from now.

"I'll go crazy if I have to wait twelve days."

She holds out her phone with her cousin's number pulled up on the screen. "I'll bet he could work you in today."

I bat it away. "Not happening."

"Okay. Twelve days it is. Guess you're going in to work today?"

I hate how passive-aggressive she's being right now. But I also know I'm not going to cave and go somewhere local. "What if we go to an emergency room in the city?"

She eyes me like I'm crazy. "To get an ultrasound?"

"I could say I'm from out of town and I'm spotting and want to make sure everything's okay."

She thinks on it and shrugs. "Get dressed. I'll tell my brothers not to expect me at work until this afternoon."

An hour later, we're sitting in a busy emergency room. Unlike me, there are people here with *real* emergencies. Broken bones. Flu. A guy comes in with a nail in his shoulder. Babies are crying. Kids are complaining. A man is yelling at the admit nurse that he's been here for four hours.

I lean to Mia. "What do I say when they ask how far along I am or what my due date is?"

"Give them your best guess. By the time you get the ultrasound and they figure out you were lying, you'll have your answers."

A kid comes in with a bloody nose. His mom carries him to the front desk, droplets of blood trailing behind them. "I feel guilty about taking a room from someone who really needs it."

A woman stands up and stomps out. "I'm going to the free clinic. It'll probably be a shorter wait."

I raise a brow. "What if we did that? There must be free clinics all over the city."

"Yeah, if you want to risk life and limb to go there. I'm sure they're in shady areas."

"Maybe not." I search on my phone then grab Mia's arm. "Check this out. There's a women's clinic a mile away. It says they offer free ultrasounds to confirm pregnancy, estimate gestational age, and detect cardiac activity." I stand. "Come on."

She takes my phone and looks at the pinned address. "You sure you want to go there?"

"I'm sure."

She eyes me up and down. "Got any valuables on you?"

"It's not going to be that bad."

When we get there, I try to pretend Mia wasn't right. But, oh my god, she was. We are so out of place here. Most of the women waiting to be seen aren't even wearing clean clothes. A lot of them have two or three kids in tow, many of them in soiled, ripped clothing.

I run a hand through my hair to mess it up, and I untuck my shirt to appear more disheveled. I sigh, feeling even guiltier here than at the ER.

"You lost?" the woman at the counter asks, popping her gum.

Mia nudges me forward. I approach slowly. "I, uh… would like an ultrasound."

She huffs. "Don't want it showing up on Daddy's insurance?" She rolls her eyes and hands me a clipboard. "Fill this out, princess."

Mia steps in front of me and puts her hands flat on the desk. "Looks like you missed the etiquette training. You have no fucking idea what she's going through, who she is, or what she's lost. So why don't you keep your judgmental thoughts to yourself?"

That's my best friend. Brusque as she is. But she always has my back.

I spend two hours trying not to make eye contact with women who are obviously judging me the same as the receptionist. Just when I think I can't take another under-the-breath comment or turned-up nose, my name is called. Not my real name. The name Mia put on the form when she filled it out for me.

"Miss Anderson?"

Rolling my eyes at the mention of Asher's last name, I stand and pull Mia with me.

We're escorted to a large room with five or six curtain separators. The lady points to the third one. "That's yours. Undress your lower half. A tech will be in shortly. Mondays are our busiest days since we're closed on the weekend. The wait might be a bit longer than normal, especially since one of our techs called in sick. Sorry."

"That's okay."

Once the curtain is drawn, there's barely enough room for the bed and one small chair. I almost fall over while removing my pants, then sit on the table and cover my lower half with the provided paper sheet.

I hear sobs from across the room. A woman is crying and saying, "I can't be pregnant. I just can't. He'll kill me."

Mia shoves her AirPods in my ears and plays music. I'm grateful I don't have to listen to anyone else. I'm fairly sure I'm the one who will be sobbing as soon as it's my turn.

Lying flat, music in my ears and Mia stroking my arm, I almost fall asleep and am startled when the music stops. I look up to see a young woman. Girl is more like it. I give Mia's AirPods back to her.

"I'm Clara. I'll be doing your ultrasound." The baby-faced tech rolls an ancient-looking machine up next to me, disturbing the closed curtain to my right.

Mia and I share a look. We're both thinking the same thing. Is this kid even out of high school?

Clara's cheeks pink. "I'm young, I know. But I've been working here over a month, and I've done a hundred of these." She laughs and tries to make a joke. "It's not like I'm performing surgery."

I throw an arm over my eyes. "Let's just get this over with."

The machine beeps as it turns on and I hear the squirt of lube knowing it's going on the wand thingy she's about to impale me with. When she tells me to relax, I want to kick her with the foot that is inches from her face, because relaxing is the last thing I'm about to do.

The wand moves around inside me as I try to go to a better place in my mind. A beach. A blanket. A bottle of champagne. And Asher. That's my place. It's the place I dream of. It's where my mind goes when I think of him. When I don't think of him. When I try to think of life without him.

"There it is."

I don't look at the screen. Because I know what 'it' means.

"Do you want to hear the heartbeat?"

My eyes are squeezed tightly shut as I shake my head. Maybe if I don't hear the heartbeat, I won't have the instant connection I had when I heard Christopher's heartbeat. Maybe if I don't let myself connect with this baby, I won't be so devastated when I find out something is wrong with it.

Mia holds my hand, squeezing it reassuringly. I'm sure her eyes are plastered to the screen. She knows my story almost as well as I do, but it's not her story. She's not scared of being pregnant. Of falling in love with another human being only to have that love ripped to shreds and her world torn apart.

"It looks like you're about eleven weeks," Clara says. "But let me take a few more measurements."

My mind is reeling. Eleven weeks. Almost three months. How did I not know this before now?

You did.

"We need a bed!" someone yells. "Got a laboring woman out here. She's crowning."

I rise up on my elbows. "I'm done here. Use this bed." I'm scooting up so the wand thing just kind of falls away as the girl looks up at me. "I got what I came for. You need the room."

I take tissues off the stand, wipe up, and quickly put on my jeans and shoes. Then I pull Mia out to the front and drop three fifty-dollar bills in the nearly empty plastic jar labeled "Contributions appreciated."

Mia wraps her arm around my shoulders as we walk to the train station.

All I can think of is the word eleven.

I'm eleven weeks pregnant.

Eleven weeks ago, Asher's sperm unknowingly fertilized my egg and now I'm pregnant with his baby.

For eleven weeks, there's been something growing inside me. It started as just a few cells. But now it probably has arms and legs and might even look like a person.

Eleven weeks.

Eleven weeks is too far along to terminate.

I press my forehead against the train car window knowing that even if they'd said *four* weeks, I wouldn't do it. It's a part of me. A part of him.

I swallow the bile rising in my throat and take a sip of water, positive my heart is about to be put through a blender and pulverized as visions of Christopher appear in my mind.

And when our train goes over the bridge on the way to Calloway Creek, I contemplate if this is the one I'll jump from when everything goes to shit.

Chapter Sixteen

Asher

I'm forty years old. I shouldn't have to play games. So why am I letting her play me? If she's going to end this, she should be mature enough to come right out and say it.

I haven't seen her since Antigua. Since the night she said maybe this was getting too complicated but then slept with me anyway. Was that goodbye?

I swore the next time we saw each other I would tell her how I really feel about her. But maybe I waited too long. Or perhaps I misread her the entire time and she was never that into me.

Twice now, I've been to New York City, and twice she's come up with excuses why she couldn't meet me. Granted, each visit was only for three days and two nights. Should I really expect her to drop everything on a whim and rearrange her entire schedule to see me?

But the thing is—I'm pretty sure that's what she did for the previous sixteen months.

Maybe my daughter got to be too much for her. I get that her adolescent antics threw a wrench into our plans. And yes, it's something we'll have to deal with if we move forward. But to ghost me because of my kid?

She hasn't exactly ghosted me. She does reply when I text her. It's just not the playful responses I usually get. The anticipatory winky faces. The sexy innuendos.

There are just so many things I want to tell her. Things I can only tell her in person. I never told her that when we first met, I had this incredible sense of déjà vu, like we'd met before. Like maybe it was kismet and we were meant to be together.

I never told her because I knew it would scare her away. She's this incredible, strong, independent woman on the outside, but on the inside, it's like she's battling demons. Demons she won't let anyone see. And those demons keep her from showing her true self. They won't let her give as much of her as I need. They hold her hostage.

It very well could be that I'm not the right man for her. The right man would be able to slay those demons. The right man could protect her from them. *Fuck.* I want to be that guy.

So, yes, I'm going to let her continue to play me until I have my say. Until I can be face-to-face with her and tell her everything I've kept bottled up for well over a year. Because I swear that's how long I've loved her. Even when I didn't think I did, I did. It's so goddamn cliché. Hell, songs have been written about it. But I truly believe I loved her even before I met her.

I scrub a hand across my face. *Jesus, Ash, get it together.* I hit the bathroom and splash water on my face just as Bug bursts through the front door, tosses her backpack across the room, and runs into her bedroom.

"Hello to you too," I yell.

"Whatever. My life is over."

I stand in her doorway, prepared to hear how a boy has broken her heart. She's thirteen. It was bound to happen sooner or later. "Want to talk about it?"

"No." She buries her head in a pillow and screams.

I don't say anything. I just stand here wondering what Marti would do.

She kicks off her shoes, which doesn't look easy considering she's lying face-down. Finally she says, "I want to change schools."

This is when I know something huge happened. Was she humiliated in front of a boy? In front of a class? I pull out her desk chair and sit, facing her. "Okay. I guess we could consider it. But there's only a month left, why not stick it out?"

"I mean change high schools, Dad."

"High school? Why would you want to change high schools when you've never even been to the one you'll go to in the fall?"

"Because I'll be a freak. I won't have any friends. Everyone else I know will go there with their group of friends. And they'll all laugh because I won't have anyone."

I move to sit on the edge of her bed. "Sweetie, did you and Mel have a fight? Is that what this is? I'm sure whatever it is will blow over."

"We didn't have a fight."

I brush her hair aside to see if her face will give me a clue. Because I'm confused. "Bug, I know I don't speak teenager, but you're going to have to explain. If you didn't have a fight, then you *will* have a friend in high school, so why—"

"She's moving." She sits up and throws her pillow angrily across the room. "My best friend since birth is fucking moving." She looks up sheepishly. "Sorry, I know I shouldn't say that. But Dad, this is *so* bad. She's abandoning me when I need her the most." She's back on her stomach, head down. "I'm in my formative years. What am I going to do without her? I'll be a loser with no friends, and she'll be all the way across the country. I'll be alone. Alone and in high school. I'll probably turn to drugs and alcohol."

I decide to cut her a break on the cursing. After all, this is about as bad as it gets. First Marti and Charlie move away, now Mel. I can hardly blame her for her choice of words.

"Ah, Bug. I'm so sorry. How far away?"

"Her dad got some big promotion. Some stupid state like Oregon."

I want to comfort her, but as soon as she says Oregon, my mind goes back to that haunting day years ago. And for the millionth time over the past ten years, I wonder what happened to that girl. The sad girl on the bridge. The one I scared away.

"You'll make new friends." I pat her reassuringly. "Your high school will get kids from more than just your middle school. Surely there will be other kids just like you. Maybe someone who just moved here."

"Yeah, but at least they have an excuse. That's why I need to change high schools. If I go to one that has nothing to do with my school now, it's expected that I won't have friends. Can we move? Mel said I should ask you to move to Winter Springs or something. They have good schools there and nobody will know me." Her eyes light up like she has the best idea ever. "Oh my god, we should move to Oregon. You don't have to be here for your job. You can live anywhere. Especially now that Aunt Marti and Charlie are gone. Dad, can we?"

"Whoa. You're getting way ahead of yourself, Bug. I own a house. We can't just up and move. Listen, you have a month left of school and then we'll have the whole summer to figure this out. Can't you apply for programs at a high school out of our district? Like if you wanted to do ROTC and your school didn't offer it?"

Her eyes roll. "ROTC. Really? You see me carrying a gun and getting up at the crack of dawn for drills?"

I ruffle her hair. "It was an example. Give me a break, kid. I couldn't think of anything better. Okay, theater. Business." I raise a brow. "IT security?"

"She's my best friend in the whole entire world. Please please please think about it? Oregon could be cool. And there's literally nothing keeping us here anymore."

She's right. There is nothing keeping us here.

But when I think of moving, Oregon is about three thousand miles away from the location that pops into my mind.

Man, for a second there, Bug's problem took my mind off my problem.

My problem being that I'm in love with Allie Montana. I'm in love with her and I can't tell her. I'm in love with her and she almost certainly doesn't love me back. I'm in love with her and all I can think about in this very second is putting a For Sale sign in my front yard so I can move to Calloway Creek and convince her of all the reasons we should be together.

I get up to leave.

"Dad?"

"Yeah?"

"You didn't answer."

I sigh. "I'm not saying we won't ever move. And I'm not entirely opposed to you switching schools. But Bug, I'm not going to lie. I don't think Oregon will ever be an option. Most of my business is on the East Coast."

She throws her other pillow on the floor. "I knew you'd say that."

I face her head on. "Almost everything I do in life, I do for you. I love you more than you'll ever know. But Oregon? Sweetie, it's just not going to happen. Now what should we make for dinner?"

She studies me, pouts for ten more seconds, then gets up and passes me on the way to the kitchen. "I'm making spaghetti. Everyone needs carbs when they're depressed."

I follow, knowing exactly how she feels. "We might want to make a double batch then. I'll get the meat. And definitely some extra garlic bread."

Chapter Seventeen

Allie

I'm running out of time. And I'm running out of luck. But it's becoming apparent my 'luck well' ran dry a decade ago. I've been faking flu symptoms for over a week. I think Mom is almost to the point of dragging me to the hospital if I don't get back on my feet soon.

Natasha and I have all but swapped rolls. I'm doing her admin duties from home while she's running the tastings and handling events. I swear if my last name wasn't on the sign, I'd have been fired long ago.

I'm also getting bigger. If I was eleven weeks when I went to the clinic, I'm close to thirteen now. Maddie was right. I'm showing earlier this time. I'm not sure others could see it. But I can. I used to have a concave stomach. Now I have a little pooch. I don't look pregnant yet, but those who know me well could notice if I wore form fitting clothes.

I've been doing yoga every night before bed. I've been meditating. Maybe I've even been praying. At this point, I need all the help I can get.

But the time has come. I can't put it off any longer. I call Mia. "Do you have any idea where I could find your cousin at this hour?"

Her relieved sigh comes all the way through the phone. "I'm glad you're going to see him. I can call him if you want, and I'm sure he can work you in tomorrow. Cousin favor."

"Are you crazy? I'm not going to his office. If there's something wrong with this baby, I don't want the town gossiping and looking at me with pity. I'll do what I did last time."

"Go to Washington?"

"It wasn't Washington," I remind her.

"Right. Sorry."

"I was hoping to talk to Hudson in person before I lose my nerve."

"He's probably at Donovan's with his brothers. Wait, does this mean you're ready to tell people? Have you told your mom? Asher?"

"I'm not ready to tell anyone yet. Especially not Asher. What he doesn't know won't hurt him if I can spare him what I went through last time."

"You really believe he wouldn't want to be there for you?"

I sigh, knowing he probably would.

"He might hate you for hiding it from him."

"Yeah? Well, I'd rather have him hate me than have to live with what I've had to live with."

"Allie, the chances are—"

"I know what the chances are, Mia," I say a little too sharply. "They're the same as they were last time. No more. No less. But as long as there's a chance, I'm not telling him."

"And if you find out the baby is healthy, what then?"

"Then I'll tell him, and we'll decide what to do."

"What do *you* want him to do?"

"Honestly, Mia, I haven't thought that far ahead. Do you know how much planning Jason and I did, and it was all for nothing. I'm not doing that again. Day by day is all I can manage right now. Can you please just be a friend and support me?"

"Okay. Meet me at Donovan's in twenty minutes. I'll pull him aside and then you can tell him what you need."

"Thank you."

I pull on an oversized sweatshirt even though it's probably too warm out to be comfortable. It's stupid to think anyone would notice yet, but I'm starting to be self-conscious about it, knowing if anyone even suspects, I'll be gossip fodder for months.

Eighteen minutes later, I'm waiting in the parking lot behind the pub for Mia. She spots me, parks, and comes over.

"I saw him on the patio. I'll text him to come out to my car, then you can get in and talk to him."

I nod, feeling sweat trickle down my back despite the mild evening temperature.

Mia sits in her car. Hudson looks out at the parking lot, waves at her, then holds up a finger. He speaks to his brothers then walks over to her car. I wait a minute to make sure Hawk and Hunter aren't looking, then I get out of my car and move quickly to hers, getting in the back seat.

Hudson turns, looking between Mia and me. "What's this about? Wait, who needs medical advice?"

I hold his stare. "You're bound by law not to talk about anything I say, right?"

"That's right."

"I have a problem, and I need your help."

He cracks a slow smile. "There are antibiotics for that."

Well if that isn't a lovely reminder of how the Montanas and the McQuaids aren't exactly friendly. The feud that divided this town a hundred years ago still exists today. You're either Team Calloway or Team McQuaid. And the Montanas are Team Calloway. Somehow, regardless of the fact that Mia is a Cruz and Cruzes are Team McQuaid, we're still best friends and always will be.

Mia hits him in the arm. "Don't be an asshole."

Hudson must key in on my total lack of reaction to his jab, not to mention my red-rimmed eyes and all-around shitty demeanor. His smile falls. "What's up, Allie?"

I briefly look down as I say the words. "I'm pregnant."

He raises a brow. "Congratulations?"

The way he says it lets me know he understands this isn't exactly a happy occasion.

"But seriously, why the clandestine meeting? There are a hundred OBs you could go to within thirty miles. Why me?"

"Because you can be discreet. And because you deal with high-risk."

"What makes you think you're high-risk?"

I close my eyes and swallow, barely able to get the words out. "I had a baby once."

"You…" I don't need to see his reaction. I can hear the surprise in his voice. "Okay, well obviously not many people know that. Did you give it up for adoption?"

I shake my head, open my eyes, and stare right at him.

He's a doctor. He can read between the lines.

He sighs. "Shit. What was it?"

"Chromosomal abnormality."

His entire attitude changes. He's in full doctor mode now, displaying all the empathy Dr. Miller did when she was my doctor. "Which one?"

I can hardly say it. "Trisomy 18."

He sighs again. A deep, almost painful sigh. "I'm sorry, Allie. I had no idea." His eyes flutter to my stomach. "But you know the odds—"

"I know the odds, Hudson. I still have to find out anyway. Before I tell anyone. I need the blood test. The one that checks for all that stuff."

"The NIPT. Sure, we can do that. But you should be at least ten weeks along first. If you just found out—"

"I'm more like thirteen. Well, almost. I went to a clinic in the city. They did an ultrasound and found a heartbeat."

He nods. "I'm sure I can work you in tomorrow. I can bring you in through the back."

"No. No way. You aren't my gynecologist. If anyone sees me there, people will talk." I feel my pulse race and I swear I'm about to hyperventilate. "If anything is wrong with this baby, nobody can know. I wouldn't be able to live with all the questions. The 'when are you due' and 'who's the daddy.' I can't. I just can't."

Hudson gets out of the car and joins me in the back seat. He puts a hand on my arm like his family doesn't hate mine. "Allie, it's okay. We'll figure something out. After hours maybe, you could meet me there tomorrow after everyone leaves."

"It's still too risky, and besides, I don't want to wait. Do you know how hard it was for me to come here and talk to you about this? Can we do it now? But not there. At my place. Or in the car even. Hudson, you don't know what I went through. Nobody can know."

"Okay, okay." He looks back at the pub. "Let me go back to my brothers. In about ten minutes, I'll say I was paged. I'm on call, so they won't think anything of it. I'll go to the office and get what I need and meet you at"—he looks at Mia—"the autobody shop? We need somewhere with good lighting for the blood draw."

"That works for me," Mia says.

I nod. "Thank you..." I glance over at his brothers.

"Allie, nobody will know about this. I promise. The blood draw will be quick and painless. I'll send it out in the morning. We should have the results early next week. But try not to worry."

"All I do is worry, Hudson."

"I'm sure you do. But more than likely, come next week, there won't be anything to worry about." He goes for the door then turns back. "Out of curiosity, who *is* the father?"

I sneer at him. "Do you ask that of all your normal patients?"

He sweeps an arm at our surroundings. "You're hardly a normal patient, Allie."

"You don't know him."

"Sure I don't." He opens the door. "I guess I'll find out soon enough. Nothing stays a secret in this town. See you at the auto shop in thirty minutes."

Nothing stays a secret in this town.

I spend the next thirty minutes, and then the next thirty-six hours in a state of constant panic.

Chapter Eighteen

Allie

Every time my phone rings, I jump. Hudson said the results would take about three days. This is day three.

My parents sat me down last night and said they were worried about me. I lied and said Asher and I broke up. It was the only thing I could think of to explain my recent behavior. And it wasn't so much a lie. Not that we've technically broken up. But can you even break up if you were never officially together?

Whenever Asher has texted about coming to town since Antigua, I've responded with a simple *'I'll check my schedule'* or *'Sorry, can't make it this time.'*

He's starting to get the message, however, because I haven't heard a thing from him in twelve days. The fact that I know exactly how many days have passed since I've heard from him is something I try not to think about. Because right now, there's no room inside me to think about anything but the impending test results.

I run a hand across my belly pooch and think of Christopher. The first time I felt him move inside me was surreal. I was sure the test was wrong even when Dr. Miller assured me a false positive occurred some infinitesimal amount, like less than a fraction of a percent. My pregnancy was so normal I just knew there had been a mistake, which is why I refused further testing. As he grew inside me and I loved him more and more each day, I thought my sheer love for him would be the miracle he would need. And that he would be *my* miracle. And we would live happily ever after, me and Christopher. Mother and child.

I'm startled when my phone rings. When I see Hudson's number on the screen, my body goes completely numb. I can't raise my hand off the bed to answer it. Because this is it. I'm about to find out if the next six months are going to be a living hell.

For a moment, I pray that the results show a different kind of abnormality. Maybe Trisomy 21: Down's Syndrome. At least then I'd get to raise my baby. Interact with my baby. *Love* my baby. I sit here, bargaining with God, or maybe the devil. I can take something else. Just not that. Not Trisomy 18.

My mind flips through all the other things that could be wrong. All the other chromosomal issues or birth defects I researched way back then. To me, there were few that were worse than going through a normal pregnancy, having what appeared to be a normal baby, and then watching that perfect, tiny human pass away right in front of you.

My screen goes blank before I work up the courage to answer.

I immediately press the number to call Hudson back. But it goes to voicemail. I hang up and call again. Same thing. I squeeze my eyes shut, cursing myself for not answering. The torture just continues to pile up as I dial him over and over. Sweat dots my brow. Shivers of fear crawl up my spine. My hands are shaking.

Am I having a panic attack?

Finally, on the ninth or tenth try, he answers.

"Allie. Sorry about that, I just got paged into an emergency C-section. I only have a minute."

I can hear him shuffling about. Maybe changing clothes or running for his car.

"You have the results?"

"I'd like you to come into my office tomorrow."

"I told you, I don't want to do that."

"You said you had an ultrasound at eleven weeks?"

"Yes."

"Did you get a video or a printout?"

"No. It was a free clinic. Why?"

"Allie, I really have to get to surgery, but I want to go over these results with you in person."

I almost drop the phone as I slide off my bed, sinking to the floor. I pull my knees up to my chest and a sob bellows out of me. "The baby has it. That's what you don't want to tell me over the phone."

"Ah, shit. No, that's not it. No Trisomy 18. I promise." His next few words are muffled, but I think he's speaking with someone else. Then he talks to me again. "Listen, I have to hang up. Come whenever you can and I'll fit you in."

The phone goes dead. I stare at it, crying. He promised the baby doesn't have Trisomy 18. He *promised.* A doctor wouldn't lie about something as critical as that, would he? But there's definitely something he's not telling me. I can feel it all the way to my bones. He'd have reassured me if everything came back normal. He'd tell me not to worry and to just make an appointment at my leisure. He wants me to come in tomorrow. To go over the test results. That means there is something to go over.

I crawl back up on my bed, curl up into a fetal position, and cry myself to sleep wondering if tomorrow I'll be going out to find that bridge.

"Push," the nurse urges again. "You can do it, Allie. You've got this."

Mom squeezes my hand and offers an encouraging nod.

I hold my breath and bear down as hard as I can.

"Okay, stop." The doctor's head pops up. "Stop pushing. The head is out. There, okay, now one last push."

I lock eyes with my mother, hers aren't as hopeful as mine. I've prayed so much these past months, surely my prayers will be answered. He's going to be fine. He's going to have ten fingers and ten toes and he's going to outlive me by twenty years. I even have a name picked out for him. I'm naming him after my father.

I can feel the relief as his body slips out of me. I rise up on my elbows, waiting to hear the sound every new mom wants to hear. When I hear it, I smile. He's okay. He's going to be okay. Dr. Miller was wrong.

His cry is everything I want to hear, but it's not loud. And when I glance around the room, people are shuffling quickly and hovering over him. Someone puts a tiny oxygen mask over his face.

"What's happening?"

I look up at my mother as if she'll have all the answers. She just rubs my arm in that soothing manner mothers do when they know you're hurting.

Mom hasn't come out and said it, but I know she hasn't believed like I have that the test could have been wrong. She's been supportive. She flew out here a week ago so she'd be here when he came. She's been staying with me at Aunt Lucy's, where I've been living for the past four months.

The doctor is busy delivering the placenta and doing whatever else needs to be done down there. A nurse helping with Christopher looks over at me with a sad smile. Nurses don't look at new moms with sad smiles. Nurses look at new moms with happy smiles, and sometimes with happy tears.

"No," I say, shaking my head over and over. "No, no, no."

Mom climbs on the bed next to me as soon as the doctor is done with me. She pulls me into her arms and cradles me like how I should be cradling my son. "Shhh." Her breath flows over my hair as she tries to calm me.

A man, the neonatologist I think, steps forward. "Miss Montana."

I hold out my hand to stop him. "I know. You don't have to say it."

He clears his throat. "Miss Montana, your son is breathing on his own at the moment, but he's weak. We're taking him to the NICU for evaluation. I'll report back soon."

The three words that keep cycling through my head are 'at the moment.' What he's really saying is that at any time, he could stop breathing. I turn and press my face into Mom's shoulder and scream.

I wake, drenched with sweat, shaking and nauseous. I can't move. I can barely breathe.

I need Mia. She's always been good at calming me down. I call her, not caring that it's four in the morning. It goes to voicemail. When I text her, I see she's set her notifications to silent. I try again and again, hoping that my sheer determination will have her waking up and checking her phone.

My heart races. Then stops. Then races again. I feel like I'm going to pass out. I'm having a full-on panic attack, and I don't know how to stop it.

Without even realizing what I'm doing, I tap Asher's name. The phone rings. He answers on the third ring. "Allie?"

"I…I…" I break down in sobs. "C-can't breathe."

"Allie. What's wrong? Do you need an ambulance?"

"N-no. I… just… c-can't… breathe. Dream. I… Ash…"

"Okay, okay. You had a bad dream?"

I can't respond. Because it's now when the true reality hits—I'm on the phone with Asher. I never call Asher. *Ever.* And it's four o'clock in the morning and I'm calling him in a frenzy.

"Listen to my voice, Al. Whatever it was, it was just a nightmare. You're okay. Do you hear me? Breathe. Just breathe in and breathe out. Do it with me. Come on, let me hear you. Breathe."

His voice is soothing. He just keeps talking, and eventually the calm, quiet cadence of his words slows my racing heart. Soon I stop shaking altogether. I actually grow sleepy again. I imagine this is how he talks to Bug when she wakes up from a nightmare. Or after she has a bad day. Or if she gets hurt riding her bike or dumped by a boy. He's a good father. A good man. I should tell him. Now's my chance to get it all out there.

But I don't. I can't. How can I tell him that tomorrow I'm going in to the doctor's office to find out what's wrong with our child—the child he doesn't even know about.

"Allie, are you still there?"

"I'm here," I say quietly.

"Must have been one hell of a nightmare."

"Yeah."

"Are you okay now?"

"I don't know. I guess. I mean, I will be." Suddenly, I'm crying again. I'm sniffing and snotting and sobbing because I know I *won't* be okay. Nothing will ever be okay again.

"Allie. Seriously, what's wrong? I can hear you crying."

"It's n-nothing. I'm gonna go now. I'm sorry I woke you up."

"Al—"

I hang up the phone before he has a chance to talk me into telling him what's wrong. Because a part of me wants to. Because he's not my ex and he would never abandon me like Jason did. Because he deserves to know. And because I'm a terrible person for not telling him.

But I have to know. I have to know before I go ruining his life. I can't ruin his life. I refuse to. I love him too much to do that. *Oh my god. I love him.*

I press my head into my wet pillow and cry at the revelation.

Then for the next ten minutes, I stare at my phone. My *silent* phone. The phone that hasn't received a single text or call from him since I hung up on him. So I cry even more, because now I know I finally did it. I pushed him far enough away that he doesn't care. Time and distance have made him lose feelings for me while all it's done to me is the opposite.

I love him.

And he's gone.

Dawn starts breaking. My sleep shirt is soaked with sweat. I take it off and pull on the first thing I can find—the yoga pants and sports bra I left by the side of the bed. I scoot to the other side of the mattress where the pillow is dry. Pulling it to me, I fall back to sleep as Asher's soothing words play through my mind, fearing the only place I'll ever hear them again is in my dreams.

Chapter Nineteen

Asher

I dress quickly and am out of the hotel before the sun rises. In less than an hour, I'm ascending the outside stairs and knocking on the door to Allie's garage apartment. There's no answer. I contemplate ringing the doorbell to the main house. If she's having some sort of crisis, maybe she went to her parents after calling me.

But then I check the knob. It turns.

"Allie?" I call quietly so as not to alarm her. I don't know if she has a bat or a gun. I'm an unexpected intruder. She has no idea I was in the city. I didn't tell her I was coming. Not after she begged off the last two times I was here. This time, the plan was to do my job then come to Calloway Creek and catch her off guard—and to not let her leave until I'd said what I came to say.

God, she sounded gutted on the phone. She was too wrecked to even speak. I wanted to crawl through the phone and wrap her in my arms. Let her cry on my shoulder. Hold her all day and tell her that whatever it was, it'll be okay. That I'll never let anything or anyone hurt her. That I love her more than I ever thought I could love another woman.

As I turn the corner, I quietly call her name again. The living room is dark. The place is quiet, the only light being that of the rising sun starting to shine through the skylight. I lean against the back of the couch pondering my next step when I hear a sound from the bedroom.

Springing up and crossing the room, I stop dead in the bedroom doorway when I see her lying on the bed sleeping. Her phone is on the floor. That's what I heard. Her phone dropped onto the carpet next to the bed. She turns over again, eyes closed as she continues her fitful sleep as if her body still hasn't recovered from the nightmare.

I want to go to her. Climb in bed and hold her still. Comfort her in her sleep.

I don't. Because I'm pretty sure she doesn't want me in her bed anymore. Or maybe even her life.

But she called.

All I can do is stand here and stare at her. Like in the living room, there's a skylight in her bedroom. The more the sun rises, the brighter the room becomes. She's on her side, facing me but still sleeping. Her features become clearer to me and my heart clenches. My soul hurts. Her face is puffy. Her eyes swollen. How long had she been crying before she called? How long after? What sort of nightmare could cause that visceral reaction?

Still wrestling sleep, she turns and lays flat on her back, the sheet falling to the side. She's not even in pajamas. It looks like she's wearing workout clothes. A sports bra and those tight pants women wear when—*Wait, what the hell?*

There's a small protrusion on her belly. Over the past seventeen months, I've gotten to know every inch of her body. This is not the body I know. Stepping forward for a closer look, I think my eyes are deceiving me. Until my brain finally catches up to what I'm seeing.

She's… she's… *pregnant.*

"What the fuck?" I say loud enough to wake her.

She startles awake and looks around the room like she's still in a dream. Her eyes land on me. "Asher?" She rubs her eyes with the palms of her hands. Then she looks back at me. Realizing I'm not, in fact, an aberration, she pulls the sheet over her. "What are you doing here?"

"Allie," I say sternly, my eyes trained on her stomach. "Is it mine?"

The words echo in my head and fear grips me as I wait for an answer.

Of course it's not mine. That's why she's been avoiding me. In an instant, it all starts to make sense. The complete one-eighty she did on me in Antigua. I thought it was because of what Bug did. But the way she avoided my texts the day of the wedding. And how sad she looked when I arrived at her bungalow. Sex that night *was* goodbye. Because that was the day she found out she was pregnant with another man's baby.

I lean over and put my hands on my knees, feeling all the life drain out of me. I want to scream at her. Hit the wall. Curse God. But all I can do is think of how much I still love her. And how I still want her. Even if she is having a baby that's not mine.

Is that why she panicked and called? Does she still have feelings for me even though she was with someone else?

All sorts of shit goes through my head as I await her answer. The answer I fear will destroy me.

She doesn't respond. But she does nod.

"What?" My head is reeling. "It's *mine?*"

She nods again. Sadly.

I want to smile and take her in my arms, but then the reality of the situation hits me. She's pregnant. She's so pregnant she's starting to show. And she kept it from me. And she's… sad. Really, really sad.

My momentary elation turns to anger. "What the hell, Allie? Is this why you've been avoiding me? Why haven't you told me? What kind of game are you playing?" I turn and pace, hands running through my hair as my anger continues to grow. "Did you think I'd bail? You know how much I love kids."

Ah, shit, maybe it's the opposite. I turn and face her. "You decided you were done with me and then this happened and you didn't want to be tied to me in any way? Is that it? Are you so goddamn selfish you would keep my own child from me?"

Through my rage, I almost miss the fact that she's crying again. No, not just crying. She's having another panic attack. *Shit.*

I race to the bed. "Calm down. This can't be good for the baby." I sit and put a hand on her arm. "I'm sorry I yelled."

So many emotions are raging through me right now, I don't even know how to process them. I'm excited because I never thought I'd have the opportunity to have another child. I'm pissed because she didn't take my feelings into consideration. I'm sad because it seems like this isn't at all the fairytale ending I'd wished for us. Most of all, I'm worried because of how she's reacting.

If she loved me—if she even just liked me a whole lot—she'd have told me.

There's no time to deal with my own emotions while she's breaking down next to me. All I can do is try to comfort her.

"Breathe, Allie."

My touch seems to calm her, something I'm grateful for even if I *am* still pissed as hell.

"I need a minute," she says, getting off the bed and crossing to the bathroom.

I hear the faucet run. Then the toilet flushes. Then the faucet runs again. Finally, she emerges.

The few minutes she's been in there have my anger growing again.

She sits in the chair across the bedroom, legs pulled up, arms around her knees, apparently wanting to be as far away from me as she can.

I stand, trying to maintain a modicum of self-control, but doing a shit job of it. "There isn't a single goddamn thing you could tell me to justify withholding this from me."

Tears start to fall down her cheeks. "I lost a baby."

My heart falls into my stomach and I want to throw up. It's like all in one fell swoop, I've been given everything I wanted, but just as quickly, it was yanked away. "You… lost the baby?" The words are stuck in my throat and barely come out past the forming lump. "Are you having a miscarriage?"

She shakes her head. "Not this baby. I lost another baby."

Again, my emotions are all over the fucking room, plastered to the wall in spits and spatters. I'm elated yet saddened all at the same time. I don't know which way is up. I've no idea what to think, how to feel. I can barely feel my own skin.

"Al, you're confusing the shit out of me. Can you please start from the beginning? This is *my* baby?"

"Yes."

"And it's okay?"

A painful sob heaves out of her. "I don't know."

My head is about to explode. I try to remain calm because me freaking out is not going to help this situation. I walk over to her and get on my knees. "Allie, what's going on?"

"I had a baby. His name was Christopher." She sniffs and wipes at a tear. "I was nineteen."

Was. His name *was* Christopher. Past tense. And she was nineteen. *Fuck.*

There are so many questions on the tip of my tongue, but I hold them all in. Because I get the feeling this is why she called. This was her nightmare. And I have to let her get it out. After… that's when I'll ask her everything I need to know.

Her tears just keep coming, streaming down her face in a never-ending flow. When her body begins shaking, I gather her into my arms and carry her to the bed. Setting her down, I crawl in beside her and wrap my arms around her. "Shhh. It's okay."

Her chest rises and falls rapidly, but soon her breathing evens out. "When they put him in my arms, he was perfect. He was smaller than average babies, but he looked like every other new baby I'd ever seen. He had ten fingers and ten toes—but his fingers were different, overlapping in an odd way. He cried sometimes, but it was so weak, like a mouse squeaking. And occasionally, he'd struggle to breathe." I watch a tear roll down the side of her head. "Every time it happened, *I* also struggled to breathe.

"My mother was there. She's the only one who was. But even she had a hard time watching it. I think it was my agony that she couldn't bear. So she'd have to leave every few hours, probably so I didn't have to see just how sad she was.

"The neonatologist reiterated what the obstetrician told me. That comfort measures were what was important. That interventions like intubation and medication wouldn't make a difference and would only prolong the inevitable. That the best thing I could do for him and myself was to hold him, cuddle him, feed him"—she chokes up—"and love him for as long as he would hold on."

Hot tears flow down the side of my face as I picture a young Allie, just a kid herself, holding a dying child.

"He lived for thirty-one hours and eighteen minutes." She bellows out a sob. "And then he just looked up at me. Just for a second, he looked at me like he knew me. Like he knew I was his mom and that I loved him. Then he fell asleep and he was gone. He was just… gone."

I squeeze her tightly and she clutches onto me like I'm saving her from drowning. I kiss the side of her head, letting her distress settle, when it occurs to me that she was nineteen—the same age she was when she said she was in Australia.

"You never went to Australia, did you?"

Her head shakes against my shoulder. "It was the only way to explain why I was away for so long."

"Oh, sweetheart. I'm so incredibly sorry."

She sighs and sniffs a few times. She's not trembling as much as she was a few minutes ago.

"My mom was out getting food. It was just me and Christopher. And even though they prepared me… They prepared me from the day I had the blood test and found out his fate. Even knowing what was going to happen and how, it still destroyed me." I feel her hand cradle her small belly. "I can't… I just can't go through it again."

That's when it hits me. *Oh, Jesus.* Is that same thing going to happen to this baby? *Our* baby?

"Allie," I say, my voice cracking. "What was wrong with Christopher?"

"It was a chromosomal abnormality called Trisomy 18."

The urge to pull out my phone and research it is strong.

My need to comfort her is stronger.

"Allie?" I close my eyes and force out the words. "Does this baby have the same thing?"

"I don't know." Her body trembles against mine. "I mean, the doctor said no, but he wants to see me and go over the results. That means something is wrong. Not *that*, but something else. I'm scared. Asher, I'm so, so scared. I can't do it again. I'm not strong enough. I didn't want you to know. Not until I was sure. I couldn't put you through it. Jason left. He couldn't handle it. Nobody should have to. I just couldn't tell you, not until I knew."

I turn her until she's fully facing me. "Slow down. You had some kind of test?"

She nods.

"A test for this Trisomy thing?"

She nods again.

"And the baby doesn't have it?"

"No. Not that. But, Asher, the doctor wants to see me. In person. Today. He wouldn't go over the results on the phone. Everyone knows that means bad news."

All at once, my anger and confusion start to abate. I'm still upset that she's gone through this alone. I'm sad that she didn't trust me enough to tell me and allow me to support her through it. But I do understand. As a father, I understand how devastating it must have been to watch your own child die right before your eyes. And as a father, I also understand the need to protect those I love from that kind of despair.

Instantly, I have to know the answer to a question totally unrelated to our baby.

I take her face in my hands. "Allie, I love you. I think I've loved you since the day we met. Before that even. And I have to know. Do you… love me?"

She has a hard time answering. But she does nod. And it's all the affirmation I need. My lips instantly find hers. I kiss her salty lips with a chaste kiss that has more meaning than any other kiss has ever had in my entire life.

"I love you. And whatever happens, we'll deal with it. We'll get through it. There are rules doctors need to follow. Maybe he *has* to tell you in person. You know, bring you in for a visit so they can bill your insurance."

She shakes her head. "Not this doctor. He's Mia's cousin. He took my blood at her autobody shop. I know he would have told me if the results were normal. He *did* tell me about the Trisomy 18 at least."

I kiss her forehead. "When is your appointment?"

"He said come anytime today and he'd fit me in."

I blow out a deep sigh. I don't want her to feel my own tension, but I think she's onto something. Him being a family friend but not wanting to give her the full results over the phone. Telling her she can come in any time. That doesn't sound like something a doctor would say if everything is okay. It sounds like what you do when there's bad news to deliver.

"What time does the office open?"

She shrugs, and I sit up and check the time. It's seven. I urge her up. "Take a shower. I'll make breakfast and cancel my day. We're going to be his very first appointment."

She cocks her head. "You want to go with me?"

"Sweetheart, I'm going to be with you every goddamn step of the way."

Her lips momentarily curve into a half-smile, but then fall back into a frown.

Usually when two people declare their love for each other there are kisses, flowers, sex, champagne, and celebration. I can't think of a single other scenario but the one we're in right now that would have us crying instead of laughing.

But she loves me. And right this second, when there's nothing I can do about anything else, that's the only thing that matters in the world.

She. Loves. Me.

Chapter Twenty

Asher

Over breakfast, she tells me about Jason. About how she didn't want anyone to know about the baby—not because she was ashamed, but because she didn't want people's misplaced well-wishes when they saw her pregnant belly. Or their sympathy when they eventually heard how it turned out. She tells me how she went out west to her aunt's house. Alone, afraid, and abandoned by the man she loved.

I'm doing everything I can to assure her that is not going to happen this time. No matter what the test results say, I'm going to stick by her side.

Which is why when we enter the doctor's office, I grab her hand and don't let go.

She was going to make me sit across the room. She said the only reason men accompany women to a gynecologist's office is if they're pregnant. She didn't want rumors starting.

Screw that. I don't care about rumors. All I care about is being here for her and getting her through whatever we're about to find out.

I'm scared shitless, however, even as I'm putting on a brave face for her. I researched Trisomy 18 when she was in the shower. It breaks my heart thinking about what she must have gone through. Knowing for months and months that she was carrying a baby who was surely going to die, either in the womb or shortly after birth. That has to permanently mess with a person's psyche. And although I'm still upset she didn't tell me, I do understand it. And a part of me kind of admires her for wanting to protect me from the sheer devastation she experienced.

There are three other women in the waiting area. The older lady pays no attention to us. The other two look at Allie. Allie is completely unaware as she's sitting here with closed eyes as if it somehow makes her invisible.

One of the lookers leans over and whispers to the other looker. They both stare at me now, smiling.

"Allie?" someone calls.

I can feel the tension through her fingers. She doesn't move. She's cemented to the seat. I stand, pull her up then lean in. "Whatever happens, I'm here. You will not go through this alone."

Slowly, her glassy eyes open and she gives me a small nod.

I'm escorted back to an exam room while her vitals are taken. As I sit in the chair next to the patient table, I examine the posters on the wall. Pregnant women looking happy. A list of what to avoid during pregnancy. A month-by-month fetal growth chart.

I try not to get too excited, but I am. She's pregnant. I'm going to finally have another child. It's something I've craved for a decade but thought would never happen. Stella and I tried for years. We went through five miscarriages. Rounds of fertility treatments. It was a constant roller coaster of ups and downs.

I know we still have to get through these test results, but if Allie really is thirteen weeks, she's in the second trimester, where odds of miscarriage go way down. Stella never made it past nine weeks. And no matter what, I'm going to love this baby as much as I love Bug.

Bug. I wonder what she'll think about becoming a big sister. Will this be the thing that finally gets her to accept Allie?

I'm getting ahead of myself. First, we need to get through the next fifteen minutes. Then we can start planning the future—whatever that may be. But one thing's for sure, it's a future where we'll be together. Me. Allie. Bug. And hopefully a happy, healthy baby. A son maybe, one who looks like me? Or a daughter who has Allie's beautiful hair and who also gets hiccups after she eats?

The door swings open and Allie walks in, followed by a nurse who announces, "Dr. McQuaid will be in shortly."

"Thank you," I reply when Allie remains quiet.

I can see the fear in her eyes. She's trying to keep it together after her breakdown. And I'm not really sure what to say. I've assured her fifty times already that I'm going to be here for her. At this point, I think all I can do is hold her hand.

Luckily, we don't have to wait long. I'm not sure if that pleases me or bothers me. He said he'd work her in, but it seems like he's taking her before anyone else. That could mean there's a reason he needed to see her first. Or it could just mean she's a friend of a friend and she's getting preferential treatment.

When he sees me, he stops and takes me in. Though I've been to Calloway Creek several times since Marti and Charlie moved here, I don't know many residents. The Montanas of course, some of the Calloways, and a few other random people.

I stand and offer my hand. "Asher Anderson."

His eyes flit amusingly between Allie and me when he shakes my hand. "Hudson McQuaid. I've heard your name once or twice. Nice to put a face to it."

It's strange, but the way he seems to be amused at my presence puts me at ease. If he had horrible news to share, he wouldn't be quite so entertained by Allie bringing me here.

He pulls over a rolling stool and taps around on his iPad.

Allie visibly tenses. I take a seat and grab her hand. Instinctively, she tries to pull away, but I don't let her. I hold on. I hold on tightly.

"Just say it," Allie belts out. "I know it's bad news or you'd have told me yesterday."

"There's nothing to freak out about. I just saw something in the blood test that didn't make sense based on what you told me. You said you had an ultrasound at eleven weeks?"

"Yes," she says, clearly scared and frustrated by his hesitation. "God, Hudson, just spit it out."

"I'm getting to it, Allie." He sets his iPad down and looks her in the eyes. He has something to say. *Now* I get concerned. "While the test didn't show any chromosomal abnormalities, it did show two sets of DNA."

Allie's eyes narrow. "Okay, right. Mine and the baby's."

My heartbeat suddenly increases by about a million beats per second. Because while Allie hasn't quite caught on to what he's saying, I have. *Holy mother of God.*

"Two sets of DNA *in addition* to yours," Hudson explains.

"I'm…" She looks between us. "I'm confused."

"Allie," I say, cracking a huge smile. "It's twins. We're having twins."

Before she can even react, Hudson holds up a hand. "Hold on a second. My concern lies in the fact that you had an ultrasound a few weeks ago and twins weren't detected."

My excitement, surprise, and sheer elation abate immediately. "You think something's wrong?"

His lips form a thin line. "Here's the thing. The NIPT can't tell if fetal DNA is from a viable or non-viable fetus."

I swallow hard. "Oh, Jesus. You think one of them died?"

Allie's hand rips away from mine and she protectively grips her belly.

"That's what we're here to find out," Hudson says.

Tears stream down her face. "I could have a dead baby inside me? But also a live one?"

Hudson stands but doesn't answer. He gets the ultrasound machine and rolls it over. "Lie back, lift your shirt and lower your waistband. Let's see what's going on in there."

This time, Allie is the one taking *my* hand.

My thoughts are all over the place. We could be having a baby. But there could be another one who died? What would happen? Will we lose the other one?

Hudson glides the transducer over the lower part of her stomach, studying the screen. It doesn't take long before he says, "Here we go." He presses a button on the machine and a fast *thump thump thump* fills the room.

All the breath in my lungs escapes in a relieved sigh, but then I hold it once more as Hudson's eyes become laser focused on the screen.

"Okay, yup." He smiles. "And there's Twin B."

Another *thump thump thump.*

He's smiling.

Allie covers her mouth in astonishment, her eyes filling with tears. "There are two of them? And they're both... alive?"

He points to the screen. "You're having what we call di-di twins. Otherwise known as dichorionic-diamniotic twins. That means each twin has their own placenta and amniotic sac. Compared to other types of twins, di-di twins have the lowest risk of complications." He puts a hand on Allie's arm. "Breathe, Allie. This is good news. The blood test shows everything is normal and their measurements are perfect." His head shakes as if he's pissed. "Whoever you went to for the ultrasound should be fired. Twins are pretty hard to miss at this stage."

She shrugs. "Free clinic. I doubt anyone's getting fired."

I stand and lean over to kiss her. "It's the *best* news."

She swats Hudson's arm. "Jesus Christ, Hudson. Why didn't you just tell me I was having twins last night? I had a freaking panic attack. I could kill you."

He laughs. "Oh, and you think knowing you were having twins but that one of them might have died would have settled you?"

She opens her mouth to argue, but rolls her eyes instead. Then she looks up at me. "Asher, oh my god." She turns back to Hudson. "And you're sure they're okay. Like one hundred percent?"

"Allie, they're fine. While nothing in life is guaranteed, I feel confident telling you to enjoy this pregnancy. Lord knows after what you've gone through you have every right to."

My smile is a mile wide. Only in my dreams have I imagined having a child with her. And now I get two. With the woman I'm in love with.

And she loves me.

And—*holy shit. Twins.* I sit back down, almost needing to put my head between my legs.

Hudson chuckles. I imagine he sees this a lot.

He types on the ultrasound keyboard and then prints out some black-and-white photos and hands them to Allie. She stares at them, disbelieving, as I look over her shoulder. One of the photos shows both babies, labeled Twin A and Twin B. The others show them individually.

"So they're not identical?" I ask.

"Actually, di-di twins can be identical, but yours are not. They're fraternal."

I squint at the photo. "Can you tell the sex?"

"Not based off the ultrasound, but the blood test showed it." He turns to Allie. "Do you want to know?"

I can tell she's experiencing a thousand emotions right now. Trying to process the fact that this baby—these *babies*—aren't like Christopher. And that there are two. And that since she's in the second trimester, she's already gotten past a few hurdles. And that, most likely, in six months, we'll have two healthy children.

If she's feeling the same way I am, she doesn't know whether to laugh, cry, or lose her breakfast.

"What do you think?" she asks me.

"Whatever you want, sweetheart."

Her face-splitting grin lets me know she likes the endearment. And, damn, I can't wait to get her home. I can't wait to kiss her like I want to kiss her. Touch her beautiful growing body. Put my hands on her belly.

"I want to know," she says, her eyes locked with mine.

Hudson taps the iPad. "You're having a boy and a girl."

It's an incredible sight, watching her eyes pool with happy tears as she absorbs the news that we're having a son and a daughter. I swear all the fear has drained right out of her body, leaving her filled to the brim with happiness.

I lean down and touch my forehead to hers. "You've never looked more beautiful than you do right now."

Hudson clears his throat as if he thinks we've forgotten he's here.

"Um… so when can we expect the big arrival?" I ask.

"Technically the due date is December fifth. But with twins, we consider full term to be thirty-seven weeks. That would put it at November fourteenth."

November fourteenth. I'll be forty-one years old then. Forty-one with three children.

I fucking love my life.

Chapter Twenty-one

Allie

It's nine thirty when Asher pulls my car into the garage at home. He cuts the engine and neither of us moves.

I know his thoughts are mirroring mine, but he's the first one to speak. "What are we—"

"I don't know, Asher. I don't know what we're going to do, how we're going to tell people, what we're going to say, or when. I'm still in shock."

He massages my shoulder. "Good shock, or bad shock?"

"Good." I smile. "Definitely good."

After weeks of anxiety, and let's face it, years of uncertainty, I finally feel like I can fully breathe again. And that full breath of air comes with what I think is hope. For me. For us. For a future I never allowed myself to envision.

"And what you said earlier?" He nudges me. "That still applies?"

I squint, unsure of what he means.

"You know, about being in love with me."

Warmth spreads throughout my body, and I smile again when I finally allow myself to think back on that conversation. I love him. He loves me. We're in love. I nod. "It still applies."

"Okay then." He gets out of the car and races around to open my door. "All that other stuff will fall into place. Right now, I just need to take you upstairs." He checks the time. "Do you think your folks have left for work?"

"An hour ago probably."

"So if I make you scream my name, nobody will be around to hear?"

For the first time in well over a month, tingles shoot through me. It's downright surprising considering an hour ago I was sure my life was in ruins. But now…

I take his hand and exit the car, popping up on my toes to whisper into his ear. "Not a single soul."

He smiles. It's a different smile than any I've ever seen. It's full of passion and awe and wonder and playfulness and… *love*… all mixed into one perfect grin. And it says much more than any words could say.

He sweeps me into his arms and we both laugh as he carries me upstairs to my apartment.

Laughing. I'm freaking laughing.

Suddenly, the world is a different place. I'm not the same girl I was this morning. Yesterday. Last year. The future is full of possibility. My life, as crazy as it may be, is now something I'm looking forward to rather than just existing day by day. And these tiny precious beings inside of me—these pieces of Asher and me— are like the missing pieces of a puzzle I've been working on my whole adult life. One I didn't even know could ever be completed.

Asher places me on the bed and stares down at me, his head cocked to the side.

"What is it?" I ask.

"I've never seen you look like this before."

I giggle. "Am I glowing?"

"Like the fucking sun."

His lips meet mine in a kiss so passionate it makes me feel bad for all the other kisses. Because no two mouths have ever come together like ours are now. No pairs of lips have been made to fit each other's as meticulously as ours do.

He pulls back slightly. Not enough for our mouths to part, just enough to utter the words, "Say it."

I don't make him clarify the command. I know exactly what he wants. "I love you."

"Again."

I dig my fingers into his lower back. "I love you."

"I love you, too," he breathes into me.

And somehow, the world is even more right than it was thirty seconds ago. It's more magnificent. More exciting. More… everything.

His fingers graze my ribs when he removes my top. When he palms my breasts, his touch is both gentle and electric. He pays them extra attention.

"They're different. Fuller. How did I not know?"

"You? What about me? It's my body and I missed all the signs."

He lightly pinches a nipple. "What signs?"

"Nausea. Weight gain. Boobs. I was probably in denial."

He nuzzles himself against my stomach, lowering my waistband and then touching, feeling, kissing his way around my bump. "This is the sexiest thing I have ever seen."

I giggle. "You won't be saying that when I'm as big as a bus."

"You're wrong." He raises his head. "I've always thought you were the most beautiful woman I've ever seen. You growing larger with my children will only amplify that." He kisses me just below the belly button. "And I promise to let you know it every goddamn day."

He slips a hand beneath my panties and lets his fingers do the rest of the talking. And, boy, what he says is amazing. The sensations coursing through me are inexplicable. It's like a sunrise, when you see the tip of the sun and it gets brighter and brighter and fuller and fuller and then, just as it rises above the horizon in a fiery ball of light, it's like an explosion of nature.

And exploding is exactly what I'm doing right now. After only seconds of his fingers on me. *In* me. I'm reeling. I'm winding up and down and in and out and back and forth and through. I'm rising and falling. Rolling and swelling. Dying and living. It's the most intense sensation I've ever experienced.

"I take it back," his low voice rumbles against the skin of my neck. "*That* was the sexiest thing I've ever seen."

I can't laugh. Can't speak. Can't respond in any way. I can just... *feel.*

"Wow," I say when I regain my ability to use words. "You think you could do that again?"

"With pleasure."

His clothes, along with the rest of mine, are in a pile on the floor quicker than I can pull back the covers.

His erection is hard against my hip, and I reach between us to stroke him.

He groans. "I'm assuming it's okay to go without a condom?"

I smile. "I doubt you could get me any *more* pregnant, Asher."

He studies me for a second, then shakes his head with realization. "It was that night we lost the condom, wasn't it?"

I nod. "Pretty much."

"And the birth control pills?"

"I never missed one, but the kind I took weren't as effective as regular ones."

"Oh, right. Because they gave you migraines."

"You *were* listening."

He kisses my collarbone. "I'm always listening to you, sweetheart."

I sigh. Nobody has ever called me that. I never *wanted* to be called that. The way he says it, it's sweet and sexy, and so completely honest.

He moans as my hand works him harder. But then, he brushes it aside. "It's been a minute since we've done this, so I'm not going to last long. I swear I'm going to make you come a dozen times today. But, Al, right now, I just need to make love to you."

Asher is the only man who has ever said he wanted to *make love* to me. Others have said they wanted to sleep with me. Have sex. Fuck. But never *make love*. Maybe it's because he's older. More sophisticated. A dad.

I look into his eyes knowing it's none of those things. He says it because what he does to me is so much more than just sex. The way he looks at me. Touches me. Speaks to me. He loves me with his eyes. His hands. His words. Every part of him is invested in these moments. And as he enters me, softly, slowly, gently, it's like our very souls are connecting.

I always assumed I knew what love was.

I didn't.

This. Here. Him. He's larger than life. He loves like he lives—with everything inside him.

I watch his face as he comes inside me, and a foreign emotion overcomes me. One I never thought I'd feel again. One I hope will become a frequent visitor.

Happiness.

~ ~ ~

He laces his fingers through mine, both of us spent and satiated after hours and hours of sex. "I have a question," he says lazily.

"Shoot."

"If you only found out you were pregnant two weeks ago, why did you pull away from me after Antigua?"

I turn and face him, tucking a hand under my pillow. "So we're moving on to the serious conversations?"

"As if what we've been doing all day isn't serious, Allie?" He tugs me closer. "Come on, no more secrets between us, okay?"

I nod. "Okay." I try to collect my thoughts and put them into words. "I guess my feelings got too big."

He traces my jawline with his finger. "You mean you realized you were in love and you didn't want to be. But why?"

"You're a great dad."

He narrows his eyes. "You didn't want to love me because I'm a great dad?"

I shrug. "Great dads usually want more kids. I knew how long you and Stella tried for a baby. And since I'm only twenty-eight, it would make sense that you'd want one with me."

He blows out a frustrated sigh. "I wish you'd just talked to me. If you'd told me about Christopher and your fears. If you'd said you loved me but never wanted to have another child, I'd have accepted that. The truth is, I gave up on the idea of having more kids a long time ago. Did the thought cross my mind over the past eighteen months? Sure. But I knew you didn't want them. Or couldn't have them. I never knew which. So it wouldn't have been a deal breaker."

I lay my head on his chest. "So I'm an idiot."

He plants a kiss atop my hair. "A beautiful idiot."

"I guess we got lucky. It's sort of strange how fate intervened. If I hadn't accidentally gotten pregnant, we wouldn't be together."

"We'd be together."

I lift my head and look at him. "How do you know?"

"I knew from the moment we met. I can't even explain it. It's like I knew we *had* to be together. There wasn't even a choice in the matter."

"Well, I'm glad one of us has their shit together."

He laughs. "I would hardly say that." His head shakes. "If you only knew. Bug is going through a bit of a crisis. Her best friend is moving, and she's been asking to go to a new school because she won't have any friends."

His eyebrows shoot up, and he pulls me on top of him and kisses me. "Sweetheart, this couldn't have been better timing." He looks around my apartment. "But with five of us, we're going to need a bigger place."

"*We?*" I bite my lip in nervous anticipation.

"Allie, of course I'm moving here."

A slow smile creeps up my face. "You're moving here? And you want to live together?"

"I want to do more than live with you. I want to *marry* you. But I'm not about to ask until I have a ring to slide on your finger. Out of curiosity, though, when I ask, will you say yes?"

My heart thunders as blood pulses through me so fast I'm sure he can hear it. He wants to live with me. Marry me. Have babies with me. Grow old with me.

Yesterday, I'd have said all those things were impossible. But today, my world is full of possibilities I never imagined.

I swallow, wanting to say yes. But one thing stands in the way of the word. "Only if Bug agrees."

"You won't marry me unless my daughter gives her blessing? You're having my babies, Al."

"I think it's only fair to her."

"And if she doesn't agree?"

I raise a shoulder. "Then I guess we'll live in sin until we die and go to hell."

He laughs. "So you'll live with me if my kid hates you, but you won't marry me?"

"How do you think she'll take the news?"

"I think she'll be excited to be getting a brother and a sister."

"Do you think it will change how she feels about me?"

"I don't see how it couldn't. Look at you. You're carrying my babies. Her siblings. We're going to be a family." He pulls my hand to his lips and kisses it.

We're both laughing when the alarm system indicates a door has been opened. I look at the time and realize we've been in bed for seven straight hours. I sit up. "We should tell my parents."

He momentarily looks worried. As if my parents would have a problem with this.

They won't.

"Don't worry," I say, getting up and pulling him toward the bathroom. "They love you. Now let's get in the shower."

We don't make it downstairs for another ninety minutes.

~ ~ ~

Mom and Dad are eating dinner when we enter the kitchen. Mom smiles brightly when she sees who's coming in behind me.

"Asher," she says with delight. "What a nice surprise." She winks at me.

It's as if in this moment she understands that my entire existence wasn't right without him. And the past six weeks make sense to her now that she sees us together. I feel bad for putting her through what I did. I swear she was about ready to send me to either an emergency room or a shrink.

Yeah, my mom is about to be super happy.

She motions to the table. "There's plenty of food if you want to join us."

Before we can even answer, she's getting two more place settings.

I dish some casserole onto a plate for Asher. "So, we have some news."

A hand flies to Mom's mouth. "You're getting married!"

Asher tosses me a look and smiles as if to say *'see?'*

"Well, um, no. We—"

"Yes," Asher interrupts. "Someday."

"Okay, yes, someday. When Bug agrees. But that's not our news."

"Spit it out," Dad says impatiently as if he can't enjoy his dinner until he hears whatever it is I came down to say.

"Asher and Bug are going to move to Calloway Creek."

Mom's eyes narrow to slits. She senses that's not all. "Aaaaaaand?"

"And I'm moving out."

Mom claps her hands together, happily. I once told her that it would take one hell of a guy to get me to move out of Montana Manor. So she knows. She knows Asher is *that* guy. Hell, she knew it even before I did. "Oh, that's fantastic. We're so happy for you."

Asher and I share a look.

Dad doesn't fail to notice. His eyes dart back and forth between us. "Aaaaaand?"

I blow out a cleansing breath. "And I'm pregnant. With twins."

My parents' reaction is somewhat expected. It's a mixture of surprise, excitement, and deep, deep concern.

"It's okay," I say. "I had the blood tests. They're fine. No abnormalities." I smile at Asher. "We're happy about this."

Mom breathes a huge sigh of relief, hops out of her chair and practically topples me out of mine. "I'm so, so, so happy for you." She reaches over and touches Asher's arm. "Both of you."

Once my mother calms down, we settle in and eat as I fill them in on the reality of what I've been dealing with over the past few weeks. Other than Mia and Jason—and now Asher—my parents are the only people who know about Christopher, so they fully understand what I was going through. That doesn't mean I don't get a few harsh looks and stern statements about not coming to them earlier.

"We need to have a family dinner." Dad claps his hands once like he's making a proclamation. "We'll make it a celebration."

"That would be nice," I say. "I think I'm ready to tell everyone."

"Well, I'd hope so." Mom stares at the ultrasound photo. "With twins you'll hardly be able to hide it much longer."

"That's not what I meant. I mean, yes, we'll tell them I'm pregnant." I turn and take Asher's hand. "But I'm ready to tell everyone about Christopher."

Chapter Twenty-two

Asher

I haven't stopped smiling for two straight days. While I had to extend my time in New York for a day to finish the business that took me there, most of the visit was spent with Allie. Contemplating our situation. Planning our future.

Our future. One that involves us being together. Thus, the smile.

It was hard leaving her this morning. But I have a lot to do. I have to finish a few home renovation projects, sell the convertible, and put the house on the market. But most importantly, I have to tell Bug.

As the plane touches down, I wonder how she'll take the news. I think she'll be happy about having a little brother and sister. But she's a teenager. I don't pretend to know anything about the workings of an adolescent brain. Not even when I was one myself.

I pull into Mel's driveway and exit the car. Mel's mom is weeding the flowerbeds.

"Thanks for keeping her an extra day."

"It's fine. I know they appreciate every minute they have together." She sits back in the grass, rubs her knees and shields her eyes from the sun as she looks up at me. "You're not really considering moving to Oregon, are you?"

I laugh a little. "Is that what Bug said?"

I'm not sure why I'm surprised. For the entire week after she found out Mel was moving, she left not-so-subtle hints. Printouts of Crater Lake National Park and Mount Hood. Information about schools. Even house listings.

She shrugs. "Teenagers say all kinds of crazy things."

"It was a bit of wishful thinking on her part. She knows I can live anywhere since I'm not tied to an office."

"You like it here?" Barb asks.

I nod. "I do like it here. And I'm going to miss it."

She looks at me confused. "You're… moving?"

I thumb to the door. "I'd better grab Bug. We have a lot to talk about."

"You were in New York." She stands and brushes off her jeans. "We know all about New York. Bug gives us an earful every time you go. Does this have anything to do with Hannah Montana and the extra day you spent there?"

I roll my eyes. "Hannah Montana, huh?"

"That's what she calls the woman—or the *'girl who's barely older than she is'*—whenever it comes up."

"Her name is Allie. And she's twenty-eight."

Her head moves from side to side as she studies me. "Ahhh. So not Oregon. New York."

"What makes you say that?"

"Asher, the second you said her name, it was written all over your face."

"Please don't say anything to Mel yet. I have to tell Bug." I sigh. "I'm just not sure how she's going to take it."

"Bribery works." She climbs the porch steps. "When we told Mel we were moving across the country, we softened the blow by increasing her allowance, buying her a new gaming system, and promising to get a dog."

"Bribery. Right."

"Dad!" Bug comes bounding out the front door.

I hug her and she squeezes me tightly. I love that about her. While a lot of kids her age act too old to get a hug from their parents, she's never been shy about it.

"I missed you, Bug. Sorry I had to extend by a day."

"It's okay. Mel and I had fun."

She runs back inside, grabs her bag and backpack, and hugs Mel. They share a look. A conspiratorial one. And I fear I may be in for a long night.

"Where should we go for dinner?" I ask, pulling out of the driveway. "The Rainbow Room?"

She puts down her phone and stares right at me. "Why do you want to take me to my favorite restaurant? The one we only go to when it's my birthday or other special occasion?"

"I just feel bad about leaving you so much. It was a lot easier when Aunt Marti was around, don't you think?"

Her eyes are back on her phone and she shrugs. "The Harrells don't mind when I stay with them."

"I'm glad. But that doesn't keep me from feeling guilty. Don't you miss the times you got to stay with Aunt Marti and Charlie?"

Another shrug. "Sure, but they've been gone for a while now. Plus, you take me up there every few months."

"How's Mel feeling about Oregon? I'll bet she's excited to get out of the heat and humidity. It sure does get sweltering here in the summer. The idea of living somewhere where you don't sweat the second you walk outside is kind of appealing, wouldn't you say?"

"Never bothered me," she says, tapping away on her phone. Probably texting or snapchatting or whatevering Mel even though we literally just left.

"So is Mel upset about moving?"

"She's still pissed. But the idea of getting a dog is growing on her. She says she's going to get the biggest dog there is. What do you call them, Great Danes? Those dogs are huge. Did you know their poops are bigger than human poops? We read their poops can be as big as a size fourteen shoe."

At a stoplight, I turn and stare. "You researched Great Dane poop?"

"We researched a lot of things."

Those two together are dangerous. On more than one occasion, Bug had enlisted Mel's help in getting rid of the woman I'd been dating.

"Bug, is she trying to get back at her parents for moving?"

"Of course she is. Why wouldn't she? They're ruining her life. *And mine.*"

"That's not really fair, sweetie. Her father got transferred. It's his job."

"He could have found a new job."

"It's not that easy."

"When you have kids, you have to do what's in their best interest. By choosing to become a parent, you have to put their needs first. That's what you always tell me."

My eyes close briefly. It's true. I do say that.

Why do I feel like this is going to go badly? I'm about to drop a lot of bombs on her. Her world is going to change. That's not something I should tell her in a public place.

"Maybe we should just go home."

"Home? No way. You promised me The Rainbow Room."

"I just didn't realize how tired I'd be after the flight. It's been a long week."

"Da-ad," she says in that whiney but endearing way.

"Fine. We'll go."

I'll just wait until we're home to tell her.

~ ~ ~

"Dad, will you just say it?"

I push mashed potatoes around my plate. "Say what?"

"Whatever you came here to say. One: you never bring me here on a random Thursday. Two: you've never been this quiet at a meal. *Ever.* Three: you're starting to freak me out. Are you sick or something?"

"Sick, no. I just may have misjudged the situation. I do have something to discuss with you, but I think it's best we do it at home."

Her eyes narrow to slits. "At home? As in you don't want to tell me here because you think I'll get mad?"

"Something like that."

"Dad, I'm thirteen. I'm not a baby. Just tell me."

I look around the crowded restaurant. It's loud enough in here that any reaction she'll have shouldn't ruin anyone's dinner. I'm just not sure what to start with. Moving or babies.

"Bug, sweetie, we can't move to Oregon. It's just too far away from most of the clients I work with. We need to stay on the East Coast."

"*That's* what you brought me here to say?" She shrugs nonchalantly. "Not a problem. Mel and I came up with a plan. I'm going to do homeschool high school. That way I can go visit her all the time, like one week a month. She swears it will be okay with her parents. The house they're buying even has an extra bedroom. And you can afford the airfare, right? You get so many points or whatever because you travel all the time. It's the perfect solution, don't you think?"

"You're not going to homeschool."

"What if it's in my best interest? Think about it, I wouldn't have to worry about going into high school without a friend. And we wouldn't have to move. I'm happy. You're happy. Mel's happy. Everyone's happy."

"Bug, I said it's not an option."

"You have to at least consider it. You never say no without giving things consideration."

"Okay, fine. I'll consider it."

She smiles. "Good. Good talk. I know all the websites and stuff we need to make it happen and—"

"I'll consider it, sweetie, but we're moving."

She looks at me. She studies me. *Hard.* Then she huffs loudly, drops her fork, and looks out the window. Her lips purse. She sits back in the booth and crosses her arms.

"It's because of *her* isn't it?" She looks disgusted. "Oh my god, you're moving us to that Podunk little town. That's what this is all about. The *'it's too hot in Florida'* and the *'don't you miss Aunt Marti?'* Is that what you were doing up there all week? Did you lie to me about going up on business?"

I reach across the table and grab her hand, but she pulls away.

"Bug, I need you to listen. There's more."

Suddenly, her face turns from disgust to sadness. Her eyes become glassy. "Please please don't tell me you're getting married."

"I'm not getting married. Not yet anyway. The more is that…" I'm looking into my daughter's teary eyes, praying what I'm about to say will excite her and not destroy her. "You're going to be a big sister."

Her jaw drops. The tears balancing on her lashes fall. She pushes herself out of the booth and runs to the bathroom.

Fuck. I definitely should have waited.

I sit here for a while, waiting for her to return. She needs a minute to let it all sink in. But then ten minutes become fifteen and I begin to worry. I settle the bill and walk past the bar to where the bathrooms are. When a woman and child come out of the ladies' bathroom, I peek inside and don't see anyone around. She must be in a stall. I knock loudly. "Bug?"

No response.

"Bug, let's go home and talk about this."

The woman who just left turns around. "Are you looking for the girl with the blue hair?"

"Yes. She's my daughter."

"She left a few minutes ago. I saw her using the Uber app on her phone."

"Oh, Christ."

I run out the front door, cursing myself for setting up the app on her phone. I'm a single father. I did it for emergency purposes. I never wanted her to be in a situation where she felt trapped if I couldn't get to her. Yet here I am being the one to trap her. I just tossed her whole world upside down. I'm the worst damn excuse for a father.

I look all over, but can't find her. I call her. I text her. She doesn't answer or reply. When I track her phone, I see she's moving. She's already in a car. A stranger's fucking car.

I race to my car and start driving. When her location doesn't go in the direction of our house, it dawns on me that she's probably going back to Mel's.

I drive way too fast and nearly catch up, arriving at Mel's house just as she's exiting the Uber.

Storming out of my car, I snap, "Get in the car, Bug."

Her hands fly to her hips. "No."

I step forward. "Darla, get in the car. Now."

Her hands ball into fists and she stomps a foot as she reluctantly obeys. But not before she says, "Don't talk to me."

The ride home is unbearable. There is so much I need to say. It breaks my heart to see her this upset. But it saddens me that she hates Allie so much that she's not even the least bit excited about becoming a big sister.

Before the car is even in park, she's out the door, running into the house, and probably locking herself in her room.

I get our things out of the trunk, counting to ten in the process. In the house, I go to my bar, unlock the cabinet, and take a shot of whiskey to settle my nerves. I give her thirty whole minutes to calm down and come out of her room. But all I hear is loud music blaring.

My phone vibrates with a text.

Allie: How's it going?

That's code for 'have you told her yet?'

I want to lie and say it's fine, because I'm hoping eventually it will be. And while Allie doesn't know Bug all that well, she seems to be in tune to her even more than I am. She expected her not to take the news very well given how Bug feels about her. But I know we both hoped she'd be wrong.

Me: Well, she's locked herself in her room if that tells you anything.

Allie: I'm sorry.

Me: It's a lot to process. I think she'll come around.

Allie: If it's too much for her, maybe we should pause.

Me: We're not pausing. You're having my babies, Al. She's thirteen. She'd have had a hissy fit if I told her we're out of her favorite breakfast cereal.

Allie: I suppose. Being a teenager isn't easy. Especially for girls. Cut her some slack. Don't be mad at her because she's having negative feelings about this. You've been her entire world for how many years? And now you're throwing a girlfriend and two babies into the mix.

I go back to my room, open my dresser drawer, and pull out a box. Inside it is my mother's engagement ring. She died when I was sixteen and Marti was one. When my dad died eleven years later, I knew he wanted to be buried with their wedding rings, but years earlier, he gave Mom's engagement ring to me to give to my future wife. Why I never gave it to Stella, I'll never understand. Because I love this fucking ring. It represents family and love and commitment. And though it's not big and flashy and super expensive, I know it's the perfect ring for Allie.

Me: We need to upgrade that title. You won't be my girlfriend for long.

Allie: One thing at a time.

Me: I'm going to marry you come hell or high water.

Allie: That's the issue. Marrying me shouldn't be hell for anyone, Asher.

This woman. She's carrying my babies. She loves me. But she won't marry me without the approval of my temperamental, judgmental, pissed-off kid.

Me: It won't be. We just need to give it time. Think I should use my key to go into her room?

Allie: Absolutely not. That's her safe space. You're going to have to wait it out.

Me: I'm not sure I can. I'm just sitting here thinking of how upset she is and how upsetting that is for me. How in the hell do I pass the time?

She sends me a few links in the next text. I smile for the first time in hours. They're links to houses for sale in Calloway Creek.

Me: You've been looking at houses? Damn, I love you.

Allie: Call me later? After you talk with her?

Call her. Yes. I'm done with this texting crap. We've texted for nearly a year and a half. But now that we're together, I want to hear her voice. Feel the emotions in her words. I want to tell her I love her, not type into a text box.

Me: Will do.

Allie: Good luck.

Me: Thanks. I think I'll need it.

I peruse the listings she gave me, shaking my head at the modest four-bedroom houses. One of the things we've never really talked about is my finances. She asked about my house once, so she knows it's not anywhere near the twelve-thousand-square-foot mansion her parents own.

While I'll never be as well-off as her family, I can certainly afford an upgrade. I get out my laptop and do some searching of my own. Five- and six-bedroom houses with large yards for kids. I send the ones I like back to her, hoping she doesn't take it wrong and assume I'm counting on her money to make up the difference.

Bug's voice in my ear causes me to jump. "Looking at houses already? So this is a done deal, whether I like it or not?"

I close the lid and sit back. "Kiddo, Allie *is* pregnant—whether you like it or not. And just like I did with you, I'm going to step up and raise them. Weren't we *just* talking about how being a parent means doing what's in your kids' best interest? That means me being there for *all* of my kids."

She's trying to come up with an argument, but she kind of backed herself into a corner with this one.

"It's totally not the same."

"It's exactly the same, Bug. Remember how excited you were when you found out Stella and I were trying to have a baby? You begged for a little brother or sister."

"You're too old. Can't she find some younger guy who's more suitable?"

"I'm not that old, kid. What if I'd made that decision about you? Abandoned you? Given you to someone else?"

"I don't know, then maybe I wouldn't be moving to New York and away from everything I've ever known."

I ignore her insinuation that maybe she'd be better off without me. She's upset.

"*You're* the one who said you wanted to move."

"To Oregon, or to somewhere else in Florida. Not some hole-in-the-wall town."

"I love her, Bug. I'm *in love* with her. And she's in love with me."

"Of course you have to say that *now*."

"This isn't anything new. I've loved her for a long time. I just wasn't sure if she felt the same. And then there's you. You know I'd do anything for you. But whether we planned it or not, it's not just the two of us anymore. Maybe that doesn't seem fair to you now, but I promise I won't love you any less just because there are more people to love."

She finally stops pacing and plops onto the large chair in the corner. It's the chair we used to cuddle in when she was little. A thousand books were read to her there. I haven't seen her sit in that particular chair for years. Is she already mourning what she thinks is the end of our father-daughter relationship?

I get up, go over, and sit down beside her. We're far too big to be sitting side-by-side in the chair, and we're squeezed in tightly, but I need her to hear me.

"Darla, I love you so much, my heart bursts every morning when I see you. And you don't know this, but sometimes I still watch you sleep like when you were little. I just stare at you and think how lucky I am to be your dad." I take her hand, and this time she doesn't pull away. "Nothing is going to change that. Not the babies. Not Allie. Nothing."

Her head whips to the side and she widens her eyes. "Babies? As in you're already planning on having more?"

It's now when I realize I haven't given her all the relevant details.

"Babies as in you're going to have a brother *and* a sister. Bug, Allie is having twins."

For a fraction of a second, I could swear I see a smile flash across her face. As if the thought of having twin siblings is exciting for her. But I may have been mistaken, because she rips her hand away and wiggles herself out of the chair.

"Just great. Like you're going to have any time left for anything else."

I stand and follow her to the kitchen. "Will things change? Yes, they will. It will be hectic and chaotic and I honestly have no idea how we're going to do it. But I can promise you, we're still going to be us. And I hope you'll help me with decisions like what house we'll get, and what kind of car. And just think about it, Bug. You'll get to go to a brand-new school like you wanted. Everyone in Calloway Creek seems nice."

"It's a small town, Dad. People there have been born and raised there. They already have friends. They don't want outsiders."

"Allie has a huge family. Lots of friends. I'm sure over the summer we can introduce you to other kids your age."

She huffs with displeasure.

"I'll make you a deal."

"You're going to bribe me like Mel's parents?"

"No. I'm not going to bribe you. I said I'll make you a deal. If you go through the summer up there and still decide you want to be homeschooled, I'll let you do it."

"Oh, right, and have Allie homeschool me?"

"I'll do it myself."

"You have a job."

"So does Allie. Parents can have jobs and still homeschool their kids, you know. Especially high schoolers. Come on. What do you say?"

"Are you going to marry her?"

"Eventually. Yes."

"Why not now?"

I'm not about to tell her Allie is requiring her approval. She may never give it.

"We have a lot to do. Moving across the country is a big deal."

"She's going to live with us, isn't she?"

"Yes. That's the plan."

"And you don't think that's going to corrupt me?"

I laugh. "Bug, you're old enough to know how babies are made. You understand the situation. And like I said, Allie and I are in love. People who are in love want to be together."

"When would we move?"

"After the school year is over. When is Mel moving?"

"June thirtieth."

"Then that's what we'll shoot for. That gives us a month to sell this house."

"I want my own room. A bigger one. Preferably with an attached bathroom. And a theater room. Mel's parents bought a house with a theater room. And…" She thinks on it. "A pool."

"Are you blackmailing me?"

"You said I could help pick the house."

I snort laughter. "I did indeed." I go to the living room and get my laptop. "Come on, let me show you what I've found." I turn to her. "But Darla, you ever pull that shit again, taking an Uber like you did today, and you'll be grounded for six months. Got it?"

She nods. But she also grins just a little. Just for a second. Like she's amused I'm not going to just roll over and capitulate in order to make her happy. I'm still her dad. I'm still going to protect her. Punish her. But mostly, I'm going to love her.

Chapter Twenty-three

Allie

There isn't a dry eye in the room. All my friends are here. And with the exception of Mia, they're all shocked to the core at my admission.

Telling them about Christopher has been difficult. But I've had a bit of practice breaking the news. I told my brothers and their wives a few days ago when Asher was here.

Marti was beside herself. She had no idea she and I shared such similar experiences. While Marti didn't know she was going to lose her infant girl, it still hit her just as hard as my loss hit me. Somehow, it's strengthened our sisterly bond. She's been calling us *double sisters* as we're marrying each other's brothers.

At least I hope that's how it turns out. So much is riding on Bug's acceptance of this whole situation, which so far, hasn't been what we'd hoped. It is, however, what I expected.

"So that's why you never wanted to talk about your time in Australia," Ren says.

I nod. "Never set foot on the continent."

Maddie and Ava are speechless as they grip each other's hands.

Sophie is sitting silently, still in tears, shaking her head in disbelief. This happened before she moved to town to become the nanny for Quinn and Amber's kids, but it's still hitting her hard. As it is all my friends.

Regan and Ellie already knew, having heard my news the other night along with Marti, but that doesn't mean their eyes are any drier.

Addison McQuaid pulls me in for a long hug. "You underestimate your friends, Allie. I hope you know we're here to support you through thick and thin."

"I'm actually glad to hear you say that," I say with the hint of a smile. "I might need a little support."

Mia's grin grows as we share a look. My sisters-in-law also begin smiling.

Addy looks from me to the others. "What is it?" she asks, confused by the sudden shift in our behavior.

"There's a reason I chose now to tell you about Christopher." I can't contain my full-on grin when I turn to the side, press my shirt flat against my belly and showcase my small bump with hands gripping it above and below.

Jaws drop. Mouths open. Gasps are audible.

"You're pregnant?" Maddie squeals, jumping up from her chair.

My eyes fall on Ava, then Serenity. Both have been trying to get pregnant, and I know every time someone they know and love has a child, it's just one more reminder of their failed attempts. I'm closer with Ren than I am with Ava. Ren and I have been friends practically our whole lives. She's already a mom, having adopted Cody years ago, but she and Cooper have been trying for a biological child for at least a year. Still, she looks nothing but happy for me and she's crossing the room nearly as fast as Maddie.

Ava is trying to show excitement over my news, but I know the tears in her eyes are both happy and sad. She and Trevor have been trying for a child forever. He's a military doctor, stationed overseas for the past seven years. Every time he's on leave, they disappear for days at a time. And if her cycle doesn't match up with his leave, they freeze his sperm through a local lab and she self-inseminates when she's ovulating. It's been painful to watch her roller-coaster of emotions every time she thinks she could be pregnant and then isn't. After Regan and Lucas had Mitchell earlier this year, Ava and Trevor decided that when he's permanently back home next year, they'll move on to more aggressive measures.

Ava gives me her best attempt at a smile, but I can tell it's forced. I don't hold it against her. She's had to watch her two very best friends—Maddie and Regan—have babies in the past year. I truly can't wait for the day she becomes a mom. No one deserves it more.

"There's more," I say, after accepting all their hugs.

"You're getting married!" Ren shrieks.

I shake my head. "No. I mean, maybe in the future." I touch my bump again. "It's twins."

For the third time today, I've shocked my friends. Hell, I've shocked myself. Every time I say the word twins, or even think it, my heart flutters.

I'm being squeezed by Serenity as I look behind her to Ava, who is putting on a brave face but is obviously conflicted by my news. She can't get pregnant and here I am accidentally having two. It makes me feel guilty.

But I also can't help feeling oh so happy, because this time I get to enjoy it. Times two!

My ultrasound pictures get passed around the room.

Marti comes up by my side and slips her hand around my waist. "Do you have any idea how happy you've made my brother?"

I'm still trying to come to terms with the whirlwind that's been this week. Asher and I are in love. We're moving in together. We're having babies. It's a lot to wrap my mind around in such a short period of time. But sometimes, in the back of my mind, I wonder if, when the dust settles, either of us will have a change of heart.

I push aside the intrusive thought and return Marti's hug, reminding myself to bask in this newfound happiness for as long as I possibly can. Because I know as well as she does that nothing in life is guaranteed.

Chapter Twenty-four

Asher

The past two weeks have been unpleasant to say the least. Not just because I haven't seen Allie, but because life with Bug hasn't exactly been a bed of roses. When she's home—which isn't much as she's practically been living at Mel's—she's moping around. I really thought she'd come around after getting used to the idea. But she's fighting it, unwilling to give in to the major changes coming.

It could just be that she's getting closer to losing her best friend. Or leaving the only house she's ever known. But my greatest fear is that she just won't accept the fact that there's a woman in my life. And I honestly do believe it has more to do with Allie than it does the babies. I overheard her talking with Mel on the phone about becoming a big sister. I dare say she even sounded excited about it. But it's not enough for her to be on board with the twins, she needs to be on board with Allie.

I have my job cut out for me. And getting the most important person in the world to me to accept the other most important person may well be the most significant undertaking of my life.

Excitement courses through me as the cab pulls up to Allie's parents' house. Even Bug manages to crack a smile when she sees Charlie and Marti waiting for us out front. As soon as the cab comes to a stop, she's out the door, racing over to give them hugs.

Bex, Charlie's dog, is all too happy to lick Bug's face as she sits on the porch stairs. It warms my heart to see all of them together, and I know it will be good for Bug to be around family again.

Movement to the left draws my attention. The air crackles when I see her. I didn't think it was possible for her to look more beautiful than she did a few weeks ago. But, damn, she does. And she's visibly showing now. I dart over to her, loving how her face lights up with a full-on smile.

Allie has changed. She was always fun to be around when we got together in the city, but there was always something missing. Something under the surface that kept her from completely letting go and being her true self. I know now that something was Christopher. And although the pain of him will never fully disappear, this Allie is on a whole other level. She's full of hope and wonder and dare I say… happiness.

I cup her face with my hands, look down into her blue eyes, and lower my lips to hers. "God, I've missed you."

It's hard to kiss when we're both smiling so much, but we manage. I don't even care that we have an audience. We don't have to hide anymore. And Bug needs to see this. She needs to understand how I feel about Allie. How every time I look at her, I see my entire future. I see fifty years or more of loving her. I see growing old together with our kids, grandkids, and maybe even a few pets. I see everything I've ever wanted but didn't know was possible.

I put a hand between us when our lips part. "I can't believe how much you've grown."

"Ugh. Don't remind me. If I'm this big at almost sixteen weeks, imagine what I'll be like at thirty-seven."

I trace her jawline with my finger. "You'll be even more beautiful than you are right now."

"You say that now, but—"

I put two fingers against her lips to shut her up. "I'll say it every day, sweetheart. Because there is nothing more beautiful than you growing larger with our children."

She kisses my fingers, then lowers my hand from her mouth and motions to Bug. "Did you talk to her about the sleeping arrangements?"

"She'll stay in one of your parents' guest rooms." I squeeze her hip. "She wasn't thrilled that I'd be staying in your apartment, but she's going to have to get used to it sooner or later."

A look of sadness washes over her. "She's still upset."

"I'm not sure upset is the word I'd use. Brooding maybe."

"I should go say hello."

I lace our fingers together as we walk over. Bug's eyes go to our entwined hands, then to Allie's stomach.

"Hey, Darla," Allie says, trying to sound chipper. "How was your flight?"

"Boring." She turns to Charlie. "Want me to take Bex for a walk?"

I take a step toward my daughter and whisper, "We talked about this. Do *not* be rude to her."

She rolls her eyes and turns back to Allie. "Our flight was boring because the Wi-Fi wasn't working and the meal sucked and the landing was a tad bumpy." She looks back up at me. "*Now* can I walk the dog?"

I flick my wrist. "Go."

"Give her time," my sister says, looking empathetic. "Lots of changes going on in her life. Not to mention she's a teenager and that alone makes her difficult."

I want to agree, but I can't. Because Bug has never been difficult. Compared to horror stories I've heard from friends and co-workers, my daughter has been a dream. Until now.

Chris and Sarah come out to greet us, and Sarah goes along with Bug as she walks Bex down the sidewalk. Bug seems to like Allie's parents. She likes Allie's brothers. She likes Allie's house. She just doesn't like Allie.

Chris takes Bug's suitcase. "Come on, let's get you settled."

We didn't bring much, just a carry-on each. We'll only be here for three days. If it were up to me, we'd already be living here. We'd be living here yesterday. But Bug only has a few more weeks with Mel and I don't want to take that away from her with everything else going on. I did insist, however, that she be involved in our house-hunting process. I want her to feel like she's part of everything we do moving forward. If there's any hope of her and Allie having a relationship, she needs to feel included every step of the way.

Once inside, I set my bag by the stairs that lead from the kitchen up to Allie's apartment. What I really want to do is take her in my arms and carry her upstairs. Have a repeat of the day we went to the doctor when we spent hours upon hours worshiping each other's bodies.

It's evident she's thinking the same thing when she catches me looking up the stairs. She wraps her arms around me. "Was your flight really that awful?"

I shake my head. "She likes to be dramatic."

"Do you know that when you leave here on Monday, it will be the last time you leave as a Floridian? When you come back in two weeks, you'll be a bonafide New Yorker."

I swipe a piece of hair off her forehead. "I like the sound of that."

She pulls me toward the kitchen counter. "You must be hungry if the meal sucked. Want me to make you a sandwich?"

"A sandwich sounds great. Thank you. How about I take my things upstairs and wash up?" I kiss her cheek. "Be back in a minute."

I park my suitcase in the living room of her apartment and quickly use the bathroom, not wanting to waste any time. When I go back down the stairs, I hear two voices in the kitchen—Bug and Allie. I stop, wanting to give them a minute. Maybe I shouldn't stand here eavesdropping, but the two of them need time together if we're going to get Bug past this.

"My dad doesn't like mustard," Bug says.

"Oh. Okay. Let me get another piece of bread."

I hear something being tossed in the trash, presumably bread with mustard on it.

"He doesn't like tomatoes either."

Allie blows out a sigh. "I guess I never knew that." Something else gets tossed in the trash.

"Ham, not turkey," Bug says in frustration. "Here, just let me do it."

I close my eyes and lean against the wall, wishing their conversation would take a turn.

"Darla, there's a lot your dad and I don't know about each other. Like what kind of sandwiches we like to eat, what fruit we like in our smoothies, and how brown we like our toast. But, honestly, right now, those things don't matter. What matters is how much we mean to each other. All that other stuff will come in time. And Darla, I hope you know that you mean something to me as well. I'm not trying to step on your toes or take your dad away."

"Whatever. Here." I can *sense* the eye roll.

"That looks like the perfect sandwich. Thanks for teaching me how he likes it. You're coming with us to look at houses, right?"

"Dad says I have to."

"You don't want to?"

I step into the kitchen, but neither of them sees me.

Bug shrugs.

"Buying a house is a big deal, and we want you to like it as much as we do," Allie says.

"It's just a house."

It saddens me that Bug is acting this way. After all the 'requests' she shared with me over the past few weeks about what she desires in a house, she's acting like it's no big deal now that she's talking with Allie about it.

"Your opinion is important to us."

"*Us*," Bug says, repeating the word like it's a curse word. "You say that like you're my mom or something. Me and my dad, we're the 'us.' You're not my mom. You'll never be my mom. You're just someone he slept with and accidentally got pregnant and now he has to *'do the right thing'.*" She emphasizes that last bit with air quotes.

I've had all I can take, so I stride forward. "That's enough, Darla. You need to apologize to Allie."

"For what?"

"You're being disrespectful."

"I'm being truthful."

I sidle up to Allie and wrap an arm around her shoulders. It fucking breaks my heart that she looks sad. And it guts me that my own daughter is the reason for her sadness.

"We aren't together because we're *doing the right thing*."

"That's not what you said two weeks ago." She pops a potato chip in her mouth.

Allie stiffens, and I know Bug sees it.

Bug continues, "Did you or did you not say that you were going to step up and raise them because it's what's in their best interest?"

I scrub a hand across my face. "Well, yes, but—"

Allie shrugs my arm off. "You said that?"

I blaze a punishing look at my daughter. "Go unpack. Now."

The smirk on her face makes me want to ground her for a month. "Fine."

When Bug is out of the kitchen, I turn to Allie and put my hands on her shoulders. "Do not take that out of context. And please don't let her get to you. I promise I'll deal with her attitude."

She rubs her belly and sits on a barstool. "Asher, if I weren't pregnant, would you be moving here?"

"I think I would be."

"You *think?*"

"I *know*. With Mel moving and Bug wanting to start over at a new school, and with Marti and Charlie living here, I absolutely would have moved here. It just might have taken me a bit longer to figure it out is all." I take her hands in mine. "Even if these babies weren't coming, I'd still be here. I would have been moving here because I love you. And if you hadn't said you loved me, I'd still be here trying to convince you that you do."

I watch as her eyes become glassy. She swipes a finger under one. "Sorry. Hormones."

I laugh. "Please take what Bug says with a grain of salt. I don't know if she's going to try and pull shit like she has in the past to break up a relationship, but it's not going to fly this time. I swear to you, I'm going to figure this out."

Her eyes focus on the bar. "How are the three of us going to live together in just a few weeks?"

"She'll come around."

"What if she doesn't?"

"She will."

Someone clears their throat, and Allie's father comes into the kitchen. "Sorry to interrupt, but your realtor just arrived."

"I'll go get Bug and meet you in the foyer," I say, kissing her forehead then scarfing down the sandwich in just a few bites as I walk away.

I find Bug sitting on the guestroom bed, staring at the wall. I'm mad as hell at her, but I'm also trying to be sympathetic to her situation. I sit next to her and take her hand. "You have to go easier on Allie. None of this is her fault. If you want to be mad at someone, be mad at me. I'm the one moving us here. I'm the one who fell for her. I'm the one disrupting your life."

Her head falls to my shoulder. It's like she knows exactly what to do to remind me how much I love her.

"Nothing will ever be the same," she squeaks out in a voice so small it breaks my goddamn heart.

I move my arm around her and pull her tightly against me. "You're right about that. It'll be better. Just wait until you see those little eyes staring up at you. Bug, you're going to be a big sister. You'll be just about as old as I was when I became a big brother. And, oh my god, how they're going to love you and look up to you and count on you. You are going to be their favorite person in the whole world."

"It's not the same. You and Aunt Marti had the same mom and dad."

"You think they aren't going to love you because you don't have the same mom?"

She shakes her head.

"Then what is it?"

She looks at the door. "She's not my mom."

"Bug, do you think Allie is incapable of loving you because she's not your mom?"

"How could she?" she scoffs.

"Do you think Dallas doesn't love Charlie because he isn't his biological child? And how about Ellie—do you think she doesn't love Maisy?"

"That's different."

"Different how?"

"None of them have other kids, Dad."

I get on my knees in front of her and lift her chin so she's looking at me. "Sweetie, is this because you don't think Allie will love you as much as she'll love the twins?"

"No," she says, not at all convincingly.

"Well, I hesitate to say you're not making it any easier." I sit on the bed again and run a hand down her back. "This isn't easy for Allie either. She thinks you hate her. She's about to share a household with a teenager who she's terrified will stop at nothing to break up our relationship. How do you think that makes her feel?"

"Maybe she shouldn't have gotten herself in this situation then."

"Darla, that's it. You need to stop blaming Allie. *I'm* the one who got us in this situation."

"*She's* the one who got pregnant."

I laugh disingenuously. "It takes two, and I know you know that." I sigh, taking a beat to breathe in and out so I don't say things I'll regret because I'm mad. "Listen, getting used to this is going to take time, but I'm telling you right now, I'm not going to stand for you disrespecting her in front of me. That shit ends right now. I don't want to ground you or take away your phone, but I will if I have to, is that understood?"

She rolls her eyes.

"Darla?"

"Yeah. Fine. Whatever."

I stand and hold out a hand. "Now let's go look at some houses, okay?"

"Do I have to?"

"Yes, you have to. Otherwise we'll end up with a two-bedroom house without a pool or a theater room where you have to share a room with the babies."

Her eyes practically roll out of her head. But she stands and follows.

Allie meets us at the front door. "Ready?"

Bug pastes on the fakest smile I've ever seen. "All set." She turns and heads out the door. "My bedroom better be gigantic."

Allie and I share an amused look, then I take her hand and we trail after Bug.

Chapter Twenty-five

Allie

"This one really does check off all your boxes," Julie, our realtor, says, standing in the kitchen and twirling around as if to showcase it.

"Nope." Bug shakes her head. "I don't want to sleep in a room that shares a wall with babies who will be crying all night."

Julie is getting frustrated with Bug. We've seen three houses, and in each one, Bug comes up with a reason why we shouldn't buy it. I can tell Asher is regretting his promise to let her help choose where we live. If she keeps this up, it'll be next winter before the perfect house comes around. Then again, maybe that's the game she's playing.

"Maybe we should reconsider the first one," Asher says. "That upstairs bonus room could easily be converted into a game room or home theater, and there's plenty of room for a pool." He turns to Bug. "And no common wall with the babies' rooms."

She crosses her arms. "But I *need* my own bathroom, Dad. We agreed."

"Maybe we should expand our search outside town limits," I say.

"And give up the running trails you love?" Asher says. "No. We'll just have to make one of these work."

"But *none* of them will work," Bug says. "And you said I could help pick out the house."

Asher stares down his daughter. "*Help* being the operative word. Maybe when you're the one footing the bill you'll get more say."

She stomps out of the house.

"I'm sorry she's being so difficult, Julie. All three of these houses are beautiful. Maybe if we let her sleep on it she'll get on board."

I can just tell Julie is trying to keep her eyes from rolling. She thinks Asher is letting his thirteen-year-old drive this train, and she'd be right. Asher is trying to include Bug to make it easier on her. But all it's really doing is making it harder on everyone else.

"There is one more possibility," Julie says, tapping around on her laptop. "It didn't come up in the search because it's only listed as having three bedrooms."

"That's not enough," I say. "I'd like the twins to eventually have their own rooms."

She waves us over. "Look here." She points to a picture of the floorplan. "There's an office off the kitchen that could potentially be converted into a fourth bedroom, and there's even a garage apartment."

I shrug and look at Asher. "You could use the apartment as your home office." I point to the room off the kitchen. "This room is pretty big. We could add a closet here and there's a full bathroom just across the hall. Think Bug would go for it?"

"It's vacant," Julie says. "We could go see it right now if you want."

Asher looks at me to see what I want to do.

"I guess it's worth a look. It's a lot closer to the park and McQuaid Circle than the others. I do like that."

I don't exactly say it with enthusiasm, though. I already know Bug won't like it. It's an older home and there's no chance for a theater room.

Julie shuts her laptop. "Let's go."

When we drive down McQuaid Circle, Asher tries to sell Bug on the location. "You could walk to the movie theater," he says. "Lots of kids hang out here. There's an ice cream shop and a bowling alley too. I'll bet you could get your hair dyed at that salon right over there."

"Like I have anyone to hang out with," she pouts, staring out the window.

I turn to face her as we're both sitting in the back. "I've been thinking about that. I have some friends with kids about your age. I could introduce you. Serenity has a son, Cody. He's super sweet. He's eleven."

"Eleven?" Her mouth hangs open like she's appalled I'd even suggest such a thing. "You want me to hang out with an eleven-year-old? As if I won't already be an outcast."

"Okay then, Maddie has a daughter, Gigi. I think you guys would get along great. She's twelve, but I think she might turn thirteen at the end of the year."

Her eyes roll to the heavens. "I'm going to high school this year. *High school.* I'm not going to be seen hanging out with middle-schoolers."

I sigh. I should have just kept my mouth shut. It wouldn't matter if I had a slew of thirteen-year-olds for her to meet, she'd find fault in every one of them. Which is why I vow to keep my mouth shut at this next house. If I seem uninterested in it, maybe she'll actually go for it.

Asher turns and gives me a sympathetic smile. He knows how hard I'm trying. But it seems the harder I try, the more pushback I get from her. I don't know how to do this. I'm sure there's some delicate balance I need to find between saying too much and too little. I just don't have a clue where that balance lies.

"Here we are," Julie says, pulling her SUV into a driveway and parking in front of the three-car-garage.

Bug's face is pressed to the side window. "Looks old."

"Don't judge a book by its cover," Asher says. "Sometimes older houses have the best features."

"Whatever."

I'm beginning to think the word *whatever* is one of the primary words in Bug's vocabulary.

Exiting the car, I instantly key in on the yard. It's amazing. And I do my best to keep how much I love it off my face and inside my head.

These older neighborhoods tend to have larger yards and more room between houses. The driveway is long and wide, lined with a beautiful bed of flowers along the outer edge. There's a massive oak tree in the middle of the front yard and I can almost see Asher hanging a swing from the sturdy branch about ten feet up.

"This was one of the first established neighborhoods in Calloway Creek," Julie says. "While new neighborhoods tend to have houses of similar sizes and price ranges, this one is quite eclectic. This house is one of the larger homes, and it undoubtedly has the most expansive yard. There's also plenty of room for an addition if you ever needed more space. The unfinished basement can easily be converted into a theater room." She turns to Bug, knowing what her hot spots are. "Just wait until you see the back yard. You could practically put in an Olympic sized pool."

A lawnmower starts in the yard next door. I turn to see a familiar face. Carter Cruz, one of Mia's brothers, raises a brow when he sees me. I'd forgotten he lives in this neighborhood. Makes sense. It's close enough to their autobody shop that he can walk there.

I eye his house. It's on the smaller side. Three-bedroom, two-bath I'd guess. It sits atop the same small hill this house is on, making me wonder if he's got a walkout basement.

Though the Cruzes and the Montanas don't usually mingle, Mia and me aside, I give him a wave and cordial smile, wondering what it would be like living next to Mia's oldest brother.

On the left side of the house, there's an outer stairway that looks like it leads up to the apartment over the garage. It reminds me of my own setup in my parents' house, and I hope there's an interior set of stairs, too. That would definitely make it easy for Asher to use the apartment as an office.

The house is red brick with off-white trim. Most of the house is single-story with tall columns towering over the large, welcoming front porch. I can already tell this house has character.

When Julie lets us in the front door, my jaw drops. Being an older house, I expected a closed floorplan with separate, boxy rooms, maybe even with wood-paneled walls. But it's evident this house has been remodeled from top to bottom. My eyes are drawn across the expansive, open-plan living area to the wall of sliding doors in the back that overlook a massive deck, and beyond that, a backyard that's so deep I can't see the end of it.

Bug must see what I do and she strides to the windows. "You weren't kidding," she says to Julie.

Julie unlocks the slider on the far right. "These doors all slide back into the wall, making a great indoor/outdoor space when the weather is right. Perfect for entertaining." She turns to Asher. "And what all men seem to want—a large outdoor kitchen."

Asher elbows me and we share a look like we're both thinking the same thing. He offers me an encouraging smile.

I like it. I really, really like it. But I try to keep my face impassive. And I definitely am going to keep my mouth shut.

Like a lot of older homes, there is a cluster of bedrooms all in the same area. Bug's hands land on her hips. "This won't do."

"Come with me," Julie says. "I had something else in mind for you." We follow her through the large living room, past the kitchen, and to the back hallway where there is a big, empty room with an impressive view of the backyard. "What do you think of this?"

Bug looks around. "It's so… boring. And there's not even a closet."

Asher steps forward and pounds on the wall. "We could put one right here, the room is certainly big enough. And I'm thinking we might even be able to put in a door to the bathroom that sits on the other side of that wall there so you could have your own entrance to it."

She shrugs, looking unimpressed. "No pool. No theater room."

"We'll put in a pool," Asher assures her. "And remember what Julie said about the basement. So how about we at least finish the tour before you start listing all the reasons we shouldn't get this one either?"

She stares out the window. "Fine."

That word joins *whatever* at the top of her word list.

Julie leads us back through the kitchen, that I love, by the way. Double ovens, an industrial-sized refrigerator, and enough counter space for an army. Behind the sizeable walk-in pantry is a door that opens to a staircase. "And this goes up to what would be your office, Asher."

Bug parks her ass on the counter, seemingly ending her tour right there. I guess she's already made up her mind about this one. I try not to get too upset about it. Maybe Asher is right and she'll change her mind about one of these houses after she sleeps on it.

The three of us leave her in the kitchen and go up the stairs. I stand and look around, smiling as I'm reminded of my own apartment, but on a smaller scale. There's even a skylight. The big difference is that this 'apartment' is all one room, more like a studio. There are three large windows overlooking the back yard and two more with a view of the front. An alcove area that was probably used for a bed would be perfect for Asher's desk. I can picture a couch along the opposite wall, and maybe a grouping of chairs or a small table. There's even a wet bar with a small refrigerator and microwave. It's anyone's work-from-home dream office.

"This is amazing," I say, finally feeling like I can share my thoughts now that Bug isn't around.

I start telling Asher everything I was picturing in my head, when I see a flash of blue. I guess Bug was curious after all. Instantly, I shut up, not wanting her to know how perfect I think the house is.

Her eyes go wide as she takes in the expansive room. The three of us watch her in silence as she runs a finger along the counter of the wet bar, then peeks into the closet and attached bathroom.

"We should get this one."

Three pairs of stunned eyes stare at her.

"You… *like* this house?" Asher asks.

"I like this *room*." She walks to the back windows and looks out. "*This* should be my bedroom."

Asher strides up next to her. "Bug, this would be my office."

Her hands land on her hips. "That makes no sense whatsoever. This is clearly a bedroom. It has a private bathroom. It has a closet. The room downstairs should be your office. You wouldn't have to remodel anything that way. And that room is still big and has a killer view of the yard."

Asher cocks his head and looks around the room. When his eyes find mine, all I can do is bite my lip and shrug. It is a rational argument. But I don't dare say so, otherwise she's likely to retract her words.

He walks to the door with the deadbolt on it, opens it, and sunlight pours through. "On one condition," he says, turning to Bug. "I'm sealing this entrance until you're thirty."

She thinks on it, then says, "We could still put in a pool, right?"

"It's the first thing we'll do."

She smiles. She smiles for the first time today. Maybe the first time since I've been in her presence. She skips over to Asher and holds out her hand. "Deal."

"Did we just… buy a house?" I ask tentatively.

Asher puts his arm around Bug. "We sure as hell did."

Julie lets out a long sigh, as if she was beginning to think she'd never be able to close any deal that Bug was a part of. She must see the way Asher and I are holding in our excitement. "Darla, why don't I take you out back while your dad and Allie discuss their offer. You can show me where you think the pool should go."

They leave the room, and as soon as Julie's voice becomes distant, I practically jump into Asher's arms.

He wraps me in a hug and kisses my head. "Do you really like it?"

"I really *love* it. The twins' rooms will be right next to ours. You'll have your large office. And Bug is a teenager, she needs her own space. It's perfect."

"I'm serious about sealing the outer door."

I laugh. "I never doubted it. Besides, I know firsthand that you should."

He raises a questioning brow, but I don't elaborate. He doesn't need to know how often Jason used to visit me using the outside stairs to my apartment.

He swipes my hair behind my ear and dips his head. "I can't wait to live with you. To build a life with you. To have these babies with you. To christen every room in this house with you." He kisses a spot on my neck. "To fucking marry you."

Sparks dart through me at his words. The warmth of his body. His confidence in our future.

"We're one step closer, you know." He pulls back and looks me in the eye. "We're moving here. We have a house, one Bug loves as much as we do." He squeezes my hand. "It's only a matter of time before she loves *you* as much as I do."

I look down at the floor. "I'm not holding my breath."

He puts a finger under my chin and forces me to look at him. "It'll happen, sweetheart. But this is a marathon, not a sprint."

His words hit me square in the chest. He's so right. I keep thinking I have to get her to like me *today*. *Now*. But that's just unrealistic. I have to play the long game here.

I lean up on my tiptoes and kiss his cheek. "Have I ever told you how smart you are?"

"I don't think you have."

"Well, you are."

"I like the way you pump my ego." His eyes grow dark and dangerous. "What else do you think I am?"

"Let's see." I lick my lips. "Handsome." I kiss his shoulder. "Strong." I kiss his neck. "Charming." I kiss the edge of his mouth. "And oh, so sexy."

His eyes are ablaze when his lips crash against mine and he kisses me for the first time in the house that will soon be our home.

The place we'll raise our kids. Maybe even the place where we'll grow old together.

"I love you," he says against my lips.

"I love you too."

Chapter Twenty-six

Allie

I've been grateful for work lately. It's kept my mind off missing Asher. I don't know why it's been harder and harder going without him when we've rarely ever been together more than a few days at a time. But since signing the contract on the house, all I've been able to think about is living with him, building a future with him, maybe even marrying him.

We don't close on the house for another few weeks, so Asher and Bug will stay at my parents' until then. I trace my finger over the outline of the house on my laptop. I can't stop looking at photos and dreaming of how it will be.

Still, part of me is scared. I'm just not sure how it's going to work with Bug. With the three of us living under the same roof. It's different when they're at Montana Manor where my parents can be a buffer. What's it going to be like when it's just Asher, Bug, and me eating dinner together every night? Or... *oh, Lord...* when Asher travels and it's just me and Bug.

I close my eyes. Why haven't I thought of that until just now? He travels at least one week out of every month. The thought has anxiety gripping my insides and I feel my stomach turn.

Wait… that's not my stomach turning.

I press a hand to my belly and concentrate hard, willing it to happen again. When it does, tears flood my eyes. I wonder which one is moving. Maybe they both are. Maybe they're fighting for space in some sort of prenatal sibling rivalry. As I bask in emotions while feeling the tiny flutters, my mind flashes forward to a hazy picture of them when they're older. Will she look like me? Will he resemble Asher? Will they be as close with each other as I am with my brothers? As Mia is with her twin, Dax? Will he protect her and always be there for her?

As much happiness as I'm feeling right now, I can't help it when my tears turn sad. Christopher is the one who should be their protector. The big brother who would watch over both of them. He'd have been ten years old by the time the babies come. He could have held them, fed them, rocked them.

"I miss you, Christopher," I whisper.

My mind shifts to thoughts of Darla. Is *she* going to be their protector? Or is she simply going to view them as an extension of me? Two more beings to be avoided. Possibly even resented.

Movement in my doorway has me wiping my eyes.

Natasha is holding a clipboard. "The Nelson wedding is this weekend. Do you want me to do it?" She looks up and takes a step inside my office. "Allie, are you okay?"

"I'm fine. It's just hormones. And no, I'll handle the wedding myself. You've covered for me a lot recently and I'm going to need your help even more when these guys come."

She leans against the doorway. "Are you planning on coming back to work after?"

My eyes snap to hers. "Of course. I can't imagine walking away from the winery. I mean, yeah, I'll probably cut back a bit, but I plan on being here as much as I can."

"I'm sure your parents wouldn't mind if you set up a couple bassinets in the corner."

I laugh. "I imagine they wouldn't. But I doubt I'd get much work done."

"You should hire a nanny."

I cock my head. "I haven't even thought that far ahead."

She pushes off the wall. "Well, unless you need me for anything else, I'll head out."

"Go ahead. I'm leaving shortly myself."

I don't even notice I'm smiling until she points it out. "Based on the look on your face, I'd guess today is the day Asher is moving to town?"

I nod. "Their flight lands in thirty minutes."

"I'm really happy for you, Allie."

The way she says it is filled with both happiness and sadness. It's no secret anymore how I once had and lost a baby. After telling my doctor, family, and friends, it didn't take long until the entire town was filled in. Thankfully, most people have enough tact not to bring it up. But there have been a few instances. Like when I ran into Jason's aunt and she had the audacity to scold me for 'running away' and keeping her from her great nephew. Or when that bitch Trina Sutter asked me if I even know what birth control is, this being my second accidental pregnancy and all.

"Thanks, Natasha. See you tomorrow."

When she's gone, I pull up the Delta flight tracker and start to get excited all over again. And apparently, I'm not the only impatient one based on the flutters I feel again inside me.

~ ~ ~

I'm waiting outside, practically bouncing from foot to foot. When I see the cab pull up, there's not a thing in this world that could keep the monumental smile off my face.

But when I see Bug get out of the back, I realize how wrong I was.

Her face is red and puffy. She stares at the ground as she slings her backpack across one shoulder.

I want to throw my arms around Asher, but feel it would be wrong when Bug's entire world just imploded. "Um… hi."

Darla looks at me and I go to speak further, but she holds up a hand. "Don't. Just don't." She stomps toward the front door, opens it, then disappears inside.

I turn to Asher, smiling sadly. "I'm not sure I've ever been so happy and sad at the same time."

He draws me into his arms. "You took the words right out of my mouth." He leans down to kiss me. "Hi," he whispers just before his lips graze mine.

"Hey, you." I squeeze his arms. "I guess I don't have to ask how the flight was."

His head shakes. "Bad day all around. Mel left this morning. We all stayed at the same hotel last night since both our houses had been packed up. We got Bug and Mel their own room. I'm sure they were up all night. It was torture pulling them apart this morning and then watching the Harrell's car pull away."

"I'm sorry. I know how upsetting that must have been."

"There doesn't seem to be anything I can do or say to make her feel better. I guess she just needs time." He nods to the house. "She'll probably go to bed and sleep until tomorrow."

The cabbie clears his throat behind Asher, presumably wanting help unloading suitcases from the trunk.

I eye the four large bags. "I'm surprised these even fit back here."

"They almost didn't," the irritated cabbie says, tugging one until it breaks free of the lip of the frame.

Asher shrugs, moving the suitcases aside as they're pulled out, then he gets out his wallet and gives the guy a sizable tip.

As the cab pulls away, I grab the handle of one of the suitcases, but Asher immediately takes it from me. "Let me. They're all heavy."

"They do roll, Asher."

"Allie, just let me do this. Please?"

I want to be offended—him treating me like I can't do it just because I'm pregnant—but I kind of like this protective side of him. Still, I tease, "Are you going to treat me with kid gloves for the next nineteen weeks?"

"Baby, I'm going to treat you with kid gloves for the rest of our lives. Not because you're pregnant, but because you're mine."

My swoony sigh is audible. "You're such a romantic."

His lips pass over mine. "Only with you, sweetheart. Now let me get these inside." He pats my backside, urging me along.

"Fine. I'll get dinner started. It's just us tonight. My parents get back from their Napa Valley trip tomorrow."

He follows me inside with two of the four suitcases then goes back for the others. But he only brings one of them into the kitchen and sets it near the stairs to my apartment.

I laugh. "Are you telling me this is your only suitcase?"

"She's thirteen. Apparently she couldn't live without her entire wardrobe for the next two weeks. The only clothes she allowed me to pack for the movers were her hoodies."

I set the salad bowls down. "I can't believe we're moving in together in two weeks."

He walks up next to me. "Al, we're moving in together *today*."

"I know. It's kind of spectacular, isn't it?"

His arms come around me. "Damn straight." He sucks in a breath as our bodies press together and he's reminded once again of what's between us. He looks down. "It's hard to believe we're almost at the halfway point."

"Speaking of that." I crack a smile. "I felt a kick today."

His eyebrows arch. "Which one was it?"

I giggle. "I have no idea."

He drops to his knees and puts both hands on my belly.

"I doubt you'll be able to feel it. It was super light, like little bubbles or butterfly wings. Maybe in a few weeks."

"I can't wait. I never got to feel Bug move in the womb."

He stands and picks up a knife to cut some vegetables.

"Will you tell me about Bug's mom? Wasn't she your girlfriend? How come you never got to feel the baby move?"

"Her name was Lisa. She wasn't my girlfriend, just a woman I dated a few times." He narrows his eyes. "Haven't I ever told you this story?"

I shake my head. "Not completely. All I know is that her mom didn't want her." I look down at the counter. "I guess when it came to talking about babies, I wasn't very receptive, huh?"

"Understandable." He puts a hand on my shoulder and squeezes. "You always seemed to zone out whenever I started talking about how I came to be a single dad, or what Stella and I went through, so I just stopped bringing it up." He kisses my temple. "I wish I'd known about Christopher."

"I was just wondering today, earlier when I felt the kicks, what kind of big brother he'd be."

"I'm sure he would have been their protector."

I smile. "That's exactly what I was thinking."

I put noodles in the boiling water and listen to him tell me about becoming Darla's dad.

"Lisa wanted to have an abortion. She only told me about the baby because she couldn't afford to pay for one." He finishes with the salad and leans against the counter, crossing his feet at the ankles. "My dad had just passed away and I was trying to figure out life with twelve-year-old Marti. It would have been so easy to just give her the money and be done with it. But I couldn't bring myself to do it. The baby was a part of me. And every time I thought about Lisa having an abortion, I'd think about my mother. She found out she had cancer when she was pregnant with Marti. The doctors told her she should terminate and get treatment. She refused because she already loved the baby growing inside her. I knew if my mom could make that kind of sacrifice, that I could handle anything."

My voice is thick with emotion when I say, "I think I would have loved your mom."

He smiles. "She would have loved you too. Anyway, it took a lot of convincing to persuade Lisa to have the baby. She hated being pregnant. We were never together again romantically because she resented me. I was never close enough to her to feel I had the right to touch her or feel the baby. I wasn't invited to any of her appointments. I was terrified that she wasn't taking good care of the baby or that she was drinking or worse, but the more I pressed her, the more she cut me off. I didn't even know she'd had Bug until a nurse at the hospital called and asked me to come in."

He expels a gush of air. "Lisa didn't even stay the night. She signed herself out against medical advice. She gave the nurse the papers I had a lawyer draw up. The ones naming me the father and legal guardian. The ones rescinding her parental rights. And then she just left. We never saw each other again."

My jaw is slack as I realize just how much Asher and I have in common. "So we both had a baby the other parent wanted to abort."

"Wow, I guess we did." He blows out a long breath. "God, how I wish your story would have turned out differently."

I nod. "Have you told Bug about Christopher?"

"No. I figured it wasn't my place to. If you want her to know about him, you can tell her when you feel the time is right."

"You know, we have the anatomy scan in a few weeks. What would you think about inviting Bug to come?"

He looks surprised. "You'd do that?"

"They're her siblings."

Fire blazes in his eyes as he traps me against the counter. "Do you know how much I love you?"

The oven beeps and I kiss him swiftly then get the garlic bread out. We take all the food to the table. But before we eat, I make up a third plate and hand it to Asher. "You should take this to Bug in case she's hungry."

He gazes deep into my eyes. "Damn, I hit the jackpot with you."

I look at him, confused.

He takes the plate. "You're already a great mom, Al."

As he leaves the room, I cradle my belly, savoring his words, hoping he's right and that I can be a good mom to *all* of our kids.

Chapter Twenty-seven

Allie

I look around the table, suddenly aware of how much I'm going to miss these family breakfasts.

We've had them for as long as I can remember, going way back to when I was little. Even as we got older and my brothers moved out, they would randomly show up for Mom's famous bacon pancakes. It's down to only once or twice a week now, but you can be sure Mom is always prepared and never runs out of fresh batter.

"Everything okay?" Mom asks me, putting a heaping plate down as Lucas stabs a pancake before the platter even hits the table.

I shrug. "I was just thinking how I'm going to miss these spontaneous family gatherings."

Her hand lands on my shoulder. "You're not moving to the moon, Allie."

I frown. "Aren't you even a little bit sad that I'll be moving out in ten days?"

"Well, sure." She cocks her head. "Actually, no. I mean, I'll miss our late-night talks and how we sometimes ride to work together.

But I think it's wonderful, sweetie. I've had you here far longer than most parents get to enjoy their children. Besides, you know you're always welcome."

I reach out and take her hand. Mom and I have always been so close. I know I'll only be ten minutes away, and it's ridiculous to be having these feelings when I'm almost twenty-nine years old. But with the babies coming, it's all getting a bit overwhelming. Sometimes a girl just needs her mom.

"Geesh," Lucas sighs. "Cut the cord already."

Mom swats him on the back of the head.

Asher squeezes my hand under the table, and when I look at him, he gives me an encouraging smile. Then he nods to the other side of the table where Bug is holding a squirming Mitchell. At almost five months old, he's at the point where he doesn't want to sit still.

"When can he eat pancakes?" Bug asks.

"Not for a few months," Regan says. "We just started him on some baby food last week. His favorite so far is peaches."

"Cool. Can I feed him?"

"Sure." Regan looks over at me and smiles. "I'll just go get some out of my bag."

Mom pulls over the highchair she keeps in the corner. "Guess I'm going to have to get a few more of these," she says happily.

Regan gets Mitchell situated in the highchair. It's amazing how far he's come since he was released from the NICU. He seems fully caught up to full-term babies. He's even sitting with support, which, according to Regan, is apparently when you can start feeding solids.

I suppose I should start reading those parenting books everyone keeps giving me. But every time I do, I'm reminded of Christopher, and it feels almost like a betrayal.

Bug dips the small baby spoon into the jar then touches it to Mitchell's lips like Regan showed her. His mouth opens wide and we all laugh. He loves being the center of attention and reacts to our laughter more than the food, so peaches drip down his chin, resulting in even more laughter. He slaps his little hands against the tray.

Bug is smiling from ear to ear.

Asher and I steal a glance at each other, both of us hoping this is just one more step in her acceptance of our situation.

"You're going to make a great big sister," Regan says.

I go completely stiff. It's like I'm bracing myself for Darla's typical snarky, petulant reaction.

So it surprises me when she says, "Kids are pretty cool." But then her eyes momentarily flit over my way. "It's some adults I have a problem with."

And there it is.

Asher doesn't call her out on it because it's not like other times when she blatantly disrespects me. These days that only seems to happen when he's not around. I gather he threatened her to within an inch of her life at some point.

I'm not about to rat her out, however, and tell him she gets in her digs when he's not here to listen to them. If I did that, there's no way in hell I'd ever earn her trust or her respect.

Asher stops eating, pulls his phone out of his pocket, then excuses himself from the table. My eyes are on him as he quietly talks to whoever it is from the far side of the kitchen. He looks over at me guiltily as he's speaking, and his chest heaves with a frustrated sigh that I can see but not hear.

He tucks his phone away and sits back down. "I'm really sorry to do this to you after only being here a few days, but there's been an emergency with a tech firm Rich has been trying to get to sign with us for years. They've had a massive data breach. Rich and Arjun are both flying in later today, but I'm going to have to get over there and get started immediately."

"Get over where?" I ask.

"The city."

I shrug. "That's not so bad. At least you were close."

"Yeah, but…" He looks over at Bug, who's still happily feeding and playing with Mitchell. "It only makes sense for me to pack an overnight bag. I could be working very late tonight and there's no way this issue will be resolved by the end of the day. I'm hoping it will be by tomorrow night though." He shakes his head. "God, I hate to do this to you."

"It's one night, Ash. I think I can handle it. Plus, if you're worried about Bug, my parents are here to run interference."

He lowers his head and says softly, "You shouldn't *need* interference. I'll talk to her, make sure she treats you with respect."

"Don't. We need to come together on our own terms."

He checks the time. "Damn. I really need to get going. Every minute I'm delayed is costing them money." He stands. "Bug, I have to go to work, and I won't be back until tomorrow night."

Her hand holding the spoon drops to the table like a lead weight. "You're leaving me here. With *her?*"

Asher shoots her a warning look. I squeeze his elbow in an attempt to keep him from scolding her in front of everyone.

"We'll make a day of it," Mom says. "How about you come in to work with me? I have a light day. It'll be fun. And we can invite Marti, Charlie, and Dallas for dinner."

Thank you, I mouth at her when she catches my eye.

Asher holds out his hand. "Help me pack?"

I smile and put my palm in his, because that's definitely code for *'I want to kiss you senseless before I leave.'*

Chapter Twenty-eight

Asher

It's been a long, long day. It's nine thirty, and Rich, Arjun and I are just finishing up dinner in the hotel restaurant.

Rich lifts his drink. "To earning our paychecks today. Nice job, gentlemen. Today we stopped the bleeding, tomorrow will just be cleanup."

Arjun and I tap our glasses against his.

"We make a great team," Arjun says.

Rich nods. "That we do. And it was a damn stroke of luck that you were close enough to get here quickly, Asher. We saved their asses today."

Rich lives in San Diego and Arjun lives in Omaha. Both of them arrived this afternoon, but with me able to get here by nine fifteen this morning, we may have saved the company millions of dollars in the data breach. And as such, they've contracted our services going forward in what I assume will be akin to a windfall for Rich.

I grip his shoulder. "Should we be expecting bonuses? I *am* about to close on a four-thousand-square-foot home, you know."

He laughs. He knows he's got talent with Arjun and me, and he's always been one to share the wealth. "As long as I'm invited to the housewarming party."

Rich pays our tab, all of us eager to get to bed after an arduous day.

Walking through the bar on the way to the hotel lobby, I'm shocked when I see a familiar face.

"You go on ahead," I say. "I'll see you both in the morning."

They leave, and I'm standing here not quite believing what I'm seeing. I walk over to the bar. "Stella?"

I'm not exactly sure why I didn't keep on walking. Did I stop just to give her a well-overdue piece of my mind?

She looks up at me with sad eyes that turn as big as dinner plates. "Asher! Oh my god."

She pulls me in for a hug like I'm her long-lost friend, not her ex whom she abandoned without warning, leaving me and my eight-year-old daughter stunned and heartbroken. I don't wrap my arms around her.

"Still pissed?" she asks, releasing me.

"Seriously? Stella, you left me with little more than a note to expect to hear from your lawyer about divorcing me."

At least she has the decency to look guilty. "You know how that last miscarriage wrecked me, Asher. I just couldn't do it anymore."

It's a day I'll never forget as long as I live. We'd been through four of them previously. We'd done eight rounds of IVF. Each day, she'd wake up and smile because we'd gotten one day further than the others. She was nine weeks along. Both of us were beginning to get excited. In just a few more weeks, we could've started to relax.

But then she'd climbed out of bed, gasping at the bright-red stain on the sheets. She'd gripped her stomach and ran to the bathroom, where she sat on the toilet, screaming and crying through cramps. What she did next is burned into my memory for all eternity.

She kneeled on the floor in front of the toilet and fished out all the tissue and blood clots, sifting through it on the tiled bathroom floor, looking for anything that could be the baby. It was the most heartbreaking, yet terrifying thing I'd ever witnessed. She was insane with grief, searching for our baby among the remains.

I'd pulled her away, refusing to let her continue. She hit me, called me names, cursed me as I gathered her into my arms and took her back to our bed.

I called Marti to come watch Bug and took Stella to the hospital. After it was all over and we came back home, she slept for three days straight. On the fourth day, when I came home from picking Bug up from school, all of Stella's stuff was gone and there was a note on the counter telling me she was done. She wanted a divorce.

This is the first time I've seen her since that morning.

"I know how devastated you were. I was too. I just think I deserved more than a *Dear John* letter." I laugh disingenuously. "Hell, even a Dear John letter would have been better. What you left me was cruel. A fucking memo that you were leaving." I release a devastating gush of air. "And what you did to my daughter… that was the most unforgivable thing of all."

She lowers her eyes to the bar top. "How is she?"

"She's thirteen. How do you think she is?"

She motions to the seat next to her. "Sit."

"I don't think so."

"Please, Asher? I mean, what are the odds we'd be at the same place at the same time like this? Maybe this was meant to happen."

"I'm *with* someone, Stella."

She flashes me her left hand. "Me too. I married Jeffrey two years ago. I'm not looking for a hookup, if that's what you think.

You're obviously not with someone this very second. So stay, just for a few minutes."

"What *are* you looking for, Stella?"

She shrugs. "Closure? Come on, for old times?"

My chest heaves with a rush of air. I should be sleeping after the day I've had. But maybe she's right. Maybe a bit of closure on that chapter in our lives would be nice.

"Bourbon on the rocks," I say to the bartender as I take a seat. "So, what are you doing here?"

"I live in Albany now. I'm in town for my dad's funeral."

"Gerry died? Damn, I'm sorry. But where's your husband?"

"Flying in from London. His plane lands early tomorrow. He was visiting his son."

I raise a brow. "You married another single father?"

She nods.

"Do you… have any kids?" I ask hesitantly.

She shakes her head sadly then asks, "Do you? I mean other than Darla?"

I shake my head, because technically, I don't. Not yet. And as much as I dislike the woman, I did love her once. I don't need to be rubbing it in her face that I'm about to have two more while she still has none.

"What brings you to New York City?" she asks.

"Work. I'm only here for the night."

"Long way to go for just one night."

"Not such a long way now. I live just outside the city."

Her jaw drops. "You said you'd never move out of Florida. You loved it there."

I shrug. "Found something I loved more."

Her face softens. "She must be really special."

"She is."

She traces the rim of her wine glass. "Are you going to try for any kids?"

"I'm not sure that's something I want to talk about, Stella."

A tear comes to her eye. "With my dad dying, it kind of puts everything into perspective—how fragile life is, and how important family is." She looks away. "Jeffrey and I have tried for years, almost since the moment we got together. I thought maybe with another guy things would be different. But I haven't even been able to conceive. Turns out the doctors were right all along. It *was* all me."

"I'm sorry."

"Late last year, we decided to try adoption."

"Sounds like a great idea."

Her head shakes. "We can't get approved. Jeffery has a history of drug use. He used to steal cars to support his habit, so he also has a criminal record. It's why his ex left him. He's fine now. He's been sober for years, even re-established a relationship with his son. But that doesn't matter to the people who need to approve our application."

"That's got to be tough."

She swallows what remains of her wine and raises her hand for a refill. "Tough doesn't begin to cover it. I love him, I really do. More than anything." She takes a long drink. "But I can't go through life without having a child."

"What are you saying?"

"I'm saying I have a decision to make. I either have to leave the man I love and adopt as a single mom, or go through life never experiencing what it's like to have a child."

I want to refute that fact and tell her she *did* have a child. A stepchild who loved her and bonded with her and who called her *Mom*. One she could have raised with me into adulthood. One she permanently fucked up when she left without so much as a hug goodbye. But I don't say any of that. I don't say it, because she's clearly broken. At this point, her grief may be more about her father's passing, but whatever it is, she's torn up inside and beginning to cry.

I put my hand on her arm. "Stella, I'm so, so sorry."

A throat clears behind us and I turn around to see Allie. I rip my hand away from Stella, utterly surprised to see her here. "I, uh… hey." But Allie's stare remains where it was, on Stella's arm.

She steps forward and gets in Stella's personal space, jutting her hand out like she wants Stella to shake it. "And you must be Rich," Allie asserts with venom in her words. "Or maybe Arjun." She glares at me. "I guess I'll just go. I can see how *hard* you're working."

Confused, Stella looks at Allie's pregnant belly and says, "Um, I'm Stella."

Allie's face falls into devastation. "Stella?" Her eyes dart between Stella's and mine. Then she turns and walks out.

"Allie!" I call. I point at the bar. "Stella, I have to go. I'm sorry. Please stay here and don't follow me."

"That's your girl? And she's… pregnant?"

"Yeah. Gotta go. I wish you all the best. And my condolences about your dad."

I rush out into the hotel lobby, looking left and right, but Allie's not here.

The doorman points outside. "Miss Montana just left, sir."

Oh, Jesus. I rip the door open before he can do it for me, and I run after her.

Chapter Twenty-nine

Allie

"Allie!" Asher yells behind me.

It's not like I can run with two babies growing inside me. I'm down the street and around the corner, doing something between a shuffle and a fast waddle.

"Allie!"

I duck into a diner to evade him, but also because I feel like my legs might collapse out from under me. Not because of the exertion, but because I need to cry. And possibly throw up.

Moving swiftly into the ladies' room, I plow into a stall, shut the toilet lid and plop down on it, my head slumping low until it meets my hands.

Should I even be surprised? Everything went at warp speed with us. As soon as he found out I was pregnant, he was uprooting his life and moving here. Across the country. Buying a house with me. I mean, one minute we were having a cross-country fling and the next we're tied together forever.

Maybe the stress of Bug and me not getting along is finally getting to him. Or maybe Bug was right when she said Asher is just *'doing the right thing.'*

Could he be *that* good at faking his feelings for me? At putting on a smile and pretending what we have is everything he wants? Are all these unfamiliar hormones making me so gullible that I've gone so far as to buy a house and agree to a future with him?

I'm trying my hardest not to cry. I refuse to cry over another man who doesn't want to be with me through less than perfect circumstances. He never asked for this. And he certainly never asked for *two* of this. My resolve crumbles and tears stream down my face and drip onto my blouse right over my baby bump.

"Miss?" a woman says from outside my stall.

I clear my throat and wipe my nose. "Are you talking to me?"

"There's a guy outside who wanted me to check on you."

I pinch my brow. "Please ask him to go away."

"Are you okay?"

"Yes. But I need him to leave."

I hear her feet shuffle. She's hesitating. I think I even hear her talking to herself. But then the bathroom door closes.

"It isn't what you think, sweetheart."

My heart clenches inside my chest when I hear Asher's voice.

"I think you just lost the right to call me that."

"Will you come out so I can explain?"

I laugh pitifully. "Explain why you got a phone call and *had* to rush to the city. And oh, how convenient that you just *had* to stay overnight when you could have taken the train home and back again in the morning. Was there even a job, Asher? Or do you just like fucking chippies in the city? Is that your thing? Maybe you need a twelve-step program, because there's something seriously wrong with you."

"Please come out."

"No."

I stare at his Cole Haan Oxfords as he enters the stall next to mine. Then suddenly, he's on his back on the floor, scooting under the partition into my stall.

"What the hell are you doing?"

He rises up in front of me, unlocks the door, and says, "Do the adult thing and follow me out. We'll get a cup of coffee and I'll explain everything."

"You had your hands on your ex-wife, Asher. That's all the explanation I need."

His head shakes in frustration. "Allie, what you saw was sympathy not infidelity. I promise you that's all it was. She was having a bad day."

"A bad day at the same hotel you were in? At the same bar. At the same time. That's too many coincidences for it to be random." Sobs begin again and there isn't a damn thing I can do to stop it. "That's *our* hotel, Asher. How could you?"

The door opens and someone walks in. "Is there a problem in here? I'm the manager. Do I need to call the police?"

Asher looks at me, his eyes begging me to follow him out.

"No," I say. "No problem."

"She was feeling lightheaded," Asher says when I emerge.

The guy carrying a baseball bat can clearly see I'm pregnant. "Oh, well, go take the booth in the corner. I'll bring you some juice and crackers."

"And coffee," Asher says. "Coffee would be nice."

The manager studies Asher like he knows we're lying, but he backs off anyway, holding the door for us so we can pass. "Right over there." He points.

When I sit in the booth, Asher tries to slide in next to me. I hold up a hand. "No."

Dejected, he takes the seat across from me as a waitress hurries over with the manager's offerings. "You okay, sweetie?"

"Sure. Thanks," I say, my gaze focused on the juice glass that I've no intention of touching.

"Stella's father died."

I huff. "And that excuses your deceit? I don't care if the supreme ruler of the world died, you should have told me instead of lying so you could come comfort your ex."

He runs a hand through his perfect hair. He's frustrated with me, but I couldn't care less. "Let me start over. Allie, I *did* come for work. We worked all day. Come with me to the hotel and I'll beat down my boss's door and he'll confirm it. We had a late dinner. On the way back to my room, I spotted Stella at the hotel bar. It was only natural to ask why she was there. I wasn't going to stay. I wasn't even going to sit. But then I saw how sad she was, and when she told me her father died and her husband's plane hadn't landed yet, I figured that no matter how I felt about her, she probably needed a friend in that moment."

I shove two crackers in my mouth as I contemplate his words. Then I wash them down because my mouth is too dry to speak. "Her... husband?"

"Yes, sweetheart, her husband." He reaches across the table and puts his hands on mine. "I promise you it was a random meeting. She's in town for her dad's funeral."

I sniff, now feeling humiliated that I thought the worst of the man who has only ever treated me with love, kindness, and respect. A man who cares so much for people in general, he would sit with someone who treated him so badly simply because she needed someone to care.

"She's… very pretty."

A smile cracks his face. "Baby, she doesn't hold a candle to you."

He gets up and sits back down on my side of the booth. This time I let him. His arm comes around me and he tugs me to him.

"I love you, Allie," he whispers into my hair. "My heart, body, and soul belong to you. Nothing in the world could change that. Not ex-wives, difficult teenagers, surprise twin pregnancies, or whatever else might get thrown our way."

I wallow in embarrassment. "I'm so stupid. I thought I'd come and surprise you. Maybe relive a few moments at our old stomping ground." I look up and catch his eyes with mine. "Are you sure nothing would have happened if I hadn't shown up?"

His smile grows into a full-on chuckle. "I've never seen this side of you, you know. As long as I've known you, you've never been the jealous type. It's kind of hot." He smirks. "Makes me think you sort of like me a whole lot."

I stab his ribs with my elbow. "No need to rub it in. I *am* a hormonal pregnant lady. Times two."

He stands and throws a ten-dollar bill on the table. "If you don't mind, I'd like to take my hormonal pregnant lady back to the hotel and do unspeakable things with her." He leans close. "Times two."

My heart, that was squeezed like a vice just a few minutes ago, is suddenly pounding with anticipation.

"As long as you promise never to speak of this again."

A finger glides from side to side over his chest. "Cross my heart." He holds out his hand.

I slip my hand into his. It's large and warm and feels like home. How could I ever think he'd do something like that to me?

I'm still scolding myself over my stupidity when we walk back inside the hotel. William smiles from ear to ear when he opens the door for us. "Miss Montana. Mr. Anderson."

Asher turns back to him. "The next time you see us here, it'll be Mr. and Mrs. Anderson."

William's eyebrows shoot up, and he looks upon us proudly, as if he somehow played a part in us getting together. "Great to hear it. Congratulations on your engagement."

"You're engaged?" I hear from behind.

When I turn, I see Asher's ex staring at my stomach.

"No," I say, at the same moment Asher says, "Yes."

I shake my head. "It's complicated."

"How… how f-far along are you?" she stutters.

"Nineteen weeks."

"You're really showing for nineteen weeks."

"It's, uh… twins."

My declaration visibly hurts her, and she bends over slightly as if I'd punched her in the gut. Part of me expects Asher to rush to her side and comfort her again. He doesn't. He simply squeezes my hand. I feel sorry for her, I do, but she doesn't own the rights to grief and heartache. Some of us have just as much of a right to all those things. Asher knows it too, which is why I think he stands by me. We may seem like this happy family now, but nobody can really know what's under the surface.

"I suppose I should give you my congratulations," she says dryly.

"Stella," Asher says. "I feel bad for you, I do. I'm sorry your dad died, and I know what seeing this must do to you. But honestly, the day you walked out of my life is the day I stopped being responsible for your feelings. I wish you the best in whatever you decide to do. Goodbye, Stella."

And with that, Asher pulls me toward the elevator, not once looking back.

Chapter Thirty

Asher

As soon as the door to my hotel room shuts, I'm pressing her into the wall, kissing her. She came here for me. Because she didn't want to spend the night without me. Because she wanted to remember the good times we had here.

My cock dances against the fly of my pants. I slowly shift my hips from side to side, pressing into her so she can feel what she does to me. When my hands land on her hair, she pulls away, a look of distaste on her face. I sigh. She's still not over it.

She points to the bathroom. "I'm not doing anything with you until you wash your hands and change your clothes. You crawled on a public bathroom floor. It's disgusting."

I laugh, happy that's her one and only reservation. On my way to the bathroom, I strip out of my clothes, leaving a trail on the floor. After washing my hands, I go back in the room, but I don't put on new clothes. I stand completely naked, dick hardening even more when I say, "Let's watch a movie."

She looks me up and down, from head to naked toe, then back at my face. "You want to watch TV?"

I retrieve my phone from the front pocket of my pants. "Not TV."

Walking to the bed, I pull up one of our videos and pat the mattress next to me.

She sits and looks at my screen, her jaw falling open. "You want to watch *this*?"

"I want *you* to watch this." I run the slider across the screen to fast forward to the exact place I'm looking for. Then I hand it to her. "See how I looked at you? I loved you even then."

She watches silently, her breaths becoming quick and audible the more she sees.

I slip behind her and wrap my arms around her. "Never question how I feel about you. I'm yours, Allie. Lock, stock, and barrel."

I kiss her neck, but she shrugs me off. "Wait. I want to see the ending."

I watch over her shoulder as she orgasms on top of me, me following right behind her. I've watched our videos more times than I care to admit. Mostly because I missed her when we were apart. But through all those viewings, I've come to learn one thing: she looked at me the same way I looked at her.

"You loved me too," I say when it's over. "You just didn't know it yet."

She tosses my phone aside and spins around in my arms. "It must be your advanced years that makes you so cocky."

I laugh. "Cocky? Or wise?" I guide her flat onto the bed and remove her top, still stunned every time I get to touch her growing breasts. "Either way, this dirty old man is about to do unspeakable things to you."

She moans when I lightly pinch a nipple. "Please."

My mouth is on her left breast before the entire word is out of her mouth. I suck and tease and even nip her a little. Her eyes close as she breathily says my name. I work a hand over her jeans, pressing my fingers against the seam running over her clit. This is all it takes to send her spiraling into orgasm.

"Fuck," I say in awe as she crumbles beneath me.

"One of the benefits of pregnancy," she says giggling when she stops shaking.

I lower the front panel of her maternity jeans and kiss her stomach. "Just how long will we be able to do this?"

"I suppose as long as I'm comfortable and can—"

Her hands go to her belly.

"What is it?" I ask, concerned.

She takes my hand and presses it against the left side of her stomach. "Can you feel that?"

I realize what's happening and my eyes go wide with anticipation as I muster every ounce of concentration. When I feel a small flutter under her skin, I gasp.

"Did you feel it?" she asks.

I can't respond. All I can do is wait for more. I put my other hand on her and lean close. It happens again. My heart is stuck so far up my throat I don't think I can speak. I need more. Feeling my child or children moving inside her has to be one of the most incredible things I've ever experienced. I don't want to move. I don't want to eat, sleep, or work ever again, I just want to lie here and feel the life inside her.

"Ash?"

"Shh."

She giggles. Then the movement abates, making me sad.

"Asher, we—"

"I'm not moving. I need to feel it again."

"You know… I think it was the orgasm that brought it on."

I lift my head to look at her. "Really?"

She nods. "So maybe if we—"

Before she can finish that sentence, her shoes are on the floor along with her jeans and panties. I crawl on top of her, careful not to put weight on her stomach. "Sweetheart, be prepared to go for the record. Because if they move every time you come, you're going to come all night long."

She laughs and pulls my head toward hers. "This night is turning out far better than expected."

~ ~ ~

I'm sure we both have bags under our eyes when we hit the hotel restaurant for breakfast. I insisted on not getting room service. If we'd stayed there a minute longer, I'd have had her naked and under me again. Last night was amazing. Between making her come as many times as I did, and feeling the babies, it was definitely the best night we've spent together. Which is kind of surprising considering how the night started.

I wave over Rich and Arjun when I see them enter the restaurant.

"Allie Montana, meet Rich Jennings and Arjun Bhandari. Gentlemen, please join us."

Rich takes the seat across from me. "I can see why Asher didn't want to go a single day without seeing you. Nice to finally meet you, Allie."

"Actually," Allie says. "I'm the one who crashed his party. I hope it's okay. If you need to talk about work, I can go."

"There will be plenty of time for that," Arjun says, extending his hand to her. "You wouldn't happen to have any sisters, would you?"

Allie blushes. "Sorry. I'm the only girl of my parents' four children."

"Three brothers," Rich says in amusement. He turns to Asher. "And you're still alive?"

We're all sharing a laugh when Stella walks into the restaurant. A man is with her. I guess her husband's flight arrived. Allie doesn't fail to notice. She tenses, but all Stella does is offer me a sad smile. She and Jeffrey stroll right past us as if he has no idea who I am. Maybe she didn't even tell him.

They take a seat somewhere behind me. I never look back at her. She's my past. The woman sitting next to me is my future.

Thirty minutes later, I escort Allie to the train station.

"Do you expect me to take your name?" she asks.

I cock my head. "That kind of came out of nowhere."

"What you said to the doorman last night about us being Mr. and Mrs. Anderson. Is that what you want?"

A slow roll of air leaves my body through my nose. "Of course it's what I want, Al. But I know keeping the name of your family business means a lot to you. How about we compromise? You be Allie Montana at work, but Allie Anderson everywhere else, especially in our bed."

She bites her lip in contemplation. "I think that could be arranged."

I'm jumping for joy inside. She's thinking ahead. I step close and put my lips to her ear. "Thinking about marrying me, eh?"

She brushes away the tickle. "I do think about it, Asher. I think about it all the time. But we still have hurdles to overcome."

"One hurdle," I say holding up a finger. "One."

"It's a pretty big one."

"Allie, we've been in Calloway Creek less than a week. Rome wasn't built in a day."

Her lungs expel a harsh sigh. "No. It took about eight hundred years. I know. I wrote a paper on it in high school. So if you're trying to make me feel better, that's a horrible analogy."

I'm trying not to laugh, but it's hard. "Sweetheart, it'll happen. You and Bug will find your groove. Whether it's her seeing you as a mother figure or just a friend, I truly believe she's going to accept you."

"And if she doesn't?"

"She will."

"Just humor me. If she never accepts me. Then what?"

I shrug. "I guess she'll go off to college in a little over four years."

I cover my face with my hands. "Oh, god."

He takes my hands off my face and kisses them. "It's not going to come to that. We're going to find a way for all of us to live together peacefully."

"I hope you're right."

"I'm right." I kiss her temple. "Listen to me. I'm older and wiser." I point. "There's your train. Today will be a long day, and I'll be home late. But I'll be home. I promise."

It's a promise I intend to keep. Even if we're not done with the job and I work until midnight, I'm going home to her. I never want her to have a reason to doubt me. And I intend on keeping every single promise I make to her. Especially the one that has her becoming my wife.

Chapter Thirty-one

Allie

"This is so stupid," Bug says from the back seat when we're almost there. "Why can't you just show me the pictures after?"

Asher looks at her in the rearview mirror. "We want you to be a part of this, Bug. The anatomy scan is a big deal. Plus, it's pretty cool."

"Whatever." She huffs. "It's still stupid. Who takes their kid?"

"We do," I say.

"I was asking my father."

Asher reaches over and squeezes my hand. He knows to pick his battles, and I've asked him more than a few times not to interfere when it comes to my interactions with Darla. For the most part, he's been accommodating. He's gotten to the point where he'll allow the typical teenage attitude, but he doesn't hesitate to step in when it crosses the line into blatant disrespect.

And Darla, well, let's just say she's pretty darn good at straddling that line when he's around. When he's not—the gloves usually come off. But that's for me to know and deal with on my own.

Inside the waiting room, Asher sits and peruses the baby magazines like the expectant father he is. Bug plays on her phone. When a few more women come in and wait in the chairs across from us, she says, "It's embarrassing. People probably think I'm pregnant or have an STI or something. There's no other reason I'd be here with you."

I clear my throat and say way louder than I need to, "Oh my gosh, I'm so excited for my ultrasound. Aren't you excited to see the babies, Darla?"

She rolls her eyes overdramatically and goes back to her phone.

Asher cracks a smile as he turns a page.

I'm called back so a nurse can take my vitals, then Asher and Bug meet me in the exam room. We don't have to wait too long for Hudson to join us.

"You're doing the ultrasound?" I ask. "Don't you have techs to do them?"

"Sometimes." He rolls the machine over. "I like to do the high risk and twin pregnancies myself." He notices Bug. "I see you've brought an audience."

"This is my daughter, Darla," Asher says. "Everyone calls her Bug."

Hudson nods. "You excited to be a big sister, Bug?"

"I guess. Whatever."

I guess? I look over at Asher. He heard it too. It's the closest she's ever gotten to admitting it out loud.

"Allie, go ahead and lie back and pull your waistband down and your top up so I can measure you." He gets a measuring tape out of his pocket. "Have you been feeling okay?"

"I've been feeling great."

"Taking your prenatal vitamins?"

"Every day."

"Any vaginal bleeding or discharge?" He notes the measurement on his iPad.

"Nope."

"Pelvic pain? Headaches? Swelling?"

"No."

"Have you felt movement yet?"

My cheeks flame. I look over at Asher and we share a smile. The babies move a lot. Especially when we're being intimate. Which we are. *A lot.* "Yes."

Hudson raises a brow but doesn't dig in further. "Any concerns?"

I shrug. "Not really."

"Well, then, let's get started." He squirts gel onto my abdomen and works the transducer around.

"What are you looking for exactly?" Asher asks.

"At twenty weeks, we look for proper development of organs and limbs and assess the placenta and amniotic fluid. I'll measure the size and shape of their heads, look at the four chambers of their hearts, assess the spine, abdomen, and facial features. Even the fingers and toes."

I rise up on my elbows, suddenly gripped by anxiety. In my head, I'm hearing all the things he's not saying. That he's looking for abnormalities. Defects. Horrible things that could affect one or both babies. My heart begins racing and I feel nauseous.

Hudson looks up. "Allie, are you okay?"

I shake my head repeatedly, suddenly feeling panicked. There are still so many things that could be wrong.

Asher slides his arm under my head and around my shoulders, cradling me. He leans close to my ear and softly says, "Hey, it's okay. Breathe, Allie."

"What's happening?" Bug asks.

"She's experiencing a little anxiety over the ultrasound," Hudson tells her. "It's perfectly normal. Allie, lie back and relax. Your pregnancy has been going well. There's no reason to believe it won't continue to go well. Just give me a few minutes. They're awake and moving around which makes this a bit more difficult. Okay, here we go."

A fast heartbeat thumps and echoes through the room, calming me momentarily.

"Is that one of the babies?" Bug asks, taking a step closer for a better view.

"That's Twin A," Hudson says.

"How do you decide which is A and which is B?" Asher asks.

"Twin A is the one closest to the cervix. At twenty weeks, there's still room for them to reposition, so they may flip-flop a bit, but with boy-girl twins, it's easier to keep track of which is which." He concentrates on the screen while moving the wand. "Right now, Twin A is the girl." He types on the keyboard with his other hand.

"Does she look okay?" I ask, still trying to slow my heartbeat.

"So far so good," he says, taking more measurements. "There." He points. "See her feet?" He presses a button that freezes the screen and types some more. "Ten toes."

Asher squeezes my shoulder.

"Femur is measuring perfectly," he mumbles more to himself than to us. "Spine looks good. There's a hand. Wait, that's not hers. Looks like we've got a little sibling rivalry going on in there."

I release a drawn-in breath, relaxing a bit at his playful manner.

The more time he spends pointing out parts of their anatomy, the closer Darla comes, until she's standing right next to Asher, her eyes glued to the ultrasound screen.

We hear Twin B's heartbeat and then get to see all his fingers and toes.

"Looks like you're carrying two healthy babies, Allie."

I smile when Asher leans down and plants a quick kiss on my lips.

"Can you show me their faces again?" Bug asks.

"Sure." Hudson moves the wand around until the profile of one comes into view.

"Which one is that?" she asks.

"This is Twin B. The boy."

"There's his hand," she says in amusement. "He's not sucking his thumb, is he?"

"Could be," Hudson says. "Another fun fact: it's not uncommon for them to use their placentas as play toys." He prints out a photo and hands it to her, somehow knowing she may want one for herself. Then he finds the other one. "And here's Twin A, your little sister."

It's hard to keep my face from breaking into a massive grin.

He prints that one as well. She stares from photo to photo, then looks up at Asher. "Twin A and Twin B sound like Dr. Seuss names. I think you should name them for real."

"Oh, you do?" Asher says, loving her sudden interest.

"Why don't *you*?" I say on a whim. "I mean, I really want your dad to name the boy, but Darla, how about you name the girl?"

"Hold on there." Asher flashes me a look of concern. "Maybe we should talk about this."

Hudson clears his throat, wipes the gel from my stomach and hands me several ultrasound photos. "I'll see you back in four weeks."

"Okay, thanks, Hudson."

When he leaves, I pull up my waistband and Asher helps me sit. "Asher, I'm just so happy to be having two healthy babies, I couldn't care less what we call them." I spare a glance at Bug. "You know, within reason. And I think a father should name his son. I just have one request."

"Which is?" Asher asks.

"His middle name. I want to choose it."

His face is full of compassion. "Christopher?"

I nod.

"After your dad," Bug says. "I guess that's cool."

Asher and I share a sad smile.

Bug stares at the photos. "You really want me to name her?"

"I really do."

She doesn't even hesitate. "Nobara Kugishaki Anderson."

My head snaps to the side, as does Asher's.

"Well that's… specific," I say, trying not to show my shock, which I'm sure is what she's going for. "You think she should have an Asian name?"

"Nobara is a first-year sorcerer alongside Yuji Itadori and Megumi Fushiguro in *Jujutsu Kaisen*. Hmm, maybe I should pick one of those." She rubs her thumb and forefinger across the tip of her chin. "There are just so many to choose from."

"She's a first year *what?*" I look at Asher to clarify. "In Jujutsu *who?*"

"Bug is going through an anime phase."

"Oh, okay." I turn back to Bug. "You think about it. You don't have to decide today. It's a big responsibility, you know, choosing the name someone will have for their entire life."

She belts out unhinged laughter. "You're actually going to let me choose. Like for real?"

"She's going to be your sister, so yes."

Bug looks at Asher. Asher looks at me. "We have veto power, right?"

"I don't think so. I want her to make the decision. Whatever name she picks will go on the birth certificate."

He takes my elbow and says in a low voice full of unease, "Allie, I'm not sure this is the right way to handle this."

I head for the door. "I'm sure they need the room. Bug" —I realize my blunder— "uh… Darla. You have seventeen weeks." I nudge Asher. "So do you."

Chapter Thirty-two

Asher

"You call this a date?" I look up at the Donovan's Pub marquee. "I was thinking more Lloyd's Steakhouse."

She elbows me on the way in. "It's where all the cool kids hang out on Friday nights."

Her saying that just reminds me that Bug is sitting home sulking. She's made zero effort whatsoever to make friends. Maybe it'll happen once we move into the house and things settle down.

I've been so busy with our new client, I haven't been able to case the neighborhood. The realtor said there are lots of families. I just hope Bug can find someone. Maybe even a new 'Mel.' Because at this point, she barely leaves her room since she's video chatting with the old one day and night.

I take Allie's hand. "I've been here once before, you know."

"Oh, right. You were here for Lucas's birthday party. I almost forgot." She smiles as we pick a booth along the back windows. "And just look at you now, a full-fledged resident."

"In theory. But I can't get a New York driver's license until I have the closing papers on the house and at least one utility bill."

"I'll get a new one, too," she says. "That way we'll both have our new address on them."

"I think you should wait."

She furrows her brow.

"You don't want to go through the hassle of getting *two* new licenses in one year."

When it occurs to her what I'm saying, her head cocks. "Oh, so you want me to *legally* become an Anderson?"

"Haven't we discussed this?"

She shrugs. "I thought since I was keeping my name for work purposes, Montana would be my legal name, but that I'd 'pretend' I'm an Anderson the rest of the time."

She peruses the menu as if she hasn't eaten here hundreds of times in her life. Also as if she didn't just deliver me a blow to the gut. Then she looks up and laughs at my expression. "Of course I'm going to change my name. But that was a lot of fun."

I give her a playful nudge under the table.

After we order drinks, I continue the conversation. "Speaking of names. How long do you intend to let this go on with Bug? It's getting a little out of control, don't you think?"

"It's fine."

"Fine? She's threatening to name the baby something like Bertha, Henrietta or Clementine."

Her mouth twitches with a grin. "She won't do that."

"How do you know?"

"I know because Darla has to live with the name just like we do. You think she wants to run after her little sister shouting *'Bertha'?"* She shakes her head. "I don't think so."

"She's being pretty stubborn. She might just do it out of spite. I'm afraid this whole thing may backfire on you."

She puts her hand on top of mine. "We can always change the name on the birth certificate later when she comes to her senses. I'm trying to build trust."

My jaw drops. "You'd really be willing to put a name like Mildred on our daughter's birth certificate?"

"It's not like the baby will know her name. I'd give it a few weeks before the guilt of it gets to Bug."

"But what would we call her in the meantime?"

She shrugs. "Sweetie? Baby girl?"

"Still. It's a dangerous game you're playing just to make Bug feel like she's a part of this."

Dallas and Blake walk through the front door, see us, and come over. Before Dallas's ass hits the seat across from us, Allie stops him. "Sit somewhere else, guys. This is a date."

He eyes her like she's crazy. "At Donovan's?"

"Thank you," I say, turning to glare at Allie.

She points across the restaurant. "Go. We'll talk to you later."

"Nice to see you too," Blake says, winking before turning to walk away.

At least a dozen other people come up and talk to us before our food comes. By the time Allie's grilled chicken salad gets placed in front of her, she's apologizing. "Maybe Donovan's wasn't the best place for our date."

"How about we go for a walk through the park after? That could be nice."

She nods. "We probably should have gone someplace further away. After Monday, we'll likely come here a lot as it's a short walk from the new house."

I lace her fingers through mine. I don't care if that means it'll be difficult to eat. "I can't wait."

"How do you think it's going to be? With Darla? Be honest."

I sigh. "Honestly? I just don't know. She'll probably never leave her room." I run my thumb across her knuckles. "I'm just sorry I'm going to have to leave for a business trip the next day." Other than the one night in the city, I haven't traveled in over a month, what with getting my house ready to sell and the move. I shake my head. "I should cancel."

"You can't do that. It's going to happen sooner or later, so we might as well get used to it. Asher, it's going to be fine." She steals one of my fries and dips it in ketchup. "Well, maybe not fine. But we'll get through it. It might even be good for us. You never know."

"I'm glad you're being optimistic." I squeeze her hand, kiss the back of it, then release it.

Allie takes a bite of her meal, then completely tenses when a group of guys walk in the front door.

I tickle her ribs and joke, "Ex-boyfriend?"

She swallows, looking a bit green around the gills. "Actually, yes. Blue shirt."

Her eyes close and it seems like she's trying to sink into the booth and become invisible.

"Wait, that's not *the* ex-boyfriend, is it?"

She nods, still not opening her eyes.

"I thought he moved away," I snarl.

"He did. But he still has friends here. I haven't seen him in, I don't even know how long. At least five years. Has he noticed me?"

"No."

The reason I know this is I haven't taken my eyes off the snake since she told me who he was.

"He's sitting at the bar with his back to us."

Finally she opens her eyes. But she's lost all interest in eating, and I can tell she no longer wants to be here. I raise my arm as the waiter walks by and ask for the check. "I think it's time we go on that walk. If you're still hungry, we'll go for ice cream after."

She nods, looking sad.

I hate it when she's sad. I live my whole goddamn life now with one objective: making her happy. After everything she's been through, she deserves it. She doesn't need to sit here and be reminded of her tragic past.

I pay the tab, never letting my gaze stray from the asshole at the bar. When we get up to leave, I block her view of him with my body. "Come on. Let's get out of here."

On our way to the door, Blake yells, "Leaving so soon, Allie?"

Fuck.

My head whips around at the same time the asshole's does. His eyes immediately land on her face. Then her belly. Then me. He stands and takes a few steps toward us. I hold up my palm. "That's far enough."

He has the audacity to snicker. "Guess my reputation precedes me." He stares at Allie's stomach. "Looks like you did it again. Is this one going to stick, or is it going to be gorked out like the other one?"

I don't even think about it before my fist meets his jaw. It just happens—like I'm out of my body and not even me. His head snaps back and blood spatters the floor behind him. He stomps his foot three or four times at the pain, then stands straight up and squares off. "What the fuck?"

He raises his fists, but before he can retaliate, a dozen people stand behind me, including two of Allie's brothers. Word spreads fast in this town, and apparently everyone knows what a loser this guy is.

Cooper Calloway, one of the owners of the pub, comes over. He stares Jason down and points to the door. "I think you should leave."

"Seriously?" Jason looks at Cooper like he's the one who's been wronged. "This guy just fucking hit me. *He's* the one you should be throwing out."

"Go. Now." Cooper steps closer to him. "Everyone in this town knows what you did. You're a sorry excuse for a man, spreading lies about how she ran off and left you, when it was you who was the pathetic loser all along."

Jason looks at Allie, surprise all over his face. Apparently he thought he'd have the upper hand here. He assumed she still hadn't told anyone about Christopher or what a coward he was for doing what he did. But it's quite the opposite. I guess his friends hadn't gotten the memo. Either that, or they were waiting to get drunk before telling him.

"Come on, man," one of his friends says, tugging on his arm. "Let's go next door."

"If by next door, you mean the bowling alley," Dallas says, "don't expect a ticker tape parade there either. You're a loser, Platt. Best go back under whatever rock you crawled out from. This town doesn't want you anymore."

As the three men leave, Allie lets out a sigh so big you'd think she'd been holding it in for days.

Blake walks up and puts his arm around her. "You okay?"

She nods.

"If you hadn't hit that fucker," he says to me, "I would have."

A bunch of "Me toos" echo in the space behind us.

I stare down at my fist, now aching and red. "I've never hit anyone in my life."

"You picked a good one to start with." Dallas holds out his hand to shake mine. "You're a good man, Asher."

"You okay?" I ask Al.

"Yeah." She looks at the door. "I'm not sure I want to leave though."

"How about we go back and finish dinner?"

Our waiter is just walking past, our barely touched food sitting under a pile of used napkins and other crap.

Cooper hands me an ice pack and looks at the tray. "I'll make up some new plates. On me."

"Thank you," I say, leading Allie back to the booth we just vacated.

I set my hand on the table and put the ice pack over it.

"I can't believe you hit him," Allie says. I think she's going to cry, but instead, she surprises me with a half-smile. "Thank you."

I laugh. "You're welcome."

She scoots closer so our thighs are touching. "I mean it. You're good at this."

"At… punching people?"

"At taking care of me."

I remove my hand from under the ice and wrap it around her. "I'm always going to take care of you, sweetheart. I promise."

~ ~ ~

Allie's been tossing and turning all night, but when she wakes up crying, I pull her to me, my front to her back, and whisper, "What can I do?"

She turns around in my arms and faces me. I can just make out her features in the moonlight coming through the window overhead.

"He never got over the fact that I didn't abort the baby. And then he actually had the gall to ask if I wanted to get back together after I came home."

"Jesus, really?"

"I told him to fuck off and never talk to me again. He moved out of Calloway Creek a few weeks later."

I kiss her forehead. "Good girl."

She falls asleep in my arms. And she stays there all night, never suffering from another bad dream.

Chapter Thirty-three

Allie

Yesterday was moving day. Other than my personal belongings, I didn't bring a whole lot from Montana Manor. Everything there pretty much belongs to my parents.

Most of our new house is being furnished by Asher's things. Although we'll still have to go shopping to fill a few spaces, not to mention all the baby stuff we'll have to get. One thing I couldn't part with, however, is my favorite chair. It's one of those big comfy ones you can just sink into and get lost in a book. I have a feeling it's going to get a lot of use in the coming months.

Today is all about unpacking boxes. It's also about me being here all alone with Bug. And not just today, for three whole days.

She's barely said two words to me. Every once in a while she'll go out to the garage, where most of the boxes are stacked, and she'll carry another one up to her room.

It's almost noon when she comes for another.

"I've got stuff for sandwiches in the kitchen. Want one?"

She puts down the box. "I could eat."

I get a little nervous, wondering what we're going to talk about for the length of time it takes to make, then eat, a sandwich. But as it turns out, I didn't need to be. Darla slaps turkey and cheese on bread, wraps it in a paper towel, and walks out of the kitchen.

She turns back, saying only one word. "Gertrude."

I know what she's doing. For days now, she's been spouting out names to get under my skin. Does she sit around and think of the most hideous names just to annoy me? I'm not going to let her win this game.

"Gerty." I nod. "That's actually not bad. Did you ever see the movie *E.T.*? That little girl was adorable."

She huffs loudly through her nose, spins around, and hoofs it up the stairs.

I get a text.

Asher: Just landed in Atlanta. Is the new house still standing?

Me: Barely. But it's fine. I don't want you worrying about us. We'll work through it. She's actually being quite entertaining, and might I say innovative, with the baby names.

Asher: I still can't believe you're going all in on that.

Me: Have a little faith, will you?

Asher: My ride is here. Gotta go. I'll call you tonight. I love you.

Me: I love you too. Don't work too hard.

I finish my sandwich, clean up the counter, and head out to the garage. I promised Asher I wouldn't lift anything too heavy, so I sift through the boxes until I find one marked 'towels.' I take it into the laundry room and dump everything into the washing machine.

Later, when I go out for another box, I stop short of the garage door. It's sitting ajar and I hear voices. I lean against the wall and listen.

"I'm Christian. I live next door."

My eyebrows shoot up. I totally forgot about Carter and his son. I'm not sure how, considering Christian is Mia's nephew, whom she loves more than life itself.

"Darla. But everyone calls me Bug. I guess I live here now."

"You guess?"

"I'm being forced to. I used to live in Florida. Why do you use those things? Is your leg broken?"

I take a chance and peek out into the garage. Christian and Bug are standing about ten feet apart on the far side. She's leaning against my car. He's balancing himself on his forearm crutches.

"I have cerebral palsy," he says matter-of-factly in his distinct tone of voice that's slow and deliberate.

"What's that?"

"Basically, something happened to me when my mom was pregnant or during the delivery. Something that affects muscle movement and coordination and fine motor skills. There are all kinds of degrees of CP. Mine's not so bad."

"Oh, okay. That's cool."

"How old are you?" Christian asks.

"Thirteen."

"Me too. Are you going to attend Calloway Creek High this year?"

She shrugs. "Haven't decided yet. I might do the whole home school thing."

I watch Christian walk through the garage on his crutches like they aren't even a bother, like they're just an extension of him. I rub my belly thinking of Christopher and how I wish he could have had CP instead of Trisomy 18. Some people look at Carter and Christian with pity. I look at them with envy.

"Why would you want to home school? Seems boring."

"Because I hate Calloway Creek."

"It's not so bad here. Maybe you need to give it a chance."

"You're only saying that because you aren't a freak."

He holds up a crutch. "You think I'm not a freak?"

I like the way he says it jokingly. Christian is an amazing kid. He's never let his disability define him. He does well in school, he works the front desk at the autobody shop in the summer, and he's incredibly outgoing and friendly.

"You think because you walk funny and have coke bottle glasses that you're a freak?"

He laughs. "Nobody ever says stuff like that to me. I kind of like that you aren't afraid to."

"Because *I'm* a freak," Bug says. "Try to keep up."

"You think you're a freak because of your blue hair? Then dye it. But personally, I think it's kind of cool. Nobody else in town has hair that color."

"I'm a freak because I'm new. I'm sure you've lived here your whole life. People don't look at you like you don't belong. Nobody wants to make friends with the new girl."

"I do. And you should totally come to high school. We'll start a club. The freak club."

I want to be appalled by their conversation. I mean, they keep using the word *freak*. But now it seems they've said it so much, the word has lost all its power.

I smile to myself, feeling guilty for eavesdropping, but not guilty enough to stop doing it. I like that Bug is possibly making a friend.

Christian looks back at his house. "I'd better go. I promised my dad I'd clean the kitchen by the time he gets home from work."

Bug cocks her head and studies him.

"What?" he says. "You don't think a freak on crutches can clean?" Then he laughs. "Okay, so it might take me two or three tries to pick up anything that falls on the ground. And I'm sure it takes me way longer than the non-freaks—"

Darla throws up her hands. "Will you stop calling yourself a freak? It's self-deprecating."

"I will if you will." He holds out a hand.

I'm fairly sure she rolls her eyes but shakes it anyway. "Deal."

Feeling their conversation is coming to an end, I shuffle back into the kitchen and pretend to be oblivious to their meeting.

A minute later, Bug walks through carrying another box. "Ursula."

I tilt my head. "Like from *The Little Mermaid*? Or from *Friends*?"

"Does it really matter?"

"Nope," I say flippantly, putting away some plates I'd washed earlier. "I suppose not."

Out of the corner of my eye, I can tell she's staring at me. She doesn't like how I won't engage with her attempts to annoy me.

"Do you need any help decorating your room?" I ask.

"No."

"If you need anything, we could run to the store. Curtains?"

"Nope."

"You don't want curtains?"

"I do. I just don't want to go to the store."

I lean against the counter. "With me. You mean you don't want to go to the store *with me?*"

"This box is getting pretty heavy." She starts for the stairs.

"We could get baby stuff. That might be fun."

She turns. "Why would that be fun?"

"Well, we need pretty much everything. I thought we could go pick out a few outfits. Maybe even the ones they'll wear home from the hospital. Or… we could get you some new clothes for school."

"Not sure I'm going." She rests the box on her hip. "I have a lot to do upstairs."

"Maybe tomorrow?"

"I'll still have a lot to do."

I force out a deep sigh and hold up my hands. "Fine. You win. Go."

I change over the laundry, then bring in a few more boxes. I have no idea what to do about dinner. I guess I'll just make something and if Bug eats, she eats. Up in her room probably. If Asher were here, he'd make her sit at the table with us. I'm not going to force her to do that.

I'm contemplating what to make when I come across the box with Christopher's ashes. They're not in a traditional urn. After all, few people knew what happened, so I wasn't about to display something in my apartment that anyone would question. It's simple. A ceramic heart tinted blue that could be something I picked up at a flea market. There's no engraving. No picture. And for almost ten years it's been on my nightstand. I set it carefully on the coffee table, thinking I might put it somewhere else now.

There's a box on the floor without a label. I pull a few things out of it. Magazines. No, not magazines, comic books. I flip through one just as Bug comes through the room. "I found your comics," I say, holding one out and picking up a stack.

She scoffs as if I just said the stupidest thing in the history of things. "They aren't comics."

"Oh, right. These are your what… anime?"

"You don't know anything," she says, striding across the floor. "Anime is what you watch. These are manga."

She reaches me, and forcefully pulls it out of my hand, accidentally knocking a few things off the coffee table in the process.

When I see the broken pieces of the urn along with Christopher's ashes scattered on the floor, I fall to my hands and knees. "No!" I pick up the base of the heart to see barely any ashes still inside. "Oh my god. No."

On my knees, I use my hands to sweep his ashes into a pile. Tears stream down my face and drop onto his ashes as I vaguely process Bug's startled reaction.

"You're kind of overreacting about a broken vase full of sand."

She leaves the room as I cup my hands, picking up ashes and depositing them back into the bottom part of the urn.

There's a noise behind me, and before I can even process what's happening, Darla is next to me sucking up his ashes into a handheld vacuum cleaner.

I push it away. "No! Stop it!" I rip the vacuum out of her hand and look into the clear collection container that is filled with dust, hair, even a few bugs. And now, my Christopher.

Sobbing, I lean back against the sofa, vacuum in hand so she can't suck up any more.

"What the heck is wrong with you?" she asks, looking at me like I'm a crazy woman. "Does my dad know about this mental instability, or have you been hiding it from him?"

I draw more of the ashes on the floor into a small pile. "This isn't s-sand. It's C-Christopher."

She looks at me, confused. "Who's Christopher?"

I touch the broken remains of the urn. "My son."

She gasps. And that's when I see it. Empathy. I see it along with all the other qualities she's never displayed in front of me but that Asher keeps telling me she has.

"Oh my god. Seriously?" She looks at the vacuum cleaner in horror. "I… I didn't know."

I shake my head, still crying. "It's not your fault. It was an accident."

She sits next to the coffee table, drawing her knees up to her chest, clearly unsure what she should do.

Asher never told her. Just like he said he wouldn't. He wanted me to tell her in my own time. I guess it's time.

"I was nineteen. I hid the pregnancy from everyone because I knew he was sick. He had what you call a chromosomal anomaly that is incompatible with life." I absently sweep more ashes into the pile. "He only lived for thirty-one hours."

"Does my dad know?"

I nod.

She looks down at my stomach and swallows like her world just turned upside down.

"Don't worry. They don't have it. They're fine."

She stands, clearly not knowing what to say. "I'll go make dinner."

I nod again, staring at the floor.

I don't even say anything when she takes the small vacuum with her. I know I'd never be able to bring myself to empty it into the trash myself. And maybe she knows it too.

When I look up, she's walking away, but she turns once and looks right at me. "I'm really sorry."

"It wasn't your fault."

"No. I mean I'm sorry about Christopher."

It's now when it dawns on me that she's no stranger to infant death. Bug's own cousin died as a baby when she must have been only ten. I'm sure she saw how destroyed Marti was when it happened. She may well be one of the only thirteen-year-olds who could understand. And that understanding is written all over her face.

For the next hour, I meticulously clean up the rest of Christopher's ashes, putting them in a sealed bag until I can get another urn. This time, I'm going to have his name engraved on it.

I can't get myself to unpack anymore. I take a nap instead. And I sleep for hours, right through dinner.

When I finally get up and go to the kitchen, there's a note that my dinner is in the warming drawer. But it's not the note and the dinner that mean anything to me. It's the small baggie next to the note. I can see what's in it plain as day. She must have spent hours going through the contents of the vacuum container, because I can't see one single hair, dust mote, or carpet fiber. What's inside is all Christopher.

A single tear rolls down my cheek.

Because this girl who hates me has just done the nicest thing anyone has ever done for me.

Chapter Thirty-four

Asher

Coming home to this house—to Allie—is like a dream come true. This is my home base now. She's my true north. I can't believe what a lucky man I am.

"Dad!"

I drop my bags inside the front door as Bug rushes through the living room and wraps me into a hug.

I was worried she'd hole up in her room the entire three days I was gone, but she's here greeting me as she always has after a business trip. It gives me hope.

"Hey, sweetie. How did it go?"

She shrugs. "Fine, I guess."

"Is your room unpacked? You need help with anything?"

"Nah. I'm good."

I look around. "Where is Allie?"

"Shopping with her mom."

"You weren't invited?"

"I was busy."

"With your room?"

She pulls me through the house to the very back. Through the sliding doors, I can see bright orange spray paint all over the back yard.

My eyes narrow. "You graffitied our back yard?"

"That's going to be our pool."

"Our pool?"

I open the sliding door and step out onto the deck, studying the outlines before I turn to her. "*You* did this?"

"I had help."

The smile on my face is a mile wide. I knew my being gone would somehow bring them together.

"Hi, Bug." My head whips around and I see a boy on crutches standing on our property line. He walks awkwardly, yet somehow confidently, toward me. When he's within arm's length, he loosens his grip on the right crutch, still keeping his forearm clipped in, and extends his arm. "You must be Darla's dad. I'm Christian Cruz. I live next door."

I shake his hand, suddenly realizing it wasn't Allie who helped with this whole elaborate pool layout. It was him. "Nice to meet you. I'm Asher Anderson."

"You picked a nice house for a big pool, Mr. Anderson."

"Isn't it great?" Bug says. "Christian had the paint in his garage. We looked up a bunch of stuff about pools. He said we should get a sports pool, which means it's shallower on each end but deeper in the middle."

"You could install a net in the center for pool volleyball," the kid adds.

I study the young man. "You seem to know a lot about pools. Is your dad in the business?"

"No." He holds up a crutch. "Pools are good therapy for people with CP."

I crane my neck and look into his back yard. No pool. Why do I get the idea this kid will be spending more than a little time in ours? I look up at the outdoor entrance to Bug's room and know I need to get busy padlocking the door.

I'm happy she's making friends, but I was sort of hoping the first one would be a girl.

"Are your parents around?" I ask. "I'd like to meet them."

"I don't have a mom." He juts out a crutch. "She didn't want to deal with this. And my dad's at the shop. I work there a few hours a day. It's just down the street and around the corner."

"On McQuaid Circle?"

"Near it, anyway. It's the Cruz-In Auto Repair Shop. My aunt and uncles work there too. If you ever need work done on your car, it's the best place to go. Even if you're a do-it-yourselfer, we have a supply store."

"I'll keep that in mind." I laugh. "I can see why they want you working there."

"It'll be partly mine one day. I'm going to be a mechanical engineer and work on engines. I'd prefer to work on race cars, but I guess you take what you can get." He turns around. "I'd better get back. I like to have dinner started when my dad gets home. Nice meeting you, sir."

"You too, Christian."

I wait until he's out of earshot to raise a brow at Bug. She rolls her eyes. "Oh, please."

"First thing on my agenda today will be taking care of your outside entrance."

"You saw him, Dad. He has trouble walking. You think he can climb a flight of stairs?"

I laugh. "You'd be amazed what people can do for love."

"Gross."

"Hey, you two," Allie says from the back door. She scans the yard. "What's all this?"

I hurry over and take her into my arms. "I missed you." I kiss her chastely, saving the inappropriate stuff for later. "*This* is what my daughter and the neighbor kid have been working on while you were shopping."

Her mouth falls open. "Christian and Bug did this?"

I narrow my eyes. "You know about Christian?"

"He lives next door. He's Mia's nephew. Great kid. Darla could do much worse in the friend department."

"But he's a… boy."

Allie giggles. "Beggars can't be choosers. You wanted her to make friends, Ash." She looks beyond me to Bug. "My mom is waiting for you out front." She holds out a small bag. "But first I wanted you to see these."

Bug looks at the shopping bag with great hesitation. As if there's nothing in the world Allie could buy her that she would like, even if it was something every teenage girl wanted. She pulls two tiny outfits out of the bag. One is pink and one is blue. The pink one reads: "Little Sis." The blue one reads: "Little Bro."

"I thought maybe these could be what they wear when they come home from the hospital. What do you think?"

Bug shrugs. "I think it's not really my choice." She shoves the bag into my arms. "Mrs. Montana is waiting."

"What's that all about?" I ask when Bug trots inside.

"She's going for a sleepover at my mother's. So is Charlie." Her face cracks into a smile. "We'll have the entire house to ourselves."

I lean in and kiss her neck, right below her ear. "I like the way you think."

Ten seconds later, we're back inside and Bug is rushing down the stairs with a backpack slung over one shoulder. "Bye, Dad. See you tomorrow." She starts to walk away then turns and looks at Allie. "Um, see ya."

I'm stunned. It wasn't much, but it was an acknowledgment.

I stare down at Al. "Something's changed. She doesn't look at you with such a sour face anymore."

"She still won't let me help her decorate her room or go shopping. And we've yet to sit at the same table for a meal whenever you're gone. But, yeah, I feel something's changed."

"What happened?"

She shrugs. Because either she honestly doesn't know, or she just doesn't want *me* to know. I don't push her, respecting her repeated request that I let them navigate this on their own.

"How was your trip?"

"Uneventful."

"As in no ex-wives showed up at your hotel bar?"

"It wouldn't have mattered." I draw her close. "Because, sweetheart, I only have eyes for you."

She grins. "Do you practice being so charming?"

I chuckle. "It comes naturally."

Allie takes my hand and presses it to her stomach. "They've started kicking a lot more this week."

A gentle tapping sensation against my palm occurs repeatedly. I take note of where it's happening. "That must be our little boy."

"I think so too. He's slightly more active than she is." She watches me enjoy the movements. "You pick a name yet?"

I don't answer. Still concentrating hard, I don't remove my hands until I feel the very last movement.

She smooths out her shirt. "If you want to name him Asher, I'd be okay with it. We could call him AJ."

"Technically, a son needs to have the exact first, middle, and last name to be a 'junior'."

Sadness washes over her. "You want him to have your middle name?"

I gather her hands in mine, bring them to my mouth, and kiss them. "Not on your life. That's already been decided."

Her face softens. "We could still call him AJ informally. I mean, if that's what you want."

"I don't know. Having a son named after me isn't all that important. Honestly, I'm just elated to be having another child." I swipe her jawline with my thumb. "And to be having *two*… you'll never know what a gift you've given me. We can call him Ralph, Ignatius, or Pikachu and I'll still love him to the ends of the earth." I touch her lower belly. "And her."

She giggles. "I'm glad you'll love them no matter what their names are, because Bug has been coming up with some real doozies."

"Just how long are you going to let that go on?"

"Do you really want to talk about this again? Because we could be getting naked right now."

I sweep her into my arms. "I'll take option number two."

She laughs as I carry her to our bedroom. "You won't be able to do this much longer."

"Not true." I lean down and peck her forehead. "In case you haven't noticed, I feel like Superman every time I'm around you." I stop cold when I step inside the bedroom. My eyes dart from one side of the room to the other. "You did all this in just a few days?" I set her down. "Allie, please don't tell me you lifted all those boxes."

"Mia helped. And my brothers. Even Bug brought some stuff in."

I draw back and study her. "Stuff that wasn't hers?"

She pulls her shirt up and over her head. Then she shimmies her skirt to the floor, making me forget what I was asking. I'm not sure how she's become even more beautiful over the past few days, but she has. My gaze shifts to her full breasts that are covered in black lace, then down to her protruding belly, where just beneath is a matching set of panties.

I hastily remove every stitch of my clothing and sit on the bed, drawing her to me so I'm eye level with her chest. When I inhale her scent—a mixture of subtle perfume and pheromones—my cock is instantly hard. They say smell is the strongest of all the senses because of its close connection to memory and emotion. I'd have to agree. Because right now, all kinds of emotions are swirling around inside me. Gratitude. Love. Awe. Desire. Admiration. But the one standing out the most right now? Happiness.

Lowering my head, I place a kiss on her rounded belly. "How did I get so goddamn lucky?" Then I look up into her intense, loving eyes. "Every day with you feels like Christmas."

She runs her hands through the top of my hair, then her lips meet my forehead. "I'm glad to hear I've got you fooled. *I'm* the lucky one."

Hooking my thumbs into the sides of her panties, I ask, "While we're debating which one of us is the luckiest, mind if I remove these?"

Her flirtatious giggle answers the question.

A quick flick of my fingers has her bra joining the panties on the floor. She's standing gloriously naked before me and I take a long moment, allowing my eyes to devour every inch of her body. I want to remember her at every stage of pregnancy, because just when I think she can't get more beautiful, I'm proven wrong.

One of her hands comes between us and works my cock. I'm glad to see she's as impatient as I am after being apart. It's true what they say about the second trimester. How a woman's libido goes into overdrive. And while I don't have any previous personal experience with it, I'd say having twins just heightens it that much further. Because she's been horny. And I fucking loving it. I'm all too eager to help her scratch the itch whenever she needs me to. Especially since I know it may not last.

She pushes me back onto the bed and climbs on top of me, straddling me and rubbing her wetness along my stiff erection. I can tell she's about to sink herself onto me, so I lift her off and move her to the side. "You first," I say, dipping my head to her chest. "Always you first."

The sounds emanating from her when I suck on her nipple have me reeling. Holy shit, I love how she's not afraid to let me know she likes what I'm doing to her.

I kiss down her body, tickling and teasing with my tongue until I hit the apex of her thighs. She's practically coming by the time my lips meet her clit. I pull away for a second. "Not yet."

She groans and I laugh.

Damn, she smells good. Whatever these pregnancy hormones are doing to her, it has her smelling and tasting even better than before. It makes me want to keep her pregnant until the end of time.

When my tongue flicks across her nub, her back arches. When my fingers find their way inside her, she moans loudly. When I finally make her come, she shouts my name and I feel like the most powerful man in the universe.

I nestle into her side, allowing her a minute to recover.

She takes my hand and presses it to her stomach. I chuckle. "Do you think they like it when you come, or are they kicking in protest?"

She sighs happily and climbs on top of me. "Don't know. Don't care. But *I* like it when you make me come, and I'd be most appreciative if you'd do it again."

I undulate my hips beneath her. "Your wish is my command."

Before the last word leaves my mouth, she lowers herself onto my cock. My eyes close at the exquisite feeling of being inside her. How the two of us fit together, as if made precisely for each other, is beyond my comprehension. I've been with my share of women in my life. Never has one of them had me believing in soulmates. Or destiny. Or forever. Until Allie.

It's her.

The words bounce around in my head like a pinball. The same two words I've felt before. If I'm being honest, I heard them the moment we met. It was like being hit with a sledgehammer. All the misconceptions I'd ever felt about women and relationships just exploded right out of me. Instead, I was filled with a sense of completeness I'd only experienced one other time in my life—the moment I first held my daughter.

"I love you."

She stops moving and gazes down into my eyes. "Good, because I think you're stuck with me."

"I don't think you understand." I reach up and put my hands on either side of her face. "I really fucking love you. I love you so much it hurts when we're not together. Hell, I love you so much it hurts even when we *are*." I trace a finger down her jaw then take her hand and place it over my heart. "You own me, Allie Montana. Heart and fucking soul. Right down to every decision I make and each breath I take. My heartbeats belong to you. My heart beats *for* you. *Because* of you. I'm talking forever here. More than forever. Eternity." I pull her head toward mine. "You are my beginning and my end. My ebb and my flow. My heaven and my hell."

She cocks her brow as a tear falls onto my chest. "Your hell?"

"Yes, my hell. Because if I ever had to live without you, that's what my life would be." I urge her lips closer. "You are everything." A faint chuckle works its way out of me as her mouth brushes against mine. "I'm not sure why I needed to tell you all this right here and now. I didn't mean to ruin the moment."

I can taste her salty tears when she says, "You didn't ruin anything. In fact, this will be a moment I always remember." She kisses me softly then pulls away. "All of what you just said, I feel it too. I feel it like a freight train, Asher."

"Marry me," I command.

"I will." She touches her fingers to my lips. "I promise."

It's not an acceptance. But it's enough. It's enough for now.

A gush of air exhales through my nose, because I know I'm lying to myself. It's *not* enough. It'll never be enough. I will never be able to get enough of this woman, not even when she's wearing my ring and bearing my name. It's a primal, visceral feeling that guts me to my very core.

I do the only thing I can in this moment to make my physical craving catch up to my emotional one—I flip her over, sink myself into her and make love to her. I make love to her so sweetly, so tenderly, so passionately, I swear by the end of it, I've met the Almighty Lord himself.

Chapter Thirty-five

Asher

I glance out the back window. "She's at it again with Christian."

Allie cranes her head to see. "There are worse things than Bug playing soccer with Christian every day."

I study the two teens. *Playing* soccer is a stretch. With Christian's mobility limitations, he pretty much stands there and kicks the ball when she sends it his way.

"She used to do this with Mel, you know. They were on a rec team together for a few years when they were younger."

"You should be happy she's making friends."

I scoff. "You mean friend. As in singular. Even with all our attempts to introduce her to every other teen in Calloway Creek, he's the one she clings to."

"He's a great kid, Asher. And it's nice that she's not staying locked up in her room texting Mel all hours of the day like she did last month."

"I suppose."

I watch Christian through the glass, amazed at his determination. His drive to be so confident and cheerful in the face of his disability.

His dad, Carter, and I have become friends despite Allie not holding him in high regard—other than raising the amazing kid he's raising. But I think that just stems back to some old family feud. It's still a bit confusing why she's best friends with Mia but has an aversion to her brothers, even her twin, Dax.

Oh, right… Mia is a twin.

"Has Mia given you any pointers on having twins?"

She laughs, taking our dirty breakfast dishes to the sink. "Mia *is* a twin. She didn't *raise* twins. Big difference. If you want to know about all the mischief she and Dax got into as kids, then, yeah, I have a lot of stories. Other than that…"

I rub my brow. "No, no. I don't want to know. I'd rather live in ignorant bliss thinking our kids will be little angels."

"What fun is that?" She sets down the dish she's rinsing. "You're not going to be the kind of dad who doesn't let his kids get into a bit of trouble now and again, are you? It's all part of growing up."

"You're going to have to cut me a break. My only experience has been with Bug, who's been the perfect kid." I hear my own words and backtrack. "Present circumstances notwithstanding. I mean, the most rebellious thing she's ever done was take an Uber without my permission."

"The most rebellious, huh?" She takes the seat next to me. "How about the texts she sent to the women you were dating? The note with the flowers. The pool incident? The—"

I close my eyes. "Okay, I get it. So she's not perfect."

Allie grabs my hand and rubs it gently. "No child is perfect, Asher. All we can do is try to give them the proper tools to deal with whatever comes their way. You're a wonderful father. And Darla is a good kid. You should be proud."

"Proud, huh?" He gazes back outside. "I'm not proud of the way she treats you."

"It's not as bad as it was. At least she eats dinner with us now."

"We've been living in Calloway Creek for weeks, and all we have to show for it is that she eats dinner with us? I'm doing this all wrong."

"You're doing nothing wrong. You're letting her accept things at her own pace. Believe me, that's better than forcing it on her."

I turn and look her right in the eyes. "But sweetheart, I want to marry you. At this rate I'll be old and gray before that happens."

She touches my temple. "Who says you already aren't?"

I laugh. She takes every opportunity to joke about our age difference. It doesn't bother me, though. It just reminds me how lucky I am to have her.

"Speaking of that, how would you like to celebrate your upcoming birthday?"

I shrug. "Forty-one isn't that important."

"Every birthday is important."

"Well then…" I wrap an arm around her and whisper in her ear, "I'd like to celebrate by making love to my beautiful—"

I stop talking. Because what I want to say is *wife*. Or at the very least… *fiancée*. But I can't. Because the woman I love, who is carrying my babies and sleeping in my bed, is nothing more than my girlfriend. I pick up her hand off my thigh and trace her finger. "I can't fucking wait to put a ring on this finger. Maybe that's what I want for my birthday."

"One, your birthday is only a month away, so I believe that will take a miracle. And two, if I'm still capable of making love by then, that will also be a miracle."

"It'll still be possible," I say with a grin. "Believe me, I've googled ways."

She caresses her stomach. "Maybe if I were only carrying one. Asher, I'll be as big as a dump truck by then. I'm already waddling around. I can't understand how you can even be turned on."

"I'm turned on alright." I run a knuckle along her cheekbone. "Every damn time I look at you."

She smiles and leans in to kiss me when the back door flies open.

"Gross." Bug slips off her shoes and motions to Allie's middle. "Haven't you done that enough?"

Allie hops up as quickly as a pregnant woman can and resumes doing the dishes.

This time, I get up too and take over. "Let me do this. You need to get ready for work." I kiss her cheek and push her toward the hallway.

"I can do the dishes," Bug says. "You can finish your coffee."

I smile, wishing Allie were still in the room to see that Darla can in fact be an incredibly kind person. When I turn to what I think will be an empty doorway, I see Allie hasn't left the room. She's standing, watching Bug do the dishes. But the expression on her face isn't pride like mine. It's something else. If I'm not mistaken, it's almost as if she's annoyed that my daughter is doing a chore. She shakes her head slightly, never looking over at me, then walks away.

"I'm thinking of trying out for the soccer team."

Bug's declaration rips me from my thoughts and stuns me into silence. I wonder if I heard her correctly. "Um… what?"

She turns off the water and dries her hands on a dish towel. "Christian says in small towns like this, you don't have to be very good to get on the team. He said last year some girl made the cheerleading squad without even being able to do the splits."

"Hold on." I try to gather my thoughts. "Don't you have to attend the school for the team you're trying out for?"

"Technically, no. Homeschooled kids are allowed to be on sports teams in the school they're zoned for. But…" She shrugs. "I'm thinking about going."

It's not even nine in the morning and she's dropped two unexpected bombs on me. Good bombs in the overall scheme of things. Still, my jaw is in my lap. "You're going to attend Calloway Creek High School. *And* you're trying out for soccer?"

She spins back around and turns on the faucet. "I said I was *thinking* about those things."

Knowing how fragile this situation is, I decide not to push it or get too excited about it. We still have six weeks until school starts. Lucky her, she got an extra-long summer as school in New York starts much later than school in Florida. Here, they don't start until after Labor Day. Which is another reason not to count my chickens. That's a lot of time for her to change her mind about everything.

"Christian said the tryouts are next month, but practices start next week for anyone who wants to go. It's not official practice because coaches aren't allowed to hold practices outside of the season. But he said it's like a thing that all the girls who are going to try out get together and play a few times a week leading up to tryouts, and that players from the previous year's team lead the practice. What do you think I should do?"

"I think Christian sure seems to know a lot about the girls' high school soccer team."

She shrugs. "He's like the equipment boy or something."

I raise a brow. "For the girls' soccer team?"

"And the boys lacrosse and baseball teams."

"But he's not even a student at the high school yet."

"It's something about his dad knowing the athletic director and how he tends to get a lot of favors because people feel sorry for him."

"People feel sorry for his dad?"

She shakes her head matter-of-factly. "People feel sorry for *him*. Because of his cerebral palsy."

"And he's okay with that?"

She picks up the dish towel and starts drying plates. "Christian is smart, Dad. Like super smart. He wants to become a mechanical engineer. That doesn't mean fixing cars like his dad, that means actually designing engines and stuff. And he says that if people pity him and that pity results in him getting what he wants, like maybe getting into one of the top engineering schools in New York, then why should he care what people think?"

"How does that have anything to do with him being the equipment boy for sports teams?"

She giggles. "I guess it doesn't. I was just pointing out that people let him do stuff because they think he's some charity case or something."

"That's kind of disgusting, Bug. He should be treated just like everyone else. You know, within the scope of his abilities."

"Hey, if it doesn't bother him, it shouldn't bother you."

I cock my head. "Is that why you hang out with him so much? Because you feel sorry for him?"

She scoffs, adding another plate to the pile. "I think you have that backwards. I'm *his* charity case."

I give her a hard stare.

"What? It's true."

Allie reappears in the kitchen, ready for work. She grabs an apple off the counter, and I try not to grin or mention how she just ate thirty minutes ago.

"I'll walk you out." I follow her into the garage and shut the door. "Bug might try out for the soccer team. And she's considering going to Cal Creek High School." I rub my temples. "My head is sort of exploding right now." But when I look down at her, she doesn't seem surprised at all. "Why do I feel this isn't news to you?"

"Mia told me a few days ago. She takes Christian out for dinner once a week."

"And you didn't think it was important enough to tell me?"

She opens the passenger door and tosses her shoulder bag inside. "I thought it was more important that you hear it from Bug when she was ready to tell you."

"I'm calling bullshit. You just didn't want to break confidence and have her think poorly of you."

"You mean *more* poorly."

I pull her to me. "Al…"

"She's thirteen, Asher. For all I know, she was going to change her mind. I didn't want to get your hopes up. And yeah, maybe I didn't want to tell you because she'd be mad at me and Mia, and maybe even Christian. She has kind of a good thing going here, if you hadn't noticed."

"With her one friend?"

"How many friends did she have back in Florida?"

I shake my head. "Yeah, okay. You're right. And maybe this soccer thing will be good for her. At least she'll be around other girls and may end up with a few friends out of it."

She leans up to kiss me. "I have to go. Don't want to be late. Who knows how long I'll be able to keep working full time."

I chuckle. "Good thing you have an in with your bosses." I tilt my head when something occurs to me. "You know, we've never talked about what's going to happen after the babies come. Are you planning on working?"

She cracks a grin. "You want me home, barefoot and pregnant?"

"No. Or yes, if that's what *you* want. It's really up to you."

"I can't imagine not working. I mean, I have Natasha and I know she'll be a huge help. And maybe I won't want to work full time when they're little. But honestly, I just don't know yet. Like you said, good thing I know the bosses." Then her eyes narrow. "You said you'd want me barefoot and pregnant if that's what I wanted. Do you mean to tell me you want *more* kids after these?"

"Baby, I'll take as many as you want to give me." I lean in and sweep my lips across hers. "But how about we just start with these and take it from there?" I open the car door for her. "Drive safely, you're carrying a lot of precious cargo."

"I will. You guys have a good day. Don't work too hard. And don't worry about Bug. Everything that's happening is good. She's growing up."

"Yeah." My eyes close for a brief second. "That's exactly what I'm worried about."

Chapter Thirty-six

Allie

Asher is out of town again, for the entire week no less, and Bug is either depressed about it or is rethinking her decision to attend school rather than do it online. She's left the confines of her room even less than normal these past few days, not even to hang out with Christian.

Browsing through Truman's Grocery, I'm wondering what food I can get to lure Darla to the dinner table. Ever since the urn incident, she seems to have a bit of a softer side when it comes to the babies, but that doesn't necessarily extend over to me. When Asher is around, she's cordial at best, but when he's not, she keeps her distance. We live in the same house, but the two of us might as well be worlds apart.

"Allie!"

I turn away from the rotisserie chickens to see Ava Criss pushing her cart over. Instinctively, I try to camouflage my belly the best I can, but at twenty-four weeks, it's pretty much a losing battle.

Her eyes never stray from my baby bump as she approaches. "Wow, I haven't seen you in a while. You look great."

Don't touch your stomach, Allie, I repeat over and over in my head. Don't touch your stomach.

It's a habit all pregnant women have. And it's really, really hard not to do it, especially since one of the babies is jabbing me in the ribs right now.

"Thanks. So do you. I love your new highlights."

"I'm trying different things out. Trevor's coming home early next year. I've started working out and eating right."

"It shows. You look fantastic."

She moves a few things around in the top of her cart. "It's going to be strange having him home all the time. For seven years, we've never had more than a few weeks together. And that doesn't even count when he was away at college. It's exciting and scary at the same time. What if he's changed? What if I have?"

I step closer and put a hand on her forearm. "Ava, you and Trev have been together since you were, what, thirteen? You guys are perfect for each other. Sure, life experience may have changed how you perceive the world, but not who you are inside."

She nods. "You're right. I'm being silly." She eyes my stomach again. "And with any luck, by this time next year, I might look like you do now."

"Hopefully you won't be quite this big." *Now* I touch my belly. "Carrying two is no picnic."

"You make it look easy. And I'd carry an entire litter if it meant getting to be a mom."

I laugh. Then wince when one of the babies stomps on my bladder.

Her eyes go wide. "Are they moving?"

"I think the boy is dancing on my bladder."

"Can I?... Would you mind?"

Ava and I aren't the closest of friends, more like we're in each other's outer circles. She and her friend group are older than me and my friend group. But we're tied together by a lot of people. And her best friend is married to my brother. Which is why she was there when I told everyone about Christopher.

I grab her hand and put it where the baby is moving.

Tears flood her eyes. "I'll never get over this. I think it's the thing I crave the most, feeling life inside me."

"With Trevor being home full-time soon, I'm sure it will happen."

"Well, I'm not getting any younger, and it can't happen soon enough. It amazes me how easily some people get pregnant."

"I'm sorry. You must hate me."

"God, no. I envy you. But Allie, I'm happy for you. Believe me when I say that. Especially after what you've gone through." Her jaw goes slack. "Oh my gosh, I really felt that one."

"I think the girl is doing flips and the boy isn't happy about it."

"You know which one is which?"

I nod and move her hand lower. "She's more down there. He's on top. They've pretty much been like that the whole time."

She scoffs. "Typical guy, wanting to be king of the hill."

I laugh.

Reluctantly, like maybe she could stand here and do this all day long, her hands fall away. "Well, I'd better get going before the milk spoils."

"It was really nice seeing you, Ava."

"You too."

After she leaves, I run into at least four more shoppers, and every one touches my stomach like it's public property. *This* is why I left town the first time. But now, even if I don't know the person well, I try not to let it bother me. Because this time is different. I'm savoring every kick. Enjoying every curious touch. Thanking every well-wisher. But mostly… I'm loving how it feels to be able to dream about a future I never thought possible.

~ ~ ~

"Dinner!" I call up the stairs.

"Not hungry!"

Disappointed she won't even come down for her favorite meal, I eat in solitude then make her a plate anyway, write her name on the tin foil, and put it front and center in the fridge hoping she'll change her mind.

I'm just about done with the dishes when the doorbell rings.

Our front door has three small square windows just above eye level, so I rise on my toes and peer through to see Christian on the stoop. I open the door.

"Hi, Miss Allie."

"Hello, Christian."

"Is, um, Bug here?"

"She is. Would you like to come in and I'll get her?"

I hold the door open and he comes through.

"Have you eaten? I made lasagna, and with Asher away, there's a lot."

"No thanks. We had burgers."

I point to the couch. "You can wait there okay?"

"Thanks, ma'am."

I chuckle. "Not ma'am. Just Allie. I'll be right back. Make yourself at home."

Deciding not to yell in front of a guest, I trudge to the top of the stairs, completely out of breath from the short climb when I knock.

"I said I'm not hungry!"

"Darla, you have a visitor. Christian is here."

"Tell him I'm sick," she answers in a muffled voice, then I hear footsteps and the slamming of her bathroom door.

I carefully navigate down the stairs and find Christian sitting at the kitchen bar staring at the cookies I made earlier. I pick up the plate and offer him one.

"I'm sorry. Darla isn't feeling well."

He takes a cookie and picks at it. "She's been saying that all week. She hasn't shown up for practice since Monday."

My eyebrows shoot up. "She hasn't?" I pour a glass of milk, and push it across the bar to him, sparing a glance to her stairway. I don't exactly keep tabs on her. I do work almost every day, and I take a lot of naps. And she *is* thirteen—a confusing age if I recall. But I had no idea she'd quit playing soccer. Maybe she really is sick.

"No. I just hope she hasn't changed her mind about tryouts. They're next week."

"I'm sure it's nothing. The flu maybe." But in my mind, I'm running through everything it could be. When I've seen her, which hasn't been often, she hasn't looked physically ill. But now that I think of it, something is most definitely off. I've been attributing it to anxiety over all the upcoming events in her life. Or depression over being stuck with me for the week. But could there be more to it? I sigh. I'm totally failing at this stepmom thing—or whatever it may be.

Christian finishes his cookie, drains his glass, then stands. "Thank you for the snack, Miss Allie."

"My pleasure. I'm sure Bug will feel better soon." I follow him to the front door. "Christian?"

He looks back at me with a questioning stare.

"Is she any good at soccer? She never wants us to go to practices, and she's pretty much forbidden us from attending tryouts."

"Honestly? She's not great, but she doesn't totally suck either. I'd say there's a good chance she'll make the team, because there are a lot more girls who suck way worse than her." His face reddens. "I didn't mean… I probably shouldn't have said suck, because she doesn't, and those other girls don't really either… I just meant…" He shakes his head, clearly flustered. "I think I'll just go now if that's okay."

I hold in my laughter. "Yes. It's okay. And yes, I know what you meant. Bye, Christian."

As soon as he leaves, I'm slogging back up the stairs again. Dang, it's getting harder to do this.

I knock on her door. There's no answer.

"Darla? Do you need to see a doctor?"

"I didn't say I *am* sick, I said *tell* him I'm sick."

I lean against the door. "Did something happen between you and Christian?"

"No."

"If something did, you can tell me."

"Nothing happened!"

"Then why have you been hiding up here for days?"

"I like my private space."

"But you've missed going to soccer practice."

"Are you checking up on me?"

"Christian was worried. He asked why you haven't been showing up."

She doesn't answer, she just turns on music.

I pound on her door. "Darla, can we please talk about this like adults?"

The volume increases even more.

I pound harder then press my palms against the door and raise my voice. "I'm worried about you. Is it tryouts? School? Have you changed your mind? Sweetie, you should talk to someone about it."

Stomping feet cross the floor. "Do *not* call me sweetie!"

The door flies open unexpectedly, and with all my weight against it, I fall into the room. At the last second, just before I hit the floor, I stretch out my arms hoping to break my fall. But my stomach protrudes too much and it hits first, maybe not as hard as if I hadn't used my hands, but hard enough. I immediately roll to the side and cradle my belly.

Darla looks down at me in horror. "Oh my god. I didn't know you were against the door. Are you okay? Should I call an ambulance?"

Still stunned, I crawl over and lean against the wall, trying to catch my breath. I put a hand over my stomach where each twin should be and pray to feel something… anything. I press down. When I feel movement from up top, I breathe a small sigh of relief. But I don't feel anything below, despite poking her a few times.

"No. No ambulance. But can you get my phone? I think it's in the kitchen."

Looking as guilty as sin, she rushes down. When she's back and handing it to me, she says, "You're calling my dad, aren't you?" She sinks to the floor a few feet away. "I'm going to get into so much trouble for this."

"I'm not calling your dad."

I dial Hudson's number. He answers on the third ring. "Everything okay, Allie?"

"I'm sorry to bother you after hours, but I just fell down."

"How did you fall, and did you hit your stomach?"

I tell him what happened, leaving out the part about Darla ripping open the door.

"Are you bleeding?"

"I don't think so."

"Have you felt any movement?"

"Yes." I lower my voice, not wanting Bug to feel worse than she clearly does. "But only from one. Hudson, I'm totally freaked out here. What if—" I can't even get myself to say it. "Should I go to the hospital?"

"Do you think you can drive?"

"Yeah. I think so. I mean I feel fine physically."

"Meet me at my office. I'll do an ultrasound."

I'm relieved he's not dismissing me as just being a nervous mom-to-be. Because in all honesty, I did downplay how hard I hit the floor in an attempt to not freak out Darla.

"Thanks, Hudson. I'll leave right now." I hang up and tell Bug where I'm going.

She stares at my belly. "Do you think…"

"I don't think anything. I just want to be sure. Will you be okay here?"

She nods, guilt eating away at her features.

"Hopefully I won't be gone too long. There's lasagna in the fridge if you get hungry, and I made cookies."

I'm trying to make it seem like everything is okay, like I'm not screaming on the inside over all the things that could be wrong. What if one of the placentas has a tear? What if I fell right on one of their heads? What if I'm going to go into early labor?

But I hold off on showing any emotion in front of Darla, making it all the way to my car before breaking down in sobs. The last three months have been pure bliss. Is the other shoe about to drop?

I let myself cry for just a brief minute. Then I check my pants again for any bleeding. There isn't any, thank goodness, and I finally back out of the garage, saying a little prayer.

Actually, it's a huge prayer.

It's *all* the prayers.

Chapter Thirty-seven

Allie

When I return home an hour later, Darla is at the kitchen table, folding a load of Asher's laundry. She looks relieved but guarded when I enter. I'm sure she understands if something were wrong, I wouldn't be back so soon.

"Everything's okay," I say, taking the seat across from her. "I'm fine. The babies are fine."

She doesn't make eye contact. "I didn't know you were behind the door."

I want to reach across the table and touch her hand, because the way she looks right now is like the weight of the world is on her shoulders.

"Darla, it's not your fault. How could you have known I was leaning on the door? If it's anyone's fault, it's mine. I was trying to get you to open the door, yet I was putting all my weight against it. It was stupid of me. But listen, everything is okay."

She stares at my stomach over the pile of laundry. "You swear?"

"I swear." I pull out a few pictures of the babies Hudson took during the ultrasound and slide them across the table. "See?"

She stops folding one of Asher's shirts and looks at the pictures. I'm not even sure she realizes the huge sigh of relief that leaves her lungs.

"You do too much for your dad," I say, pulling the shirt over and folding it. "You shouldn't be home doing laundry and cleaning up after your father. You should be going to the movies and eating ice cream."

"You say that like there's anyone to do it with."

"There was someone here earlier who I'm sure would love to do all those things with you. Or how about some of the girls you've been playing soccer with?"

"They all think I'm a freak."

"Darla, I'm going to be honest here. I think the only one who thinks you're a freak is you. Yes, you're the new girl in town. And maybe they need time to get to know you. But I'm telling you right now, if you believe you're a freak… well, have you ever heard of a self-fulfilling prophecy?"

She shakes her head.

"It means if you believe something about yourself hard enough, it's likely to come true."

"That's crap. So if I believe I'm as good as Mia Hamm, I'll suddenly be some star soccer sensation?"

"Well, sometimes they can be positive, but more often, they're negative. A self-fulfilling prophecy is a belief that influences behavior, which in turn makes the belief come true. In your case, you think you're unworthy of friendship, so you may be putting out signals to support that. You're expecting people to reject you. That leads to withdrawn behavior which can push away potential friends."

"So now you're a philosopher?"

"It has nothing to do with philosophy. More like sociology or psychology."

"Whatever."

Aaaand, there she is.

"Anyway, I just wanted you to be aware that if you act a certain way because you think you are something you aren't, it can and will affect how others see and interact with you." I pull over the entire laundry basket. "Let me do this. You shouldn't have to."

She snatches it back. "I know how he likes it."

"Okay. Why don't you teach me?"

"It's just easier for me to do it."

"Darla, I'm not trying to take your place, you know."

She practically doubles over, clenching her stomach. Then, clearly in pain, gets up from the table. "I'm going to bed."

My eyes go wide when I see the red stain on the back of her shorts. "Darla!"

She turns and spouts, "What?"

Suddenly, everything over the past few days begins to make sense. I motion to her shorts. "You've gotten your period."

Embarrassed, she tries to look behind her but can't see the stain. Then her eyes catch on the chair she vacated where a small smear of blood remains. Looking horrified, she runs to the stairs, taking them two at a time. I contemplate not following her—I *have* climbed them a lot today—but she's obviously in need of a little support.

I pause at her door, not wanting to open it and invade her space. I'm sure it's locked anyway. I knock softly. "Darla? Why don't you hand me your soiled clothes and I'll get them soaking." I chuckle, wanting to add levity to the situation. "Wow, you know, this explains a lot about the past few days. I thought maybe you were re-thinking the whole school thing. Do you always get cramps that bad?"

"I don't know!" she shouts from what seems the far end of the room, or maybe the bathroom. "I've never had it before. Now leave me alone!"

Shocked, I sit on the top step. She's never had it before? As in this is her very first period? She's thirteen—fourteen in less than six months. I was eleven when I got mine.

She's going to need someone to talk to. Maybe I should call Asher. But even as close as they are, I'm not sure that's the way to go. Marti maybe?

I hear Bug's shower running so I go downstairs and pick at a cookie as I call Marti. It goes to voicemail, and I decide not to leave a message. Then I convince myself that calling anyone else would be a mistake. Darla might be upset with me if I did. If this is her first period, she's probably embarrassed and confused, not to mention hormonal.

Fifteen minutes later, I hear the water stop upstairs so I trek back up yet again. But before I can knock, I hear her voice. Her phone must not be on speaker because I only hear one side of the conversation.

"I don't have anything, Mel. And Aunt Marti isn't answering her phone."

"I'm not about to go to the store."

"No way am I asking her. She's pregnant. She won't even have that stuff."

Blowing out a long sigh, because I've now done this far more than any pregnant woman should have to, I descend the stairs, head to my bathroom, and gather various size pads I've accumulated over the years along with the smallest size tampons I can find. I fish around my underwear drawer until I find a pair of brand-new period underwear I'd never gotten around to opening. I put it all in a small box and head back up to Darla's room.

No longer hearing her on the phone, I knock. "I have some things you might need. Can I come in?"

"Just leave it by the door."

I contemplate doing just that. But she seems pretty freaked out. Has no one ever talked to her about this? Until I know, I can't just leave her to fend for herself.

"It would be nice if I could come in and show it to you."

She laughs disingenuously. "You want to give me a demonstration?"

"I just thought I could explain some stuff. You know, in case nobody has. I mean, we're sort of lucky if you think about it. When my mom was my age, it wasn't so easy. Now they have underwear and even swimsuits that are more absorbent than tampons."

The door opens hastily, but at least this time she doesn't practically rip it off the hinges. I guess the thought of watching me fall on my face two times in one day doesn't excite her.

"Easy? I have to bleed between my legs every month until I'm what… sixty? And I don't even want kids." She shakes her head, then takes the box from me and sifts through it.

"You don't have to have a period every month."

Now I seem to have gotten her interest, though she still doesn't respond.

"There are pills you can take that will allow you to go a long time between periods. But it's birth control, and I'm not about to counsel you on that."

"How can I get it? Can your doctor give it to me without Dad knowing?" She cocks her head showing a hint of excitement. "Can you take me?"

"Hold on. It's hardly my place—"

"Oh, right. You're living with my dad. You're trying to be my friend or whatever. You want to marry him, right? But you don't want to help me with this one little thing."

"It's not little. This is a big deal. It's your first period. I'm kind of surprised you haven't had one until now. Has nobody spoken with you about this?"

She shrugs. "Aunt Marti sat me down about five years ago. Mel got hers when she was ten, but she didn't warn me about all this. She claimed it was no big deal."

I lean against the wall, my feet hurting from all the up and down, but I don't presume I'm welcome in her room enough to take a seat. "It's different for everyone. Some women get bad cramps, some get migraines, some get nauseous. But a lot of women, like Mel, don't have any problems their time of the month. I'm somewhere in between. I'll usually get a bit depressed and crave chocolate. I do a lot of binge-watching TV." I nod to the box in her hands. "Do you want me to show you how to use any of that?"

"I'm not stupid."

"Of course not. It just might be confusing to figure out what sizes you need. If you choose to use tampons, always use the smallest size that will work. And never ever leave it in longer than eight hours. You could get really sick from something I can't remember the name of."

She rolls her eyes. "Great. More crap to worry about."

"Believe me, you'll get used to it after a few months. You'll figure out what works the best. My advice, be sure to always carry a few things in your school backpack. And when it's approaching your time, wearing period underwear or a small pad might ease your mind."

One of the babies kicks hard, and I rub my stomach with a small wince.

Her eyes follow the motion. "Dad's going to be so pissed at me."

"That you got your period?"

"That I made you fall."

"Not your fault. It's forgotten. I'm fine and there's no reason he should know. Now, do you have any questions?"

She sighs. "I just want to go to bed."

"I get it. But at least let me wash out your clothes."

"I threw them away."

"Those shorts are really cute on you. It would be a waste to get rid of them." I hold my hand out. "Please let me do this for you."

She hesitates, then puts the box down, walks into the bathroom, and comes out with her trash can, looking more than a little embarrassed.

"It's nothing to be ashamed of." I reach in and get her shorts and underwear in a way that I hope shows her it's not disgusting, but just a fact of life. "Some peroxide and a little soaking will have these looking as good as new." I turn and head out the door. "Get some sleep. You know where I am if you need anything."

Once I'm at the bottom of the stairs, I hear my name being called. I look up and Darla's door is cracked just enough so I can see her face.

"Thanks," she says, the word coming out with zero inflection and little emotion, like it's the hardest word she's ever had to say to anyone ever.

But that's not the point. The point is, she said it.

"Anytime."

Her door slams shut before she can see the magnificent smile spread across my face.

Chapter Thirty-eight

Asher

Allie tugs on my shirt, pulling me back behind the school concession stand. "She'll see you."

I'm more than a little surprised she even wanted to come with me considering what day it is. Today would have been Christopher's tenth birthday. I know she knows it. She's been quieter than normal. More introspective. And she's spent most of the day by herself. But now she's here. For *my* daughter. God, how I love this woman.

I take a step behind the small building and wipe my sweaty palms on my pants. "Looks like she's up next for the free kick."

"She's doing great. Much better than I anticipated after Christian alluded to her 'sucking but not sucking as much as some of the other girls'."

"Alluded?" I raise a brow.

"Well, not so much alluded as told me outright."

I peek out. "He thinks she sucks? That's a shitty thing to say."

"He didn't say it to her. I flat out asked him if she was any good. He said she 'doesn't totally suck' and is probably decent enough to make the team. But he said it in the nicest way possible."

A shout comes from across the field. "Yes! Way to go, Bug!"

I look over to see that Darla has made her first free kick and Christian is celebrating. I watch intently as she makes two of the next four attempts. Christian celebrates each successful kick. I turn to Allie. "Why am I so goddamn jealous of a thirteen-year-old boy right now?"

"Because you want to be the one down there cheering for her."

"How is she okay having him there but not me?"

"She probably thinks you'll embarrass her."

I motion to Christian. "More than that?"

"Friends cheering on friends is different than a parent cheering for a child."

I shake my head. "I don't care what she says. If she makes the team, I'll be at every game."

Allie squeezes my arm. "I will be too. Do you know when they'll post the results?"

"Not for a few days. I hope she's okay and doesn't get depressed like she was last week. Do you think that was soccer related, or school related? I could barely get her to respond to my texts let alone talk to me on the phone."

She draws in a long breath and lets it slip out between her lips. "I'm going to break the girl code here because as her dad you should know."

I'm not sure I like the sound of that. "Ah, shit. Is she dating? Is there a boy I need to be worried about?" I brace myself for unwanted news. "Is it Christian?"

"Nothing like that. Bug had her very first period last week when you were gone."

My eyes snap to hers. "What do you mean her very first period?"

"I mean, she'd never had one before." Her eyes narrow. "How do you not know this being as involved in her life as you've been? Don't you think she'd be asking you to buy products if she'd been having her period?"

I scrub a hand across my jaw. "I guess I just assumed she was using her allowance to get that stuff. And Marti said she took care of 'the talk' a long time ago."

"Yeah, about five years ago. I'm sure at that age it went in one ear and out the other."

My eyebrows meet in the middle. "Shouldn't this have happened long before now?"

"It did for me, but I looked it up, it's perfectly normal. But she wasn't prepared and was pretty embarrassed."

"She shouldn't be."

"It's not unusual. She'll get used to it soon enough. But don't be surprised if she asks to go on birth control."

My jaw drops so low it almost hits my belt. "I know you didn't just suggest putting my thirteen-year-old on the pill. Jesus, Al."

"To control her period." Her eyes roll. "Being on the pill makes it more predictable, which is super important for teenagers who are planning trips to the pool and sleepovers."

"But… it's like giving her permission to…" I can't even say the words.

"Calm down." She touches my shoulder. "This is something every parent of girls needs to deal with sooner or later. I'm not saying do it now. I'm just saying it's probably going to come up and I wanted you to be prepared."

I sink against the wall of the concession stand. "I'm not sure if I should be happy she wasn't reconsidering her choice to attend school, or sad that my little girl is growing up."

Allie chuckles. "I think you're allowed both." She runs a hand across her belly. "And oh joy, we get to do it all over again when this little girl hits puberty."

Christian's cheers hit my ears again and I look out once more. But when my eyes land on Darla dribbling the ball across the field, it's like I'm seeing her in a whole new light. I'm not sure why, because I assumed she'd been having her period for some time now. But my daughter, my little Bug, has somehow just grown up right before my eyes.

"We should go." I tug on Allie's hand. "It looks like they're wrapping up and we don't want to get caught."

Back at the car, I sit in the driver's seat, still feeling as if my head is spinning, when something occurs to me. I look over at Allie. "How did you know? Wait… did she tell you?"

Before I can get too excited about Darla sharing that monumental moment with Allie, she says, "I was there when it happened. There was a little blood. I gave her some supplies and washed her clothes. I'm not sure I'd have known otherwise."

Those last few words have her looking sad. It kills me that we've been living together as a family for months now but Bug isn't treating her much differently. It's true, she isn't getting in the digs she used to… at least I don't think so. But who knows what goes on between them when I'm not around.

I put a hand on her thigh. "I'd hoped that my time away would somehow bring the two of you closer together."

She shrugs. "We're making a little progress. Baby steps are better than no steps at all."

She reaches into her purse and pulls out a granola bar, munching on it on the way home. I smile when she hiccups a few times after. She's so darn cute when she hiccups. By the time we're pulling into the garage, she's laughing.

"What is it?" I ask.

"Baby girl has the hiccups."

She takes my hand and sets it low on her belly where I feel incremental little jerks. "Does he get them too?"

"Sometimes. Not as much as she does."

I look into her eyes. "I hope she's just like you. Beautiful. Fun. Kind."

She smiles, the gleam of a tear in her eye. "And I hope he's just like you. Charming and thoughtful."

I open my door and race around to help her out. I lower my lips to within an inch of hers. "Come inside. I have something to show you."

She lowers her gaze to my pants. "I've seen it, Asher. Quite a lot." I know she's making a joke, but her smile fades. "And as glorious as it may be, I just don't think I'm in the mood for it today."

"I knew you wouldn't be, considering the date. I have something else in mind."

She narrows her eyes but allows me to help her up and take her inside. When she sees the birthday cake with ten candles on top, a hand flies up to cover her gasp. "Asher."

"I know it's a bit unconventional. But you'll be an Anderson soon if I have anything to say about it. And Andersons celebrate *all* birthdays, even heavenly ones. It's tradition. One I'm sure you heard about from Marti, or maybe Dallas."

She nods. "I had, but I'd completely forgotten." She touches each of the ten candles, one at a time.

"I'm sorry we don't have a picture of Christopher, but you can still light the candles and remember what it was like to hold and love him. You can say a few things about who he would have been."

"I can't believe you remembered the date."

"Babe, when are you going to get it through that pretty little head of yours that I hang onto your every word?" I gesture to the lighter next to the cake. "Can you do the honors?"

Carefully, and with tears pooling in her eyes, she lights each of the candles.

"I *do* have pictures. I never showed Jason. He didn't have the right or privilege to know even a little piece of Christopher." She turns to me with red-rimmed eyes. "Do you want to see them?"

"I'd be honored, sweetheart."

She scrolls through her phone and hands it to me. What I see almost wrecks me. A young, beautiful, devastated Allie is holding what looks to be a totally healthy baby. She isn't looking at whoever's snapping the photo. She's looking down at her son. The love in her eyes practically jumps through the phone and pierces my heart. I know right here and now what an amazing mother she's going to be to our children.

She scrolls to the next photo of Christopher in his hospital bassinet, sleeping peacefully. There's another with Sarah. In the last photo of Allie and the baby, she's in a rocking chair holding him against her chest. A flexible tube snakes over her shoulder and is pointed at his face. Oxygen, I presume. His skin is much more ashen than in the other photos. This one must be shortly before he died.

"Does it hurt to look at these?" I ask.

"I look at them almost every day."

"Does it ever get any better?"

"Are you asking me if time heals all wounds?"

I shrug.

"I've always hated that saying." She scrolls back to the first picture. I think it's her favorite. "Time doesn't *heal* all wounds. Just ask Addy. It's not like her leg grew back after a time. And ask Marti and Dallas and Serenity and anyone else who's lost something this significant. I think they should change the saying to 'time *deals* with all wounds.' That would be more accurate. Because the hole in my heart left by him will never be healed. There's a big ugly scar in its place. And sure, when the babies come, I'll be happy, and maybe I won't even look at these pictures every day. But that won't mean I'm missing him less. It won't mean I still don't dream about the kind of boy he would have been or the man he'd have grown up to be. Christopher will always be my first child. When the twins come, I'll be the mother of three. One of them just happens to be in heaven. So, yeah, time may be helping me deal with his loss in healthier ways, but it will sure as hell never heal me."

"Wow. That's… existential."

She laughs sadly and puts her phone away.

"Tell me about the kind of person Christopher would have been."

"He'd have been like you." She threads our fingers together. "Caring. Protective. Loving. He'd have loved chocolate—that I'm sure of considering how much of it I ate when I was pregnant with him. He'd love playgrounds, especially swings, and he'd swing so high I'd get scared he would fly off. But he never would because he'd hold on tight and say *Don't worry, Mommy*.'" Tears make her eyes sparkle. "He'd have been very smart. But the one thing I'm sure of is that he'd have done something important and altruistic with his life, like become a doctor or firefighter."

"Sounds like someone I'd want to know."

She nods, and lets the tears roll down the sides of her face. I kiss them, wanting to absorb all her pain. Needing to be the one who helps her deal with it. Work her way through it. Live with it in a way that brings her peace.

"Thank you," I whisper into her hair.

"For what?"

"For trusting me with who he was and who he would have been."

She leans up and kisses my cheek. "Help me blow out the candles?"

"On three," I say.

We blow, then I get two forks, handing her one before I dig in, shoving a gigantic bite in my mouth. Her eyes bulge at my lack of manners. After all, I didn't even cut the cake.

She turns up her nose. "We haven't even had dinner yet."

I chuckle. "I'm guessing you missed the part of the tradition where we have to *eat* the cake."

"Oh, okay." She takes a dainty little bite and puts the fork down.

"No, no, no." I pick it back up and hand it to her. "The *whole* cake."

Chapter Thirty-nine

Allie

Every morning, as if by instinct, the very first thing I do is hold completely still and wait for the babies to kick. Some days I don't have to do this, because at seven months pregnant, it's not unusual for one or both to be moving during the night and into the wee hours of the morning. Sleep has become harder to come by with two little ones vying for space as it becomes tighter and tighter. But I'm not complaining. I'll never complain.

The second thing I do is look over on the dresser where the brand-new urn with Christopher's ashes sits atop a mirrored tray. His name and the outline of his tiny footprint are engraved on the front. Next to it, also on top of the mirror, is the picture of Christopher and me that Asher printed four weeks ago after we ate Christopher's entire birthday cake.

I stretch my arm across the empty side of the bed, missing Asher. Pulling his pillow close, I inhale his scent. It's a mixture of his manly body wash, laundry detergent, and something that's just pure him. Can other people smell it, I wonder, or is it some sort of pheromone meant only for me?

More and more lately, I've come to believe Asher is right. That we're meant to be together. That even if it weren't for the babies, we'd have somehow ended up with each other. Maybe not today or tomorrow, but someday. He often says he feels like he knew me before he met me, like something from an old love song. I thought he was just being romantic. But in the back of my mind, far beyond the reaches of my mortal memory, I feel he's onto something.

I may have been spiritual before Christopher, but I've never been a religious person. And I never thought everything happened for a reason. What reason could there possibly be for Christopher having a rare chromosomal anomaly? For Addison losing her leg? For Ava and Trevor not being able to conceive? And there sure as hell couldn't be a reason why Dallas lost his wife and son in a tragic accident.

But this—Asher and me—it niggles away at me that there is a reason for it. And it goes beyond the babies.

Smiling when an elbow or knee jabs me, I poke back. It's near the top of my stomach by my ribs, so I know it's the boy. *The boy.* That's how I've come to think of them. *The boy* and *the girl.* Because somehow, in my hormonal stupidity, I've made others responsible for naming them.

It's hard not to roll my eyes at Bug's outlandish suggestions. I think she's suggested the names of the entire female cast of *Game of Thrones, Dune,* even *The Hobbit.* I never react, which is why she hasn't done it as much lately. A few weeks ago, when she suggested Khaleesi, I simply asked her if the baby girl was going to be the queen, would that make *her* the princess? She stomped away, not at all getting the reaction she'd hoped to get from me.

I have all the confidence in the world that Bug will come up with an appropriate name. And despite Asher's disapproval of the whole situation, I'm dead set on being true to my word and going with whatever she ultimately decides.

Confident after feeling several rolls, kicks, and punches from all sides, I get out of bed, put on my robe, and barely make it to the toilet without peeing all over myself.

I love being pregnant. But one thing I won't miss is having to run to the bathroom every thirty minutes.

I stare in the mirror, replaying the words that just flew through my brain. *I love being pregnant.*

This is what most women experience. The joy and anticipation. The bonding with a baby or babies they know won't be ripped away from existence and reduced to ashes in a jar on their dresser. This is what makes life worth living. And I leave my room with a smile.

My good mood is soured when I enter the kitchen to see Darla sitting on a bar stool slumped over a cup of coffee.

I raise a brow. "Drinking coffee now?"

"I'm in high school, so yeah."

I don't touch that with a ten-foot pole. I'm sure if I did, we'd end up in another meaningless debate or with her storming off like she normally does.

She's been in school for two weeks now. She rarely talks about it. She leaves the house at seven fifty-five every morning without ever needing to be woken up. She returns at six after soccer practice, because thank the Lord for small favors, Christian was right and she made the team. I fear if it weren't for that, she'd be home by three thirty, back in her room on the phone to Mel. Or maybe texting Christian.

I get eggs, milk, and bacon from the refrigerator. I don't bother asking if she wants any. I know what her answer will be. *'Whatever.'* I just make breakfast and set it out without any fanfare. Sometimes she eats it. Sometimes she doesn't.

Waiting on the bacon to cook, I watch as Darla gets a Ziploc bag from a drawer, throws in a granola bar and a banana, and tucks it into her backpack.

I get money from my purse. "Here." I put twenty dollars on the table. "In case your dad forgot to give you lunch money."

She looks at it but doesn't take it. "Nobody pays with cash. He puts money into an account at school. Believe me, there's plenty."

I cock my head. "You don't like school food? I don't remember it being particularly horrible."

She shrugs. "Don't know. Haven't tried it."

I stir the eggs, not wanting to seem overly interested in the conversation because that will usually put an end to it. "Well, if you do, just don't try the pizza. Anything but that. Unless it's a Tuesday and they order in bulk from a pizza chain. Do they still do that on Tuesdays?"

She shrugs again. "Don't know. I've never been in the cafeteria."

"Never?" I turn as my eyes bug out. Then I catch myself and spin back around, making myself busy so I appear much less interested than I actually am.

She doesn't answer, and I don't dare push. I just put out the food and start eating.

"It's pointless to go. Christian and I don't even have the same lunch. He has lunch A and I have lunch B. School pretty much sucks all around because we only have one class together."

"If you don't go to the cafeteria, where do you eat?"

"Courtyard mostly. But when it gets cold I'll be scoping out other places."

"What about the girls from the soccer team? Can't you eat with them?"

She scoffs air through her nose. "Right. Those." She takes a strip of bacon and shoves the entire thing in her mouth. "They're still trying to decide if they like me."

"I'm sure that's not the case. They just need time to warm up to you. Because I'm here to tell you, anyone who knows you will like you, Darla."

She stands, puts her coffee cup in the sink, takes another strip of bacon, and walks out the front door with her backpack.

Damn. I crossed the line into giving parenting advice. I should know by now how anytime that happens, she puts up the wall I've yet to penetrate.

We've had a few conversations. Mostly about things that don't matter much. Like when we're breaking ground on the pool or how Charlie did at T-ball. Conversations may be a stretch—it's more like we share a few sentences here and there. But one thing I've noticed is that she has been more respectful. Quiet and disengaging, but civil all the same. It happened after I fell into her room. I think she still feels guilty over it. I never told Asher, and maybe that's why she doesn't give me as much push-back as before.

I finish breakfast, clean up, and go to work, glad that it's Thursday and Natasha is running the wedding this weekend. Because I'm definitely getting too big, too scatter-brained, and too damn exhausted for such large events.

~ ~ ~

After a long day at work, I go right from the garage into the bedroom, only stopping to pee before I collapse on my bed and fall asleep before I can even think.

Ninety minutes later, feeling more rested, and with my ankles almost back to normal size, I change out of my work clothes, put on something more comfortable, and waddle out into a dark kitchen.

There's no sign of Bug having even been here. No backpack in the corner. No cookies missing from the platter. But it's almost seven. She should have been home by now.

I go back to the bedroom and get my phone. It's now when I see the text.

Darla: Spending the night at Aunt Marti's.

It's not an unusual occurrence. Not even for a weeknight. And it happens at least once every time Asher is away, so I don't really have a problem with it. Not that there's anything I could do if I did. I just wish she didn't feel the need to escape this house when her dad is gone. Maybe once the babies come she'll want to spend more time at home.

Me: Thanks for the text. Your dad will be home by 4 tomorrow.

There's no reply. Not even a thumb's up. I wasn't expecting one.

Still, I sit and stare for a moment, wishing the three dots in the bubble would show up and just once she'd acknowledge my text.

A short time later, I'm sitting at the table, pushing my dinner around my plate. It's not like there's room in my belly to fit any more. It seems like if I eat more than a few bites of food, I get intense heartburn. Which is why I feel like I'm constantly eating just to get enough calories. But this time, my being pregnant is not the real reason for the food pushing.

I'm concerned about Bug.

More than once last week, I heard her telling Asher she doesn't fit in. How she still feels like the new girl and thinks she always will.

I hate to bring it up to her again, but I feel it's her that's the issue. She's putting out the wrong vibes. And sitting by herself in the courtyard is not exactly an invitation to be approached.

Asher and I were hoping after she made the team she'd begin to bond with the other players. But it seems she's sabotaging those efforts without even realizing it.

I get it though. I grew up here, in a town where everyone knows everyone. We'd all picked our friends by the third grade. Sure, there were friend shifts from time to time. I remember when new kids moved to town because it was such a big event. The questions would start the moment the SOLD sign went up out front. Would he be hot? Would she be a bitch? Would he be a star football player who could help us get to the state championship? Would her parents go out of town and leave the liquor cabinet unlocked? And while we all sat back and sized up each new student, eventually they found their place within one group or another. I'm praying that will happen to Bug.

Without anyone here to keep me awake, I go back to bed right after dinner, propping myself up on a mountain of pillows so my few bites of chicken don't try and make their way back up due to the limited space. How am I going to have room for anything a month from now? Two? I rub my belly, marveling at the capacity of the human body to grow to accommodate multiples.

~ ~ ~

My alarm goes off. But it's still dark outside. Really dark. I grumble as I turn to look at the clock. It's only one in the morning. Why is my alarm going off?

Then I realize it's not my alarm. It's my phone. And it's ringing. While I usually put it on silent at night, I never do when Asher is away. Which is why my spine stiffens and my stomach lurches. Why am I being called in the middle of the night? Has something happened to him?

I pick up my phone, but it's not some random number that could potentially be a hospital or police station. It's not Asher's face that appears either. It's Bug's.

"Bug? Uh, I mean Darla?"

She doesn't answer for a second. Maybe she rolled over on her phone while she was sleeping. I almost hang up, but then I hear muffled music in the background. The bass is pounding. I go on high alert because I'm pretty sure Marti and Dallas do not play loud music in the middle of the night.

"Darla, what's wrong?"

"I… I need you to come get me."

At least I think that's what she says. Her words are slurred and she sounds really tired. Maybe she's dream-calling me.

Still confused, I ask, "Come get you? If you're sick, can't Dallas or Marti drive you home?"

She mumbles something unintelligibly through the phone.

"Darla, you need to speak up."

"I can't. I'm in a closet."

I sit up, heart pounding. "In what closet? Where?"

"Some guy's house."

Oh, holy shit. "What guy? Where?"

Her voice trembles as she slurs, "I d-don't know."

I'm off the bed and pulling on clothes. "Drop me a pin. Right now, Darla. Do it. I'll call the police."

"No!"

It's the most coherent word she's said.

"Darla, it sounds like you're scared and maybe in trouble."

"I just need to get out of here. I won't drop a pin unless you promise no cops."

Her words are slurred and it's obvious now that it's not from being sleepy. She's been drinking.

Seriously? This is the position she's putting me in? I have absolutely no idea what to do. If I do call the police, I'm breaking trust. If I don't, she could be in serious danger.

"Is there a lock on the door? Are you feeling threatened in any way?"

"I locked the door. Just text me when you get here. And please, please don't call my dad."

Double shit. It's the first thing I was going to do after hanging up. But then I have another thought—I shouldn't hang up at all. I need to keep her on the line. That way I'll know if anything else happens.

"I won't call anyone because I'm going to stay on the phone with you the whole time. Drop the pin, Darla."

"Okay."

When nothing comes through, I ask, "Are you doing it?" There's no reply. I think she dropped the phone. I pray she doesn't hang up on me.

Finally, a text comes with her location. I'm already in my car when it does. She's only a few miles away.

"Talk to me, Darla."

"I don't feel like talk—"

Her words are cut short and then I hear an awful noise like she's vomiting before the call ends. *Oh dear Lord.*

I may be driving faster than the law allows, but the streets are deserted this time of night and it doesn't take long to arrive. When I do, it's clear which house. There are several bikes and skateboards in the driveway, and a few cars clearly belonging to teenage boys line the street. I hear music even before I open my car door. I'm surprised the police aren't already here. I do spy a neighbor peeking from a window shaking his head. His phone is in his hand. I really want to get her out of here before any police arrive.

I don't bother knocking. I walk right in the front door. Then I text her.

Me: I'm in the house at the front door.

As I await her reply, I contemplate ripping every door open to find her. Instead, I'm looking around at all the baby-faced teens. A few girls I recognize from soccer tryouts.

A boy walks over and hands me a can of beer, then he eyes my stomach. "Um… you drinkin'? Hey, how old are you?"

All of his words are slurred. It's a good thing I have a lot of experience in 'drunk teenage boy speak,' having grown up with three brothers.

I shove the beer forcefully back at his chest. "No, I'm not drinking, you little shit. And neither should you. What are you, twelve?"

He stands taller. "Fifteen."

I see a streak of blue flash past me and realize Bug is darting by me and heading outside. I follow her, not bothering to close the front door.

Bug doesn't go straight for my car, she heads for a nearby bush instead and pukes on it. Well, I suppose that's better than in my car. I just hope she can make it five minutes before it happens again.

I don't bother saying anything to her in the car. It might make her sick. I remember the first time I got drunk. All I could do was sit and focus on something so my head would stop spinning. I didn't want anyone to talk to me or touch me. I just wanted to stare at one immobile point.

I want to laugh, because I know she'll be in for a world of hurt tonight and tomorrow. But I can't laugh. Because she was in a fucking closet. And the implications of that scare the life out of me.

My own stomach turns when I inhale her putrid scent. She must have vomited on herself. I lower the windows and turn on the air.

As I wait for the garage to fully open, she flings open the car door, hurries out, then graces the front bushes with more rejected alcohol. I close my eyes, praying alcohol is really *all* it was.

She's nowhere to be found by the time I park the car and get inside. I gather supplies—a few bottles of cold water, some Advil, a cold washcloth, a mop bucket in case she can't make it to the bathroom—and knock on her door before opening it, glad she didn't have the wherewithal to lock it.

"Darla?"

She groans, lying face down on her bed.

"Darla, I need to know if you're just drunk or if you took anything else."

"I'm not stupid," she says into the mattress.

That point is fully debatable but now is not the time for a lecture.

"Did you ever pass out or even fall asleep?"

"No. I didn't even drink that much."

"If this was your first experience with alcohol, it wouldn't take much to make you feel this way."

Still, I suspect it was far more than she'd have me believe. It's almost as if she thinks the less she drank, the less trouble she'll be in. I'm not about to break it to her that, knowing Asher, quantity will have absolutely no bearing on her punishment.

I put a bottle of water and the Advil on her nightstand. "You need to hydrate. Being dehydrated will make it worse. And you should take Advil. Two of them. If you throw them up, it's okay to take two more." I put the cold washcloth on her hand so she can feel it. "This will help. Try and keep it on your head. There's a bucket right next to the bed if you can't make it to the bathroom. And we should probably get you out of these clothes. You puked on them."

"I can't move or I'll throw up."

"You don't have to. I'll help."

I untuck her shirt and lift it up. Her arms are like Jell-O when I maneuver them out of it.

"Just lift your head for one second."

She groans as she does it. I toss the horrid-smelling shirt on the floor. Luckily, her shorts have an elastic waist, and I shimmy them down her legs. Once she's down to just a bra and underwear, I pull the sheet over her.

"I'll be right back. I'm going to toss these clothes in the laundry. Can I bring you anything?"

"A gun?"

I put my hands on my hips even though her eyes are closed and she can't see how angry her comment made me. "Please don't joke about that."

"My dad's pregnant girlfriend had to rescue me from a party. I'll never be able to show my face again." As soon as the words leave her mouth, so does another round of vomit—right into the bucket next to the bed.

I pick up the washcloth and put it on her forehead before going downstairs.

In the laundry room, I lean against the washing machine and contemplate calling Asher. He's her father. He would know what to do in this situation. But it's almost two in the morning and he's had such a long week. Besides, there's nothing he can do from there but stress about it, so I decide it can wait.

I get a few more cold washcloths, a sleeve of saltine crackers, my kindle, and head back up.

~ ~ ~

Darla's room is just beginning to become light. She rolls over, groans, and opens her eyes to find me sitting in the chair next to her bed. I'm weary after only getting a few minutes of sleep here and there. It seems every time I'd fall asleep, she'd moan or say something about the room spinning, or puke. I was afraid she might vomit in her sleep and aspirate, so I tried my best to stay awake all night. But with the exhaustion of growing a pair of tiny humans, it proved to be a Herculean task.

"Uuuuuuuuugh." She throws a hand over her eyes to keep out the light. "What are you doing up here?"

"I slept here." I snort. "Well, I didn't really sleep much for fear of you choking on your vomit."

"Oh god." She rolls over. "Kill me."

I hand her a bottle of Gatorade I'd brought up in the wee hours of the morning. "You should drink. Even if you don't want to. It'll make you feel better."

She bats it away.

"Darla, it's either this or I drive you to the hospital and have them give you an IV. You threw up a lot last night. You have to replenish your fluids." I hold out the half-eaten sleeve of saltines. Half-eaten by me. "You probably won't feel much like eating today, but you can try a few crackers. If you keep those down, I'll make you some toast or soup."

"Can I have some more Advil?"

I take two tablets from the bottle and hold them out. "Just as soon as you tell me what happened."

"What did it look like?" she asks sarcastically.

"It looked like you lied to me about spending the night at Marti's and went to a party instead. Darla, what was all that bullshit about not having any friends? Was Christian there? Who took you?"

"It had nothing to do with Christian." She pulls the dry and crusty washcloth over her eyes so I change it out with a fresh wet one. "Noelle invited me."

"Who's Noelle?"

"Captain of the soccer team."

"And the boys there, who were they?"

She shrugs. "Don't really know. Students I guess."

"Darla, did any of them… Did they try to…"

"Nobody touched me, if that's what you're asking."

"Are you sure? You were pretty drunk. How do you know?"

"I just know, okay?"

I sigh. "When your dad and I hoped you'd make friends with teammates, you do understand this is not what we had in mind?"

"He's going to kill me, isn't he? What did he say?"

"I haven't told him."

Finally her head turns and she looks at me, surprised. "You haven't?"

I shake my head.

"That's pretty cool of you, I guess."

"Have you met Addison Calloway?"

"Who?"

"Addy. She's a friend of mine. The one with the prosthetic leg."

"Oh, her. Yeah, I've seen her around."

"Do you know how she lost her leg?"

She rolls back over and pulls a pillow to her chest. "I'm not in the mood for any lectures."

"Maybe not, but you sure as hell deserve one. Addy was eighteen when she got drunk and then drove a car. She crashed into an overpass and got pinned, crushing her leg. They couldn't save it. They had to cut her leg off. All because she'd been drinking."

"What does that have to do with me? I wasn't driving. I'm nowhere near old enough to drive."

"Okay, we'll let's unpack that, shall we? You are thirteen. You just started high school. You aren't old enough to drive. You're barely at the age where you can even get a job. What about that makes you think you're qualified to be able to drink alcohol?"

"Like everyone isn't doing it."

I sigh. "I was a teenager once, Darla. I'm not going to lie and say I never had anything to drink. Of course I did. I even ended up throwing up on my parents' lawn a few times. So believe me, I get it. But you're thirteen. What's going to happen when you're fourteen? Are you going to try pot? And when you're fifteen, will it be cocaine? The earlier you go down that path, the worse it will be."

"Gee, thanks, *Mom*."

The sarcastic way she spits out the words sends a dagger straight through my heart.

"I'm only telling you the same things your dad would say if he were here. That he loves you and cares about you and his top priority is keeping you safe. All of that goes for me as well."

"But you're not going to tell him?"

"No. I'm not."

Her sigh tells me how relieved she is that she believes I'll keep her secret.

"I'm not going to tell him. But *you* are."

"Me?" She turns over again, her face softening as if she's having a conversation with a trusted friend. "I've learned my lesson, Allie." *Allie?* She never uses my name, and now she's saying it as if we're BFFs. "I guess I was caught up in trying to make friends. I'll figure out some other way. I'll even sit in the cafeteria if you want. I promise. And no more coming up with stupid baby names. I'll pick a good one. One you'll really like. And I'll babysit whenever you want. Just ask Aunt Marti how good I am with babies. I would watch Charlie all the time. And I'll eat with you. Even when Dad is gone. I swear I will."

The bullshit she's feeding me just keeps getting deeper and deeper. I feel like I'm in it up to my knees. She's all but saying she'll get along with me as long as I don't tell Asher. She's putting me in a hell of a position. And I resent her for it.

"Darla, stop it. I'm not going to let you try and manipulate me."

"I'm not. I swear I'll do all that."

"*If* I don't tell your dad. That's manipulation. Actually, it's blackmail."

"Forget it," she scoffs. "It's not as if I expected you to do it anyway. When have you ever cared about what I want?"

I stand. "Listen. This stops now. I've bent over backwards to make this work. I've ignored your disparaging comments and downright disrespect. I've explained away your behavior as typical rebellious teen angst. But this—what happened last night—isn't something I can overlook. It's serious, Bug."

"It's Darla!" she shouts, then holds her hands on either side of her temples.

I walk to the door. "I'll call the school and tell them you're sick. I'll stay home too since I got pretty much zero sleep being on vomit watch. I'll make pancakes and toast, that might sit well. You need to shower and change your sheets. But, Darla, you *will* tell your dad. You have until the end of the weekend."

I shut the door and something, probably a shoe, hits it behind me.

I slump down and sit on the top step, wishing like hell Asher hadn't picked this week to be away.

Chapter Forty

Asher

This weekend has been unusual. There's been a lot more tension between Bug and Allie than normal. I thought they were getting along better, but the pointed stares between them, the downright evil glares Darla is giving Allie, and the stilted conversation all indicate otherwise.

I get to the breaking point Sunday morning during breakfast. "Did something happen last week when I was gone?"

I glance between the two of them. They look at each other as if sizing each other up, confirming my suspicions.

"You two have been dancing around each other since I got home on Friday. What's going on?"

Allie taps her wrist as if tapping a watch, never losing eye contact with Bug. Bug shakes her head defiantly and puckers her lips.

I put down my fork. "Well, somebody better tell me something."

Allie puts her plate in the sink—not bothering to wash it or anything else, which is very unlike her—and says, "I'll be in the bedroom resting."

Now I'm confused, and a little concerned. I know she tires easily, but we've only been up for an hour. "Are you okay?"

"I'm fine. I'm also not the one you should be asking." She nods to Bug then leaves.

My eyes rest back on my daughter, who hasn't eaten much. She's just pushed eggs from one side of her plate to the other.

"Okay, kiddo, what's going on?"

She looks at the door Allie walked through as if she wants to spit fire at it. "As always, she's making a way bigger deal out of it than she needs to."

I cock my head. "Actually, I've never known Allie to make a big deal about *anything*. What is it?"

"It's stupid. And she's *forcing* me to tell you. Your girlfriend gave me an ultimatum. How's *that* for good parenting?"

"Bug, quit dancing around it and just tell me. If Allie is concerned about something, I trust her gut." When she hesitates, I think of all the things that could have happened. "Did you quit the soccer team? Did you quit school?" I rub my temples. "Did… something happen between you and Christian?"

Her head shakes, looking down at her lap. "None of that."

"Then what?"

"Promise you won't get mad?"

I push away from the table and stand up. She's starting to piss me off, let alone scare the shit out of me.

"No, Bug, I can't promise you that. I promise I'll try to keep my cool. But if you tell me you're pregnant, all bets are off and I will hunt down whoever did it and pulverize him into the ground before locking you away for the rest of your young life." I scrub a hand across my jaw. "Jesus, you aren't, are you?"

"I'm not pregnant." She rolls her eyes as if it's the stupidest thing I've ever said. Then she lowers her voice. "I just went to a party and had a few drinks is all. It's not that big a deal."

I step back, feeling like I've taken a punch to the gut. "You went to a party? And you *drank?*"

"You promised you wouldn't yell."

I pace the kitchen, breathing in and out so I don't take her by the shoulders and try and shake some sense into her.

"You're thirteen fucking years old, Darla."

Tears well in her eyes. She's not used to me yelling at her like this. But all I can think about is my baby at a party with alcohol, maybe even drugs, and undoubtedly… boys.

She sniffs. "I'll be fourteen soon."

I laugh hysterically. "And *that* would make you getting drunk okay?"

Calm the fuck down, Asher. You're scaring her. I turn my chair around and sit in it as if somehow the back of the chair is a buffer between us that will soften this blow.

"What the hell were you thinking?" I ask in a somewhat controlled tone.

"I was thinking that you've been on me to make friends. It's all you ever talk about. So I made some."

"And who are these… friends?"

"Just some girls from the soccer team."

I close my eyes. The one good thing I thought she had going. "Great."

"Noelle invited me. She's the captain. The *captain*, Dad. She's a senior. I *had* to go."

"So the whole team was there? Where were Noelle's parents?"

"Not the whole team. And it wasn't exactly at her house. It was at her boyfriend's."

Both my heart and my brain want to explode. But I attempt to control my anger. "You went to a strange boy's house. I suppose I don't even have to ask if *his* parents were home."

Her glance out the window tells me all I need to know.

"Did Allie know you were going to a party?"

She looks away, her head shaking.

"What did you tell her?"

"Dad, I had to go or I'd be an even bigger loser. I only had one drink, I swear."

"Oh, you swear? A minute ago it was *'a few drinks.'* Better get your story straight, because you do understand I'll get to the bottom of this, don't you? Allie obviously knows a lot more than she let on. Lying to me about the details will only get you in more trouble."

"So I had a few drinks. It wasn't a big deal."

"Darla, what did you tell Allie about where you were going?"

She picks at her napkin. "That I was spending the night at Aunt Marti's."

"Spending the night?" My chair falls over when I stand up too quickly. "As in you were planning on staying out all night?"

"I... I don't know. I guess it was stupid."

I scoff. "Ya think?" I right my chair and sit back down, dreading the answer to my next question. "And where did you end up sleeping?"

"Here. I slept here."

"And how did that come about?"

"I called Allie to pick me up."

She called Allie? For a moment, I'm happy that she felt she could trust Allie enough to call her. But that happiness turns to disgust when I think of all the things that could have led to her calling the one person I'm one hundred percent sure she didn't want to have to call.

"What happened at the party that made you call her? Did a boy do something—"

"Nobody did anything. It just got crazy. Some of the kids started playing strip poker."

"So Allie picked you up? What time?"

She shrugs. "I can't remember. After midnight I think."

"How much did you drink?"

She shrugs again.

"How much, Darla? Did you get sick?"

She nods.

"A lot?"

She nods.

"Good. Maybe you'll think twice about doing it again."

"Am I in trouble?"

I throw my hands up in frustration. "Yes, you're in trouble. Jesus, Bug."

She glances over at the doorway. "It's all her fault."

"*Allie?* You think this is *Allie's* fault? Grow the hell up. I'm so goddamn tired of you blaming her for everything bad in your life. It's not her fault she got pregnant. It's not her fault I love her so much I want to marry her. It's not her fault you and Mel live across the country from each other. And it's definitely not her fault that you chose to lie to her, put yourself in danger, and then presumably try to convince her not to tell me. Do you realize the position you put her in?"

"She's not my mother. She never will be."

She stomps off toward her room.

"We're not done here!" I follow her up, pressing my foot in the door before she can close it.

She falls onto her bed, crying. "Why does she have to go and ruin everything? Everything was perfect before her."

Torn between consoling her and yelling at her, I sit on the edge of her bed. "Everything *wasn't* perfect, honey. Mel was still moving. You still wanted to go to a different school."

"It's *so* not about that." She sobs into a pillow.

"Bug, talk to me. I know this has been a hard adjustment for you. But it would have been hard if we'd stayed in Orlando. Surely you understand that."

She shakes her head, still face down on the pillow. Her words come out muffled. "At least there it would have been just us."

I brush her hair aside to try and see her face. "Sweetie, even if it weren't Allie, I would have met someone else I wanted to be with. This was bound to happen sooner or later."

"But why? We were happy just the two of us. We don't need anyone else to come into our lives just so they can…" She buries her head even deeper into the pillow.

"Just so they can what?"

"Nothing. Forget it."

I roll her over so she has no choice but to look at me. "Bug, just so they can what?"

She swallows. It looks almost painful. "Leave, okay? Just so they can leave." She rips herself out of my arms and turns away.

My heart is lodged in my throat. Allie was right all along. This isn't about me having a woman in my life, it's about Bug's insecurities over women leaving *her*.

I try to console her but she just cries harder. "Nobody wants me because I'm such a freak."

"That's not true."

"My mother didn't want me. My own mother, who gave birth to me, just gave me up with one scribble of her signature. Has she ever once tried to find me? Asked how I was doing? Sent me a freaking birthday card?"

"But it's not because she knew you and thought poorly of you. She was young. She didn't want to be a mother. It had nothing to do with you."

"Nothing. Right. And Stella?"

"Oh, baby, Stella left because she was sad over not being able to have a child."

"B-but she had m-me. *I* was her child. And she left. She didn't even bother to say goodbye. She just decided I was too much trouble. What happens when…" She looks over at the door. "When *she* decides I'm too much trouble?"

It all comes together and hits me like a Mack truck. Her behavior around women I've dated. Her aversion to Allie. Her overall attitude since we moved. She's being difficult on purpose, perhaps in an attempt to push Allie away before she becomes too attached to her.

"That's never going to happen," Allie says from the doorway, holding a plate of food. She cringes, looking guilty. "Sorry, I saw she didn't eat anything. I didn't want her going hungry." She holds out the plate to Bug. "I thought you might want this."

"You thought wrong," Darla bites. "And you shouldn't eavesdrop on private conversations."

"Asher, do you think I could have a minute with her?"

I'm hesitant to leave. But I feel maybe they need to hash this thing out after Darla finally spoke her fears.

"Dad, don't," Bug says when I get up.

"This is between the two of you more than it is anyone else. Listen to her, Bug. For me."

She rolls over, turning her back to us. "I'm done talking."

Allie gives me a sad smile and nods to the door, letting me know she still wants to do this. I leave knowing this could very well be the moment that defines their entire relationship. I leave praying it won't be the moment that completely destroys it.

Chapter Forty-one

Allie

I don't sit on her bed. She wouldn't want that. I pull over the same chair I slept in Thursday night, sit down, and try and figure out what to say. It gutted me when I heard her say what she did about me deciding she was too much trouble. All of this stems from her being afraid.

"Life is scary," I say.

She scoots further to the other side of the bed.

"It's scary for everyone. Some people are afraid they won't make enough money to put food on the table. Some worry they'll never find someone to spend their lives with. Some are so fearful of the entire world that they won't even leave their homes. Everyone has something they're afraid of."

"Says the girl who has everything."

"You really think that? Darla, you saw the urn and the ashes. You know about Christopher."

"What does that have to do with anything?"

"You really have no idea, do you? I've lived in fear for ten years. Losing him was the worst thing that ever happened to me. And guess what? After it happened, I wasn't about to let it happen again. I was never going to have more kids. *Ever.* I was never even going to be in a long-term relationship, because those usually lead to kids."

She exhales a deep throaty cackle. "And how'd that work out?"

"These babies weren't planned. Falling in love with your dad wasn't either. Both of those things just happened. And I'm glad they did. I wouldn't change a thing.

"For so long I was so afraid of being hurt by having another baby, I refused to allow myself to live and be happy. But now? Now I'm already part of a new family. You and your dad are that family. The babies are too."

I lean forward and touch the bed, not that she can or wants to feel it, but I need to do something with my hands. "My brother Dallas lost his first family, you know that. He was never going to love anyone again for fear of another loss. Then he met your aunt. Look at them now."

"I still don't see what any of this has to do with me."

"Darla, I get that you're afraid of letting another woman into your life. One who will only let you down. I'm not going to let you down. But I'm also not going to try and be your mom if that's not what you want or need. We can be friends."

"Whatever."

"I love you, you know."

"Yeah, right."

"It's the truth."

"How could it be?" she says, her voice still muffled by the pillow.

"Because you are a part of your dad, and I love everything about him. You are an extension of him." I take a chance and move over to the bed, relaxing a little when she doesn't try and push me off. "I'm not going anywhere. I plan on being in your lives until the day I die, which will hopefully not be for another sixty or seventy years."

"I'm sure Stella thought that too. You shouldn't make promises you can't keep."

"I guess you're right. I can't predict the future. All I can do is show you how I feel and hope you'll believe it to be genuine."

"Friends don't narc each other out."

"Your dad had to know about what you did. And if it happens again, or anything like it, I'll still make you tell him. Being your friend doesn't mean letting you make bad choices."

Finally she turns to face me. "He actually had no idea. I thought you would have at least told him I lied to you about sleeping at Aunt Marti's."

"I didn't tell him anything."

"Yeah. Obviously. He freaked out."

"He was worried about you."

"And if I didn't come clean today? What would you have done?"

I shrug. "I knew you'd tell him. You're a good kid, Darla. But being a kid myself once, I also knew you needed a little time to get up the courage."

"You really wouldn't have told him?"

I shake my head. "Nope."

She sighs into the pillow. "How much trouble do you think I'm in?"

"A lot probably. My advice? Take it like a grown up. You're old enough to understand what you did was wrong. You're mature enough to understand why we were scared ourselves."

"You? Why were *you* scared?"

"Have you not been listening? If anything had happened to you, I would have been devastated. The thought of you being hurt or in trouble guts me to the core. Darla, I was scared because I love you."

Tears well in her eyes. "You barely know me."

"I still love you. And guess what?" I rub my hands across my belly. "They're going to love you too. They're going to love you so much. Because you're their big sister and nothing will ever change that. The three of you will be tied together for life. They're going to look to you for guidance. And one day, they might even find themselves calling *you* in the middle of the night because of a bad decision *they* make."

She stares at my stomach. "You think so?"

I laugh when I get jabbed by an elbow or foot in the ribs. I touch the spot. "This little guy just confirmed it."

"Is he kicking?"

I nod. "Want to feel?"

She contemplates it for a second, and suddenly I'm sure that whatever she does next may impact our entire future. She holds up a hand. "Can I?"

I scoot closer and show her where to put her hand. "Here."

Slowly and carefully, like she's not sure she wants to, she puts her hand lightly on the spot. I smile when he kicks.

Bug looks up, open-mouthed and awestruck. "Oh my god, do they do that a lot?"

I chuckle. "All the time. It's becoming harder for me to sleep with all the somersaults they do in there."

"Is she moving too?"

I take her hand and move it to the girl baby. "Give her a little poke and she might."

She gently taps.

"Really poke her. Like this." I depress the skin over my lower belly a few times.

Darla follows suit then freezes. "I can actually *see* her moving under your clothes."

"Oh, that's nothing." I lift my shirt and push down my waistband.

She stares at my stomach, both twins fully awake now and kicking in different directions. Her eyes are wide as she watches the show, then she puts her hands back on my stomach. "Do you ever feel like you're in that movie, *Alien*, and something is going to pop out of your stomach and eat you?"

I smile at the absurdity. I smile because it's the funniest thing she's ever said to me. I smile because it's the very first time she's spoken more than a few words to me without animosity, hostility, or disrespect. But mostly, I smile because we're sitting here sharing a moment I hope will be as memorable for her as I know it will be for me.

She looks up. "You're naming him after your son, not your dad, aren't you?"

"Christopher was named after my dad. But, yes, this little guy's name will be after his."

"What do you think about Christina?"

"Who's Christina?"

"I mean for a name. Christina is kind of like Christopher."

My heart leaps. I hold back tears so as not to seem like an over-emotional hormonal pregnant lady. "I think Christina is a beautiful name. And I know Christopher would approve."

Her hands are no longer on my belly, but she lowers her head. "Hey, Christina." She narrows her eyes at me. "What's *his* name going to be?"

I shrug. "Don't know, your dad hasn't told me yet."

"He should consider Alex."

I raise a brow. I'm guessing it would be a tribute to Marti's daughter who died as an infant. But she might think differently if she knew Alexandra is my real name.

When I don't say anything, she elaborates. "It kind of makes sense. That way he'd be named after your son, your father, my cousin… and you."

My eyes snap to hers. "Me?"

"Alexandra, right?"

"That's right."

"Christina and Alex Anderson. Cool names, don't you think?"

I try not to smile too broadly. "I'm on board. But you have to ask your dad, and more importantly, your aunt."

"I'm not about to ask my dad anything right now. I feel like I'm going to be grounded until the end of time and anything I ask for will be immediately dismissed."

"Maybe you're right. Give it a few days. He might be super mad right now, but it's only because of how much he loves you."

She pulls her knees to her chest. "And you? Are *you* mad?"

I rein in my emotions, because I know exactly what she's asking. "Yes, Darla. I'm steaming mad." I wink at her and get off the bed. "I also have to pee before one of these babies kicks my bladder again and I burst all over your bed."

She laughs. *Laughs!*

At the door, I turn. "Are we good?"

She nods and I smile.

I'm almost through the door when she says, "Allie?"

"Mmm?" I look at her over my shoulder.

"You can call me Bug."

Chapter Forty-two

Asher

"How many clothes do two babies need?" I shake my head in amusement as I unload the car.

I never knew two women could shop so much. Don't we already have everything?

Allie and Bug have been shopping together. *A lot*. When Bug was grounded, it was the only way she could leave the house other than school and soccer. But she hasn't been grounded for a few weeks, and it makes me so incredibly happy that she still wants to go shopping. So, even knowing we have little room for anything else in either nursery, I shouldn't be too hard on them.

I hate that my thirteen—now fourteen-year-old—had to go through what she did in order for them to finally form a bond. But I can't deny it's been worth it. Watching the two of them get closer over the past few months has brought me more happiness than I thought I could feel. And with just a week to go before the babies come, there's no time to spare.

I've thought about bringing up the marriage thing again. After all, I've been carrying around Mom's ring in my pocket for so long now I'm surprised I haven't lost it. But there's a lot on our plate being so close to D-day.

"You'll be amazed at how quickly they grow out of things," Allie says, out of breath as she walks from the garage to the kitchen.

I pull out a chair for her. "Sit. You shouldn't be on your feet so much."

I remove her shoes and pull her feet onto my lap and rub them. She shifts uncomfortably in the chair. For weeks now, she's been unable to find good positions to sit and sleep in, not to mention having sex. That's pretty much been off the table. The babies are taking up so much room, there isn't room for anything else—including her own internal organs or my cock.

"Just one more week," I say, kneading the balls of her feet.

Bug comes into the kitchen and starts getting out ingredients for dinner. She cooks three nights a week. I cook three nights a week. The other night we go out or order in. Allie balked about being left out of the rotation when we insisted on it about a month ago, when it started to get hard for her to get around. But now she's come to appreciate everything that gets done for her so she can stay off her feet.

"Mel wants to come visit the babies," Bug says. "After Christmas maybe? During her holiday break?"

I laugh. "I think Mel wants to come visit *you* and you're just using the twins as an excuse."

"It'll be okay, though, right? Please? After visiting her, we vowed never to go more than a few months without seeing each other."

The first thing Bug asked for after her six weeks of being grounded, was to fly out to see Mel for a long weekend. It was the least I could do after she took her punishment so well. She never once complained about being stuck in the house.

I was a wreck, putting my teenage daughter on a plane all by herself. But we got her a non-stop flight and, since she's no stranger to flying, at least she knew how it works.

"Yeah, I think that'll be okay. I'll even spring for the flight. It'll be my Christmas gift to her."

Bug squeals and shoots off a text. Then she proceeds to make a delicious chicken casserole from Allie's recipe.

After I'm done with the dishes, I peek over at the couch where Allie looks like she can barely stay awake.

"How about I draw a bath for you?"

Her eyes flutter open. "A bath sounds heavenly."

"Dad!" Bug shouts from the back door. "I'm going to Christian's."

"Is his father home?"

She peeks out from around the corner. "Would you stop? I don't *like* him, you know. He's my Mel."

That doesn't make me feel much better. I was fourteen once. *And* a boy. Best friend or not, the kid is still a red-blooded guy with teen hormones running amok.

"You didn't answer the question."

Her eyes roll. "Yes, *warden*, his dad is home. Want me to have him call you?"

I let the 'warden' comment slide due to the obvious sarcasm in her voice. It's something she called me a few times when she was grounded. But since she was the perfect inmate, I gave her a pass. "Nope. I trust you. But that doesn't mean I still won't check up on things from time to time."

"Whatever. Come spy through the windows if you want, we'll just be playing video games."

"Be home by ten."

"Yup. I know my curfew. Bye."

Once the door shuts, I turn to Allie. "Do you think her curfew should be nine? What was yours when you were fourteen?"

She shrugs. "I can't remember. Ten seems fair for a freshman in high school."

"She'll probably ask for it to be eleven next year, then midnight. By the time she's a senior, she'll want to stay out until one in the morning." I pinch my brow. "I'm not ready for this."

"Not ready for her to grow up?" She touches her stomach. "We're going to blink and these two will be Bug's age. Promise me we're going to cherish every second and not waste it on trying to be perfect parents raising perfect kids."

I laugh. "Since when have I ever been close to being a perfect parent?"

She squeezes my thigh. "You're an amazing father. I'm so glad it's you."

"So glad what's me?"

"Who knocked me up."

"Sweetheart, you have no idea." I kiss her belly. "I'm going to draw you that bath."

~ ~ ~

"This is exactly what I needed," she says, settling into our large soaking tub.

"You don't have to keep taking her shopping. It's probably hell on your feet."

"It's become our thing."

I sit on the edge of the tub. "Who'd have thought the two of you would ever have a thing?"

"Yeah. It's pretty great."

"*You're* pretty great."

"I don't *feel* pretty great. In fact, I don't feel pretty *or* great. I feel like a beached whale."

I stand, crack a smile, then undress. Stepping into the tub, I work my way around her so her back is leaning against me. I reach a hand around her and whisper in her ear, "I know just what to do to make you feel both." Then I touch her clit.

Her head falls back against my shoulder, and she groans. I love the sexy little noises that come out of her when I touch her. I love how she's not afraid to moan and mewl and tell me what feels good. She's the most sexually compatible person I've ever been with—just one more reason we're meant to be together.

My dick grows hard against her back. "Fuck, I love the way you feel."

She moans her appreciation when I slip a finger inside her. I alternate playing with her clit and her pussy, driving her to the brink and then pulling back. It's been a minute since we've done this. She needs a good release. Maybe that will help her sleep tonight.

"Oh… yes… Ash… right there… don't stop."

I smile against the side of her head. "You like it when I do this." I swirl a finger around her clit.

"Yes."

"You like it when I do this, too." I plunge two fingers inside her.

"Mmmmm," she moans.

"You love the way I make you come," I mumble slowly in her ear.

"Please… Ash… do it."

I've teased her long enough. I use my finger like I'd use my tongue, flicking her clit back and forth, keeping up constant pressure. Her head presses back into me. Her back arches. She shouts out with her explosive release. It's so damn sexy, I almost come myself. It doesn't matter that I don't. This is about her, not me. Her body. Her pleasure. Her comfort. I don't move my fingers until she pushes them away, drawing every last quiver out of her body.

Her chest heaves with a huge sigh. "Wow. Thanks, I needed that."

"Anytime. And I mean that." I move my hand up to her stomach. "Did it calm them down or wake them up?"

"It—"

Her entire body stiffens, a complete contradiction to how relaxed it was just a moment ago.

"Allie?"

"I felt a pop. Asher, I think my water just broke."

My eyes go wide. "Oh, shit. But how will we be able to tell given you're *in* water?"

"I'm pretty sure. It's a fairly distinct feeling. And I remember it from… before."

I gently get out from behind her, pull the drain on the tub, and wrap her in a towel.

"Wait. Do you see any blood or anything? Hudson will want to know if it was clear fluid or not."

I scan the tub. "It looks clear." I pull over her makeup chair and help her sit on it. Then I dry her off. "I'll get my phone."

With only a towel around my waist, I race to the kitchen to get it, then call Hudson.

"Allie's water just broke. Well, she thinks so. She was in the tub."

"Was the fluid clear?"

"Yes. That's good, right? Is it too early?" I stop and lean against the wall, my heart racing.

"She's right at thirty-six weeks. Babies born now have the same chance of being healthy as full-term babies. But I do want you to get her to the hospital right away. Has she had any contractions?"

I push off the wall and go back to the bathroom. "Hudson is asking if you've had any contractions."

"Braxton Hicks, I guess, for a few days now. Or at least I thought they were Braxton Hicks." She sighs, clearly upset with herself for missing the signs. "But my water definitely broke. I can feel it trickling out of me."

I relay the message.

"I'll meet you there," Hudson says and then ends the call.

I fall to my knees in front of Allie. "Is this really happening?"

She swallows and looks at me, terrified. Allie has been so upbeat during the entire pregnancy, I'm shocked to see her like this. Is she thinking something will go wrong? Is she thinking about Christopher?

"Sweetheart, it's going to be okay. It's not too early. They are going to be fine." I cup her face in my hands. "We're doing this. And tonight or tomorrow we're going to meet Alex and Christina. And, oh my god are they going to love their mom."

She nods over and over, unable to speak.

I stand and hold out my hands to help her up. "Let's get you dressed and go have some babies."

Chapter Forty-three

Allie

I can't help but make comparisons to when Christopher was born. Laboring this time is like night and day. With him, all the doctors and nurses knew the situation. Every time one of them looked at me I could see the sadness in their forced smiles. They all knew I was having a baby just to watch him die.

This time, the room is filled with nothing but excitement.

We decided a while ago to invite Bug to be here when the babies were born. I've been doing everything I can to make her feel like we're a family and in this together. And while some teenagers would surely shy away from watching their siblings enter the world, she has embraced the idea with open arms, stipulating only that she not be 'down there' to see the 'gross stuff.'

At the moment, however, it's quiet. There are no doctors or nurses milling about, and Bug is asleep on the couch since it's three in the morning. I dozed off a few times earlier, but since I'm having contractions now, I doubt that will happen again.

Asher repositions the pillow behind me. "How're you holding up?"

"It's not too bad. You should try and get some sleep. It might be a while yet, and you may not get a chance later."

"I'm not sleeping if you're not. We're in this together."

There was a whirlwind of activity when I got to the hospital seven hours ago. I was immediately induced, given an epidural, and hooked up to two baby monitors. They also did an ultrasound to make sure each of the twins are still presenting head down.

But now, it's a waiting game. My contractions are getting closer together. They don't hurt necessarily, but I do feel pressure which is keeping me from sleeping. Or maybe it's the excitement that's doing it. Or the anticipation. Or the underlying fear.

For over five months now, since the blood tests and ultrasounds showed everything was normal, I've been good. No panic attacks. And as far as I can tell, not much more than the usual pregnancy stress, albeit doubled for twins. But I've been generally happy, relaxed, and optimistic.

So why now, when the babies are mere hours away from being here, are all my nerves suddenly coming out to play? What if one or both is deprived of oxygen during the birth? What if one is born vaginally but the other has to be C-section? What if they missed something on the blood test or ultrasounds?

"Allie? You okay, sweetheart?"

I open my eyes to see Asher studying the monitor by my head that's reporting my vitals.

"I'm good."

"Your heart rate just went up. I should get the doctor."

"No. Don't. I suddenly got super anxious over everything that can go wrong."

He sits on the sliver of exposed bed next to me and draws me into his arms. "Nothing is going to go wrong."

"You don't know that for sure."

"Babe, we made it this far. And just think, this time next week, when the babies are keeping both of us up all night, you'll probably be wishing you were still pregnant."

I shake my head. "You can bet your ass I *won't*. I'm ready to evict them, Asher. I'm just not ready for anything bad to happen. I'm not sure I could take it." I close my eyes. "Does that make me selfish? Am I a horrible person for wanting *two* perfectly healthy babies? What if that's more than I deserve?"

He holds me tight. "Allie, *everyone* deserves healthy babies. But, sweetheart, if anyone deserved them more than others, it would be you." He kisses my temple. "There's no reason to believe anything bad will happen. If you end up having a C-section, it's okay. Women have them all the time. If the babies need a little oxygen, that will be okay too. They have an excellent NICU here—just look at what they did for Mitchell. We're going to deal with whatever happens because they're our children. But I just know in my heart that everything will be all right. You need to trust in that even if you can't trust your own feelings, okay?"

I nod. "Okay."

The door opens and Hudson walks through. I haven't seen him since before midnight.

"Didn't you go home?" I ask.

He puts on a pair of latex gloves. "Shut my eyes for a few hours in the on-call room."

"You're staying here?"

"I wanted to be close for the big event. Now, let's see how much progress you've made." He checks my cervix and removes his gloves. "You're about eight centimeters. It may go quickly now. I'll check back in an hour. Try to get some rest."

"Is it time?" Bug asks sleepily from the sofa.

"Not yet," Asher tells her. "Go back to sleep."

She rolls over and is out before Hudson leaves the room. Oh, to be a teenager. And *not* be in labor.

Asher crawls into the bed next to me, wraps me in a hug, and holds me until I drift off.

~ ~ ~

"Allie."

A light overhead is turned on.

"Allie, wake up."

When I fully realize where I am and what's happening, I get nervous and excited all over again.

"Hey, sweetheart. I'm glad you got some sleep, but Hudson needs to check you again."

"What time is it?"

"Just after four-thirty."

I touch low on my stomach. "I feel pressure. But this time it's different. It's more."

Hudson sticks a hand inside me for the fourth time since I've been here. It's strange how it doesn't even bother me. As if being pregnant and in labor somehow makes me immune from the embarrassment of having strangers, acquaintances, and near-enemies poke and prod me in my intimate places. "I think we're ready."

"Yeah, I feel ready." I shift around. "Definitely stuff going on down there."

"Don't push yet, Allie. We're going to move you to the OR." He puts a hand on my arm. "I'll see you in there."

We know the drill. Hudson told us long ago that twins always get delivered in the operating room, even if they come vaginally. There's always a chance the second one will turn breech or develop a situation where they need to convert to a C-section.

Asher leans over and kisses me. "You ready?"

Tears flood my eyes. Tears of stress. Tears of anticipation. Tears of hope.

I nod. "Can you call everyone and let them know what's happening?"

Two nurses come in the room and start unhooking me from all the stuff I've been tethered to for the past nine hours. There's a lot of activity and all the lights are on, but Darla is still sleeping. Lucky duck.

"Better wake her up or she'll miss the big show," I say.

A third nurse enters and hands Asher two sets of scrubs. Not all hospitals require dads to wear scrubs for a vaginal delivery in the OR, but this one does. Luckily, he won't have to wear a mask—unless I do end up having a C-section—because I want to see every emotion on his face the first time he holds our children. I choke up even more at the thought of it.

Normally the hospital doesn't allow more than one family member in the OR for a twin delivery. But Hudson pulled some strings, and we got approval for Bug to attend. The second set of scrubs is for her.

Asher looks around the room. "When we come back to this room, we'll be a family of five." He almost falls onto the chair next to the bed. "Oh my god, this is really happening."

It's the first time I've ever seen hesitation on his face. As if he's just now realizing the scope of the situation.

I clutch my belly, feeling a buildup of pressure. "You think?"

He stands confidently, pushing aside his own feelings or fears, strides over, and pulls my hand to his lips, kissing it. "We'll see you in there," he says, as my bed gets wheeled toward the door. "I love you."

I crane my neck. "I love you too."

My bed is pushed down a long hallway, through two sets of double doors, and then into a very cold, very bright, sterile-smelling operating room. I'm asked to scoot from my bed onto another—the OR table I presume, although it's been modified for a vaginal birth.

I shiver. "It's so cold."

"Sorry about that," a nurse says. "I'll get you a warm blanket."

As people shuffle around me, I glance around the room. There are two infant warmers, tons of trays of various instruments, and lots and lots of people. Hudson warned us how crowded the room would be. There is a nurse assigned to me, and two more for the babies, a neonatologist, an anesthesiologist, and a surgical scrub tech on stand-by. I'm surprised there's enough room for Asher and Bug, who are escorted in moments later wearing full scrubs and hats, masks dangled around their necks just in case.

While Darla seems interested in everything going on around us, Asher's eyes are laser-focused on mine. "You doing okay?"

I shrug. "It's not exactly the intimate birth experience I'd hoped for."

He laughs, finally looking around at all the commotion. "No, I guess it's not."

Hudson comes in the room, all doctored up in scrubs, a scrub cap, and a mask, looking ready for anything. "Let's get started," he says, taking a seat at the end of the bed as the nurse helps situate my lower half.

In going over my birth plan, I'd stressed how I despise stirrups. Hudson said they wouldn't be necessary unless he needed to increase medical intervention. Meaning if there was a problem and he had to use forceps or vacuum extraction. He has the nurse move the stirrups aside as his gaze sweeps across Asher and Bug. "You each want to take a leg?"

Bug steps back. "Um… I'm just here to watch, not participate."

Hudson chuckles and motions for the nurse to step to the side opposite Asher.

"Are you feeling pressure?" Hudson asks, looking at one of the monitors. "It looks like you're having a contraction."

I nod.

"Okay, go ahead and push."

I bear down and give it my all. Then I do it again. And again. And again. It seems like hours pass, but I'm sure it hasn't been that long.

"How much longer is this going to go on?" I ask, feeling completely exhausted.

"Not long. I can see the top of Twin A's head," Hudson says. He motions to Asher. "Want to take a look?"

"Yeah. Yes. Of course." The excitement in his voice is evident. He looks over my leg, his hand coming to his mouth to cover an emotional gasp. "That's amazing." He blindly reaches for my arm. "She's got hair. Allie, I can see dark hair."

"Allie," Hudson says. "Here comes another contraction. I need you to push hard on this one to get her head out.

"I'll try."

Asher squeezes the leg he's holding. "You can do this, babe. Just a few more pushes."

I flash him an annoyed stare. "A few more and then a whole other baby."

Hudson chuckles, which I appreciate more than he knows. He wouldn't be laughing if he were the least bit worried. His levity makes me breathe a little easier and push a little harder.

"There she is. Now stop pushing. Suction. Okay, great. Now give me another push. That's it. There's a shoulder. Gentle now, give me one more."

I push once more, then the pressure is gone and I hear my little girl cry. I rise up on my elbows, desperate to see her. "How does she look? Is she okay?"

"You did great, Allie," Hudson says. "She looks healthy, and a bit larger than I anticipated. Good job. Asher? Want to cut the cord?"

Asher looks over at Bug. "You do it. I'll do the next one."

"Seriously?" She looks terrified. "No. What if I screw up?"

"You can't screw up," Hudson says. "We have the cord clamped and you cut right in between." He points. "Here."

Hesitantly, she steps forward and takes the surgical scissors, eyes filled with wonder as she separates me from her sister—my daughter. *Oh my god. I have a daughter.*

"What does she look like?" I ask Asher.

"I don't really know. The doctor is examining her and you've got a death grip on my hand."

I release him. "Sorry. Go."

The nurse shows Asher where he can walk, steering him clear of the trays of instruments that thankfully haven't been needed.

"Jesus, Allie," he says from across the room. "She's beautiful."

"One minute Apgar is nine," someone says.

I strain to sit upright. "That's good, right?"

"That's *great*," Hudson says, still between my legs but taking a break.

Only a few moments go by before Asher brings our swaddled daughter to me and places her in my arms. I can barely see her perfect little face through my tears. Maybe it's the blurred vision, but I swear she looks so much like Christopher it takes my breath away. "Hey, little one. I'm your… mom." I choke out the last word because it's one I never thought I'd say again.

A nurse comes over and puts something on my wrist. "This is an ID band that matches hers. Your husband will wear one too."

Asher squeezes my shoulder, neither of us bothering to correct her.

I lean down and kiss the baby's cheek. I touch her nose. I unwrap her a bit and count her fingers. "Are you sure she's good?"

The neonatologist appears by my side, "She's presenting very healthy. We'll take her back for all the usual tests, but so far, she's doing as well as a full-term baby, all five pounds twelve ounces of her."

I look up at Asher. "We have a daughter."

"We sure as hell do."

"Bug," I say. "Do you want to touch her?"

She nods, eyes wide as she reaches out to her little sister. She touches the baby's head on top of her little blue and pink beanie. Then her cheek. Then her hand. "Her fingers are so tiny." She cocks her head to the side, studying her new sibling. "Hmmm… now that I see her, I'm thinking… Phyllis." Asher scoffs. "Elektra? Paisley?" But then a tear drops from her eye as she wipes the other. "Hi, Chrissy. I'm your big sister." She looks at Asher. "I think I already love her. Is that even possible?"

I reach out and put my hand on Bug's arm, encouraging her to look at me. When she does, I say, "You better believe it is," hoping she gets my meaning.

The new tear welling in her eye says she does. We share one more brief moment of… *something*, then she turns back to Christina, emotions swelling my heart as Bug continues to love on her.

Hudson clears his throat. "I hate to break up the party, but we need to do an ultrasound to see what's going on with Twin B."

Someone rolls over the ultrasound machine as Asher gently takes Christina from me.

Hudson glides the transducer over my belly, though I can't feel it. "Mmm," he mumbles.

My body stiffens. "What does that mean?"

"He's turned. He's in the transverse position." He moves the wand around some more. "That means he's sideways. Could be he's taking advantage of all that extra space."

He's trying to make a joke, but I know what this could mean. I close my eyes. "Do you have to do a C-section?"

"Not necessarily. I'm going to try and turn him." He hands the transducer off to the nurse and puts both hands on my stomach. "This won't hurt, but you will feel a lot of pressure."

I lock eyes with Asher and his bright smile is encouraging. He holds Christina close to me and I caress her soft face with the back of a knuckle.

"Allie," Hudson says, "I'm not having any luck. I'm going to try for an internal rotation. This will be slightly less comfortable, but it still shouldn't hurt with your epidural."

"Wait," Bug says, seemingly horrified. "You're going to stick your entire hand… up *there*?"

Hudson holds up his hand. "It's a lot smaller than what just came out of her."

"Still… gross."

"Darla," Asher warns. "How about you keep those comments to yourself?"

"Take a deep breath," Hudson says.

I feel pressure and tugging and, oh god, I don't even want to think about what he's doing right now. It seems to take forever, but then it's over.

"It worked," he says. "He's head down for now."

I look up. "For *now?* Meaning you might have to do that all over again?" I slump back onto the bed.

"There's a chance."

"If you can stick your whole hand up there, why not just pull him out?" Bug asks.

It seems like a legitimate question, so I await his answer.

"That's not how it works. In breech births, you can help them along by tugging the feet and legs. But you don't want to pull a baby out by his head. That could lead to complications."

"But it's safe to use forceps and the vacuum extractor?" I ask.

"Those are for when the baby is low enough in the birth canal. He's not there yet."

"How long will it be?" I ask, ready to have this over with.

"Minutes. Ten to thirty usually."

"Can I hold her while we wait?"

"Better yet, try and nurse her," he says. "Nursing will help the uterus contract and may even move Twin B along."

"What are we waiting for? Let's do it."

I scoot up into a more comfortable position and Asher puts Christina in my arms. I can't help the sob that bellows out of me when she latches on. I was never able to nurse Christopher. I pumped and he ate my breast milk, but I never got to feel the sensation of him nursing at my breast. I think it's the most incredible feeling I've ever had.

"Look at that," Asher says in amazement. "She's doing it like a champ."

"You should probably go tell the masses that she's here. I'm sure they're all waiting for news."

"Are you sure?"

I nod.

He kisses my head. "I'll just be a minute. Don't want to miss the second act."

By the time he returns a few minutes later, Christina is asleep on my breast. And I feel a sudden build up of pressure. "Hudson?"

"Are you feeling like you have to push?"

I nod and hand the baby off to Asher as Hudson does another ultrasound. Looking pleased, he announces, "Still head down." He puts on a new pair of gloves and checks inside. "And I can feel his head. Whenever you want to push, Allie. This one should come easier."

I close my eyes, hoping he's right.

I feel a kiss on the side of my head. When I look up, I see Asher. But he's no longer holding Christina. "Where is she?" I ask, worried.

He nods to my left. Despite my exhaustion, I smile big when I see Bug sitting on a stool holding her sister like she's made of glass.

"Come on," Asher says. "Let's meet our son."

After I push five or six times, Hudson says a bunch of stuff to the other staff and people move swiftly around down there.

"What's wrong?"

"Allie, stop pushing. Do not push, okay? No matter how much pressure you feel."

"Hudson, what's going on?"

"The cord is around his neck. I'm working on freeing it."

My eyes flood with tears. "Oh my god."

Asher grips my shoulders, wrapping me in a half-hug. I hear Bug crying.

"Maybe we should get her out of here," a nurse says.

"No, please. He's my brother. I want to stay. Please."

"I've got it," Hudson says. "Cord is free. Push, Allie. Give it everything you've got."

Still terrified beyond belief, I push until I feel I've broken every blood vessel in my face.

"He's out."

I lie back, relieved, but then I realize I haven't heard him cry. I look up at Asher. He looks as terrified as I feel as people shuffle around the room. I close my eyes and see only one thing: Christopher. Is he about to be joined by his brother? Am I about to hold another dead child in my arms? Am I destined not to ever have a son?

I hear Bug's voice. It's weak and broken. "I did this. It's my fault. It's all my fault."

A nurse takes Christina from her arms, then another nurse escorts Bug out of the room. The whole time she's mumbling how sorry she is.

I look at Asher again and ask him the question I fear more than any other question I've ever asked before. "Is he dead?"

Chapter Forty-four

Asher

Time has slowed to a halt while they work on my lifeless son. It feels like minutes have passed when I'm sure it's only been seconds. When he finally cries out, his cries are met with cheers from the healthcare team. And it's now when I start breathing too.

Allie bellows out a sob. "He's alive? Is he okay?"

I sit on the stool next to the bed, my legs barely able to hold me up as the last minute of my life has been the most stressful of my entire forty-one years. "He's crying. That's a good sign."

Allies rises on an elbow. "Hudson?"

He looks to the neonatologist for confirmation. "One minute Apgar is seven. That's acceptable. But I'd like to take him to the NICU for monitoring. Standard procedure in situations like this."

"What is the situation exactly?" Allie asks, her head likely still fuzzy from lost sleep and… everything.

"The cord was around his neck," the neonatologist says. "While he wasn't without oxygen for a prolonged period, he did require stimulation and a bag mask to get him breathing. He's looking healthy, but to be safe, we'll monitor him there for a while." He swaddles the baby and brings him to Allie. "You can hold him for a minute. This little guy is six pounds on the dot. A healthy weight."

Allie welcomes him into her arms. She studies him, crying happy tears. "You look nothing like your sister. And you definitely have your dad's nose." She glances at me. "He's all you. And that makes me so, so happy." Alex makes a noise then his eyes open and he looks directly at Allie. "Alex Christopher," she says, her voice hitching on his name. "You've got big shoes to fill." She kisses him. "And you also happen to have the world's best guardian angel."

"We should go," the neonatologist says. But before they leave, the nurse puts a second ID band on Allie's wrist and then mine.

"Go with him," Allie tells me. "He needs you. And Asher, find Bug. She needs reassurance."

It hits me again what Bug said about it being her fault.

"You'll be all right?" I look to Hudson for the answer.

"Placentas are coming out now. She should be back in her room shortly. I've got her."

"Thanks, Hudson. For everything."

"You're welcome."

I glance at Christina, who's sleeping peacefully in the baby warmer, and I follow the other doctor as he pushes Alex's warmer out the door. But then I see Bug at the end of the hallway, curled into a ball on a chair while being consoled by a nurse.

"Um, where's the NICU? I need to do something real quick."

The doctor points. "End of the hall to the right. Ring the bell and show your ID band."

I put a hand on my son's head to let him know I'll be right behind him. Then I walk to the chairs and nod to the nurse, who gets up and walks away. I sit and put an arm around her. "He's going to be okay."

"He w-wasn't crying. And they had the m-mask thing on his face."

"He just needed a little help. He's okay now. They just need to monitor him for a few hours."

"It's all my fault. He wasn't breathing. If I hadn't opened the door, she wouldn't have fallen. It's my fault. I did this."

"Hold on there, sweetie. Slow down. Start from the beginning. What do you mean she fell? Allie? When?"

She looks up at me with red-rimmed eyes, makeup smeared beneath them. "She didn't tell you?"

"Tell me what? I have no idea what you're talking about."

She shakes her head. "It was a few months ago. Allie and I had kind of a fight. She wanted in my room but my door was locked. I didn't know she was leaning against it and when I opened it, she fell."

My jaw drops in abject horror. "Down the stairs?"

"Into the room. I just know something happened. That's when the cord got wrapped around his neck, isn't it? She said the doctor told her everything was okay, but it wasn't. He wasn't breathing, Dad. What if he went too long? What if what I did makes him have CP like Christian? That's what he said caused it, that they think he may have been deprived of oxygen during birth. What if it's the same with Alex?" She rocks back and forth, hands clutching her knees to her chest. "What did I do?"

I catch a glimpse of Hudson coming out of the OR. "Dr. McQuaid?" I wave him over.

"She's doing very well. No issues with the delivery of the placentas. Allie and your baby girl will be back in their room momentarily."

"That's great, but what can you tell me about a fall Allie took a few months ago? My daughter was just telling me about it. Allie came to see you?"

"It was nothing. She was just being cautious. I did an ultrasound and everything checked out."

I rub and hand across my jaw. "She never told me."

"She probably didn't want you to worry."

I stand up and whisper. "Could the fall have caused what happened in there… with my son?"

"No, no. Of course not. More than likely, when he shifted around after his sister was delivered, he got himself wrapped up in the cord. Listen, he's going to be fine. I'm no neonatologist, but I deliver a lot of babies, even high-risk ones, and believe me when I say what happened was frightening, but there should be no lasting damage or deficiencies because of it."

I ask once more, louder this time so Bug can hear. "So the fall she had did not cause this?"

"Absolutely not."

"Thank you."

"My pleasure. You have two great kids." He eyes Bug. "Pardon me, three."

I nod and sit. "See there, the fall had nothing to do with what happened."

"You both are just saying that to make me feel better."

"Yeah, doctors don't really do that. If he thought the fall was significant, he'd have said it." I thumb down the hallway. "Come on, let's see if we can get you in to see your brother and you'll see for yourself."

"I can see him?"

"I don't see why not. You're his big sister, aren't you?"

She wipes a tear. "He's really going to be okay?"

I stand and hold out my hand. "He really is."

~ ~ ~

Thirty minutes later, we're heading back to Allie's room. I halt in the doorway, stunned to see her holding and nursing Christina. She's smiling down at her. And she's crying. Then she starts singing. It reminds me of the time I walked in on her in Antigua when she was singing to Mitchell. Oh, how that moment means so much more now that I know her past. It's the same song, and I wonder if she sang it to Christopher in the short time he lived.

"Hey," I say quietly.

She looks up and smiles. "Hey, you guys, come in." She glances at Bug then back at me. "Everything okay?"

"Yup. Alex is crying like a champ. They have no reason to believe he won't be out of there by this afternoon."

She sighs as if the weight of the world has just been taken off her shoulders. Then her eyes grow super weary and I'm reminded she has barely slept, pushed out two babies, had a bad scare with one, and now she's probably crashing. I scoop Christina up and place her in the bassinet by the bed.

"Sleep now, while you can."

"Mmmm." Her eyes flutter.

"Allie?"

"Mmmm?"

"How come you never told me about the fall you took?"

"Didn't want you to be mad."

"Why would I be mad?"

"At Bug. I didn't want you to be mad at Bug."

She drifts off to sleep and I turn to see Bug wiping at her eyes. "You heard that?"

She nods.

"You could do far worse in the stepmom department, I hope you know that."

She nods again. "I know, Dad. She's… pretty great."

I'm hoping Allie heard the compliment, but I doubt it. I'll tell her about it later. I still can't believe she didn't tell me, and she kept it secret in the interest of her own relationship with Darla. Damn, that woman is going to make one hell of a mom.

Bug and I take turns holding Christina while Allie sleeps. After a few hours, there's a light knock on the door and a nurse comes in rolling a bassinet.

I hop off the couch and race over. "Is this for good, or just a little while?"

"Dr. Bundy released him from the NICU. He's doing great."

"Oh, thank God."

"Did you hear that?" Bug leans over and says to Christina, "Our brother is one tough little dude."

Allie stirs and I roll Alex over to her. "Somebody really wants to see you."

Her hand flies to her mouth. "He's good?"

"He's better than good." I pick him up and place him into her arms.

"Beautiful family," the nurse says, then leaves.

I wrap my arm around Bug, who's still holding Christina. "I'd have to agree."

Once Allie has traced every feature on Alex's face, she asks, "Have they seen each other yet?"

"Not since they were vying for space inside you."

"I think they should meet." She motions for Christina. "I'd like to introduce them."

I gather her up from Bug and put her into Allie's free arm. "Guess we'll have to get used to balancing two of them, huh?"

She situates them both like she's already a pro. "Christina, meet Alex. Alex, this is Christina, but her big sister calls her Chrissy." Unable to wipe her tears, they flow freely down her face. "And I'm your mom." She turns to Bug. "Maybe one day, you'll let me be yours."

I can tell it's hard for Bug to contain her emotions, no matter how much she's trying. She smiles, trying to brush them off. "Maybe. But you realize you'd have to marry my dad before that could happen."

I cock my head. "Are you saying you'd be okay with that?"

"I'm kind of surprised you haven't already done it."

"It's *her* fault." I point to Allie. "She wouldn't let me marry her without your blessing."

"Wait… seriously? So all this time, you were waiting on *me* to be okay with it?" She looks more than a little guilty. Walking over near Allie, she leans close to each baby then says, "They say go for it."

I take the opening when I see it, and pull the engagement ring out of my pocket. I've been carrying it around for nearly six months waiting for this opportunity, no way am I letting it slip by. I drop to a knee beside her bed. "You've stolen my heart. You've had my babies. We have the blessing." I hold out the ring. "*Now* will you marry me?"

Since the day she told me about Christopher, I haven't seen her cry this much. The difference is, these are happy tears. Tears of joy and hope. Tears I've shared in more than once on this monumental day.

She nods over and over. "Yes. Of course I will." She holds up her left hand the best she can while still securing Alex. "It's beautiful," she says when I slide on the ring.

I lean down and kiss her. "It was my mother's."

"Oh." Allie examines it with hesitation.

When it dawns on me what she must be thinking, I add, "Nobody has ever worn it but you. I mean, and my mother."

"Stella didn't…?"

"My mother was a huge believer in soulmates. When Dad gave me the ring after she died, I knew it could only go to one person. Stella wasn't that person. I don't even know how I knew. But now I know it was meant for you all along."

"Quit being so cheesy," Bug says behind me.

When I turn, however, she's crying. Hopefully my daughter believes in soulmates too. Because I wish nothing more for my children than to find someone who completes them as well as Allie does me.

"Get over here," I say to Bug.

She joins us, her on one side of Allie's bed and me on the other.

I get out my phone, hold my arm out, and take our very first family photo.

Chapter Forty-five

Allie

I stare down at Alex as he finishes nursing, unable to believe he's been here for two weeks when it feels like he's been a part of my life forever. Gazing across the room at my mom holding Christina, it's hard for me to think of a time they weren't with us.

When I put him on my shoulder to burp him, Isla, the night nurse Mom and Dad hired us for the month, swoops in and gets him. "Let me do that, dear," she says in her proper English accent that has started grating on my nerves.

I straighten my top then look around the room. This just feels wrong. Sad, and fearing I'm suffering from postpartum depression, I pick up a few used burp rags and take them back to the laundry room. While I'm there, I switch a load from the washer to the dryer. Back in the kitchen, I find a mostly warm, half-drunk bottle of soda and throw it out. I glance around the kitchen for something else to do, but there's just nothing.

The dishes are clean. I did that earlier. The food's been put away. Bug helped with that. Even the floor has been swept. That was Asher's job.

I sit heavily on a barstool and gaze out into the living room. Mom and Isla are chatting away while holding, burping, swaying, and tending to every one of the twins' needs.

Out of nowhere, I start to cry. I full-on sob.

Arms come around me. "Hey there. What's wrong, sweetheart?"

I turn and bury my face in Asher's chest. "Everything."

His silent chuckle bounces my head around. "It's your hormones. They're all over the place. Why don't you go get some rest?"

I shake my head defiantly. "I don't need rest."

"It'll get better, Allie. Recovering from having two babies is hard. Your body must be going through a lot right now."

I pull away from him. "That's not it."

"Then what is it?"

"I don't know." I wipe a tear. "It's just… everything."

He showers me with a few quick kisses and an empathetic smile. He thinks I'm depressed.

Maybe all new moms feel this way. Like they aren't doing enough. Like they're completely inadequate. Like they can't be the supermom all their friends seem to be.

Maybe I *am* depressed.

I glance back into the other room, watching Mom and Isla holding *my* children. If it's not Mom and Isla, it's Mia and Marti, or Ren and Ellie, or Regan and Addy. While Isla is here twelve hours every day starting at six pm, my family and friends all take turns with the day shift, making sure there are always two of them around to give me a break.

"This is just… all wrong." I run to the back door between the laundry room and the kitchen and go out onto the deck. I don't even bother with a coat, welcoming the cold when it stings my face.

Asher shows up behind me, draping a blanket across my shoulders. "Sweetheart, please tell me what this is all about."

I spin around and flail my arms in the air. "This is about everything not being like I imagined."

He pulls me against him, comforting me. "I'll bet all new moms say that. Things will calm down."

I push off him, frustration crawling up my spine. "That's the issue. Things *are* calm. Asher, look at our house. It's clean. You know why it's clean? Because *we* clean it. There aren't takeout containers spilling out of the trash, because we actually have time to cook. And there isn't laundry piling up on the floor, because it's actually getting done. By *me*. By *us*. And you want to know the worst thing? I feel… *rested*."

He laughs. "And that's a bad thing because…"

I throw my arms up again. "Because I hardly even feel like a new mom. Because the British bitch my mom hired to watch the twins all night is like a dang robot." Hot tears flow down my face. "Because I feel like a guest in my own home." My head shakes. "I don't want this. We're practically freaks of nature. No new parents are like us. I want to experience being a new mom. The dirty house, eating takeout every night, even the sleep deprivation. I want to go through it all. Because right now, I barely even feel like they're *my* kids."

"Babe, I had no idea you felt this way."

"Neither did I really. I just thought I was going through normal mom emotions. But Asher, I don't want a nanny getting up with the babies at night. I don't want a nanny at all. *I* want to do it. I don't care if I'm a zombie all day. I want to change their diapers and rock them and sing to them. I want to be their *mother*."

"Oh, dear," Mom says, peeking her head through the door. "Allie, are you having an emotional moment?"

"No, Mom, I'm not. I'm having an epiphany."

She grabs her coat and joins us, Christina obviously asleep somewhere else. "About what exactly?"

I look to Asher, because I don't really want to hurt anyone's feelings.

"Allie is having second thoughts about Isla."

Mom's eyebrows shoot up. "You don't like her?"

"Isla is fine, Sarah. She's been very helpful. But I think that's the issue. She's *too* helpful. As are all of you. I mean, you've been great. But—"

"I don't feel like a mom," I say, butting in. "I'm watching all of you raise my babies. Do you know the only time I spend with them is when I'm feeding them? Because as soon as someone sees they're done eating, they take them away."

"Oh, honey. We're helping. All new moms need a little help."

"*Little* being the operative word." I wrap the blanket around me and pace the deck. "You're doing so much, all that's left for me and Asher to do is cook, clean, and sleep. But what I really want to do is raise my own darn babies. I had less than two days with Christopher. I never really got to be his mom. I want to cherish every moment I can get with the twins. I don't care if I don't get to shower or sleep or if I have to live off DoorDash food. I just want to experience what every other new mom gets to experience. I even heard Bug complain yesterday that she rarely gets to hold them. She's their sister, for God's sake, she should get to participate in their care. I appreciate you wanting to help, but I really wish you'd have hired me a housekeeper or a chef instead." Done with my tirade, I sit on the snow-covered bench and freeze my ass.

Mom sighs, shakes her head sadly, and looks at me with empathy. "You're absolutely right. I'll go break the news to Isla. She'll be gone in an hour, sent off with a full month's pay."

Before she's at the door, I call out. "Mom? I know you meant well, and I'm not saying I don't want you or the others here to help. But maybe just one at a time. And not *all* the time. There are two of us, three counting Bug. We can handle this."

She comes back and cups my jaw. "Of course you can, honey. I don't know what I was thinking. I'll go take care of this right now."

Asher and I watch as Mom goes into the living room and has a talk with Isla.

"You don't really think Isla is a bitch, do you?" Asher asks.

"No." A burst of air rushes out of my lungs. "She's actually very nice. And good. And was probably trained to be a nanny to the royals or something knowing my mom."

He laughs. "I have no doubt she was. Are you sure you're ready for this?"

"I've been ready for over ten years, Asher."

He kisses the side of my head.

Isla waves at us from inside, probably happy to have earned four weeks' pay for less than two weeks' work.

My mom is on the phone when we come back inside, so she can't help when both babies begin stirring at once. Asher and I smile at each other and go to them.

A half hour later, Mom is gone and it's just the two of us, sitting on the couch together, holding sleeping babies.

Bug comes through the back door, much earlier than curfew. She looks around. "Where is everyone?"

"Allie fired the nanny. Well, she made her mom do it."

She plops next to Asher on the sofa. "Thank goodness. She was weird. She never wanted me to hold the twins. It's like she thought I was doing it wrong."

Asher puts Christina into her arms. "Well, you'll be holding them a lot more now. I hope that's okay. Because not only did Allie fire the nanny, she put her foot down about so many people coming to help. One person at a time, and nobody here after dinner."

Bug looks excited. And happier than she's looked since we brought the babies home. "Are you going to let me change diapers?"

He snort-chuckles. "*Let you?* How else do you think you're going to become their babysitter?"

Bug smiles proudly. At fourteen, I'm not sure she's capable of handling two of them at one time. Heck, I'm still not sure *I* am since I've never been allowed to try. But it's something I'm looking forward to figuring out.

I glance around the room and smile big.

"What is it?" Asher asks.

"I was just thinking how this is the first time in two weeks we've been truly alone. Our family. With no doctors or nurses or nannies or grandmas or friends. It's just us."

"Our family," Darla says, as if trying out the phrase. "I think I like being part of a family."

"Hey." Asher looks offended. "You and I were a family before all this."

She shrugs. "This is different. It's more real. Better somehow."

I smile. Because just a few months ago, I'd have sworn she'd never want anything to do with being part of any family that included me.

"Bug?" I ask.

"Yeah?"

"Will you be my maid of honor?"

"Me?" She looks confused. "What about Mia? She's your best friend."

"She is my best friend, and she'll be a bridesmaid. But you're about to become my daughter. That's much more important. I hope you don't mind that I think of you that way."

"You think of me as your daughter?"

"I have three kids, Bug." I glance up at the mantle where Christopher's urn now sits. "Actually, I have four."

Asher elbows her.

"Yeah," she says. "Being your maid of honor would be cool."

"I think it'll be pretty awesome too. Thanks, Bug."

"So what now?" she asks. "Are you going to put me on cooking duty?"

"Eventually." Asher's face breaks out into a grin. "But not quite yet. Sarah may have fired the nanny, but she immediately turned around and hired a housekeeper to come three times a week and a chef to cook our dinners Monday through Friday."

Bug's jaw drops and her eyes go wide. "I will *never* get used to being part of a rich family."

"Good. You shouldn't," he says. "Because we're not going to forget who we are or where we came from."

"Will you still pay for Harvard if I get in?"

"Yeah, kiddo." He chuckles. "We'll pay for Harvard."

"And maybe a car when I'm sixteen?"

"How else will you be able to run errands for us or take the twins to the park?"

"Um, Dad, we live three blocks from the park."

He just shrugs.

I love the relationship they have. It's easy. It's fun. It's loving. And I love that I get to see that side of Darla now. The side she hid from me for so many months. What's more, I'm excited about how that part of their relationship is now bleeding over into ours. Bug and I have become so much closer over the past month. Even this past week. We've laughed while doing laundry. We've horsed around while cooking dinner. She even told me she has a crush on a guy at school—although she wouldn't reveal his name.

Progress. So much progress.

The babies cry. Both at the same time. The three of us all look at each other and laugh.

Asher stands. "Here we go!"

~ ~ ~

Cries wake me. I look at the clock. It's three in the morning, basically the middle of the night, but I smile. Because it's the first time I've been woken up like this since the hospital. Isla didn't even let us have a baby monitor in the room. She took care of everything.

Now, not only do we have a baby monitor, we've got two bassinets near the bed. I sit up, looking over to see which one is awake. It's Alex.

Asher hasn't even stirred. He's a much heavier sleeper than I am. I scoop Alex into my arms and take him to the nursery to change him. Then I feed him and sing to him, cherishing every single moment even though I'm dead tired.

When I return to bed and put him back down, I stare at him, watching his little chest rise and fall with every breath, knowing how lucky I am. I put my hand on his chest. "Goodnight Alex Christopher."

As soon as I'm lying down, Asher's arm comes around me. "You're amazing," he mumbles sleepily. "I was watching you."

Right. The baby monitor.

He's back asleep before I can respond.

A moment later, Christina starts to wake and whine. This time, Asher moves to get up. But I stop him. I stop him because this feels like my very first night of being a mom and I intend to enjoy it.

"I've got her," I say, in spite of my heavy eyelids.

"But you did Alex."

"I've got her." I lean down and kiss him on the cheek. "Give me tonight, Asher. You can have tomorrow."

Just like I did with Alex, I take her to the nursery, change her, then feed her and sing. I look at the camera and can almost feel Asher's eyes on me. Somehow I know he's watching. He's always watching. Always making me feel special. Always telling me how much he loves me and our life.

Most of all, he's always reminding me what a good mother I am.

When I put Christina down, I drift off before my head hits the pillow. And then I dream. I dream of a ten-year-old Christopher holding his little brother and sister. Of Bug teaching Christopher how to play soccer. Of Asher showing him how to become a man. Of family vacations to Disney World.

When I wake, it's the first time I've ever not been sad after dreaming of him. Somehow I know Christopher is going to be in a lot more of my dreams, showing me the life that should have been. In my dreams, he'll be at every birthday party. Every wedding. Every family gathering.

In my dreams, I'm going to watch him grow up and grow old. And he's going to let me be the mother I never got to be to him.

Asher rolls over and sees me awake. "So how was it? Your first real night of motherhood?"

As my eyes graze over the sleeping twins, they catch on something just beyond the bassinets. I know the rising sun is playing tricks on me, but I could swear there's a shadow behind them, protecting them somehow. And the shadow is about the size of a ten-year-old boy.

I smile at my soon-to-be husband. "It was the best night I've ever had in my entire life."

Epilogue

Asher

When I wake to an empty bed, I turn toward the baby monitor. Allie is hovering over the crib in what will eventually just be Alex's room, but is currently the crib and room he's sharing with his sister.

I guess I shouldn't be surprised Allie is in there watching them sleep. For three months they slept beside us. Each time they woke in the night, we were right there to soothe them back to sleep. Last night was the first time one of them slept through the night, so we figured it was time for the move. But this first night apart is proving to be tough. More so on us than them, I imagine.

When Alex stirs, Allie starts singing. I could listen to her sing all night long. I'm so drawn to the sound of her voice that I get out of bed and stand in the doorway to the nursery, mesmerized. I really did hit the jackpot with Allie. Not because of her family money. Because she's the most incredible woman and the absolute best mom I could ever wish for our children.

I walk up behind her, wrap her in my arms, and whisper, "Hey, you."

She leans back into me. "I love them so much, Asher. I never thought I'd be able to love another child as much as I loved Christopher."

"I know what you mean. But it's like the heart has this amazing capacity to expand and hold equal amounts of love for all of them." I kiss her neck. "And I love you, Mrs. Anderson."

I think I've said those exact words ten times a day since our wedding last weekend. I'm not sure I'll ever get used to her being my wife. But she *is* my wife. And every day I wake up and have to pinch myself because I feel as if I'm living in a dream.

She raises her hand, admiring her rings. She twists the engagement ring around her finger. "Do you really believe in soulmates and divine intervention and stuff like that?"

"I do. Don't you?"

"I suppose." She sighs heavily as if about to reveal something. "Did I tell you how I used to go on walks when I stayed at my aunt's house in Oregon?"

"No. And you never told me it was Oregon."

"Is that significant?"

I shrug, because honestly I don't know. But then again, somehow I *do*. "Tell me about your walks."

"There was this bridge a few blocks from her house. I would walk over it every day. It was so beautiful and serene. The grassy, rocky, ravine below seemed out of a fairytale. I'd always stop and stare out and dream about becoming a mom. About what life could be like with Christopher if the doctors were all wrong.

"Then after he died, before I came back to Cal Creek, I wanted to walk over that bridge again, but for a very different reason. Something called me there. Maybe it was Christopher."

She leans her head back against my shoulder. "This particular bridge didn't have water running beneath it like the other ones in

Klamath Falls, so I knew there would be nothing to break my fall. It would be quick and easy, and I felt almost at peace in that moment, knowing how simple it would be to just take one step so I could be with him, wherever he was."

I pull her close, my heart thundering in my chest as my head spins. "Did you say Klamath Falls?"

She nods. "Strange name for a town, huh? So there I was, climbing over the railing, balancing on the edge. I was all in. There wasn't a question of if I would do it, I was going to do it. But that's when the divine intervention happened. Because right at that moment—"

"A guy driving a blue SUV honked at you."

She spins around in my arms. "How do you know this? I've never told anyone."

I swallow hard. I can't believe I didn't put it together until just now. "Allie." I run a hand through my hair. "Holy shit, Allie, it was *me. I* was the guy in the blue SUV."

Her head tilts in confusion. "What? How?"

"Jesus. I thought it was all in my head. I swear the moment we met, I knew we'd met before. I felt it in my soul. I'd begun to think it was some past life thing, or we'd worked together but forgotten, or we crossed paths as kids. Whatever it was, I knew it had happened. I can't tell you how many nights I've stayed up wondering how, when, and where I'd seen you before."

I can't help it when tears well in my eyes at the realization of just how profound that moment in time was for both of us, yet we never knew.

"Sweetheart, it was me. I was in Klamath Falls ten years ago. I was driving back to my hotel after working a long day on the job when I saw a girl on the other side of the bridge. My heart slammed into my chest when I thought she might jump. But it was a divided bridge with a gap between the two sides. There was no way for me to get over to you. So I stopped the car, honked, and started yelling. I was so freaked out I can't remember what I said, but I scared you and you ran off."

"T-that was you?" she asks, still as stunned as I am.

I cup her face. "Yes, baby, it was me." I lower my lips to hers. "Now I know for sure that we're soulmates."

Her lips are salty and sweet when I kiss them. We cry into each other for what seems like hours, holding on like we're each other's lifeline.

"Wait," she says, causing me to pull back.

I cock my head, wondering why she wants me to stop comforting her.

"That's what you said. You said to wait. You were yelling, and my head was all over the place, but I remember you said to wait, and if I still felt the same way tomorrow, I could always come back."

I shake my head in disgust. "Well, that's stupid advice. Wait to kill yourself until I'm not there to see it?"

"It wasn't stupid, Asher. It saved my life. I was embarrassed, so I ran back to my aunt's house. And when I went back to the bridge the next day, I looked over the edge into the peaceful ravine, wanting to jump, but hesitated. I heard your voice in my head urging me to wait. Wait until tomorrow. So that's what I did. For weeks. I'd go to the bridge, contemplate jumping, but then I'd wait until tomorrow."

I lower my forehead to hers, my tears dripping onto her face. "Thank God tomorrow never came."

"You saved me."

"After you ran off, I patrolled that damn bridge all night, sure you were going to come back. I think I'd have staked it out the next day, too, if I didn't have to catch a flight back to Orlando. And though I couldn't remember what I said to make you run off, the image of that night never left my mind. I scoured the internet for weeks for any news of a bridge jumper in Klamath Falls, Oregon. I remember being so relieved that I didn't ever come across a story." I chuckle. "That was just a few weeks before I proposed to Stella. Maybe that's why I didn't give her the ring. It's because even then, somehow I knew that girl on the bridge would alter the course of my life."

"Oh my god, Asher. What are the odds?"

I cup her face and smile. "I'd say pretty damn good when you're two people who are destined to be together."

"But why not then? Why didn't we meet all those years ago?"

"It wouldn't have worked then. You were grieving your son. I was about to get engaged." I inwardly roll my eyes. "Not to mention I'd have been close to being arrested as you were only nineteen and I was thirty-one." I push her hair behind her ear. "We met when we were supposed to. After you went through your shit. After I went through mine." My eyes close briefly, still not believing this. "In the car at the winery—the first time I saw you—there was something in the back of my mind that said *'that's her.'* I didn't know what it meant. I assumed it was my imagination going wild and telling me I was experiencing love at first sight."

She bites her lip. "You really thought it was love at first sight?"

I nod. "Oh, yeah. Obviously, I never said anything. I was sure it would drive you away. But I knew… somehow I knew that no matter how long it took, we'd end up together. So I was patient."

She chuckles, eyes sparkling as she gathers my face into her hands. "You must be the most patient man on the planet, Asher Anderson."

I gesture to the twins. "I guess I was waiting on them. They seemed to know more than we did when we were ready."

She looks away from me, her gaze settling on the twins. "You think they were always meant to be?"

"Yes. They were just waiting for the right time."

Her arms come around my neck. "Do you know how much I love you?"

"I do." I motion toward the door. "But I wouldn't mind you showing me."

She takes my arm, leading me out of the room. "Right this way, Mr. President."

Bonus Epilogue

Allie

Twelve years later…

"Mom, I'm scared."

I squeeze Bug's hand. She only calls me *Mom* when she's sad, frightened, or needs motherly advice. The rest of the time I'm just plain old Allie. Which I'm surprisingly fine with considering how much I think of her as my daughter.

Sweat rolls off her as she pushes for what seems like the millionth time.

She's been in labor for almost two days. Which is both a blessing and a curse. Because her husband isn't here yet. He's been overseas in Italy for the past few weeks, working on Formula One cars. His dream job that he worked for years to get but that came at the absolute wrong time. Darla urged him to go, supporting him even though she knew this was a possibility. He was only going to be there for a month, set to arrive home two weeks before her due date. But this little one—our first grandbaby—decided to throw a wrench in things and come three weeks early.

I squeeze her hand. "It's okay, sweetie. I know it feels like you've been doing this forever, but it'll be over soon, and you'll welcome your daughter into the world."

She glances at the clock. She's been doing it every few minutes since she started pushing an hour ago.

"He'll be here," I say. "He just texted your dad that he's only a few miles away."

She nods then screams when another contraction hits. She's probably cursing herself right about now for not getting the epidural. The first thirty-six hours of her labor weren't that bad, only mild contractions, so she was sure she could do without. Just like the Bug from twelve years ago, she asks for, but doesn't always take my advice.

I can tell she's trying not to push. Hudson, the same doctor who delivered all four of my and Asher's kids, looks up. "Darla, I know you want to wait for him, but it's important that you push. Your little girl is getting impatient and wants to meet her mother."

She shakes her head. "I'm not ready. Maybe we did this too soon. I'm only twenty-six."

Her contraction ends and she relaxes back against the pillow.

"Bullshit," Mel says from the opposite side of the bed. "You've been ready to be a mom since Chrissy and Alex were born. By the time Sarah arrived, you could change a diaper with one hand behind your back. And then AJ. All I'm saying is if they handed out honorary degrees in motherhood, you'd have been issued one a long time ago." She takes her hand. "You've got this."

Even after Mel moved away and they lived three thousand miles apart, her and Bug's relationship never wavered. They were college roommates at NYU. And now Mel and her girlfriend live less than an hour away in the city. They've been through thick and thin together. Mel is most definitely her person.

For as much as she hated it when she first moved here twelve years ago, it amuses me that Darla ended up staying in Calloway Creek. But this is where her family is. Her dad. Her husband and his family. Her siblings. Her aunt and cousins. And me. Though I think of myself as her mother, Bug and I are definitely more friends than anything. I'm her Mel when Mel isn't around. And she's my Mia.

There's a knock on the door and Asher sticks his head through the opening. "Everything okay in here? Has my granddaughter made her arrival yet?"

"When will he be here?" Bug yells through a contraction.

"The car is pulling up now," Asher says. "He didn't even wait for his bags at the airport."

"And there's the top of the head," Hudson says. "One more push and her head will be out."

"Run!" Bug yells. "Get him up here. He can't miss this, Dad." She collapses back against the pillow then looks up at me. "He has to be here."

"He will be."

Less than two minutes go by, not even enough time for another contraction to hit, and the door bursts open. Asher pushes Christian through in a wheelchair, bringing him right over to the bed before handing him his forearm crutches. Asher shrugs, nearly out of breath. "Faster this way."

"My hero," I say to him with a smile.

"We have quite a crowd," Hudson says. "How about you all give Dad a chance to enjoy these last few moments of labor?"

"Thanks for being here for her," Christian says.

Christian Cruz has been in our lives since the day we moved into the house next door. I could see the connection they had from the very beginning. It took the two of them a while to catch up and realize they felt about each other the same way Asher and I do.

That they are soulmates.

"I'll always be here for her." I lean in and kiss Bug's sweaty forehead. "You are *so* ready for this. And you're going to be the best mother."

She reaches for me. "Only because I had an amazing example."

Tears come to my eyes as her next contraction hits and we're ushered out of the room.

Mel, Asher, and I join the others in the waiting area. AJ bounds over and climbs into my lap. Like Christina and Alex, he was an *oopsie* baby—coming even after Asher had a vasectomy after Sarah was born and we felt like our family was complete. It wasn't. It is now.

I hug my four-year-old son who is about to become an uncle. I look around the room. Christina and Alex are only a little younger than Bug was when they were born. They're both super excited to be getting a niece. Sarah is nine, and from the time AJ was born has been the best little helper.

Mom and Dad are here, happy, but not quite ready to accept the fact that they are about to be great-grandparents. Carter and his wife are here as well. So is Mia and her other two brothers.

The room is filled to the brim with people who love Bug and Christian. I hope they know how lucky they are.

Thirty minutes later, Christian appears in the doorway, beaming as he smiles from ear to ear. "She's here." His head shakes over and over. "I can't believe I'm a dad."

Carter is the first to congratulate his son.

All four of my kids ask in tandem, "When can we see her?"

Christian laughs. "Soon." He turns to me. "Allie and Asher, Bug is asking for you."

I hand a sleepy AJ off to my mom and the two of us follow Christian back to Bug's room.

Tears flood my eyes when we enter and see Bug holding her daughter. We rush to her side, eager to meet our first grandchild.

"You did it," I say, kissing Bug's forehead. "Oh, Darla, she's beautiful."

Asher gives a slow whistle. "Dang, you two kids made one good looking baby." He touches her tiny hand. "*Now* will you tell us her name?"

For months, everyone has been asking if they've chosen a name. They said they had, but refused to tell us until she arrived, claiming they didn't want to jinx it.

Bug looks into her daughter's blue eyes and rubs a knuckle against her soft little cheek. "I wanted to name her after the most important woman in my life."

I smile. "Mel will be honored."

Bug and Christian share a look, then Bug says, "Mom, Dad, meet your granddaughter, Allie Cruz."

Acknowledgments

This has been my first series of four full-length novels, and boy am I glad it happened. When I first introduced Asher back in *Loud Unspoken Memories*, I wasn't sure what was going to happen. Two books later, as I started writing *Tiny Precious Secrets*, the story took on a life of its own.

I hope you enjoyed reading not only about Allie and Asher's journey, but about how Allie and Bug finally became what the other desperately needed.

There are a few key people I need to thank. My amazing assistant and friend, Julie Collier, who always pushes me to be a better writer.

My editor, Michelle Fewer, who never fails to amuse me with her comments as she goes through my manuscripts.

And my beta readers, Joelle Yates, Kellie Shanks, and Page Levendis, I value your thoughtful comments, suggestions, and criticisms.

Navigating the intricacies of a chromosomal anomaly wasn't easy. Kudos to my medical expert Kimberly Kernek, M.D. FACOG (fellow of the American college of obstetrics and gynecology) for always answering my questions, no matter how crazy they may be.

I'm going to miss the Montana family, but you'll see glimpses of them in the future as I plan to stay in Calloway Creek for a good long time.

Samantha Christy's passion for writing started long before her first novel was published.

Graduating from the University of Nebraska with a degree in Criminal Justice, she held the title of Computer Systems Analyst for The Supreme Court of Wisconsin and several major universities around the United States.

Raised mainly in Indianapolis, she holds the Midwest and its homegrown values dear to her heart and upon the birth of her third child devoted herself to raising her family full time.

While it took time to get from there to here, writing has remained her utmost passion and being a stay-at-home mom facilitated her ability to follow that dream.

When she is not writing, she keeps busy cruising to every Caribbean island where ships sail.

Samantha Christy currently resides in St. Augustine, Florida with her husband and the two of her four children who haven't yet flown the coop.

You can reach Samantha Christy at any of these wonderful places:

Website: www.samanthachristy.com

Facebook: https://www.facebook.com/SamanthaChristyAuthor

Instagram: @authorsamanthachristy

E-mail: samanthachristy@comcast.net